# "You know, no one is watching us. You don't have to pretend to want to kiss me."

Julian smiled. "If there's one thing I've learned in my years in LA, it's that someone is always watching. But even if there weren't, I would still kiss you."

"Why?" Her dark eyes searched his face in confusion, her brows drawn together.

She honestly didn't think she was kissable. That was a shame.

"It's not that hard. Just take a deep breath, tilt your head up to me and close your eyes."

He intended it to be a quick kiss, knowing it would take a while for them to work up to a convincing one. But he found that once they touched, he didn't want to pull away.

\* \* \*

**One Week with the Best Man**
is part of the Brides and Belles series: Wedding planning is their business...and their pleasure

# ONE WEEK WITH THE BEST MAN

BY
ANDREA LAURENCE

Published in Great Britain 2015
by Mills & Boon, an imprint of Harlequin (UK) Limited,
Eton House, 18-24 Paradise Road, Richmond, Surrey, TW9 1SR

© 2015 Andrea Laurence

ISBN: 978-0-263-25286-6

51-1115

Harlequin (UK) Limited's policy is to use papers that are natural, renewable and recyclable products and made from wood grown in sustainable forests. The logging and manufacturing processes conform to the legal environmental regulations of the country of origin.

Printed and bound in Spain
by CPI, Ba

**Andrea Laurence** is an award-winning author of contemporary romance for Mills & Boon Desire and paranormal romance for Mills & Boon Nocturne. She has been a lover of reading and writing stories since she learned to read at a young age. She always dreamed of seeing her work in print and is thrilled to share her special blend of sensuality and dry, sarcastic humor with the world.

A dedicated West Coast girl transplanted into the Deep South, Andrea is working on her own happily-ever-after with her boyfriend and their collection of animals, including a Siberian husky that sheds like nobody's business. If you enjoy her story, tell her by visiting her website, www.andrealaurence.com; like her fan page on Facebook at facebook.com/authorandrealaurence; or follow her on Twitter, twitter.com/andrea_laurence.

*To my baby sister Hannah—*

Being a girl is tough. Surviving your teenage years with your self-esteem intact is a major feat. You've got a long way to go, but no matter what, I want you to remember: you are smart enough, you are talented enough and you are pretty enough. Don't let anyone tell you otherwise. You can do anything you put your mind to, and if and when you choose to fall in love, that man will be damn lucky to have you in his life. Don't settle for someone that treats you like anything less than the best thing that has ever happened to him.

# One

"Pardon me," Natalie said, leaning in toward the man sitting across from her. "Could you run that by us again?"

Gretchen was glad Natalie had said it, because she was pretty darn confused herself. The four owners and operators of From This Moment wedding chapel were seated at the conference room table across from a man wearing an expensive suit and an arrogant attitude she didn't care for. He wasn't from the South; that was for sure. He was also talking nonsense.

Ross Bentley looked just as annoyed with the women's confusion as they were with him. "You advertise From This Moment as a one-stop wedding venue, do you not?"

"Yes," Natalie said, "but usually that means we'll handle the food, the DJ and the flowers. We've never been asked to provide one of the wedding guests a date. This is a wedding chapel, not an escort service."

"Let me explain," Ross said with a greasy smile that Gretchen didn't trust. "This is a very delicate arrangement, so this discussion will need to fall within the confidentiality agreement for the Murray Evans wedding."

Murray Evans was a country music superstar. On his last tour, he'd fallen for his opening act. They were having a multiday wedding event at their facility next weekend, the kind the press salivated over. Those weddings usually required a confidentiality clause so that any leaks about the event are not from the venue. Frankly, Gretchen was getting tired of these big, over-the-top weddings. The money was nice—money was always nice, since she didn't have much—but carefully addressing thousands of invitations in perfect calligraphy wasn't that fun. Nor was dealing with the high-and-mighty wedding guests who came to these kinds of shindigs.

"Of course," Natalie replied.

"I represent Julian Cooper, the actor. He's a long-time friend of Mr. Evans and will be attending the wedding as the best man. I'm not sure how closely you follow celebrity news, but Julian has just had a big public breakup with his costar of *Bombs of Fury*, Bridgette Martin. Bridgette has already been seen out and about with another high-profile actor. As his manager, I feel like it would look bad if Julian attended the wedding alone, but he doesn't need the complication of a real date. We just need a woman to stand in and pretend to be with him throughout the wedding events. I assure you there's nothing inappropriate involved."

Gretchen knew of Julian Cooper—it would be impossible not to—although she'd never seen any of his films. He was the king of dude films—lots of explosions, guns and scripts with holes big enough to drive a truck through them. That wasn't her thing, but a lot of people loved his movies. It seemed a little ridiculous that he would need a fake date. His sweaty, hard abs were plastered all over every billboard and movie preview. While Gretchen might not appreciate his acting skills, she had a hard time discounting that body. If a man who looked like that couldn't get a last-minute date, she was doomed.

"What kind of woman are you wanting?" Bree, their photographer, asked cautiously. "I'm not sure I know many women who would look natural on the arm of a movie star."

"That's understandable," Ross said. "What I'd really prefer is an average woman. We don't want her to look like an escort. I also think it would go over well with Julian's female fan base for him to be seen with an everyday woman. It makes them feel like they have a shot."

Gretchen snorted, and Ross shot a cutting look at her across the table. "We'd be willing to handsomely compensate her for the trouble," he continued. "We're willing to pay ten thousand dollars for the woman's time. Also, I can provide additional funds for salon visits and a clothing allowance."

"Ten thousand dollars?" Gretchen nearly choked. "Are you kidding?"

"No," Ross said. "I'm very serious. Can you provide what we're asking for or not?"

Natalie took a deep breath and nodded. "Yes. We'll make arrangements and have someone in place to meet with Julian when he arrives in Nashville."

"Very good. He flies into Nashville tonight and he's staying at the Hilton." Ross reached into his breast pocket and pulled out a leather wallet. He extracted a handful of cash and pushed it across the table to Natalie. "This should cover the incidentals I discussed. The full payment will be provided after the wedding is over."

Without elaborating, he stood up and walked out of the conference room, leaving the four women in stunned silence.

Finally, Bree reached out and counted the money. "He left two grand. I think that will buy some really nice highlights and a couple fancy outfits, don't you, Amelia?"

Amelia, the caterer and resident fashionista, nodded. "It should. But it really depends on what we have to start with. Who can we possibly get to do this?"

"Not me," Bree insisted. "I'm engaged, and I've got to be able to take all the pictures. You're married and pregnant," she noted.

Amelia ran her hand over her rounded belly. She had just reached twenty-two weeks and found out that she and her husband, Tyler, were having a girl. "Even if I wasn't, I've got to cook for five hundred guests. I'm already in over my head on this one, even with Stella's help."

They both turned to look at Natalie, who was frantically making notes in her tablet. "Don't look at me," she said after noticing them watching her. "I'm the wedding planner. I'll be in headset mode keeping this show on track."

"There's got to be someone we could ask. A friend?" Gretchen pressed. "You grew up in Nashville, Natalie.

Don't you know anyone that wouldn't mind being a movie star's arm candy for a few days?"

"What about you?" Natalie fired back.

"What?" Gretchen nearly shrieked in response to the ridiculous question. They'd obviously lost their minds if they thought that was a viable solution. "Me? With Julian Cooper?"

Natalie shrugged off her surprise. "And why not? He said they wanted a normal, everyday woman."

"Just because he doesn't want a supermodel doesn't mean he wants...*me*. I'm hardly normal. I'm short, I'm fat and never mind the fact that I'm horribly awkward with men. I clam up whenever Bree's musician fiancé comes by. Do you really think I can act normal while the hottest star in Hollywood is whispering in my ear?"

"You're not fat," Amelia chastised. "You're a normal woman. Plenty of guys like their women a little juicy."

Juicy? Gretchen rolled her eyes and flopped back into her chair. She was twenty pounds overweight on a petite frame and had been that way since she was in diapers. Her two sisters were willowy and fragile like their ballerina mother, but Gretchen got their father's solid Russian genes, much to her dismay. Her pants size was in the double digits, and she was in a constant state of baking muffin tops. *Juicy* wasn't the word she would use.

"You guys can't really be serious about this. Even if I wasn't the last woman on earth that he'd date, you forget I work here, too. I'll be busy."

"Not necessarily," Bree countered. "Most of what you do is done in advance."

Gretchen frowned. Bree was right, although she didn't want to admit it. The invitations had gone out months ago. The programs and place cards were done. She would need to decorate the night before, but that didn't preclude her from participating in most of the wedding day activities. "I handle a lot of last-minute things, too, you know. It's not like I'm sitting around every Saturday doing my nails."

"That's not what I'm implying," Bree said.

"Even so, it's ridiculous," Gretchen grumbled. "Julian Cooper? Please."

"You could use the money, Gretchen."

She looked at Amelia and sighed. Yes, Gretchen was broke. They'd all agreed when they started this business that the majority of their profits would go into paying off the mortgage on the facility, so they weren't drawing amazing wages. For Amelia and Bree it didn't matter so much anymore. Bree was engaged to a millionaire record producer, and Amelia was married to a rare jewels dealer. Gretchen was getting by, but there wasn't much left over for life's extras. "Who couldn't?"

"You could go to Italy," Natalie offered.

That made Gretchen groan aloud. They'd found her Achilles' heel without much trouble. She'd had a fantasy of traveling to Italy for years. Since high school. She wanted to spend weeks taking in every detail, every painting of the Renaissance masters. It was a trip well out of her financial reach despite years of trying to save. But Natalie was right. With that cash in her hand she could immediately book a flight and go.

*Italy.* Florence. Venice. Rome.

She shook off the thoughts of gelato on the Spanish Steps and tried to face reality. "We're overworked. Things are slower around the holidays, but I don't see a three-week Italian vacation in my future. He could give me a million bucks and I wouldn't be able to take off time for a trip."

"We close for a week between Christmas and New Year's. That would cover some of it," Natalie said. "Or you could go later in the spring. If you work ahead with the printing, we can get someone to cover the decorating. What matters is that you'd have the money in hand to go. What can it hurt?"

"Yeah, Gretchen," Bree chimed in. "It's a lot of money, and for what? Clinging to the hard body of Julian Cooper with a loving look in your eyes? Dancing with him at the reception and maybe kissing him for the cameras?"

Gretchen tightened her jaw, choking down another argument, because she knew Bree was right. All she had to do was suck it up for a few days and she could go to Italy. She'd never have another opportunity like this.

"Besides," Bree added, "how bad can faking it with a sexy movie star really be?"

If Ross hadn't been personally responsible for Julian's career success, Julian would throttle him right this second.

"A date? A fake date? Really, Ross?"

"I think it will be good for your image."

Julian sipped his bottled water and leaned against the arm of the chair in his Nashville hotel suite. "Do I look that pathetic and heartbroken over my breakup with Bridgette?"

"Of course not," Ross soothed. "I just want to make sure that her management team doesn't outsmart us. She's already been seen out with Paul Watson. If you don't move on fast enough, you'll get painted as lovesick for her."

"I don't care," Julian exclaimed. "Despite what everyone thinks, I broke up with Bridgette six months ago. We only went out publicly because you insisted on it."

"I didn't insist," Ross protested. "The studio insisted. Your romance was a huge selling point for the film. They couldn't have you two break up before it even came out."

"Yeah, yeah," Julian said dismissively. "If I ever even look twice at one of my costars again, you haul me off and remind me of this moment. But now it's done. I'm over Bridgette and I'm *way* over dating someone just for the cameras."

Ross held up his hands. "It won't be like that. I swear. Besides, it's already done. She'll be here to meet you in about five minutes."

"Ross!" Julian shouted, rising to his full height to intimidate his short, round manager. "You can't just do stuff like this without my permission."

"Yes, I can. It's what you pay me to do. You'll thank me later."

Julian pinched the bridge of his nose between his finger and thumb. "Who is it? Some country music singer? Did you import an actress from Hollywood?"

"No, none of that. They tell me she's one of the employees at the wedding chapel. Just your everyday girl."

"Wait. I thought after what happened with that waitress you didn't want me dating 'regular' women. You said they were a bigger security risk than another star with her own career to protect. You said I needed to stick to women that didn't need my money or my fame." Julian had been dealing strictly with high-and-mighty starlets the past few years at Ross's insistence, but now, a regular girl was okay because he said so?

"I know, and normally that's the case. That waitress just wanted to dig up dirt on you to make a buck with the tabloids. There are a million women just like her in Hollywood. But in this scenario I think it's a smart choice. Women in Nashville are different, and it's an unexpected move. Your female fans will like it, of course, and so will the studios. I've been trying to get you a role as a true romantic lead. This could do it."

Julian didn't really want to be a romantic lead. At least not by Ross's definition. His manager's idea of a romantic film was one where the sexy blonde clings to his half-naked body while he shoots the bad guys. He'd already played that role again and again. When he'd pushed Ross on the topic a second time, he got Julian the "romantic" lead in a movie about male strippers. Not exactly hard-hitting, award-winning stuff. Hell, he'd be thrilled to just do a light romantic comedy. Something without explosions. Or machine guns. Or G-strings.

"I should fire you for this," Julian complained as he dropped down into his chair. It was a hollow threat, and they both knew it. Ross had made Julian's career. He might not be creatively fulfilled by big-budget action films, but the money was ridiculous and Julian needed every penny.

"It will be fine. I promise. It's not a real relationship, so I can break my own rules this once. In a few days, you can go back to Hollywood and date whomever you want."

Somehow, Julian doubted that. Since moving to Hollywood, he hadn't had the best track record with the ladies. The waitress had sold the story of their romance to the newspapers with some other juicy tidbits she'd gotten out of him. The dancer was just looking for a guy to pay for her boob job. So many others were after either his money or his leverage to get into show business.

Ross encouraged him to date other actresses to reduce that issue, but either way, there was usually some kind of confidentiality contract involved. Even with that in place, he'd learned quickly to keep private things private. He didn't talk about his family, his past…anything that he couldn't bear to see in the papers. An after-the-fact lawsuit wouldn't undo the damage once it was out there.

Since his breakup with Bridgette, he hadn't really shown any interest in dating again. It was too damn much work and frankly, just not that fun. How was he supposed to find love when he couldn't even find someone he could trust?

Ross got up from his seat and put his drink on the coffee table. "Well, that should do it."

"Where are you going?"

"I'm leaving," Ross said.

"Leaving? I thought you said my date was on her way over."

"She is. That's why I'm leaving. Three's a crowd, after all. You two need to get to know each other."

Julian's jaw dropped as he watched his manager slip out of the hotel suite. He should've throttled him. He could get a new manager.

With nothing to do but wait, he slumped into his chair and killed time checking his smartphone for missed calls or updates from his family. His mother and brother lived in Louisville, and that was the easiest and most secure way to keep up with them, especially with his brother James's condition. James's attendant usually kept him up to date on how his brother was doing and shared any funny tidbits to make him feel more connected. Today, there were no messages to worry him.

About four minutes later, there was a knock at the door to his suite. His new girlfriend was punctual if nothing else.

Julian got up and went to the door. He looked through the peephole but didn't see anyone there. Confused, he opened his hotel room door wide and realized it was because his guest was very petite. She was maybe five foot two if she had good posture, and she didn't. In addition to being petite, she was curvy, hiding most of her body under an oversize cardigan. She had the look of the average woman on the street, nothing like he was used to seeing around Malibu.

What really caught his attention, however, were her eyes. She had a dark gaze that watched him survey her with a hint of suspicion. It made him wonder what that was about. Shouldn't *he* be suspicious of *her*? Julian had been a part of the Hollywood scene for several years and had seen his fair share of staged relationships. The women were usually attractive and greedy, hoping they might actually charm their fake boyfriend into falling for them so they could take advantage of California's community property laws.

He waited for her to say something, but she just stood there, sort of awkwardly hovering outside his door. "Hi," Julian finally offered to end the silence. "I'm Julian, although you probably already know that. Are you the one the wedding company sent over?"

"Yes." She nodded, her dark brown curls bouncing around her round face. He expected her to say something after that, but she continued to just hover. It made him think that at any moment, she might turn and bolt down the hallway. He was used to his fans being nervous around him, but not skittish. He was certain Ross would blame him if he ran off the woman his manager had so carefully arranged for him.

Julian didn't want a fake girlfriend. He would gladly send this poor woman back home with an apology, but Ross wouldn't have set this up without a good reason. He paid the man to make smart, strategic decisions about his career, so he had to be nice and make this work. Or he'd hear about it.

"And your name is…?" he prompted.

She seemed to snap out of her nervous daze. "Gretchen," she said, holding out her hand. "Gretchen McAlister."

Julian shook her hand, noticing how ice-cold her skin was and how her fingers trembled in his grip. This woman seemed terrified of him. Women usually had a much…warmer reaction to Julian. He had to pry them from his neck and wipe away their lipstick from his cheeks at movie premieres. He needed to warm her up or they were never going to convince anyone—much less a skeptical press—that they were dating.

He took a step back to let her into the hotel room. "Come on in, Gretchen." He shut the door behind them and gestured for her to take a seat in the living room of his suite. "Can I get you something to drink?"

"Something alcoholic would make all this easier," she muttered under her breath.

Julian's lips twisted in amusement as he went over to the minibar. That wasn't a bad idea to help break the ice. At least for her. He didn't drink, but certainly the hotel would've stocked the room with something useful. He wished he *could* drink, but that was on his personal trainer's list of no-no's: no alcohol, no sugar, no carbs, no dairy, no preservatives, no artificial colors, flavors or anything else remotely interesting or tasty.

Unfortunately, he didn't know where to start with a drink for Gretchen. "There's a collection of tiny bottles in here. Feel free to pick whatever you'd like."

Gretchen watched him curiously as she walked over to the bar and pulled out what looked like tequila. He expected her to mix it with something, but instead, watched in surprise as she twisted off the lid and threw back the tiny bottle in a few hard draws. She really must be nervous if she was doing tequila shots just to be in the same room with him.

"You know, you look like you could use one of these yourself. I'm not getting the feeling that you're very happy about this," she said as she looked at him out of the corner of her eye. She tossed the empty bottle into the trash and turned back to sit on the couch. "I know I probably don't meet your standards for a woman you'd date. Mr. Bentley specifically requested an everyday woman, but I assume I'm not what he had in mind. I'm obviously not a Bridgette, so if that's going to be a problem, just say the word and I'll go on my way."

He was doing a crappy job at making her feel welcome. "No, no. I'm sorry," Julian said, sitting down in the chair to face her. "My manager informed me about this whole arrangement literally minutes before you showed up. My reaction has nothing to do with you and the standards you seem to think you fall short of."

"So you're not on board with Mr. Bentley's plan?"

"Not really," he replied. There was no sense in sugar-coating it. "I'll do what I need to do, but this isn't my choice, no. It's pretty common in Hollywood to contract relationships, but that's not my style. I'd rather go to an event alone than with some woman I don't even know. That's probably why Ross sprang this on me—I couldn't get out of it quickly enough. But now, here we are, and I find I'm just not as well prepared as I would like to be."

"Neither am I," she said. "Does one ever really get used to being pimped out by your friends for something like this?"

"Pimped out?" Julian chuckled. The alcohol seemed to loosen her tongue. "That's one way to put it. Welcome to the Hollywood game, Gretchen McAlister. We've all sold ourselves for success. How much did it take for you to toss your good sense out the window and end up on my couch?"

A flicker of irritation crossed her face, blushing her cheeks an attractive pink. It might have just been the tequila kicking in. He'd bet her hands weren't cold any longer. He fought the urge to find a reason to touch her again.

"Apparently, ten grand for my time and another two grand to make me more presentable."

Julian looked over his date of the next few days and frowned. It shouldn't take two thousand to make her presentable, and he hoped Ross hadn't been rude enough to say such a thing. Ross was usually brutally honest, with a set of unrealistic Hollywood ideals. Whereas Gretchen wasn't the kind of woman Julian was normally seen with in LA, she wasn't unattractive. Her skin was creamy and flawless, her lips full and pink. Her eyelashes were so long and thick, he thought they might be fake, but she didn't strike him as that type.

He supposed anyone could use a haircut and a manicure. She could take the rest of the money and buy clothes. Tonight she was dressed as though she'd come straight from her work at the wedding chapel, wearing a plain green shirt and khakis with a brown cardigan, a pair of loafers and argyle socks. Appropriate for winter in the South, he supposed, but not overly dressy. She looked nice. She actually reminded him a lot of his mother when she was younger and life hadn't completely sucked away everything she had.

But instead of complimenting Gretchen the way he knew he should, he went the other direction. He felt himself being drawn in by her shy awkwardness, but Julian had no intention of getting chummy with this woman. She may not be a part of the Hollywood machine, but she'd use him just like everyone else. She was only here because she was being paid a ridiculous amount of money to do it.

"You should've held out for more. Ross would've paid twenty."

Gretchen just shrugged as though the money didn't mean much to her. He knew that couldn't be true. Who would sign up for something like this if it wasn't because they needed the money? He was a millionaire, and he still wouldn't turn down a well-paying role. There was always something he could do with it. Even socking it away in the bank put it to good use.

He doubted that was the case for her, though. She certainly didn't seem to have agreed to this because she was a fan. She was lacking that distinctly starry-eyed gaze he was used to seeing in women. The gaze that flickered over him was appreciative, but reserved. He sensed there was a lot going on in her mind that she wouldn't share with him. He knew he shouldn't care;

she was just a fleeting part of his life this week, but he couldn't help but wonder what was going on under that curly mop of hair.

"Well, now that we've established that I've been had cheaply, do we need to work out any details?"

Yes, Julian thought. It was better to stick to the logistics of the plan. "I came out a few days early to hang out with Murray before the wedding, so you've got some time to buy clothes and do whatever grooming women do. The first event for the wedding is Wednesday night. They're holding a welcome barbecue out at Murray's house. That will be our first official outing. Maybe we should get together here on Wednesday afternoon and spend some time on our story for anyone that asks."

Gretchen nodded. "Okay. I'll get the event schedule from Natalie, the wedding planner. Any special requests?"

Julian's brows went up at her question. "Like what?"

She shrugged. "I've never done this before, but I thought you might have favorite colors for me to wear, or find acrylic nails to be a turnoff, that sort of thing."

He'd never had a woman ask him something like that before. Despite how often people told him they were there for him, they rarely inquired or even cared what he might really want. He had to think about an answer for a moment. "I only have one request, really."

"What's that?"

"Please wear comfortable shoes," Julian said. "I don't know how many events I've sat through where the woman did nothing but complain about her expensive, fancy, painful shoes the whole night."

Gretchen glanced down at her practical and comfortable-looking brown leather loafers. "I don't think that will be a problem. Well, I'll get going." She got up from the couch and held out a card to him.

He accepted it, turning it over to find it was her business card. The design of it was very intricate but delicate, with a shiny ivory damask pattern over a flat white card. The text was in a blush pink, as was an edging of abstract roses, screaming wedding, but not cliché wedding.

"You can reach me at the chapel number during the day or my cell phone the rest of the time. If nothing comes up, I'll see you Wednesday afternoon before the barbecue."

Julian took her hand in his. It was warmer now, and this time, he noticed how soft her skin was against him. He swallowed hard as his palm tingled where their skin touched. His gaze met hers, and he watched her dark eyes widen in surprise for a moment before she pulled her hand away.

"Thanks for doing this, Gretchen," he said, to cover his surprising physical response to her touch. "I'll see you in a few days."

She nodded and bit at her lip as she made her way to the door. After she slipped out, he bolted the lock and turned back to face his room. It suddenly felt more empty and cold than it had when she was here with him.

Perhaps this setup wouldn't be as bad as he thought.

# Two

Gretchen felt as if she'd just lived through that make-over montage from the movie *Miss Congeniality*, although it was more painful than funny. Amelia had scheduled her appointments at the day spa they contracted with for bridal sessions, and they were happy to fit in Gretchen for a full day of beauty.

She was expecting a hair trim and some nail polish. Maybe a facial. Gretchen wasn't a movie star, but she didn't think she needed that much work.

Instead, she'd had nearly every hair on her body ripped out. The hair that was left was cut, highlighted and blown into a bouncy but straight bob. Her skin was buffed and polished, her clogged pores "extracted," and then she was wrapped like a mummy to remove toxins, reduce cellulite and squeeze out some water weight. They finished her off with a coat of spray tan to chase away the pastiness. She got a pedicure and solar nails in a classic pink-and-white French manicure that she couldn't chip. They even bleached her teeth.

Thankfully Gretchen didn't have much of an ego, or it would've been decimated. It had taken about seven hours so far, but she thought she might—*might*—be done. She was wrapped in a fluffy robe in the serenity room. Every time someone came through, they took her into another room and exposed her to another treatment, but she couldn't come up with anything else they could possibly do to her.

This time, when the door opened, it was Amelia. If Gretchen's lady parts weren't still tender, she'd leap up and beat her friend with an aromatherapy pillow for putting her through all this. Instead, she sipped her cucumber-infused mineral water and glared at her.

"Don't you look refreshed!" Amelia said.

"Refreshed?" Gretchen just shook her head. "That's exactly the look I was going for after seven hours of beauty rituals. Julian Cooper's new woman looks so well rested!"

"Quit it, you look great."

Gretchen doubted that. There were improvements, but "great" took it a little far. "I should, after all this," she joked. "If this is what the women in Hollywood go through all the time, I'm glad I live way out here in Nashville."

"It wasn't that bad," Amelia said in a chiding tone. "I've had every single treatment that you had today. But now is the fun part!"

"Lunch?" Gretchen perked up.

Amelia placed a thoughtful hand on her round belly.

"No, shopping. They were supposed to feed you lunch as part of the package."

"Yeah, they did. Sort of." The green salad with citrus vinaigrette and berries for dessert hadn't really made a dent in her appetite.

"If you promise not to give me grief while we're shopping, I'll take you out for a nice dinner."

"I want pretzel bites, too," Gretchen countered. "Take it out of my makeover money."

Amelia smiled. "Fair enough. Get dressed and we'll go buy you some clothes and makeup."

"I have makeup," Gretchen complained as she got up, realizing as she spoke that she'd already broken her agreement not to give Amelia grief. It just seemed wasteful.

"I'm sure you do, but we're going to have the lady at the counter come up with a new look for you, then we'll buy the colors she puts together."

In the ladies' locker room, Gretchen changed back into her street clothes, all the while muttering to herself about Italy. It would be worth it, she insisted. *Just think of the Sistine Chapel*, she told herself.

She continued the mantra as the woman at the department store did her makeup. The mantra got louder as Amelia threw clothes at her over the door of the changing room. Gretchen wasn't really into fashion. She bought clothes that were comfortable, not too expensive and relatively flattering to her shape, such as it was.

But as she turned and looked at herself in the mirror for the first time today, something changed. She was still the Gretchen she recognized, but she looked like the best possible version of herself. Those hours in the salon had left her polished and refined, the makeup highlighting and flattering her features. And although she wouldn't admit it readily to Amelia, the clothes looked really nice on her, too.

It was an amazing transformation from how she'd woken up this morning. This department store obviously used fun-house mirrors to make her look thinner.

"I want to see," Amelia complained. "If you don't come out, I'm coming in."

Reluctantly, Gretchen came out of the dressing room in one of the more casual looks. She was wearing a pair of extremely tight skinny jeans, a white cotton top and a black leather jacket. It looked good, but the number of digits on the price tags was scaring her. "I only have two thousand dollars, Amelia. I don't know how much we blew at the spa, but I'm certain I can't afford a three-hundred-dollar leather jacket."

Amelia frowned. "I have a charge account here. They send me a million coupons. We'll have enough money, I promise. You need that jacket."

"I'm going to a wedding. Isn't it more important for me to get a nice dress?"

"Yes, but all the formals are marked down from homecoming, so we'll get one for a good price. You're also going to the welcome party and the rehearsal dinner. You need something casual, something more formal and a few things in between just in case you get roped into the bridal tea or something. And you're going to own this stuff long after this week is over, so it's important to choose good bones for your wardrobe. I like that outfit on you. You're getting it."

"It's too tight," Gretchen complained, and tugged the top away from her stomach. "I'm too heavy to wear clingy stuff like this."

Amelia sighed and rolled her eyes. "I'm sorry, but wearing bulky clothes just makes you look bigger than you are. I wore a 34F bra *before* I got pregnant, okay? I've tried hiding these suckers under baggy sweaters for years, but I wasn't fooling anyone. If you've got it, flaunt it. Well-fitting clothes will actually make you look smaller and showcase your curves."

Gretchen just turned and went back into the dressing room. There was no arguing with her. Instead, she stripped out of the outfit and tried on another. Before they were done, she'd gone through about a dozen other outfits. In the end, they agreed on a paisley wrap dress, a gray sweaterdress with tights, a bright purple cocktail dress, and a strapless formal that looked as if it had been painted with watercolors on the full silky skirt. Gretchen had to admit the gown was pretty, and appropriate for an artist, but she wasn't sure if she could pull any of this off. In the end, she needed to look as though she belonged on the arm of Julian Cooper.

She didn't think there were clothes for any price that would make the two of them make sense. Julian was…the most beautiful man she'd ever seen in person. The movies didn't even do him justice. His eyes were a brilliant shade of robin's-egg blue, fringed in thick brown lashes. His messy chestnut-colored hair had copper highlights that caught the lights and shimmered. His jaw was square and stubble-covered, his skin tan, and when she got close, she could smell the warm scent of his cologne. It was intoxicating.

And that wasn't even touching the subject of his body. His shoulders were a mile wide, narrowing into a thin waist and narrow hips. He'd been wearing an untucked button-down shirt and jeans when they met, but still, little was left to her imagination, they fit so well. The moment he'd opened the door, her ability to perform rational speech was stolen away. She'd felt a surge of desire lick hot at her blushing cheeks. Her knees had softened, making her glad she was wearing sensible flats and not the heels Amelia had nagged her to wear.

When it came down to it, Julian was…a movie star. An honest to God, hard-bodied, big-screen superstar. He was like an alien from another planet. A planet of ridiculously handsome people. And even though she looked pretty good in these expensive clothes with expertly applied makeup, Gretchen was still a chubby wallflower with no business anywhere near a man like him.

Men had always been confusing creatures to Gretchen. Despite years of watching her sisters and friends date, she'd never been very good with the opposite sex. Her lack of confidence was a self-fulfilling prophecy, keeping most guys at arm's length. When a man did approach her, she was horrible at flirting and had no clue if he was hitting on her or just making conversation.

At her age, most women had a couple relationships under their belts, marriages, children… Gretchen hadn't even been naked in front of a man before. On the rare occasion a guy did show interest in her, things always fell apart before it got that far. Her condition seemed to perpetuate itself, making her more unsure and nervous as the years went by.

Being close to any man set her on edge, and a good-looking one made her downright scattered. Julian just had to smile at her and she was a mess. She couldn't find a normal guy to be with her; how would anyone believe a shy, awkward nobody could catch Julian's eye? It was a lost cause, but she couldn't convince anyone of that.

An hour later, they carried their bags out to Amelia's car and settled on having dinner at a restaurant that was a few miles from the mall, near the golf course.

"I'm glad we could have a girls' day out," Amelia said as they went inside. "Tyler had to fly to Antwerp again, and I get lonely in that big house by myself."

Amelia's husband, Tyler, was a jewel and gemstone dealer who regularly traveled the world. They'd hired a woman named Stella to help with catering at From This Moment, so Amelia occasionally got to travel with Tyler, but the further she got in her pregnancy, the less interested she was in long flights. That left her alone in their giant Belle Meade mansion.

"In a few more months, that little girl will get here and you'll never be alone again."

"True. And I need your help to come up with some good names. Tyler is terrible at it." Amelia approached the hostess stand. "Two for dinner, please."

"Good evening, ladies."

Gretchen turned at the sound of a man's voice and found Murray Evans and Julian standing by the entrance behind them. Before she could say anything, Julian approached her and she found herself wrapped in his arms. He smiled at her with a warmth she would never have expected after their awkward first meeting, and he hugged her tight against the hard muscles of his chest.

She stood stiffly in his arms, burying her surprised expression in his neck and waiting for him to back off, but he didn't seem to be in a rush. When he did finally pull away, he didn't let her go. Instead, he dipped his head down and pressed his lips to hers. It was a quick kiss, but it sent a rush down her spine that awakened her every nerve. She almost couldn't grasp what was going on. Julian Cooper was kissing her. Kissing her! In public. She couldn't even enjoy it because she was so freaked out.

He pulled away and leaned down to whisper in her ear. "You need to work on that," he said. Then he wrapped his arm around her shoulders and turned to Amelia with a bright, charming smile.

"What good fortune that we'd run into you tonight. It must be fate. Do you mind if Murray and I join you for dinner?"

"Not at all, please," the redhead said with a smile that matched his own. "Gretchen said the boys would be out and about today, but we didn't expect to run into you down here in Franklin." She had a twinkle of amusement in her eyes that made her seem like the savvy type who knew how to play the game. But judging by the curve of her belly and the rock on her hand, he knew why the redhead had been taken out of the running for his fake girlfriend.

"Excellent." Julian turned to ask the hostess to change the table from two to four, ignoring the woman's stunned expression. He was used to that reaction when he attempted to live a real life outside Hollywood. What bothered him more was the wrinkling of the woman's nose as her gaze shifted to Gretchen in confusion. It made him pull her tighter to his side and plant a kiss in the silky dark strands of hair at the crown of her head.

"What are you two doing out in Franklin?" Gretchen spoke at last, squirming slightly from his arms.

"Well," Murray began, "we wanted to play some golf. Since I live in Brentwood, coming down here to Forrest Hills is easier and we're less likely to run into any photogs."

The hostess gestured for them to follow her to a corner booth in the back of the restaurant. Gretchen slid into one side, and he sat beside her before she could protest. She might not be ready for their ruse to begin, but they were together in public. He hadn't seen any photographers, but one could be around the next corner. The nosy hostess could tip someone off at the local paper. If anyone saw them together, they needed to be playing their parts.

"What are you ladies up to today?" Julian asked after the server took their drink orders.

"It's makeover day," Gretchen said. "Julian, this is Amelia Dixon. She's the caterer at From This Moment. She's also very fashionable and helped me with my full day of beauty and shopping."

Julian shook Amelia's hand, but he found it hard to turn away from Gretchen once he started really looking at her. She looked almost like a different woman from the one who had shown up at his hotel room the day before. He hadn't even recognized her when they first walked in the restaurant. It wasn't until Murray pointed out that they were the women from the chapel that he realized it was Gretchen. The changes were subtle, a refinement of what was already there, but the overall effect was stunning. She was glowing. Radiant. The straightening of her hair made an amazing difference, highlighting the soft curve of her face.

"Well, she did an excellent job. You look amazing. I can't wait to see what you guys bought for the wedding."

Gretchen watched him with wary eyes, as though she didn't quite believe what he'd said. She'd looked at him that way the first night, too. She was an incredibly suspicious woman. He smiled in an attempt to counteract her suspicion, and that just made her flush. Red mottled her chest and traveled up her throat to her cheeks. It seemed as though she blushed right down to her toes. It was charming after spending time with women too bold to blush and too aware of their own beauty to be swayed by his compliments.

He'd argued with Ross that he didn't think this was going to work after their short, strained meeting, but maybe he was wrong. They just needed to deal with her nerves so her physical reactions to him were more appropriate. She went stiff as a board in his arms, but he had some acting exercises that would help. It was probably fortuitous that they ran into each other tonight. Better they work these issues out now than at an official wedding event.

As the evening went on, it became clear that Julian knew the least about everyone there. Murray had met both women at the various planning sessions leading up to the wedding extravaganza. Julian was starting with a completely clean slate where Gretchen was concerned. Ross hadn't even told him his date's name before they met, and their first conversation hadn't been particularly revealing. They wouldn't just be posing for some pictures this week. They'd have to interact as a couple, and that meant they needed to learn more about each other if they were going to be believable.

"So you said Amelia is the caterer. What do you do, Gretchen?"

Gretchen got an odd look on her face as though she

wasn't quite sure how to describe what she did for a living. It wasn't a very hard question, was it?

"Gretchen is our visual stylist," Amelia said, jumping in to fill the silence.

"I have no idea what that is," Julian admitted.

"Well, that's why I hesitated," Gretchen said. "I do a lot of different things. I design all the paper products, like the invitations and programs. I do all the calligraphy."

"So you designed Murray's invitations?"

A wide smile crossed Gretchen's face for the first time. "I did. I was really excited about that design. I love it when I can incorporate something personal about the couple, and musical notes seemed like the perfect touch."

"They were just what we were looking for," Murray said.

"They were nice. I wouldn't have remembered them otherwise."

"Thank you. I also do a lot of the decorating and work with the various vendors to get the flowers and other touches set up for the wedding and the reception. I'm a jack-of-all-trades, really. On the day of the wedding, I might be doing emergency stitching on a bridesmaid's dress, tracking down a wayward groomsman, helping Amelia in the kitchen…"

"Or pinch-hitting as the best man's date?" Julian said with a chuckle.

"Apparently." She sighed. "I was the only one that could do it."

"You mean, you ladies weren't clamoring over who got to spend time with me? I don't know if I should be insulted or not."

Gretchen shrugged and looked at him with a crooked smile that made him think maybe he should be insulted. "It's got to be better than stitching up a torn bridesmaid's dress, right? It's not so bad to be around me. At least I don't think it is. I'm fun, aren't I, Murray?"

"Absolutely. You're going to have a great time with Julian. Just don't get him talking about his movies. He'll be insufferable."

"What's wrong with my movies?" Julian asked with mock injury in his voice. He didn't really need to ask. He knew better than anyone that all the films he'd done in the past few years were crap.

He'd started out at an acclaimed theater program at the University of Kentucky. He'd gotten a full scholarship out of high school, praised for his senior performance as the lead in *The Music Man*. He'd intended to go on to graduate and do more stage work. Maybe not musicals—he wasn't the best singer—but he enjoyed the acting craft. Then his life fell apart and he had to drop out of school. Desperation drove him to commercial acting, and with a stroke of luck, he ended up where he was now. It wasn't the creative, fulfilling career he'd dreamed of when he was younger, but his paycheck had more zeroes than he'd ever imagined he'd see in his lifetime.

Everyone laughed and they spent a while critiquing the plot of *Bombs of Fury* as their food arrived. The conversation continued on various subjects throughout the evening, flowing easily with the group. Gretchen had been quiet at first, but after talking about her work and mocking his, she started to warm up. Julian actually had a good time, which was rare, considering he was having to eat salmon and steamed broccoli while the rest of them were enjoying tastier foods. It should be against the law to be in the South and not be able to eat anything fried.

When it was over, they headed out to their cars as a group. He walked Gretchen to the passenger door of Amelia's SUV and leaned in close to her. "I had fun tonight."

"Yeah," she said, nervously eyeing him as he got close to her. "It was a pleasant surprise to run into you."

"I guess I'll see you tomorrow afternoon." Tomorrow was the welcome party and their first official time out as a couple.

"Okay. Good night."

"Good night." On reflex, Julian leaned in to give her a kiss good-night. He was stopped short by Gretchen's hand pressed against his chest.

"You know, no one is watching us. You don't have to pretend to want to kiss me."

Julian smiled. "If there's one thing I've learned in my years in LA, it's that someone is always watching. But even then, I would still kiss you."

"Why?" Her dark eyes searched his face in confusion, her brows drawn together.

She honestly didn't think she was kissable. That was a shame. She was very kissable, with pouty lips glistening from just a touch of sparkly lip gloss. If he were interested in that sort of thing. Tonight, however, he was more focused on their cover and getting it right.

"I'm going to kiss you again because you need the practice. Every time I touch you, you stiffen up. You've got to relax. If it means I have to constantly paw at you and kiss you until you loosen up, so be it." He'd had worse assignments.

Gretchen bit her bottom lip. "I'm sorry. I'm just not used to being touched."

He wrapped his hand around hers and pulled it away from his chest, where she'd still been holding him back. "It's not that hard. Just take a deep breath, tilt your head up to me and close your eyes."

She did as she was instructed, leaning into him like a teenage girl being kissed for the first time. He shook away those thoughts and pressed his lips against hers. He'd intended it to be a quick kiss, knowing it would take a while for them to work up to a convincing one. But he found that once they touched, he didn't want to pull away.

Gretchen smelled like berries. Her lips were soft, despite the hesitation in them. A tingle ran down his spine, the kind that made him want to wrap his arms around her and pull her soft body flush against his hard one. He settled for placing a hand on her upper arm.

She tensed immediately, and in an instant, the connection was severed. He pulled away and looked down at her, standing there with her eyes still closed.

"You did better this time," he noted.

Her dark lashes fluttered as her eyes opened. A pink flush rushed across her cheeks as she looked up at him with glassy eyes. "Practice makes perfect, I guess."

He laughed softly. It certainly did. "I'll see you tomorrow afternoon. Be sure to bring extra lipstick."

"Why?" she asked, her brow furrowed.

Julian smiled wide and took a step back toward where Murray was waiting for him. "Because I plan to remove all of it several times."

# Three

Gretchen made her way back up to Julian's hotel suite the next day. This afternoon, she wasn't as nervous as her first visit, but she still had butterflies in her stomach. She was pretty certain that last night's kiss had something to do with it. She'd been kissed by only four men before last night, and none of them had been movie stars.

She couldn't even sleep last night. His threat to remove her lipstick several times over lingered in her mind. He was going to kiss her again. She felt a girlish thrill run through her every time the thought crossed her mind, quickly followed by the dull ache of dread in her stomach.

There was nothing she could do about it, though. She had to live through this. It was only four days. She could make it through four days of almost anything. She

knocked at his hotel room door and waited, anxiously
tugging at her paisley wrap dress.

"Hey, Gretchen," Julian said as he peeked around the
door with a head of damp hair. "You'll have to excuse
me—I was running late. Come on in. I've just got to
finish getting dressed."

He stepped back and opened the door wider. As
Gretchen entered the suite, she realized he'd been hiding his half-naked body behind the door. Just his hair
wasn't wet; all of him was. He had a bath towel slung
low around his waist, but otherwise, he was very naked.

She didn't even know what to say. As he closed the
door behind her, all she could do was stare at the hard,
tanned muscles she'd seen in the movies and on adver-
tisements. His body didn't even look real, although she
could reach out and touch it. It was as if he was Photo-
shopped.

"Gretchen?"

She snapped her head up to see Julian watching her
with amusement curling his lips into a smile. She could
feel the blood rush hot into her cheeks when she realized she'd been caught. "Yes?" she said.

"Go ahead and grab a seat. I'll be right back."

"Yeah, okay."

Turning as quickly as she could, she focused on the
couch, gluing her eyes to the furniture so they couldn't
stray back to Julian's naked, wet body.

He disappeared, thankfully, into the bedroom. The
moment the door closed, she felt the air rush out of her
lungs. Sweet Jesus, she thought as her face dropped into
her hands. She was about as smooth as chunky peanut
butter. There was no doubt that Gretchen was miser-

ably in over her head. There had to be a better person to do this than her.

"Sorry about that," he said as he came out a few minutes later. He was wearing a pair of charcoal dress pants and a navy dress shirt that made his eyes seem as if they were an even brighter blue. "I didn't want to leave you out in the hallway while I got dressed. I hope that was okay."

"It's fine," she said dismissively. Hopefully convincingly. "It's not like you don't run around like that in half your movies anyway. Nothing I haven't seen."

He chuckled as he settled down on the couch beside her. "Yeah, most of my modesty went out the window a few years ago. Once you film a sex scene with thirty-five people watching, then millions watch it on the big screen, there's not much left to worry about."

"Do you do a lot of sex scenes?" Gretchen asked. She couldn't imagine how invasive that would be. She couldn't even work up the courage to take her clothes off in front of one man, much less a roomful.

"There's usually one in every film. I typically save the female lead from the bad guy and she thanks me with her body. It's always seemed a little cliché and stupid to me. You'd think someone would be too traumatized for something like that, but apparently I'm so handsome, they can't help themselves."

"I'm sure most women in real life couldn't help themselves either. You're in…excellent shape."

He grinned wide, exposing the bright smile that charmed women everywhere. "Thank you. I work very hard to look like this, so it's nice to be appreciated."

"I can't imagine what it would take."

"I can tell you. I do high-intensity interval training four days a week and run about ten miles a day the other three. I have given up all my vices, and my trainer has me eating nothing but lean protein, vegetables and some fruits."

Gretchen's eyes grew larger the more he talked. That sounded miserable. No pizza, no bread, no cookies. He looked good, but what a price. "I, obviously, am not willing to put that much work in."

"Most people aren't, but I make my living with these abs. It's not exactly what I'd planned when I moved to California, but it's worked out. Even then, there are days where I'd kill for a chocolate chip cookie. Just one."

That just seemed sad. She was no poster child for moderation, but there had to be some middle ground. "I guess the wedding cake is out, then. That's a shame. Amelia does amazing work."

Julian narrowed his gaze at her. "Maybe I'll make an exception for a bite or two of her amazing cake. I'll let you feed me some of yours so I'm not too tempted."

She couldn't even imagine feeding Julian cake while they sat together at the reception. That seemed so intimate, so beyond where they were together. She knew nothing about him, aside from the fact that he was out of her league.

"I need to tell you something," she said. The words shot out of her mouth before she could stop them.

His dark brows went up curiously. "What's that?"

"It may be painfully obvious to you, but I'm not very good with this kind of thing. I haven't been in many relationships, so this whole situation is alien to me. I don't know if coaching will be enough for me to pull this off." She stopped talking and waited in the silence for him to put an end to this torture and terminate the relationship agreement. If they hurried, maybe they could find a more suitable replacement before the welcome dinner. Anyone would be better than Gretchen.

"I think that's charming," he said with a disarming smile. "Most of the women I know mastered flirting in kindergarten. But no worries. I'll teach you what you need to know."

"How can you teach me how to have a relationship in only a few hours if I haven't mastered it in almost twenty-nine years?"

He leaned in and fixed his bright blue gaze on her. "I happen to be an actor," he confided in a low voice. "A classically trained one at that. I can teach you some tricks to get through it."

Tricks? How could a few acting drills undo fifteen years of awkwardness around men? "Like what?"

"Like reframing the scene in your mind. For one thing, you've got to stop thinking about who I am. That's not going to help you relax. I want you to look at the next few days like a play. You and I are the leads. I'm no more famous than you are. We're equals."

"That's a nice idea, but—"

Julian held up his hand to silence her. "No buts. We're actors. You are a beautiful actress playing the role of my girlfriend. You're meant to be here with me and you're perfectly comfortable with me touching you. That's how it's supposed to be."

Gretchen sighed. It would take more than a little role-playing for her to convince herself of that. "I'm not a beautiful actress. I can't be."

"And why not?" He frowned at her, obviously irritated by her stubbornness to play his game.

"To be a beautiful actress, one must first be beautiful. Only then are acting skills relevant."

Julian narrowed his gaze at her. She squirmed under the scrutiny. They both knew she wasn't Hollywood starlet material; there wasn't any need to look so closely and pick apart the details of her failures.

He reached out and took her hand in his. "Did you know that Bridgette has a mustache she has to get waxed off? She's also not really a blonde, and most of her hair is made up of extensions. Her breasts are fake. Her nose is fake. Everything about her is fake."

"And she looks good." The money was well invested in her career if what he said was true. If Gretchen had a couple grand just lying around, she might make a few improvements herself.

"Julia Monroe is legally blind when she isn't wearing her contact lenses. If her makeup artist doesn't contour her face just right, she looks like a guy after a losing boxing match."

Julia Monroe was one of the biggest and most sought-out actresses in Hollywood. Gretchen had a hard time believing she could look anything but stunning.

"Rochelle Voight has the longest nose hairs I've ever seen on a woman, and her breath is always rancid. I think it's because all she ever eats or drinks are those green juices. I hate when I have to kiss her or film close scenes."

Was he serious? "Why are you telling me all this?"

"Because you need to know that it's all an illusion. Every single one of the Hollywood beautiful people you've compared yourself to is a carefully crafted character designed just for the cameras. We're far from perfect, and more than a few of us couldn't even be described as beautiful without our makeup and hair teams."

"You're telling me everyone in Hollywood is secretly ugly, so I shouldn't feel bad."

He smirked and leaned in to drive home his point. "I'm saying you're an attractive woman—a realistically attractive woman. You shouldn't put yourself through the wringer comparing yourself to an unrealistic ideal. It's all fake."

Gretchen's brows went up in surprise. Even with her makeover, she felt as if Julian were only tolerating her because he couldn't get out of the arrangement. Could he actually believe what he said, or was he just trying to boost her ego enough to get them through this week together?

"Everything about me is fake, too," he said.

It was easy to believe the women he'd spoken about were painted to perfection, but everything on Julian looked pretty darn real to her. "Come on," she chided, pulling her hand from his. She knew he was putting her on now.

"No, I'm serious. These baby blue eyes are colored contacts. The highlights in my hair are fake. My teeth are porcelain veneers because my parents couldn't afford braces when I was younger. My tan is sprayed on weekly. Even my accent is fake."

"You don't have an accent," she argued.

"Exactly. I'm from Kentucky," he said with an unmistakable twang he'd suppressed earlier. "I have an accent, but you're never going to hear it from me because I hide it like everything else."

Gretchen sat back against the cushions of the couch

and tried to absorb everything he was telling her. It was a lot to take in all at once.

"We may all have fake hair and wear makeup and put ourselves through all sorts of abuses to chase the elusive beauty and youth, but we're all actors. This is just our costume. So think of your new makeover as your costume. You've been given all the tools you need. Are you ready to play the role of Julian Cooper's girlfriend?"

She took a deep breath and straightened up in her seat. "I think so."

He cocked his head to the side and lifted a brow at her in challenge.

"I *am*," she corrected with faux confidence in her voice. "Let's do this. Where do we start?"

Julian smiled and turned to face her on the couch. "Okay. When I was in acting school, one of my professors was adamant about throwing the hardest scenes at us first. He didn't let us warm up or start with a less challenging part. We had to open with the dramatic soliloquy. His theory was that once you did that, everything else would come easier. So we're going to start with the hardest part of your role."

Gretchen tensed beside him. The hardest part? It all seemed pretty challenging. She'd be much happier working her way up to the comfort level she needed to pull this off. "How are you—"

He lunged forward and pressed his lips to hers, stealing the question from her lips. Unlike their quick, passionless pecks at the restaurant the night before, this kiss packed a punch. Julian leaned into her, coaxing her mouth open and probing her with his tongue.

She wanted to pull away, but he wouldn't let her. One of his hands was at her waist and the other on her shoulder, keeping her from retreating. Closing her eyes, she remembered she was an actress playing a part. She stopped fighting it and tried to relax. Maybe she could let herself enjoy it for once.

When her tongue tentatively grazed along his, he moaned low against her mouth. The sound sent a shock wave of need through her body making her extremities tingle. She wrapped her arms around his neck and pulled him closer to her. When she'd relaxed against him, his grip on her lessened and his hands became softer and exploratory. They slid across the silky fabric of her dress, finally coming to rest as they wrapped around her waist.

Just when Gretchen had relaxed into his arms and was enjoying their experimental kiss, she felt him tug hard against her. Mercy, but he was strong. Those muscles weren't just for show. The next thing she knew, she was in Julian's lap, straddling him. Her dress rode up high on her thighs and she could feel the warm press of his arousal against her leg.

She almost didn't believe it at first. Gretchen hadn't felt many erections in her time. She hadn't anticipated feeling one here, for sure. Could Julian really be turned on by their kiss, or was he just a very convincing actor? The concerning question startled her enough to make her break away from the kiss. The second her eyes opened, she regretted it. In the moment, things had felt right. Exhilarating and scary, but right. Once she pulled away, all she could do was look awkwardly at the man in whose lap she was sitting. It was a decidedly unladylike and bold place to be, and she wasn't comfortable with either of those adjectives. She could feel the heat in her chest and throat and knew she was blushing crimson in her predicament.

Julian didn't seem to mind. Their awkward parting and her extra pounds in his lap were irrelevant if the pleased grin on his face told her anything. She couldn't tell if he was happy she was doing so well, if he was that good an actor, or if he really was having a good time with it.

"Excellent work," he said. "You're an A pupil."

"Does that mean I should get off your lap so we can move on to the next lesson?"

He shook his head and wrapped his arms tighter around her waist. "Not a chance. Just because you're a quick study doesn't mean you don't need the lessons. We're going to work on this a little more."

"How much more?"

"We're going to sit on this couch and make out until it feels like the most natural thing in the world for us both. If you're going to fool the cameras, we can't stop short of anything less than authenticity."

Gretchen swallowed a chortle of laughter. She wasn't sure that making out with a man like him would ever feel natural, but she wasn't about to complain any time soon about extra lessons.

Julian's rental car was only a few miles from Murray's house, where they were hosting the welcome barbecue. Julian had spent a good part of the past hour going over their manufactured backstory with Gretchen.

"Okay, tell me again how we met. People are going to ask."

She sighed and turned to look out the passenger side window. "You came out here to visit Murray a few weeks ago and happened to join him on a trip to the venue, where you met me. We hit it off, you asked me out for a drink. We've been texting and talking since you went back to LA, and you came back to Nashville early for us to spend time together."

She nailed it. He knew she would. Beneath that shy buffer, Gretchen was one of the smartest, funniest women he'd ever met. It just took a while to get through the nerves. She could handle this; she just couldn't let her anxiety get in the way. "Have we slept together yet?"

Gretchen looked at him with wide eyes. "No, I doubt it. I think we may have traded some saucy texts, but I'm making you wait a little while longer."

"You're a little minx. Good to know."

Julian slowly pulled the car into the driveway and stopped at the large wrought-iron fence, where a small crowd of camera-toting men and fans were loitering. "Smile, you're on *Candid Camera*."

"What do I do?" she asked.

"Just pretend they aren't there. That's the easiest thing to do. Maybe play it up for them a little bit." He reached out and took her hand, holding it in an effortless way as they waited for security to open the gates. Once they pulled through there, they followed the circular driveway to the house, where a valet was waiting. He left the keys in the ignition and turned to look at her. "Any last questions before we do this?"

"Who knows the truth about us?"

That was a good question. "Murray, obviously. And I'm sure he told his fiancée, Kelly. That should be it since Ross won't be at the festivities. Everyone else here thinks you're my new girl."

She nodded and took a deep breath. "Let's get our party on, shall we?"

The valet opened her door and she stepped out, waiting for Julian to walk around and meet her. Together, they walked up the stairs to the front door. When the massive oak doors swung open, they were bombarded with a cacophony of sounds and delicious smells. Murray had spared no expense with even the smallest of events. There were easily a hundred people throughout the large open areas of the ground floor and more outside on the heated deck. A bluegrass band was playing in the gazebo in the backyard, and parked out there was a barbecue truck, smoking ribs and brisket for everyone.

There was a large bar set up in the dining room, just past the buffet of goodies that he knew was only to hold people over until the main course was ready. Shame he couldn't eat any of it.

"Would you like a drink?" he asked, leaning down to murmur in her ear.

"Please."

They went over to the bar, where he got her a margarita on the rocks and got himself sparkling water with a twist of lime. They had a huge keg of beer from a local Nashville microbrewery, which he'd love, but he knew he shouldn't. There would be enough temptations this week without starting off on the wrong foot. As it was, he hadn't worked out since he got here.

"So you don't drink?" Gretchen asked. "Is that a health thing or a moralistic thing?"

"Health. Too many empty calories. One too many beers and all my dietary rules will go out the window. You don't want to find me passed out in a half-eaten pizza, I assure you."

"Scandalous!" she mocked.

"I know, right?" He looked around and spied Murray and Kelly out on the patio. "Have you met Kelly?"

"The bride? Yes. She's been to the facility several times going over details."

"Okay, good. Let's go say hi to the happy couple, then we can find a comfortable place to hang out and hide from most everyone."

"You don't have friends here?"

Julian shook his head. "Not really. Murray and I were roommates in college. When I dropped out and moved to LA, we kept in touch, but I don't really know any of his Nashville friends. I'm mostly here for moral support."

They stepped out onto the deck and greeted the engaged couple.

"So, this is the new lady Murray has told me so much about," Kelly said with a wide smile and a twinkle in her green eyes. "It's good to see you outside of work, Gretchen. I have gotten so many compliments on the invitations. I can't wait to see what you've got in store for the wedding. I think the programs are going to be fabulous."

"Thank you," Gretchen said with a smile.

Julian watched the two women as they chatted about wedding details. From that night at the restaurant, Julian had noticed that Gretchen's reluctance faded away when she talked about her work. She was like a totally different person. She nearly radiated with a confidence that vanished the moment the attention shifted from her art back to her. He understood that. He'd much rather talk about his films, such as they were, than talk about his family or his upbringing. Those were tales better left untold.

"Do you mind if I steal her away?" Kelly asked. "I want to introduce her to my bridesmaids."

"Sure." Julian bent down and planted a kiss in the hollow just below her ear. She shivered but didn't pull away or tense up. Bravo. "Hurry back."

Gretchen gave him a wave and disappeared into the house with Kelly.

"How's that going?" Murray asked.

"Better than expected. I've got her loosened up, so that's helped."

"You're doing a good job, whatever it is. When you came out on the patio together, there wasn't a question in my mind that you two were a couple."

"Really?" Julian smiled. He was pleased they'd come so far, so quickly. Perhaps he wouldn't have to deal with Ross's sour disposition later in the week if this worked out. "I am an award-winning actor, you know."

"The golden popcorn statuette from MTV for Best Fight Scene doesn't really stack up to a Screen Actors Guild Award."

"Don't I know it," Julian grumbled. One day, he wanted a real award for a movie with substance. Once he'd told Ross he wanted to do a movie with depth and the next thing he knew, he was in a movie about terrorists who take over a submarine. Just another flick where he lost his shirt eventually.

"It didn't look like acting to me," Murray said. "You two really look like you've got some chemistry between you. Real chemistry. I'm surprised. She didn't strike me as your type, but stranger things have happened. I, for one, never thought I'd end up with my opening act."

Julian listened to his friend and thoughtfully sipped his drink. He was right. There was something building between them. He didn't know what it was—novelty perhaps. Gretchen was nothing like any of the women he'd ever dated before, and it wasn't just physical differences.

For one thing, she wasn't a vain peacock of a woman. Julian spent his fair share of time in the hair and makeup trailer during films and for official appearances, but it was always a fraction of the time his female costars put in. He got the feeling that Gretchen's day at the spa was a rarity for her. She took care of herself, but her whole self-worth was not wrapped up in her appearance. She was a skilled artist, a savvy businesswoman, and that was more important to her than clothing designers and a close, personal relationship with her colorist.

She also didn't seem that impressed by him. Gretchen was nervous, to be sure, but he got the feeling she was that way around most men. She was aware of his celebrity status, but he couldn't tell if it just didn't impress her, or she didn't care for his body of work. He'd been greeted by plenty of screaming, crying women on the verge of passing out when he touched them. If Gretchen passed out at his touch, it was probably because she'd tensed up and locked her knees.

It had been a long time since he'd been around a woman who didn't care about his money or what he could do for her. She didn't secretly want to act. He wasn't aware of her carrying around a screenplay in her purse for him to read and pass on to a producer. Gretchen was real. She was the first authentic woman he'd spent time with in a really long while. He'd been in California so long, he'd forgotten what it was like to be with a woman instead of a character.

He turned and glanced through the wall of French doors into the house. He spied Gretchen and Kelly standing by the buffet chatting with another woman. Gretchen was smiling awkwardly, carrying on the conversation as best she could. He knew the exact moment the discussion shifted to her work, because she lit up like the sun. She might not think she was a beautiful woman, but he'd never seen anyone more radiant in that moment.

Gretchen was slowly drawing him in. He never intended to let himself get that close to his fake date, but he couldn't help it. He fought the urge to text his brother and tell him about her. James always loved it when his aide would relay stories about Julian's escapades, and he thought his brother would take to Gretchen. She was a talented artist with a quick wit and coy smile. She seemed to enjoy the pleasures in life, drinking her margarita and nibbling on goodies without remorse. She knew who she was, and she lived the life she wanted to.

It was an attractive quality that made him both extremely jealous of her and desperate to have her all at once.

# Four

Gretchen crept quietly into the office Thursday morning. She didn't have any wedding-related activities with Julian today, so she wanted to get some things set up for the weekend. Despite the assurances from her co-workers that she didn't have much to do the day of the event, there was plenty that needed to be organized beforehand. And the more she could get done without her coworkers knowing she was there, the better. She wasn't ready for the inquisition.

"Look at you," a woman's voice called down the hallway just before Gretchen reached her office. "Creeping around in the hopes we wouldn't see you. Your hair might be different, but we can still recognize you, you know."

Turning around, Gretchen saw Bree standing outside her office. There was a knowing smirk on her face, and her arms were crossed over her chest.

"Morning, Bree," Gretchen tried to say brightly.

"Don't 'morning' me. You go ahead and get settled, but you'd better know we want to hear all about it."

With a sigh, Gretchen nodded and continued into her office. She hoped it would be quick. They did have a huge, expensive wedding this weekend. Amelia, especially, didn't have time to waste with all those people to feed.

Setting down her things, Gretchen didn't even bother getting on her computer. Instead, she went to the door that led to her storage area. She scanned the various box labels on the shelves, finally identifying the box with the Murray wedding paper goods.

She put it on her desk and lifted the lid. Inside were the wedding programs she'd had printed weeks ago. Beside them were the name cards, table markers and menus. Gretchen had thoroughly gone over everything when they arrived, so she knew they were good to go. She carried the programs into the chapel and left them on the small table just inside. The name cards were left on the round table outside the reception hall. Once the table linens were put out and the centerpieces placed, the cards would be laid out alphabetically for attendees to find their table assignment.

Gretchen continued on through the glass double doors into the reception hall. The large, open room was just a shell of what it would be. The bones were there—sparkling chandeliers and long draped panels of white fabric were hanging overhead, the stage and the dance floor cleared and ready to be occupied by tipsy revelers. The cleaning crew had already been through the day before to vacuum and arrange the tables and chairs.

It would take hours of work to decorate the room. She

hoped to get a head start on some of it today, although a lot of things were last-minute, such as the dishes and the floral arrangements. The wedding was black and white, following along the musical note theme, so the dry cleaning company would deliver their cleaned, pressed white and black table linens sometime this morning. Some custom hand-beaded sheer overlays were ordered to be put over them, making the white tables look like sheet music. The napkins needed to be folded. Several hundred white pillar candles had to be put out.

Gretchen nervously eyed the bare ballroom. The list of things she had to do was staggering. How had she allowed herself to get roped into this romance charade? Just because things were handled the day of the wedding didn't mean she wasn't running around like a chicken with its head cut off the days leading up to it.

"Gretchen, the dry cleaning delivery is here." Natalie stuck her head into the ballroom. She was wearing her headset, as usual, as she was constantly on the phone. She was the command center of the entire operation, coordinating vendors, talking to clients, booking future events and managing the bookkeeping.

"Awesome, thank you."

She helped unload all their clean linens into the ballroom and decided she wanted to start laying them out. She didn't have time to waste.

"I'm ready to hear about yesterday." Amelia walked into the ballroom with Bree on her heels. "My cakes are cooling and I've got some downtime."

Downtime? Gretchen tried not to snort. "Well, I don't have downtime, so if you want to hear about yesterday, you can listen while you help me drape all the tables."

"Fair enough." Bree shrugged. She reached for a tablecloth and flung it over the nearest table.

"We're alternating black and white," Gretchen explained, and they all started at it. They got through about a third of the tables before Bree gently reminded her that they weren't helping out of the goodness of their hearts.

"So, spill it. Did you kiss him?"

Gretchen felt her cheeks turn crimson again. "Yes. I kissed him a lot. He insisted we kiss until I could relax while I was doing it."

"That is just crazy," Bree said. "You're getting paid to make out with Julian Cooper. How did this even happen?"

Shaking her head, Gretchen covered another table in black linen. "I recall you all twisting my arm until I agreed to it."

"Are you getting more comfortable?" Amelia asked, ignoring Gretchen's pointed accusation.

"Yes. I think we're finally to the point where people might actually believe we know each other."

"Biblically?"

"Ugh," Gretchen groaned. "I haven't known anyone biblically, so I can't really say."

"Say what?" Bree stared her down, the linen in her hands pooling on the table. "Did you just say what I thought you said?"

Amelia narrowed her gaze at Gretchen, too. She should've kept her mouth shut about the whole thing. She'd gotten good at it after all these years, even keeping the truth from her best friends. Now the cat was out of the bag.

Gretchen straightened the cloth on the table and admitted the truth, reluctantly. "Yep."

"You're a virgin?" Bree nearly shouted. "How could we not know that you're a virgin?"

"Hush!" Gretchen hissed. "Don't shout it across the ballroom like that."

"I'm sorry," she said, her blue eyes as big as saucers. "It just never occurred to me that my twenty-nine-year-old friend was keeping a secret that big. Did you know?" Bree turned to Amelia.

"I did not."

"You didn't tell any of us?"

"She told me," Natalie said, coming into the room. "It's been a long time, but I haven't gotten any updates that would lead me to believe things had changed."

That was true. Natalie was the only one she'd told, and that had been on a long-ago college night where they'd stayed up late studying, ended up getting into a cheap bottle of wine and spilled their secrets to each other. Natalie was the right person to tell. She wasn't a hopeless romantic like Amelia or pushy like Bree. She took the knowledge at face value and didn't press Gretchen about it.

Bree dropped the tablecloth and sat down in the chair. "Stop, everyone, stop. You all sit down right now and tell me what the heck is going on. How could you keep that from us? And why would you tell Natalie, of all people?"

"Hey!" Natalie complained.

Gretchen frowned at Bree and dropped into a nearby chair. "Bree, how could you not tell us that Ian was your ex before you went up into the mountains to take his engagement photos?"

Bree's nose wrinkled, and she bit at her bottom lip. "It wasn't relevant at the time."

"And neither is my sexual inexperience."

"It might not be relevant to running the business, but as your friend, it seems like something we should've known."

"Known what? That I'm so incredibly awkward with men that I've driven them away since I was fourteen? That my self-esteem is so low that I can't believe a guy could really be interested in me and I look suspiciously at their motives?"

"You're a beautiful, talented woman, Gretchen," Natalie said. "You may not have felt that way when you were a teenager or just in college, but you're on the verge of being in your thirties. Don't you feel differently about yourself after your successes in life?"

"I did. I thought I was doing better and I was even considering putting up an online dating profile, but I have to tell you there's nothing quite like a movie star to bring out your insecurities."

"May I ask how you've gotten this far in life without losing your virginity?" Amelia looked at her with concern in her eyes. It was the same look guys tended to give her when she told them the truth. Like she was damaged somehow.

Gretchen shrugged. "I didn't date in high school. College was hit-or-miss, but nothing ever got serious enough. As I got older, it got harder. It felt more like a burden, which made it even harder to admit to it. With the few guys I've dated in the last couple of years, they push for sex until they find out I haven't done it before, then they back off. They don't want the responsibility for being my first, or they think I'm going to get clingy because of it… I don't know. It just seems like the longer I wait, the harder it is."

"We can fix this," Bree said brightly. "With your new makeover and your new attitude, we can get you a hot guy, pronto."

"I don't want a—" Gretchen tried to argue, but was drowned out.

"We don't just want to get her laid, Bree," Amelia argued. "We want her to find real happiness in a healthy relationship that includes sexual intimacy."

"I'm not sure I'm—"

"She's waited this long, it should be special."

"Just stop!" Gretchen shouted. The others were working hard at fixing all her problems, but that wasn't what she wanted. "See, this is what I wanted to avoid. I don't need to be fixed up or pimped out. It just is what it is."

"Are you happy with the status quo?" Amelia pressed.

"Some days yes, some days no. But the point of this whole thing is that it makes it harder for me to pretend with Julian. I am awkward enough without being around someone that is completely unattainable in real life."

"I don't know," Bree said thoughtfully. "I think you could have him. You're looking mighty fine today."

"You've lost your mind," Gretchen muttered. If there was one thing she hated, it was being the center of attention. It made her extremely uncomfortable. She was desperate to shift this conversation in another direction. "Now you all know my deep dark secrets, so either help me put out tablecloths or return to your battle stations. There's nothing more to see here."

Bree finished laying out one more tablecloth, then she joined the other two as they slipped out to their offices and kitchen to return to work. Gretchen was relieved to be in the ballroom by herself again.

That was uncomfortable, but it was over, thankfully. She'd never have to confess it to her friends and coworkers again. But she was sure she hadn't heard the end of it. Once this nonsense with Julian wasn't taking up her time, she had no doubt one of them would try to fix her up. They'd tried before, just attempting to help her find a guy, but now it would be a mission.

Laying out the last tablecloth, she looked across the room, which was like a checkerboard stretching out in front of her. In two days, she would be in this room as a guest instead of an employee. It was an odd thought, especially considering she'd be on Julian Cooper's arm.

She couldn't believe Bree actually thought that Julian could be the one to relieve her of the burden of her virginity. That was ridiculous, even with her secret knowledge that he was aroused by kissing her. There was a far leap between those two things. She was paid to be his date in public, not in private. If he actually slept with her, it would be because he wanted her.

There was no way in hell he wanted her. Or did he?

Julian pulled his nondescript black rental SUV into the parking lot at From This Moment. He really didn't need to come here today. Today was a day of relaxation, small errands and final preparation for the big event. At least for the men. The women had gathered for a spa day in the morning, and this afternoon, they were having a bridal tea downtown. That left their male counterparts a day to themselves.

The day had started for them at the golf course. The weather at that hour was a little brisk for Julian's California blood, but the skies were clear and they had a good time playing. They'd all had lunch at some famous hole-in-the-wall barbecue joint, where Julian had a grilled chicken breast and one glorious hush puppy, and then they returned to the hotel and went their separate ways.

With that done, Julian was able to clean up and get ready to do a few chores for the day. There were no messages on his phone from his family, nothing to concern him, so he could focus on wedding preparation. He needed to pick up the tuxedos and get the wedding rings from the jeweler. As the best man, Murray didn't ask much of him. Running a couple errands and throwing a decent bachelor party Friday night were all that was required. It wasn't hard.

And yet he found himself thinking he should pick up Gretchen and bring her along with him.

She wasn't expecting him to show up. He knew she had work to do and his sudden arrival would likely throw her off her game. He told himself he needed to keep her on her toes, because the press certainly would, and she had to be ready for anything.

But in truth, he just wanted to see her again.

It was hard to explain—a feeling he hadn't experienced in a long time. Lately, he'd dated his costars, women he saw on the set every day. He'd gotten used to that sort of immersive dating pattern. So last night, when he'd realized he wouldn't see Gretchen until Friday evening at the rehearsal dinner, he'd felt a little… lonely. He found he missed her awkward smiles and sarcastic comments under her breath. He wanted to wrap his arms around her waist and kiss her until she blushed down into her cleavage.

He didn't realize he was driving to the wedding chapel until he saw the sign ahead of him. By then, he figured it couldn't hurt to pop in and see if she had the time to join him.

Turning off the engine, he climbed out of the SUV and went in the front entrance. The lobby was huge and shaped almost like a cross, with four arched doorways leading to different areas of the chapel. In the center was a round table draped in white with a sheer fabric over it. It looked as if tiny musical notes were stitched all over with shiny black thread, beads and crystals. A tall silver tree branch came up out of the center. Hanging from it were strands of crystal, musical notes and little white cards with people's names on them.

Fancy.

To his left was the wedding chapel, and straight ahead was the reception hall, so he opted to go right, where the offices were. He found a closed door with Gretchen McAlister's name on it and knocked softly.

"No, I don't want to date your cousin!" he heard her shout from the other side of the door.

With a smile, he opened the door, peeking his head in to see her sitting at her desk, tying black and white ribbons around glass cylinders with candles in them. "But you've never even met my cousin. You might like him."

Gretchen's gaze shot up at the sound of his voice, her eyes widening. "Julian! Sorry about that. I thought you were Bree. What are you doing here? Is there a problem? I thought we weren't getting together until tomorrow."

"No problem," he said, slipping into her office and shutting the door behind him. "I just thought you might like to hang out with me today."

Her gaze narrowed at him. "Hang out? Do you mean practice some more? Go over our cover story again?"

Julian shook his head. "No, you've got that covered, I think. I've got to run a couple errands today and I thought you might like to join me, that's all."

Her eyebrows drew together as she considered his offer. She seemed genuinely confused by it. That, or suspicious again. He still didn't understand that. "I'm not dressed up for an official day out with you."

Her hand ran self-consciously over her hair, which was pulled back into a butterfly clip. Her makeup was done, but not heavy-handed. She was wearing a pair of skinny jeans and a simple V-neck sweater with boots. The dark brown of the sweater matched her eyes and made her skin look even creamier against the rich tones. She looked great to him. He actually had a hard time tearing his gaze away from the tantalizing glimpse of cleavage that her sweater teased at, without being too blatant. "You look great," he countered.

"I've also got a lot to do," she said, uncertainty in her voice.

"Well, it just so happens that I don't have a lot to do. How about a little trade-off? You come with me to do a few wedding-related chores, and then I'll come back here with you and help you do whatever it is you do."

A delicate dark eyebrow raised at him. "You're going to help me?"

"Sure," he said with a winning smile. "I have no clue what needs to be done, but I'm an actor. I can fake it."

Gretchen snorted and shook her head. "Well, I'm not sure how much help you'll be, but any help would be great."

Julian chuckled. "Well, thank goodness you have

low standards. Let's go. I have to pick up the tuxedos and the rings."

He helped Gretchen into her coat, and they left the chapel a moment later. As they got into his rental, he admitted, "I also have no idea where I'm going. Do you know where Couture Connection is? That's where I have to get the tuxedos. I can look it up on my phone if we need to."

Gretchen nodded and pointed to the right. "I know where it is. It's just a couple miles from here. Go out to the right."

That part of the day went smoothly enough. They found the store and waited a few minutes to pick up their suits. It wasn't until they were getting ready to leave that Julian noticed the guy across the street with a camera.

He sighed. They'd finally found him. It had actually taken longer than he expected. "Someone tipped off the paparazzi," he said to Gretchen, although he gave a meaningful glance at the girl behind the counter. She'd been in the back room far, far too long in his opinion. She bit her lip and handed over the suits without comment.

"What do we do?" Gretchen asked. "I told you I'm not camera-ready today."

He shrugged. "We do what we need to do. If life stopped just because someone was taking my picture, I'd never get anything done." Julian draped the suits over his arm and reached out to grasp Gretchen's hand. "Off we go," he said.

By the time they reached the jewelry store, there were three cars tailing them, and they were bolder than before. Julian hadn't even opened the car door for

Gretchen before there were four guys swarming the car with cameras, snapping pictures and asking questions.

"Who's the lady, Julian?"

"Her name is Gretchen McAlister," he said, opening the door and helping her out of the car. Normally he would just ignore them, but what was the point of having a fake girlfriend if he wasn't going to publicize that fact?

"Is this your new lady love?" another one prompted, making Gretchen blush.

Julian took her hand and looked into her eyes. It was easy to get lost there, the feelings she evoked in him lately hardly an act. "She's very special to me," he answered with a sincere smile.

"What do you think Bridgette will think of your new relationship?"

"I really don't care what she thinks," Julian said and leaned into Gretchen's ear. "Let's get inside."

The cameras stayed outside while they met with the jeweler. The woman at the counter left them for a moment to go back and find the owner. Julian watched Gretchen peruse the case, her eyes lighting up as she spied something interesting. It was always dangerous to go into a jewelry store with the women he dated. It almost always cost him more than he expected.

"What do you see?" he asked, curious as to what would spark such a reaction in Gretchen. She didn't seem to wear much jewelry.

"That necklace," she said, pointing out a teardrop-shaped opal, speckled with blue and pink fire. "That's my birthstone. I've never seen a natural opal with such bright fire in it before."

It was pretty, and not at all what he expected her to

choose in the case of flashy diamonds and other glittering and expensive gemstones. He doubted Bridgette even knew what an opal was. Julian hovered, waiting for the expectant look he was used to seeing, but Gretchen just shrugged and continued down the case. She continued to surprise him. Perhaps she deserved a surprise in return.

"Mr. Cooper," the owner of the store greeted them as he came out from the back room. "Come with me. I have everything ready for you."

They were taken to a private room in the back where they could inspect the rings and sign for them. There was a lot of gold and a lot of diamonds involved, so he wanted to make sure everything was perfect for Murray and Kelly.

"Is there anything else I can do for you today, Mr. Cooper?" the jeweler asked.

"Actually, yes. That opal teardrop necklace in the case. I'd like that for my companion, please."

The man nodded. "An excellent choice." He called out to the woman at the counter to bring it back to them.

Julian ignored the stunned look on Gretchen's face as the jeweler presented the necklace on a velvet tray. "It looks perfect, thank you."

"Would you like it boxed up?"

"No, we'll be wearing it out." Julian reached for the necklace and unfastened the clasp. Before Gretchen could breathe a word of argument, he rose from his chair to stand behind her. He gently brushed a loose strand of dark hair from her neck, then draped the necklace at her throat. When fastened, the gem fell right beneath her collarbone and was highlighted nicely by the low plunge of her sweater.

"Lovely," the jeweler said. "I'll put the box in the bag with the rings for you."

Julian handed over his black American Express card as the jeweler left the room.

"What is this for?" she finally said when they were alone. "This necklace was super expensive."

He could only shrug and dismiss it the same way she'd dismissed the idea of getting the necklace. "It made you smile," he said. "That was worth every penny."

Gretchen gripped the pendant in her hand, shaking her head. "I'm already being paid a ridiculous amount for this. You don't have to buy me anything."

Julian tried not to flinch at that unfortunate reminder. He'd nearly forgotten that she was being paid to be with him. She was so unlike all the other people in his life with their hands out that it was an unwelcome shock to remember she was getting her piece of him just like the rest. And yet he somehow knew that she was different.

In the end it didn't matter. He wanted to buy the necklace and he bought it. "It's a gift. Enjoy it."

The jeweler returned with his card and receipt. "Anything else I can do for you today?"

As they stood, Julian considered the reporters outside waiting for them. He'd spied a little café up the block, but he didn't want them following the two of them there. He wanted some quiet time with Gretchen before the wedding chaos began.

"Just one more thing. Do you have a rear exit we could use?"

# Five

"Is that all you're going to eat?" Gretchen asked. "Seriously, I can't have those camera guys show up and document me here with a full plate while you pick at a spinach salad with no dressing."

"I told you," he said with a smile, "I'm saving up for that cake of Amelia's."

Gretchen looked down at her sandwich and shrugged before taking another bite. "You could at least have the decency to order more food for appearances and just not eat it."

"No one is looking at us, Gretchen. We're hidden in the back corner of a tiny café. Relax and enjoy your food."

Gretchen took a few more bites before she worked up the nerve to ask Julian a question. "Do you ever get tired of it?"

"Tired of what?"

"Tired of being treated like a piece of meat?"

Julian smothered a snort of laughter. "Actually, yes, I do. But I won't look like this forever. I'm young, in my physical prime, so I thought I should make the most of it while I can. I suppose I can tackle some meatier scripts when I'm older and people aren't that interested in my biceps anymore."

"It's not your biceps," Gretchen corrected. "It's the abs."

One of Julian's dark eyebrows went up. "Well, thank you for noticing."

Gretchen blushed. "I didn't. I was really just saying that I…" Her voice drifted off as she ran out of argument.

"It's okay, Gretchen. You're allowed to admire the abs. It would be hypocritical of me to use my body to make money, then criticize someone for noticing it. Maybe someday I'll be known for something else."

"Have you considered doing different kinds of films now? I mean, how many big action flicks can you make in a year? You'd think you'd have time to do something new every now and then."

Julian sighed. "I'd love to. I've actually got a script in my hotel room for something I'm really excited about. It's totally different for me. A real, meaty role. The kind that might earn critical acclaim for my acting."

Gretchen noticed Julian perk up in his seat as he talked about the plot of the script. He was eyeing the role of an alcoholic who loses everything and returns home to face the family he'd left behind. It sounded like an amazing role, the kind that could change the whole trajectory of his career. "Why don't you do it?"

"My manager doesn't think it's a good idea. And

he's right. The more I think about it, the more I know it isn't the right time."

"Why? What could it hurt to try it?"

Julian got a distant look in his eyes as he turned to glance out toward the front of the café. "It could hurt everything. I'm blessed to have what I do now. I have enough money coming in to care for my family, live an amazing life and never worry about how I'm going to pay for something. But this industry is fickle, and you can lose it all in an instant."

"How could you possibly do such a terrible job that you could sink your entire career?"

"It's been a while since I've stretched my serious acting muscles, Gretchen. I may not have even been any good at it to begin with. I landed my first movie role for my body, and little has changed. What if I…" His voice trailed off. "What if I tried to do a serious movie and I'm no good? What if I get panned left, right and center, ripped apart by critics for thinking I could do anything more than shoot a gun or fly a helicopter?"

"At least you will have tried. Pardon me for saying so, but these action movies don't really seem to fulfill you. As a creative person, I understand how that can be. If you're compromising and not doing what you love, eventually you'll lose your joy for the work."

"You enjoy your work, don't you? I can tell by the way your whole demeanor changes when you talk about it."

Gretchen hadn't noticed that before, and she was surprised Julian had paid that much attention. "I'm not sure about how it changes me, but I do love my job. I'm not necessarily a traditional artist that paints or sculpts, but I get to do so many different and creative things. I never get bored. And I get to work with my best friends, so that makes every day fun."

"I have to admit I'm jealous."

Gretchen looked up at him, her eyes wide in surprise. "You're jealous of me? Really?"

He nodded. "Absolutely. You're living the life you want. You're doing the job you enjoy. You seem to be living so authentically, doing what makes you happy."

"Well, I'm also not a millionaire. There's probably a trade-off in there somewhere."

"Money isn't all it's cracked up to be. It's necessary, and I'm thankful to have enough to do what I need to do, but the thought of losing it can become what holds you back. I mean, look at me. I'm in a delightful-smelling café, near drooling over some berry tart in the case that I won't let myself have. I don't eat what I want, I don't do what I want, I don't act in the films I'd like to…all because of the money."

Gretchen shook her head. "Only someone with money could ever consider it a burden."

Julian watched her curiously for a moment. "May I ask why you agreed to participate in this charade with me?"

She had to laugh at his query. She was surprised it had taken him this long to ask. "That's a good question. For the first few days, I was asking myself the same thing. Part of it was being in the right place at the wrong time, but in the end, I'm ashamed to admit it came down to the money. It was a few days out of my life and when it was over, I'd have the opportunity to take the trip I've always dreamed of taking. Without it, who knows when, if ever, I'd get another chance."

"I love to travel," Julian said, scooting aside his half-eaten salad and leaning closer to her. "Where are you wanting to go?"

"Italy," she said with a wistful sigh. "It's been my dream since high school when we studied the Renaissance. I want to go and just suck up all the beauty there. The paintings, the architecture, the food and the people. I want to experience it all, and this money will make that possible."

Julian nodded as he listened to her speak. "Italy is beautiful. You'll love it."

"Have you been?"

"Once. We filmed for a few weeks in Tuscany and I got to visit Florence. It's an amazing place. I've always wanted to go back, but I haven't had the time."

Gretchen understood that. "I know how you feel. Even with the money, taking the time away from From This Moment is hard to do. It's been my life since we started the place."

"Well," he said, "I think you need to make the time. If you've got the money, do it. There's never going to be a perfect time, and before you know it, life will dwindle away your savings and you'll miss your chance."

"I don't think I—"

"I dare you to go next spring," Julian said with a conspiratorial smile. "Maybe late April or early May. It will be perfect. Good weather and not too crowded yet."

Gretchen nearly choked. "You *dare* me?"

"I do," he said, his blue eyes focused intently on her in a way that made her spine soften and her chest tighten. "You don't seem like the kind of woman that would back down from a dare."

She eyed him with a twist of her lips. She hadn't played many games of truth or dare in her time, but she was certain that two could play at this game. "Very well, I accept. But I have a dare for you as well."

"Oh, you do now?" He sat back in his seat and crossed his arms over his chest as though he couldn't be intimidated by her challenge. "I can't wait to hear what it is. Back in college, I always opted for the dare over the truth. I haven't turned one down, ever."

That might be true, but he hadn't gone up against Gretchen before. "Okay, Mr. Confident. I dare you to go back to the counter, buy that berry tart you want so badly and eat every bite of it. Live on the wild side for just today, Julian. Who knows, one day it's berry tarts, the next day it's a film premiering at Sundance."

Julian watched her face for a moment. She knew that he was fighting with himself, but a dare was a dare, right?

She decided maybe she should throw him a bone. She of all people knew what it was like to try to diet and have family and friends unintentionally sabotage her plans. "I'll share it with you, if you want."

At that, his expression brightened. "Done." He got up and left her alone at the table for a few minutes to secure their pastry prize.

Alone, she sat back in her chair and took the first deep breath for nearly half an hour. Julian was so intense, she sometimes found it hard to breathe when he was around. But she liked it. She liked being with him. She'd never expected that to be the case. They were so different, or so she thought.

Beneath it all, she realized they had more in common than she expected. The more time they spent together, the more easily she was able to see the man behind the actor.

As nice as that was, they were dangerous, pointless thoughts. They'd just discussed what she was going to do with the money he was paying her to be around him. Once the wedding was over, so was their time together. It might feel as if they had a connection, but he was an actor. Gretchen couldn't let herself forget that. In a few days, he would return to LA and forget she ever existed.

It was just her luck that the first guy she'd really felt comfortable with in years turned out to be a Hollywood actor who would disappear and want nothing more to do with her.

At this rate, she was never going to get laid.

Julian nearly groaned as he took the last bite of the berry tart. It was the best thing he'd tasted in…a year, maybe? Most days of his life, he didn't control what he ate. His trainers and personal chefs took care of that for him and kept the temptations far away. Bridgette was even more strict with her eating, so it was easier to get through the day knowing he wouldn't be exposed to the things he really wanted. Out of sight, out of mind.

Gretchen wasn't hung up on all that. She indulged when she wanted to indulge, and the satisfied smile on her face was evidence of that. So what if it cost her a few extra pounds? Her soft, womanly figure with a sincere smile was far better than rail-thin Bridgette and her pinched, anxious look. She never smiled with contentment. She was always looking for something more in life.

This berry tart may have been that very thing.

"So naughty," Gretchen said, putting her fork down on the empty plate. "I bet you gain three whole pounds eating that."

Julian sat up sharply. "That's not possible. Is it?"

She laughed at him and shook her head. "No. You're fine. Half a berry tart isn't the end of the world. You did get a serving of fiber-rich fruit out of it, after all."

That's when Julian noticed a small dab of strawberry glaze at the corner of her lips. He reached for his napkin to dab it away, but hesitated. He had a better idea.

"Hold still," he said, leaning across the table toward her. With one hand gently caressing her neck, he pressed his lips to the corner of her mouth, removing the last of their dessert before moving over and kissing her.

Just like every time he touched her, Julian immediately responded to Gretchen. With her soft lips pressed against his and the scent of her skin filling his lungs, he couldn't pull away. Every muscle in his body tightened with a building need for her. Each time they kissed, his desire for her grew. He knew that this was a business arrangement, but he couldn't help his reaction to her. He wanted her more than he'd wanted any other woman before.

But unlike the other times when they were practicing making it look good for the cameras, this time Gretchen pulled away from him.

He wasn't expecting it, and her sudden withdrawal left him hovering, vulnerable, over the table. "What's the matter?"

She watched him with wary dark eyes. "What was that about?"

His brows went up. "What was the kiss about?"

"Yes." She glanced around the café, her gaze dropping into her lap. "I thought you said we were done practicing that. There's no one watching us right now."

Gretchen couldn't fathom that he would kiss her just

because he could. Because he *wanted* to. "That kiss," he said, "wasn't for the cameras. That one was for me."

Her eyes met his with a narrowed gaze and a frown wrinkling her nose. "I don't understand."

Julian reached across the table and took her hand. "What is there to understand, Gretchen? I like you. I wanted to kiss you, so I did. That's pretty simple boy-meets-girl kind of stuff."

She nodded, although he wasn't entirely sure she felt better about the whole thing. "I told you before I'm not that good with the boy-meets-girl thing."

She had told him, but he didn't realize until that moment how serious she was about it. How was it possible that she couldn't understand why he'd want to kiss her? Was her self-esteem so low that she didn't think she was worthy of his attention? If so, he'd see to correcting that assumption right away.

"You said you like me. What did you mean by that?"

"I mean that I like you. And yes, that I'm attracted to you. I know this arrangement is mostly about business, and I don't want to make you feel uncomfortable, but I'm into you, Gretchen. Truly."

She responded with silence, reaching out to take a sip of her iced tea. It was almost as though she didn't know how to respond, as if he'd said "I love you" too soon in a relationship. Had he read the signals wrong? He didn't want her to think that he presumed their contract extended to extracurricular activities in the bedroom. He was about to say something to soften the statement when she looked up at him with an intensity in her chocolate-brown eyes.

"I'm attracted to you, as well," she said boldly.

Julian shelved the instinctual smile. He didn't want

her to think he was laughing at her. It was anything but. He had suspected that she was turned on by him, but he couldn't know for sure. Knowing made him feel lighter somehow. "I'm glad we got that out there."

She nodded, and her gaze returned to her lap. Any fantasies he had about taking her back to his hotel room and making love to her that instant fizzled away. One step at a time, he reminded himself. Besides, they had work they were avoiding. Even if she wanted him as desperately as he wanted her, there was a wedding coming up, and the ballroom needed to be decorated sooner rather than later.

"I guess we'd better get back to the chapel," he said. "I promised I'd help you set up all those decorations, remember?"

"You don't really have to," she said dismissively. "You bought my food, and more importantly, this necklace. I'll happily stay up all night decorating on my own to make up for the lost time."

He shook his head. "You're not getting rid of me so easily. I may not have an artistic eye, but I'm helping you and that's final."

Gretchen nodded and placed her napkin on the table. "It's been over an hour. Do you think the photographers have given up or are they still sitting outside the jewelry store?"

Julian shrugged and got up from the table. "It doesn't matter. I'm happy we had the hour alone that we had." He took her hand and led her out of the café. The cameramen had given up, and their vehicle was waiting patiently for them down the block.

The return to the chapel was uneventful, yet awkwardly silent. Not since their first night together had there been this weird energy between them. It continued until they were back in the ballroom and the work began. They lost themselves in tying a black organza bow around the back of each chair. Julian was quickly removed from that task—apparently he didn't tie bows, just knots—and he was given the job of folding all the linen napkins. Thank goodness there wasn't some fancy fabric origami going on, just a simple fold that created a rectangle with a pocket.

When the bows were finished, Gretchen laid a glass charger with silver beaded accents at each place setting. Julian followed behind her, draping the napkin across the charger and slipping the menu into the pocket. He helped her carry in about forty of the decorated hurricane vases, placing them on the stage along with some large silver vases and candelabras.

"What next?" he asked. "Do these need to go on the tables?"

Gretchen sat down on the edge of the stage and shook her head. "Not tonight." She glanced at her cell phone. "It's getting late. I'll do that tomorrow."

Julian sat beside her and eyed the room. They had gotten a lot done, but if he knew Gretchen, there was a lot more in store for the decor. "Are you sure? I can stay as late as you need me to."

"Aren't you here for Murray? Shouldn't you guys be hanging out and playing poker or something? Guy bonding?"

He shrugged. "Not really. We golfed and ate barbecue today before I came over. Tomorrow, there's just the rehearsal, the dinner and the bachelor party."

Gretchen gave him a knowing smile. "Whatcha got planned? Strippers and beer?"

"No," he said with an offended tone to his voice. "It's going to be classy! I've rented out an old piano bar downtown. I've also got a Cuban guy coming in to roll authentic cigars and a local microbrewery doing flights of all their best beers. A few ladies from the burlesque show will be performing." He tried to say it all with a straight face, but it didn't last long. She had him pegged the first time. "Okay, yeah," he laughed. "Strippers and beer. But they're expensive strippers and beer."

"I'm sure that makes it a much classier affair," she said with a smile.

"I thought so."

"We'd better get you home, then. You'll need your rest for a long night of debauchery." Gretchen stood up and dusted her hands off on her jeans.

Julian followed her out of the ballroom, waiting as she switched off lights and locked doors behind her. When they stepped outside into the parking lot, he noticed the temperature had really dropped since they went inside. In just a few short hours, it had gone from a California November day to a November day anywhere else. He snuggled into his leather jacket, but all it really did was keep the wind from cutting through him.

Gretchen seemed more prepared. She stepped outside in a dark burgundy peacoat and a scarf. He walked her over to her tiny sedan, hesitant to say good-night and hesitant to say what he needed to say to make the night last. He moved close to tell her goodbye, her back pressed to the car as she looked up at him with the overhead lights twinkling in her eyes.

"Do you have a real coat?" she asked when she noticed him start to shiver.

"Not with me. I have one I wear when I go skiing

in Aspen, but I didn't think I'd need it here." Looking at the space between them, he realized he could see his breath. It was darn cold. He should've looked more closely at the forecast before he packed.

"Well, maybe tomorrow you should take a trip to the store and pick up a nice wool coat. We can't let the best man catch cold the day before the wedding."

"That's a good idea. Perhaps you can just help me stay warm in the meantime."

With a smile, Gretchen wrapped her arms around his neck and pulled him close. Her lips mere centimeters from his, she asked, "How's this?"

Julian pressed the full length of his body against her and wrapped his arms around her waist. "Definitely getting warmer. Still a little cold, though."

Holding his face in her hands, she guided his lips to hers. A surge of heat shot through his veins as they touched. When her tongue grazed along his own, he was nearly warm enough to take off his jacket. That simple, innocent touch was enough to set his blood to boiling with need for her.

He traveled the line of her jaw, leaving a trail of kisses until he reached the sensitive curve of her neck. Gretchen gasped and clung to him as he nibbled at her flesh. The sound was like music to his ears, sending a chill through his whole body. Desperate to touch more of her, he moved one hand from her waist, sliding it up her side until it cupped her breast.

He was rewarded with another gasp, but it was quickly followed by insistent palms pressing against his chest. He moved back, dropping his hands to his sides. "What's the matter?" he asked between panting breaths.

"I…" she started, then shook her head. "It's just a little too fast for me, Julian."

Fast? "It's Thursday, Gretchen. By Monday, I'll be back in California. I don't want to make you uncomfortable, but we don't have forever."

Gretchen sighed and shifted her gaze to look over his shoulder. "I know."

"What's really bothering you?" It didn't seem as though her body and her words were lining up. "Tell me."

Swallowing hard, she nodded. "I told you I hadn't dated much, but it's more than that, Julian. It's not that I don't want you. I do. Very badly. And I would gladly take this as far as you're willing to go. But I think if you knew the truth, you'd…"

"I'd what?" He couldn't think of anything she could say to smother his desire for her.

"I'm a virgin," she said, almost spitting out the words as if to get them out before she could change her mind.

Julian's eyes widened and he stumbled back, as though her words had physically hit him. Was she serious? "A virgin?" he asked.

"Yes. Like I said, it isn't a problem for me. Frankly, you'd be doing me a huge favor by ridding me of this burden I've carried around for all these years. But I find that people don't react well to the news."

He could understand that. He wasn't reacting that well himself. It wasn't as though she'd just announced she was a hermaphrodite or something, but still, it had caught him off guard. In an instant, the idea of a fun, casual romance while he was in Nashville had just gotten instantly more complicated.

"Damn," Gretchen whispered.

Her curse snapped him out of his own head. He looked at her with a frown. "What?"

"It's happened again," she said. "I've scared you off. You can't get away from me fast enough. I can see it in your eyes."

"No, no," he said, shaking his head adamantly. "It's just not what I was expecting. But I should've…" His voice trailed away. All the signs had pointed there; he just hadn't thought it was possible.

"Well, it's getting late and you're probably freezing," he said, the words sounding lame even to his own ears. "We've got a long night tomorrow, so I'll let you get home. I'll see you here at the rehearsal at six?"

"Yeah." Gretchen didn't even try to hide the disappointment on her face and in her voice. His quick backpedaling had hurt her feelings, but he didn't know what else to do. "Good night, Julian."

Without so much as a goodbye peck on the cheek, she opened her car door and got inside. He'd barely closed the door when the engine roared to life and she backed out of the parking space.

As her taillights disappeared into the distance, Julian realized he was a schmuck. Apparently he was much better with women when he had a script to follow.

# Six

Gretchen should've kept her damn mouth shut. That was it—she wasn't telling a guy the truth again. The next time she got someone interested in sleeping with her, she'd let him find out the hard way. It might be rough going, but by the time he realized it, it would be done and she wouldn't have to go through this embarrassment again and again.

At the moment, it would be easy to believe that nothing had happened last night. She and Julian were seated together at a table with a few other members of the wedding party. The rehearsal dinner was wrapping up, and waiters were coming around with trays of desserts. His arm was draped over her shoulder, a devoted smile on his face whenever he looked at her. Ever the actor, this was easy for him. It wasn't so easy for her, especially with Bree hovering around the edge of the room taking pictures and smiling knowingly at her.

Just when she thought she'd overcome all the potential problems with this fake dating scenario, she'd screwed it up. She should've just kept it fake. By admitting in the coffee shop that she was attracted to him, it had opened up the charade to more. He liked her, she liked him…what was stopping this public relationship from becoming a private one?

A hymen, that's what.

The look on Julian's face when she said the words had been heartbreaking. One minute, he'd looked at her with blue eyes hooded with desire. She had no doubt in that moment that he sincerely wanted her. Not even her fragile ego could believe otherwise. Then, in a flash, it was replaced by panic. She knew the moment the words left her mouth that it was a mistake.

Julian wanted fun, flirty sex. A hot wedding hookup. Deflowering some thirty-year-old virgin probably didn't line up with his plans. She'd accused him of trying to escape, but at that point, she wanted out of there more desperately than he did. She needed plenty of time to get home, lie in bed and kick herself.

Fortunately, today had been about wedding preparations. She spent most of the afternoon getting things in place in the chapel before the rehearsal. That kept her busy enough that she could keep her embarrassing incident far out of her mind. When she did see Julian again, there wasn't much time to talk. First was the rehearsal, and he was on the platform with Murray and Kelly. After that, they all got ushered onto a limo bus and taken to the restaurant for the rehearsal dinner. They hadn't had two seconds alone, much less time to talk.

Part of her was okay with that. She didn't feel the need to analyze last night with him. She just needed to get through the next two days and put all of this behind her. But it was hard when he was always touching her. Holding her hand, hugging her to his side, whispering in her ear. It just made her want what she was destined not to have that much more intensely.

One of the waiters placed a piping hot ramekin of peach cobbler in front of her with vanilla bean ice cream melting over it. It looked amazing, and the thought of a tasty treat was enough to rouse her from her dark thoughts. She needed to play the happy girlfriend regardless of what was going on between them.

"That looks good," Julian said, leaning in to examine her dessert. "Decadent, actually."

"Didn't you get dessert?" she asked, already knowing the answer but trying to make polite conversation.

He shook his head and took a sip of his water. He'd spent the evening nibbling on blackened tilapia and roasted vegetables. "Just because you dared me to eat that berry tart doesn't mean I've thrown my clean eating lifestyle out the window."

"Would you like just one bite? I mean, I know you don't want to be first, but I thought you might want the second bite." She couldn't help getting that dig in under the veiled discussion of dessert so the others at the table couldn't follow the twists and turns of their relationship.

A look of surprise lit up Julian's face, his lips twisting into an amused smile. "For the record, I don't mind having the first taste. I just feel guilty getting the first bite when I know I can't stay around to eat the whole thing."

"The cobbler won't be offended, I assure you. It just wants to be eaten while it's still hot and juicy. Before long, it's going to be a cold, crusty, bitter mess."

"I sincerely doubt that. I know turning that treat down last night was a mistake, but as it was, I spent two hours in the hotel gym last night."

Her gaze met his. "Feeling guilty?"

He nodded. "I had a little pent-up energy after I left you. Ten miles on the treadmill helped, but I still felt like crap when I was done."

"You can run all you want, but if you're on a treadmill, you aren't getting any farther from your problems."

"Wise words," he agreed. "Exercise does help me think. If nothing else, I got some…clarity."

Gretchen narrowed her gaze at him, her heart suddenly leaping to life in her chest. "What does that mean?"

"It means we need to talk."

She rolled her eyes and turned back to her dessert. Talk? She'd done plenty of that already. If all he wanted to do was talk, she was going to save this poor cobbler from her own fate. She picked up her spoon and scooped up a bite, stopping as Julian leaned in.

"Soon," he whispered into her ear. The spoon trembled in her hand as she held it in midair. "I don't know when, but soon. Don't you worry about that dessert going uneaten."

Gretchen drew in a ragged breath. Suddenly, she wasn't that hungry for cobbler anymore. The idea that she might be naked in front of him in the near future was an appetite killer.

"So, Julian," one of the bridesmaids called across the table. "Are you guys ready for the bachelor party tonight?"

Julian sat up and flashed his charming smile at the

others seated with them. "Absolutely. I've got a great night planned for the boys."

One of the other women looked at her date with a warning glance. "Try to limit yourself to one lap dance, please."

The man laughed. "Why? I'm not the one getting married tomorrow. You afraid I'll be tempted by the goods?"

The brunette shook her head. "No, I'm worried you'll stick your whole paycheck in her panties and come back to me broke."

"Well, if I do, maybe Julian can help me out. I heard you made fifteen million for your last movie. Is that true?"

Gretchen felt Julian stiffen beside her. For the first time while they were together, he was the nervous one. He'd mentioned a few times about how people seemed to come to him with their hands out. This guy didn't even know Julian, not really. It was veiled as a joke, but it wasn't funny. She didn't like seeing Julian react that way.

"And exactly how much money did *you* make last year?" she piped up before Julian could respond.

The man's eyes grew wide at her sharp tone and he immediately held up his hands in surrender. "Sorry," he said. "It was a joke. I mean, if I made that much money, I'd be shouting it from the rooftops."

"And everyone, including the IRS and some guy you don't even know at a rehearsal dinner, would be knocking on your front door looking for their piece."

The large, burly groomsman seemed to disappear into himself. "I'm going to go get a drink from the bar," he said, getting up and crossing the room. The other people turned to each other and started talking among themselves to avoid the awkward turn in the conversation.

"Rawr." Julian leaned in and growled into her ear. "I didn't know you were such a tiger."

Gretchen chuckled. "Neither did I. But I couldn't sit there and say nothing. Just because you're a public figure doesn't mean it's any of his business how much you make."

Julian smiled. "It isn't as exciting as it sounds anyway. I mean, I have plenty, don't get me wrong, but the bigger the life, the bigger the expenses. The mortgage on my house in Beverly Hills is nearly thirty thousand a month."

Gretchen nearly choked on her sip of wine. "That's insane."

"That's California real estate for you. Add in the ridiculous property taxes and insurance, security, staff... it adds up. Uncle Sam gets his whopping cut, then Ross, then my accountant."

"Do I need to give this necklace back?"

"No, of course not. I wouldn't live in a five-million-dollar house if I couldn't afford to. Life is just on a different scale when you live this way, is all."

Gretchen shook her head and reached into her purse to find her phone. It was getting late. As much as she was enjoying the dinner and curious to finish her interrupted conversation with Julian, she needed to get back and finish up the ballroom for tomorrow. "I'd better go."

Julian pouted, the frown pulling at the corners of his full mouth. Gretchen wanted to kiss it away, but resisted. Instead, she leaned in and pressed a kiss to his cheek. "You have fun with the boys tonight. Don't let Murray get too hungover. Natalie hates it when the wedding party is teetering on their feet all day."

"Yes, ma'am. I'll walk you out."

"No, no," she insisted, pushing him back into his seat. "I can make it just fine. Your loyalty is to Murray tonight."

Gretchen stood up, and he scooped her hand into his own. He brought it up to his lips, placing a searing kiss on the back of her hand. The heated tingle radiated up her whole arm, making her flush pink against the deep shades of purple fabric that made up her dress.

"I'll see you *soon*," he said, emphasizing the last word. That was the same word he'd used earlier when they spoke about their physical relationship.

She pulled her hand away and tried to cover her reaction with a smile. "Okay," she said. "Good night."

Gretchen gave a parting wave to Murray and Kelly before slipping out. It wasn't until she stepped out that she realized they'd all come in the limo van, including Bree. With a shake of her head, she called a cab and waited patiently outside for it to arrive.

It was just as well. She needed the cold air to cool the fire Julian had so easily built inside her.

Julian was over the bachelor party scene. He'd done his duty and set up a great send-off for Murray, complete with alcohol, scantily clad women and billiards, but it wasn't really where he wanted to spend his time. Not since his discussion with Gretchen at the rehearsal dinner.

He'd relived that moment by her car over and over in his head since it happened. He had expected a lot of different reasons for why she shied away from him, but none of them included the fact that she'd never been with a man before. In this day and age, that sort of thing was almost unheard of.

Admittedly, he hadn't reacted well to the news, and he felt horrible about it. He'd told her about his two-hour treadmill penance, but that wasn't the half of it. He'd barely slept that night thinking about how badly he handled her confession. It hadn't been because he felt as if there were something wrong with her, or that she was strange, but because he'd felt this sudden pressure he wasn't expecting.

Being a woman's first lover was a big responsibility. When he was sixteen and horny, he hadn't thought about it that way, and he knew of at least one girl who'd had a less-than-stellar first time because of how he'd handled it. Now he was a grown man. An experienced lover. It was bad enough that he had a reputation because of his films that he was some hard-bodied Casanova. Adding the delicate handling of a woman's first time on top of that made his chest tighten.

Gretchen had made it sound as though she would be happy to be rid of the burden of her virginity. It would be doing her a favor, somehow. And he wanted her. There was no doubt of that. But was making love to Gretchen selfish? Was taking her virginity and then returning to LA a horrible thing to do, even if she'd asked him to? Just the thought of it made him feel sleazy.

Speaking of sleazy, a woman in a corset and a thong was making her way over to him. She had multiple bills tucked into her G-string and a coat of glitter across her tan skin, reminding him of his own ill-fated turn as a stripper in a movie. The kind of movies he hated.

The kind of films Gretchen encouraged him to branch out from.

The burlesque dancer wrapped her feather boa around Julian's neck to pull him closer. Putting a few obligatory dollars beneath the strap at her hip, he waved her back toward the groom. Murray was the one who deserved the attention tonight, not him.

Julian looked down at his phone to check his messages. He didn't want anything to be wrong at home, but it would give him an excuse to leave. Murray had been his roommate in college, so he knew all about Julian's family and how things tended to crop up. Thankfully, all was well, but unfortunately it was only a little after ten. Was that too soon to leave? He sighed and put his phone away. Probably. The cigar roller hadn't even finished making all the cigars yet.

Then he caught Murray's gaze across the room. His friend smiled and shook his head. "Go," he mouthed silently, then turned back to the busty blonde vying for his attention.

That was all it took. He stood and walked toward the edge of the room, trying to slowly slip out without making a big deal of it. Once he made it out the door, he climbed into his SUV, thankful that they hadn't taken the limo bus directly from the rehearsal dinner so he had a vehicle to make his escape. Inside his car, he texted Gretchen.

Where are you?

As the engine warmed up, he got a response. In the ballroom hanging seventy thousand crystal pendants. Care to join me?

He did. Putting the phone aside, he pulled out of the parking lot and headed back to From This Moment. Once again, Gretchen's little green sedan was the only car in the lot when he arrived. Apparently everyone else had already given up for the night.

He headed straight for the ballroom, as she'd said she'd be there, but he didn't see her. Her handiwork was evident, though. The room had been absolutely transformed since he'd been there the day before. The tables now had an assortment of glasses and flatware at each place setting. The tall silver candelabras he'd moved the night before stood in the center of some tables. Others had slim silver vases or small silver bowls. There were candles scattered all over and tall white trees in the corners, dripping with crystals. It looked as though the only thing missing was the fresh flowers.

"Just wait until the pin lights are on and all the candles are lit," Gretchen said, coming in behind him with a box in her arms. "It will be magical."

"I bet. You're very talented."

Gretchen snorted and moved past him to set the box on the edge of the stage where the band would set up in the morning. She was still wearing the flirty purple dress she'd worn to the rehearsal dinner, only now she was barefoot, having cast aside her heels for the sake of comfort. "You're very kind, but it's a table setting, not a Picasso."

Julian followed her path, slowly coming up behind her as she unpacked tiny attendee gifts to place on the tables. When she stood, he snaked his arms around her waist and pulled her back tight against him. The soft curve of her backside pressed into his desire, suppressing all the reasons why he couldn't be with Gretchen.

What if he could give her something without taking anything away? It might take every ounce of restraint he had, but he wanted this so badly. "I've thought a lot about our discussion at dinner."

Gretchen gasped softly, although he wasn't certain if it was his words or his obvious need for her. "And?" she asked in almost a hushed whisper.

"And it made me wonder." Julian nestled into her neck, planting warm kisses under her earlobe between phrases. "You said you're a virgin, but have you ever had an orgasm before?"

Gretchen chuckled. "Yes, I have. I might be a virgin, but I'm also a grown woman perfectly capable of managing my needs when necessary."

Now Julian had to laugh. She always surprised him, especially with her bold honesty, even in the face of potentially embarrassing questions. "Has someone else ever given you one?" he pressed.

"No."

"I'd like to."

She shivered as he pressed another kiss along the soft skin of her neck. "Um…right now?"

Not the ideal location, but why the hell not? "Yes, right now." His palm slid across her torso, venturing to her low belly, then to the side of her hip and down. He moved until he reached her smooth bare thigh, shifting the hem of her dress a few inches higher to stroke it. Then he stopped. "Unless you'd rather wait," he said.

After a slight hesitation, Gretchen arched her back, pressing the curve of her rear firmly against his erection. "I think twenty-nine years is long enough to wait, don't you?"

"I do."

Julian turned her in his arms so she was facing him. Despite her bold declaration, he could still sense anxiety in her. She bit at her bottom lip, her dark eyes both challenging him and nervously flickering toward the door and back. He could imagine that the mix of emotions was confusing, but he wouldn't let her psych herself out about this. It was happening.

Dipping his head down, he kissed her. She started to relax with the familiar activity, wrapping her arms around his neck. She let her tongue slide boldly along his own, eliciting a low groan deep in his throat. Keeping this all about her pleasure would be hard when she touched him like this, but he could do it. He was determined.

Julian encircled her waist, pulling her toward him and guiding her backward toward the stage. Once her calves met with the wooden platform, he eased her back until she was sitting on the edge. He tore his lips away from hers, lowering himself to his knees in front of her. Gretchen's eyes grew wide as she watched him put his palms on each bare knee.

With his eyes trained on hers, he pressed gently, parting her legs little by little until he could move between them. He slid his hands up her thighs, pushing the purple fabric of her dress up and out of his way, stopping just short of exposing her. He could feel her muscles tense beneath his touch, so he changed his tactic. Julian wanted her fully relaxed for this.

He kissed her again, distracting her with his lips and tongue as he slipped the straps of her dress off her shoulders. It didn't take much for the fabric to slide down, exposing the bra beneath it. He cupped one breast, slowly stroking and teasing at the nipple through the sheer black fabric. Gretchen groaned against his mouth, her reaction encouraging him to break away from the kiss and draw her nipple into his mouth.

Gretchen's head went back, a cry of pleasure escaping her lips. It echoed in the large ballroom like music to his ears. He continued to tease her through the moist fabric, the distraction it provided allowing him to move his hand beneath her skirt. He found that the panties were made of the same sheer material. When his fingers brushed across her most sensitive spot, Gretchen gasped, her hips rising up off the stage.

Julian eased Gretchen back until she was lying on the stage. She protested at first, but he didn't want her nervously watching everything he did. "Just lie back, close your eyes and enjoy it," he said soothingly until the tension eased from her body.

He started by removing her panties. He slid them down her legs, tossing them out of his way. Then he crouched down and started a trail of kisses that ran from the inside of her ankles, up her calves, to her inner thighs. He let his hot breath tease at her center. She squirmed beneath him, the anticipation of it likely building inside her.

Without warning, he let his tongue flick across her flesh. Gretchen cried out, her fingers grasping fruitlessly at the stage beside her. Julian gave her a moment to recover before he did it again. He pressed her thighs farther apart, exposing more of her to him. His fingers and tongue started moving over her in earnest now, the relentless pursuit of her release foremost in his mind.

Gretchen's gasps and groans were an encouraging melody. As they escalated in pitch and intensity, he knew she was getting close. Her thighs were tense beside him, as though they were made of steel. He re-doubled his efforts until a desperate "yes, yes!" filled the room.

Gently, he slipped one finger inside her, knowing it would put her over the edge. He felt her muscles clamp down on him and half a second later, she came undone. She gasped and cried, writhing on the hard stage even as he continued to work over her with his tongue.

It wasn't until she collapsed back against the stage, her thighs trembling, that he pulled away. Her ragged breath was the only sound in the massive ballroom as he smoothed out her skirt and sat back on his heels.

Several minutes later, Gretchen pushed herself up to look at him. Her pale cheeks were flushed red, her eyes glassy, but she was smiling. It made his chest ache to see it. The women in his life always seemed to demand so much from him. Gretchen appreciated even the tiniest of gestures.

"Well," she said at last. "I'm never going to look at this ballroom the same way, ever again."

# Seven

"Take me to the hotel, Julian."

Julian's gaze met hers, a heat in them she couldn't ignore. And yet he hesitated, swallowing hard before he spoke. "Are you sure?"

"I am." She'd never been so certain of anything in her whole life. She wasn't foolish enough to think this relationship would last past the weekend, or that she would be anything more than a faint memory in Julian's mind, but she couldn't pass this chance up. Even if she *had* been with a man before, making love to a movie star was every woman's sexual fantasy.

And yet the doubts plagued her. Of course she wanted him. But his wanting her was another matter. "Unless you don't want to," she added in a quiet voice.

Julian rolled his eyes and took her hand, tugging her up off the stage. "I want to. You have no idea how much I want to. I just don't know that I should. I can't promise you anything."

Gretchen gazed up at him and shook her head. "All I want you to promise me is a night of hot sex and enough orgasms to last me until the next guy comes along."

Julian smiled, making her relax into his arms. He wasn't turning her down, thank goodness.

"That," he said with a wicked glint in his blue eyes, "I can do."

They left the chapel so quickly, Gretchen barely had time to grab her heels and switch off the lights. The drive to his hotel seemed to take an eternity. In the dark of the car, Gretchen bit at her lower lip and tried to stay in the moment. While her body was still pulsating from the orgasm he'd given her it was easy to propose they go further, but the reality was creeping in with every mile they came nearer to his hotel. She was about to have sex. The idea of it both thrilled and terrified her.

As they walked the length of the hotel corridor together, hand in hand, she could feel her heart pounding in her chest. On the other side of the door was what she'd been fantasizing about since she was sixteen years old.

"Would you like a glass of wine?" he asked as they stepped into his suite.

"No," she shook her head. "I'd rather just…get to it."

Julian frowned at her and crossed his arms over his chest. "Gretchen, this isn't a sprint, it's a marathon."

"I know," she replied, knowing it had come out wrong and right at the same time. She wanted it done so she could put the anxiety aside and enjoy herself.

Julian dropped his arms at his side and approached her, stopping just short of them touching. He placed his large, warm palms on her bare upper arms, rubbing them in a soothing rhythm. "Relax. Enjoy yourself. Unless you change your mind or the hotel catches fire, I guarantee it's going to happen."

Gretchen let out the ragged breath she didn't realize she'd been holding in. As the air rushed from her lungs, so did the tension that had built up in every muscle. "You're right, I'm sorry. I'm just so—"

Julian's lips met hers in an instant, stealing the words from her mouth. His touch made all her worries disappear. She melted into his arms, pressing into the hard body she couldn't get out of her head. Even when she heard the sound of her zipper gliding down her back, she didn't tense up. The glide of his tongue and the hungry press of his fingertips into her flesh made her whole body soften like butter.

He tugged the straps of her dress and bra down her shoulders, planting a line of kisses along her throat and across the newly exposed skin. Julian's hungry gaze flickered over her breasts before he dipped his head to taste the flesh that threatened to spill over the top of her bra.

With her dress open in the back, she could feel the fabric slipping down, pooling at her waist, but she fought the urge to stop it. By all indications, Julian liked what he saw. Tonight it was all coming off, no matter how anxious she might be about it.

Reaching behind her, Julian unfastened the clasp of her bra, sliding it down her arms and draping it across the nearby chair. Her nakedness was immediately covered by his hands and his mouth. Gretchen's eyes fluttered closed as he drew one hard pink nipple into his mouth. A bolt of pleasure shot right through her, mak-

ing her core tighten and ache and her legs start to trem-
ble beneath her.

She was so lost in the moment that when Julian
crouched down and lifted her up into the air, she was
caught completely off guard. With a cry of surprise, she
wrapped her arms around his neck and her legs around
his waist. "You're going to throw your back out or something," she complained as she clung to him. She wasn't
some skinny-minnie supermodel, as though he could
forget with her half naked in his arms.

He narrowed his gaze at her, a challenge in his eyes.
"Gretchen, even on a bad day I can bench press twice
what you weigh. Stop worrying and let me carry you
into the bedroom to ravish you properly, all right?"

Squeezing her eyes shut, she buried her face in his
neck. She couldn't let her stupid insecurities ruin this
moment. With one arm wrapped around her waist, Julian's other slid along her outer thigh, gripping one
round cheek beneath her cocktail dress. She felt his
palm explore her skin in a curious fashion before he
spoke.

"Naughty," he whispered as they started toward the
bedroom.

"What?" She didn't know what he was talking about.

"You never put your panties back on."

Gretchen straightened up in his arms, her eyes wide
as she gasped. "Oh, my God. I left them on the floor
of the ballroom."

Julian chuckled and shook his head, continuing into
the bedroom. "Someone's going to get a surprise first
thing in the morning."

Thoughts of Bree or Natalie running across those
sheer black panties in the ballroom suddenly consumed

her. How embarrassing. Then Julian lowered her onto the bed and her bare back met with the soft, plush fabric of the comforter.

She watched as he unbuttoned his dress shirt and slipped it off, exposing the famously familiar muscles beneath it. God, he was beautiful. There was a Michelangelo-like quality to the definition of his body, as though each muscle had been carved out of flesh-colored marble with a fine chisel.

Her eyes remained glued to his hands as he unbuckled his belt, unzipped his trousers and let the last of his clothing fall to the floor. He kicked off his shoes and stepped out of it all, taking a step toward the bed in all his naked glory.

"Well?" he asked after giving her a moment to take in every inch of the glorious sight. "Will I do?"

Gretchen laughed in a nervous titter. The man was beautiful, rock hard and very aroused. Any doubts she had about his attraction to her were instantly quelled. They were replaced by the anxiety of realizing he was a large specimen of man. She covered her nerves with a wide smile and a nod. "I suppose so."

One dark brow shot up at her blasé assessment of his manhood. Without responding, he approached the bed and reached for her waist. He gathered her dress and gave it a firm tug to slip it over her hips. When he dropped it to the floor, his gaze returned to her fully naked body.

Gretchen took a deep breath and fought the urge to cover herself. Instead she raised her hand and crooked her index finger to beckon him to her.

He didn't hesitate. Julian covered her body with his own, every inch of his blazing-hot skin touching hers.

The firm heat of him pressed at her thigh, urging her to open herself to him, so she did. He slipped between her legs and rested there. She could feel the tip of him teasing at her, but he didn't press forward. Not yet.

Instead, he hovered over her, lavishing more attention on her breasts. He kneaded and tasted her flesh, nipping at the tight peaks and flicking over them with his tongue until her back arched off the bed. Then, with one nipple drawn into his mouth, his hand slid down her stomach to delve between them. As he had at the chapel, his fingertips sought out her most sensitive flesh. He stroked over her in soft circles, building up another climax.

He slipped one finger inside her, stroking in and out of her tight body while his thumb still teased at her apex. The sensations coursing through her were so intense. She was desperate to keep her eyes open, yet no matter how hard she fought, they kept closing so she could savor the feeling.

He added a second finger, stretching her body wider and intensifying the ache in her belly. She easily accommodated him, anxious and ready for everything he had to offer.

That was when he pulled away. Gretchen's eyes flew open in time to see him reach for something beside the bed. A condom, she realized, as he quickly applied it and returned to the bed. As he moved across the mattress, his hands slipped behind her knees and bent them, drawing her legs up and spreading her wider for him.

Julian hovered over her then, watching her with a curious expression on his face. Then he lowered his face to hers and kissed her. Gretchen wrapped her arms around his neck and gave herself over to the kiss.

He rocked forward in short, slow strokes, rubbing the tip of his erection against her, picking up where his hands had left off a moment ago. She felt the orgasm building up inside her again. He sped up, rubbing over her sensitive flesh again and again as her cries escalated.

She was about to come a second time. She could feel the tension in her, about to break. "Julian," she gasped, clinging to his neck. "Yes, yes!" she cried out as she went over the edge.

That's when he entered her in one quick thrust. Pleasure. Pain. It was so fast, she almost didn't realize what had happened until it was done. She gasped with a mix of surprise and release as the last tremors of her orgasm traveled through her body.

Julian held himself remarkably still, even as he was buried deep inside her. His eyes were closed, a look of near pain on his face.

"Are you okay?" she asked.

His brows drew together as he looked down at her. "Aren't I supposed to be the one asking that question?"

"I suppose, but you're the one that looks like you're being hurt."

He shook his head. "Oh, it doesn't hurt. Not at all. I'm just trying to restrain myself a little."

Testing the waters, he eased out slowly and thrust forward again. Gretchen's body lit up with tiny pinpricks of sensation, most of them wonderful. "Don't. It's done. Now make love to me, Julian. Please."

With a curt nod, he shifted his weight and moved in her again with agonizing restraint. Now it was his turn to groan aloud. The feeling was amazing, but Gretchen couldn't help watching Julian's responses. She loved that she was able to give him pleasure, something she hadn't entirely considered before this moment.

Any residual soreness faded away as his movements came faster. Feeling more bold, she drew her knees up, cradling him between her thighs. The movement allowed him to move deeper, and she gasped as she adjusted to the feeling.

Julian swore against her cheek, a low rumble of approval that vibrated to her core. "You feel so amazing, but if you keep moving like that, I'm going to lose it."

"Lose it," she encouraged. She wanted him to lose control because of her. "Like you said earlier, we've got all night."

"Yes, we do."

Closing his eyes, Julian moved harder into her, the quick thrusts pushing him over the edge in mere minutes. His muscles tensed beneath the skin, his breath labored. She watched as he surged into her one last time, his jaw dropping open with a silent groan and shudder that ran through his whole body.

And then it was done. It was official. Gretchen was no longer a pathetic twenty-nine-year-old virgin. Julian rolled off onto his side and collapsed back against the bed with ragged breaths.

Gretchen could only lie there and smile as she gazed up at the ceiling. They'd just finished, and she couldn't wait to do it again.

A familiar sound roused Julian from his satiated sleep. One eye pried open to look at the screen on his cell phone as it charged on the nearby nightstand. It was the last number he wanted to see, especially at such an early hour, but it was the one he'd been anticipating all week. He'd had a feeling something wasn't quite right with his brother, and he was usually spot-on with that.

Shooting up in bed, he grabbed the phone and answered.

"Hello?" he said in a sleepy, gravelly voice.

"Mr. Curtis?" the woman said, using Julian's real last name.

"Yes?"

"Mr. Curtis, I'm sorry to call at such a late hour, but this is Theresa from the Hawthorne Community."

He knew that. He knew the minute he picked up the phone. Now get to the point. "Is James okay?"

A hesitation, slight but noticeable, preceded her answer. "He's stable," she said. "He's developed pneumonia and we're going to be transferring him to the hospital for observation."

Julian fought the confusing mix of sleep and panic. "Do I need to come? Is he going to be all right?"

"We don't think you need to come yet," Theresa said. "Right now he's stabilized. We're going to see how he reacts to treatment. He already has so much difficulty breathing, this just makes things that much harder for him."

"Yes, I know. Someone will call me as soon as there's a change?"

"Yes, Mr. Curtis. That's what James's file says, which is why we called you at such a late hour. You're to be notified any time there's a major medical change for him."

Julian nodded at the phone. That was the way he wanted it. If anything went wrong, he wanted to know. He couldn't be there with him, but he could make sure

James had all the best doctors and treatment that a movie star's salary could provide. "Thank you."

The call ended. Julian dropped the phone into his lap and took a deep breath to expel the fear that held his lungs captive. It was only fair—if James couldn't breathe, Julian shouldn't be able to breathe, either. That was never the way it was in reality. Julian was perfect. Healthy and able-bodied. James was not. The constant stream of late-night calls over the years had proven that much.

"Julian?" Gretchen's soft, concerned voice called to him from the pillows. "Is everything all right?"

A sudden feeling of dread, more powerful than the one that rushed over him as his phone rang, overcame Julian. Gretchen was in bed beside him. She'd heard everything. This situation had the potential to go horribly wrong.

"Uh, yeah," he said dismissively, hoping she would let it go. Very few people in his life knew about James's situation. Hell, almost no one knew about James at all. Julian kept it that way on purpose. He certainly didn't need the press exploiting this story. James had never asked for anyone's pity, and making him a headline could potentially have millions of people looking at his brother as though there was something wrong with him. He didn't want that. Despite everything, James had always just wanted to live a normal life. Being at the Hawthorne Community had given him that. He had his own apartment, his own helper and a staff of professionals to care for him when he needed it. Julian didn't want to ruin that for his brother.

Gretchen sat up beside him in bed and leaned her

bare shoulder against him. "For an actor, you're not a very good liar."

Julian chuckled softly. "Three a.m. is not the peak hour for my craft, I suppose." He turned to her, planted a soft kiss on her lips and ignored the concern in her eyes. "It's nothing. You can go back to sleep."

He expected her to lie down, but instead he felt her arm wrap around his shoulders. "Julian, I told you my secret and you were able to…uh…help me out. Tell me what's going on and maybe I can help you in return."

He shook his head. "Gretchen, if this was as simple as making love to you, I'd tell you in a second. But this can't be fixed by you or anyone else." Julian returned his phone to the charger and lay down in the hopes she would do the same.

She did, pressing her naked body against his and resting her head on his chest. Normally, thoughts of desire would've rushed through his mind and he would've made love to her again, but there were too many worries in his mind now.

"Tell me," Gretchen said. "It's dark. We're both half asleep. You don't have to look at me while you say it. Just get it off your chest. You'll feel better."

Julian had never told anyone about this situation aside from Ross and the people who were a part of his life before he became a star, like Murray. Ross needed to know why he was so driven. But tonight, under the cover of darkness, he wanted to tell Gretchen the truth. She wasn't like those other women, mining for a story they could sell. If there was one person he could tell, it would be her. He didn't want to keep it from her.

"My brother is in the hospital," he said simply.

"I'm sorry to hear that. Is it serious?"

"Unfortunately, everything is serious when it comes to my brother." That was true. A run-of-the-mill cold could be near fatal, much less the pneumonia he currently had.

"Tell me," she pressed again.

He wanted to, but he had to be careful. "If I do, you have to swear that you'll never tell a single soul what I've said. It's absolutely critical that no one know about this."

"Okay," she said. "You have my word."

Somehow, Julian knew that Gretchen wouldn't spill his secrets, but he had to put it out there and let her know how serious it all was. "I have an identical twin brother named James."

"I didn't realize you had a brother, much less an identical twin."

"No one knows. I try to keep my life before I went to Hollywood very quiet for my family's sake. They didn't ask for this spotlight to be shone on them. And since my brother has so many issues, I'm all the more protective of him."

"What's wrong with him?"

Julian sighed. There were so many things. James had never had a chance to live the truly normal life he wanted, no matter how hard they tried or how many specialists they brought in to see him. "My brother has a severe case of spastic cerebral palsy. The doctors said that he sustained some kind of brain injury in utero or during his birth that impaired his ability to function."

Gretchen didn't respond. He wasn't sure if she was surprised by his tale or wanted to let him just get it all off his chest.

"He was diagnosed when we were about two. My mom was in denial, thinking he was just slower to crawl and get around than I was, as though the two minutes older I was than James made that big of a difference. She finally took him to the doctor when she couldn't ignore the disparity any longer. The diagnosis was devastating, but the hardest part was not knowing how it would fully impact him until he got older. The severity of cerebral palsy can vary widely based on the injury. Some people can live normal, long lives with only a few limitations. My mother hoped for that, but by the time we were getting ready to start kindergarten and his problems became more pronounced, it was easy to see that it was getting harder for her to stay positive. She cried a lot when she thought I wasn't looking. James was wheelchair-bound and needed constant supervision. He had an aide at school that stayed with him and helped him through his day.

"The medical bills were crippling. Even though my father had a good job at a nearby production facility with solid benefits, it didn't cover everything. James went through so many surgeries and treatments. Hours of therapy and trips to the emergency room. Cerebral palsy doesn't get worse, you see. But the complications can. He'd had trouble swallowing and breathing since he was a baby. James nearly choked to death a couple times, and every time cold and flu season came around, we lived like a quarantine facility to keep him from catching anything. Eventually, when he was about ten, they had to put in a tracheostomy tube.

"As we got older, it got harder. James wasn't a little boy anymore—he was a growing teenager. Simple things like getting him out of his chair and into bed, or giving him a bath, got so difficult. We got a home health nurse to help out when we were in high school, but by the time I went off to college, Mom just couldn't handle it anymore. He had a really severe bout of pneumonia and he ended up in the hospital. The doctors told us that he needed better care than we could provide, and they recommended we put him in a state facility that was better equipped to handle James's treatment."

Finally, Gretchen spoke. "That must've been a very hard decision for your parents. Hard on all of you."

"You have no idea. I've lived my whole life with this guilt."

"Guilt? Why would you feel guilty? You didn't do anything wrong."

Julian stroked his hand over Gretchen's soft curls. "I was healthy. I was everything James wasn't. We were identical, we started absolutely the same in every way, and yet something went wrong—something I could've caused before we were even born. It's very easy to feel guilty."

"Did the doctors ever say that? Did they ever directly blame you for it?"

He shrugged. "If they did, my mother would never tell me. It wouldn't matter, though. I was still active and went out with friends and did all the things he couldn't do. When I went off to college and he went into a state hospital, the disparities were painful. And then my father died my junior year of college. In addition to our grief, we had to cope with the fact that now the family had no income and no insurance. My father's life insurance policy was barely enough to pay off the mortgage so my mother wasn't homeless. Something had to be done, so I dropped out of school and moved to LA."

"Really?"

"Stupid, right? I was convinced that I would go out

there and get acting work and be able to support my family. I could've just as easily landed a long-term role as a waiter who couldn't afford his own rent. But I met Ross. He saw potential in me. He might be a jerk sometimes, but he got me into some commercials, then small roles in movies. The next thing I knew, my parts were getting larger, and then I was offered a lead role. I wasn't an overnight success, but it only took a few years before I started making seven figures on a film. I wasn't thrilled with the parts, but they allowed me to move James to a private residential facility that specializes in patients with cerebral palsy. I was able to buy private health insurance for all of us and send my mom money to live on. I'd achieved my goal."

"That's why," Gretchen said with an enlightened tone.

"Why what?"

"Why you don't want to take those other roles. You said you worried about screwing up and damaging your career. It has nothing to do with your ego and everything to do with supporting your family."

Julian sighed. "Yes. They depend on me. I can't, won't, do anything to risk my career. Or to risk anyone finding out about James and turning him into a tabloid headline." As he said the words, he realized just by telling Gretchen this story, he'd compromised his brother. She might not mean to tell, but things could happen. If Ross knew, he'd insist on a confidentiality agreement. Not exactly his usual pillow talk, but he supposed everything was different with Gretchen.

"I know I made you promise not to tell anyone, but to tie up loose ends and ensure my brother's protection, I'll probably need to have Ross draft up a confidentiality agreement in the morning. I know he'll insist on it. I'll also see to it that he adds another five thousand to your payment to compensate for your cooperation. It's not your fault I dumped this on you."

He felt Gretchen stiffen beneath his fingertips, and then she raised her head to look at him. "Are you serious?"

Julian frowned. "This is the way my life works. Contracts and compensation, even in my personal life."

She just watched him for a moment, but her body remained stiff as a board. Finally, she said, "I'll sign your stupid agreement, Julian." The tone of her voice was sharp. He could tell he'd offended her. "But I'm not taking any more of your money."

# Eight

Any second now, someone was going to wake Gretchen up. She sat in front of her vanity applying her makeup the way the woman at the department store had told her to. Draped across the bed behind her was the gown she was wearing to the wedding as Julian's date. That was surreal enough on its own. Knowing she'd slept with him the night before was completely in the dream realm.

She'd waited years for that moment, never once anticipating that she would end up in the arms of one of the sexiest men alive. Gretchen still couldn't quite understand why he wanted her. It annoyed him when she mentioned it, so she'd stopped. But even if she'd had a healthy sense of self-esteem going into this scenario, it would be unbelievable.

The only thing about the past few days that convinced Gretchen that all of this was real was their awkward discussion after his call about James. She had been high on the excitement of having sex for the first time and thrilled that Julian was willing to share something that personal with her. Then he started talking about confidentiality contracts and worse—paying her to keep quiet about it.

The longer they were together, the easier it was for her to forget that none of this was real and that she was being compensated for her time. She hadn't liked the idea of this from the beginning, but as they went on, she liked it even less. With sex added to the mix, she was starting to feel very *Pretty Woman* about the whole thing. The additional money for her silence just rubbed salt in the wound and reminded her that she was that much closer to being a whore.

"Ugh," she said as she applied the last of her mascara and threw it down onto the table in disgust. She needed to get out of here and distract herself with the chaos of the wedding so she didn't stew in those thoughts any longer.

Looking into the mirror, she admired her handiwork. It wasn't bad at all. She'd already straightened her hair and wrapped it into a French twist with a crystal barrette securing it. Having her hair up made her neck look longer and her face look thinner, which was great. She anticipated a lot of cameras being around today since it was the big event they'd been building up to. She had to be believable as Julian's girlfriend, and a double chin wouldn't help her case at all.

With her undergarments in place, Gretchen slipped into the gown she'd chosen with Amelia. It was strapless with a sweetheart neckline and a high waist that fell right under her bust. The top was a shiny black ruched satin, but below the waist, it was flowing white satin, painted in purple, blue and black almost like a wearable piece of watercolor art. It was beautiful and fit her perfectly.

The last piece she added was the necklace Julian had given her. The fiery opal rested nicely on the bare expanse of her chest, falling right below her collarbone.

Admiring herself in the full-length mirror on her closet door, she was stunned by what she saw. This wasn't the mousy, awkward Gretchen from a week ago. She looked confident, radiant and even beautiful. Gretchen was ready to walk out the door and be Julian's girl, which was a good thing, because it was time to go. She needed to get back to the facility.

It felt weird enough already that she wasn't there helping the others, but she'd done her part, including buzzing by this morning to meet the florist and snatch up those wayward panties. Now she was returning as a guest. Since Julian was the best man, he wasn't able to pick her up. He was in the groom's room, likely doing a shot of whiskey with Murray and helping him with his tie. They had to be ready early so Bree could take pictures of the wedding party before the ceremony.

Just in case, Gretchen threw a few last things into an overnight bag she'd packed. If she did end up staying with Julian again, she wanted to be ready and not slink back home in the morning in a gown. She had all her toiletries, a change of clothes and a slinky little red lace chemise that had been rotting in her closet since she'd impulse-purchased it several years back. She was looking forward to someone actually seeing her in it, aside from her.

After loading everything into her car, she returned

to the chapel. Gathered on the curb outside the facility was a crowd of photographers. The location had leaked, as expected, but they weren't allowed on the grounds. With very little activity outside with the winter weather, all they'd get were shots of people coming in and out. They paid little attention to her in her cheap sedan. She was able to slip in the back door as usual.

"Wow."

Gretchen paused outside her office where she was about to stow her overnight bag. Turning, she saw Natalie watching her from the hallway. She was all geared up with her headset, her tablet and fierce determination to tackle the day, but the expression of awe on her face was new.

"Do I look okay?"

Natalie nodded, coming close to admire the dress. "You look amazing. Every bit the girlfriend of a movie star, no doubt."

Gretchen beamed. She thought she looked nice, but was nice good enough? It seemed so, at least in Natalie's opinion.

"I especially like the well-bedded glow. Is that a bronzer or an all-night lovemaking session?"

Gretchen's eyes widened and she brought her hand to her lips to shush her. "Bronzer," she said pointedly. "We'll discuss the brand and how well it was applied later."

Natalie gave her a wicked grin and swung her dark ponytail over her shoulder. "You bet we will. The ballroom looks great, so relax and have fun today."

"I'll try." Gretchen put her things into her office, then went around the facility checking on a few last-minute things. All was well in the ballroom. The pin lights were perfect, and the floral arrangements added the ideal touch. Amelia's wedding cake was an eight-tier masterpiece nestled in a bed of white pastillage roses. All that was left was for the servers to light the candles and the guests to mill in.

She crossed the lobby and found Julian, Murray and the other groomsmen in the chapel taking photos with Bree and another guy who was probably from the magazine that had the exclusive to the event. Gretchen couldn't help the wide smile on her face when her eyes met Julian's, especially when his own smile returned her excitement. He looked so handsome in his tuxedo, as if he were auditioning to be the next James Bond. And he was hers, at least for now. Their relationship might be short, but it was special, and she'd always think of it that way.

Natalie followed her into the chapel, this time on official planner duties. "Okay, gentlemen, we need to get all of you except the ushers back into the gentlemen's suite. The guests are about to arrive. Ushers, please meet me back here so we can go over your instructions one last time."

The men filed out, Julian pressing a kiss to her cheek as he went by, so as not to mess up her lipstick. "I'll meet you in the lobby after these two get hitched."

"I'll be waiting," she said, trying out a seductive smile. She wasn't entirely sure that it worked, but Julian sighed and reluctantly followed Murray out of the chapel. That was proof enough for her.

"All right," Natalie shouted. "Ushers at the doors. Musicians, please cue up the string medley to take us through to the groom's entrance. Gretchen...do something with yourself. Let one of the ushers seat you. They need practice." Without another word, she disappeared from the room.

As she was told, Gretchen returned to the entrance and approached one of the ushers with a polite smile.

"Are you a guest of the bride or the groom?"

"The groom."

He nodded, handed her one of the programs she'd made and took her arm to lead her down the aisle and to a seat on the right side of the chapel. She wasn't alone for long. Guests started arriving in huge waves. This was a big wedding, putting the facility's capacity limits to the test. Every spot in the parking lot, every seat in the chapel, would be taken, and taken by Nashville royalty.

The room filled quickly. Gretchen tried not to act out of place as different country music stars were seated around her. Before long, the chapel looked like the audience at the Country Music Awards. She was pretty certain Garth Brooks and Trisha Yearwood were sitting right behind her. It was odd, but that hadn't fazed her when she was working—a guest was a guest—but as a guest herself, it felt extremely bizarre to be sitting among them. She had to keep reminding herself that her date was a movie star and she needed to be cool.

The string quartet's music medley faded, and she recognized them changing to the song they played when the parents were escorted in, then the officiant and the groomsmen entered. Julian sought her out in the crowd and gave her a sly wink as he went by. It was enough to make her heart flutter in her chest.

They assembled on the raised platform, and the music announced the arrival of the bridesmaids, then Kelly with her father. Gretchen stood with the crowd as the bride walked down the aisle in a lace-and-crystal extravaganza, custom-made for a country music diva.

As the wedding began, Gretchen felt her mind stray. Her gaze drifted to Julian, standing by with the ring and to catch Murray if he fainted. He looked so calm, so natural, compared to Murray, who'd started to sweat and could barely make it through his vows his voice was shaking so badly. Of course, Julian wasn't the one getting married.

She imagined he'd still be calm at his own wedding. Even if he felt nervous, he'd fall back on his actor training and play the part of a confident groom. He'd speak the words to her without faltering, with nothing but love and adoration on his face and in his voice…

*Oh, no.* She stopped herself. Gretchen might be in the midst of a lusty haze, but she wasn't letting herself go *there*. She wasn't a naive girl who thought the man who took her virginity would love her forever and marry her and they'd live happily ever after. She knew the truth and she'd accepted it, despite the ridiculous tangent her brain had taken. Like it or not, she was a paid companion. He wouldn't be looking adoringly at her and speaking vows of any kind, ever.

With a sigh, Gretchen let her gaze drop into her lap as she pretended to study the program. Maybe it was a good thing that their time together was coming to an end. Keeping her heart out of the arrangement with Julian was getting harder and harder.

He needed to get on that plane back to Beverly Hills before she lost the fight.

Julian couldn't wait for the ceremony and all the pictures to be over so he could hold Gretchen in his arms again. She'd hovered on the fringes during the photo shoot, watching with adoration in her eyes, as she was instructed.

Their progressing physical relationship had certainly made their public appearances easier. Neither of them really had to act anymore. They just did what felt natural and it translated beautifully. He'd already had several people ask him about Gretchen, and he couldn't help boasting about how smart and talented and beautiful she was.

It was all true.

At last, Julian's duties were over, save for his toast at the reception. The wedding party finally made their way over to the ballroom and took their places to welcome the happy couple and witness their first dance. That done, they were allowed to take their seats, eat their dinner and finally relax. The round of toasts was completed during the salad course, effectively allowing Julian to be off duty the rest of the night. Weddings were exhausting, almost a bigger production than some of the movies he'd starred in.

"You look amazing," he leaned in and said to Gretchen as the wedding cake was served. Julian wasn't interested in dessert. He had a hard time tearing his eyes away from the exposed line of her neck and shoulders. He ached to run his fingertip along her bare skin and leave a line of kisses in its wake.

Gretchen smiled at his assessment, her cheeks blushing adorably. "Thank you. You're looking pretty dapper yourself."

"Meh." He dismissed it. He wasn't interested in talking about himself tonight. He wanted the focus to be on her. "I can't wait to get you out on the dance floor and show you off to everyone."

Gretchen stiffened slightly, looking at him with concern in her dark eyes. "Dancing? We've never discussed the subject of dancing before. I've got a lovely pair of two left feet."

"You can't be that bad," he dismissed.

"No, you don't understand. My mother was a professionally trained ballerina. She tried to teach me to dance for years, then finally declared I was about as elegant and graceful as a rhino in heels."

Julian flinched. That was a horrible thing to say to someone, much less your own daughter. No wonder she'd gone this long thinking she wasn't worthy of a man's attentions. "We're not doing that kind of dancing," he insisted. "I'm going to hold you close and we'll just lose ourselves in the music. Nothing fancy, just dance floor foreplay."

"Foreplay?" Her arched brow raised curiously.

"You betcha." Julian knew a lot of guys didn't like to dance, but those guys were damn fools. If they only knew how a good slow dance could prime the pumps, they'd all sign up for ballroom dancing lessons.

As if on cue, the bandleader invited the whole wedding party out onto the dance floor. "Here's our chance," he said.

"Aren't you supposed to dance with the maid of honor?"

He turned to see her step out onto the floor with another man. "I guess not. Would you care to help a lonely gentleman out?"

Gretchen nervously took his hand and let him lead her out onto the dance floor. The song was slow and romantic, allowing him to take full advantage of the moment. He slipped his arms around her waist, pulling her close. It took a minute for her to relax, but eventually, she put her arms around his neck and took a deep breath to release the tension.

"See? This isn't so bad."

"You're right. And if it wasn't for the frantic flashing of cameras taking pictures, I might be able to relax."

Julian shrugged. He'd learned long ago to tune all that out. It was hard for an actor to stay in the moment if he couldn't ignore the camera in his face, the lights shining on him and the boom mike hanging overhead. There were really only two photographers tonight; the rest were just guests taking photos like at any other wedding. They were harmless.

"This moment is what the whole week was about. Let them take their pictures. Let them plaster it across their celebrity gossip magazine pages and make you a household name if that's the price for bringing you into my life."

Gretchen gasped softly at his bold words. He'd surprised himself with the intensity of them, but it had felt right at the moment. As time went on, he realized that he just couldn't let this go when he returned home. He didn't know how they could manage it or if it would work at all, but he wanted to try. He would be a fool to let such a sweet, caring woman drift out of his life.

The moment was perfect, like one carefully crafted by one of his directors. The lighting was dim with the occasional beam dancing across them. The music was soft and seductive, their bodies moving in time with it. Every inch of her soft curves was pressed against him. When she laid her head on his shoulder, it was as if the world had ceased to exist. The wedding guests, the cameras…all of it felt as if it was suddenly a million miles away and they were dancing all alone.

Her touch made his skin prickle with sensations,

but none could come close to the lightness inside him. With Gretchen in his arms, he felt as though he could do anything. He could take on that gritty script, he could pursue a more serious acting career without compromising his brother's care, he could have everything he wanted…including her.

It had been only a few days, but he had Gretchen to thank for opening his eyes to the possibilities. He intended to talk to Ross about it tomorrow morning. That script was everything he wanted, and a part of him needed to try out for it. He might not get it, or he might wish he hadn't when the critics got a hold of him, but he needed to try.

The song came to an end, and Julian could feel the spell drift away with the last notes. This night could only be more perfect with Gretchen in his bed again. He wanted to get out of here before something interfered.

"Are you ready to go, Cinderella?" he asked as he led her off the dance floor.

"I don't know," she said with a wrinkled nose. "The minute we step out the door, it's over, isn't it? Our little fantasy relationship turns back into a pumpkin at midnight. If leaving means it's over, then no. I want to stay and dance until the band unplugs and goes home."

Julian pulled her tight against him and kissed her. A tingle traveled straight to his toes, making his feet feel as though they were asleep. "I'm not sure what time period Ross negotiated, but I really don't care. If we walk out of this ballroom, I intend to take you back to my hotel and make love to you all night. And I'm going to keep doing that until I have to get on a plane and go back to LA. I don't know about you, but to me, what's going on between us has nothing to do with any business arrangement."

"It's not for me, either."

Julian smiled. "Then slip out of this ballroom with me right now."

Gretchen looked around the dim ballroom at the crowd on the dance floor and the others milling around their tables. "Isn't it too early to leave? Isn't there anything else you need to do as the best man?"

Julian shook his head. "I'm done. We'll see them tomorrow morning at the farewell brunch."

She was biting her lip, but he could tell he'd won the battle by the naughty glint in her eye. "Okay, let me go get my bag out of my office and we can go."

Julian took Gretchen's hand and they made their way out of the ballroom. He was moving quickly, weaving through the other guests. He couldn't wait to peel that dress off her tonight. In the lobby, he waited while she dashed down the hallway to grab her things.

Then he heard it: the special ringtone designated for his brother's care facility. Reaching into his tuxedo pocket, he grabbed his phone and said a silent prayer.

"Hello?" he said, wishing the voice on the line would tell him it was a wrong number or something.

"Mr. Curtis?" the woman said, dashing his hopes.

"Yes?"

"Mr. Curtis, I'm sorry to have to call again, but this is Theresa from the Hawthorne Community. James's condition has gotten substantially worse since we spoke last."

"He's in the hospital, isn't he?"

"Yes, but he isn't responding quickly enough to treatment. The doctors think they might have to put him on a ventilator to keep his oxygen levels high enough while the pneumonia clears up."

Julian should know more about his brother's condition and what all this would mean for him, but he didn't. His brother's tracheostomy was supposed to solve his breathing problems, but apparently it wasn't enough this time. "What does that mean? Is he going to be okay?"

"We don't know. We called to give you the status and let you know that your mother is with him and hopes you can come as well. Do you think that will be possible?"

"Yes, I'm in Nashville right now. I can be there in a few hours. Which hospital is he staying in?"

"He's at the university hospital. I'll be sure to let your mother know you're on your way."

"Thank you. Goodbye."

Julian hung up the phone and slipped it back into his pocket. He looked over his shoulder as Gretchen came from her office with her purse and a small duffel bag.

"Gretchen…" He stopped. He hated to derail everything, but he had no choice. "I'm going to have to cancel on tonight. I just got a call about James and I'm leaving for Kentucky as soon as I walk out of here."

Her dark eyes widened with concern lining them. "Is he going to be okay?"

Julian felt a tightness constrict his chest, making it almost impossible for him to get out the words. "I… don't know. I just know that I have to go. I'm so sorry. This isn't how I wanted tonight to end."

"Then let's not let it end. Let's go."

"Go?" he asked in confusion. "You mean you want to go to Kentucky with me?"

She nodded quickly, without hesitation. "Absolutely." Walking up to Julian, she placed a reassuring kiss on his lips and then took his hand to tug him toward the door. "Let's get on the road."

# Nine

Julian hated hospitals. A lot of his childhood had been spent in one while his brother was tested and treated. Julian was the lucky one—no one ever came after him with needles and scalpels—but the scent when they exited the elevator was unmistakable. Bleach and blood and God-knows-what-else.

Having a firm grip on Gretchen's hand made it easier. He'd never considered bringing her here until she suggested it, and then he'd realized he didn't want it any other way. For all his muscles, having her here made him feel stronger. He wanted to introduce her to his family; he wanted to share this secretive part of his life with someone.

As they approached the waiting room outside the ICU, he heard his mother's voice calling to him. Turning, he saw her pick up the coffee she was making and head their way.

His mother had been—and in his eyes still was—
a beautiful woman. Time and stress had aged her faster
than they should've, but you could still see the sparkle
of the vibrant young woman beneath it all. Her wavy
dark hair was more gray than brown anymore, but she
still had the same bright smile, and her blue-gray eyes
lit up when she saw him. Julian had her eyes, his own
color much more sedate without his colored contacts.

"I'm so glad you could make it." She smiled as she
approached, wrapping him in a big hug, then turning to
look at his unexpected companion. "And who is this?"

"I'm Gretchen," she said, reaching out to take the
woman's hand. "It's nice to meet you, Mrs. Cooper."

His mother smiled and shook her head. "It's Curtis,
dear. Cooper is Julian's stage name. You can just call
me Denise."

"Mom, Gretchen and I are seeing each other." It may
have only been for a week, but it was true. This was
more than just a setup relationship to him.

His mother looked them both up and down. "We've
interrupted something important, haven't we? You two
look like you came here straight from an awards show
or something."

"Just a wedding that was winding down anyway,"
Julian insisted. "You remember Murray, my roommate
in college?"

She nodded. "Oh, yes, I bought one of his albums
for James to listen to. That explains why you were in
Nashville. Convenient timing, although there's never
really a good time for this." His mother smoothed over
her hair, which was pulled back into a bun.

"How is he doing?"

She shrugged, drawing her oversize cardigan tighter

around her. "It changes by the hour. Doctors keep waiting, hoping his blood oxygen levels will start coming back up without further intervention, but they could decide to go ahead and put him on the ventilator. They worry that if they take that step, he might be on it permanently. I just hate it. He was doing so well."

His mother shook her head sadly. "That trip to Europe for the Botox treatments made a huge difference. He was able to stretch his legs out, and the casts corrected some of the alignment problems he had in his legs. We were hopeful that with enough therapy we might get him walking, but this will set him back again. He's always had the breathing troubles."

Over the years, the spastic nature of his brother's cerebral palsy had worsened as his underutilized muscles started to atrophy. He'd undergone multiple surgeries and years of therapy to lengthen his muscles in the hopes he could walk or manage other dexterity tasks on his own, but they always drew back up. The controversial Botox treatments weren't legal in the States, but they'd taken the risk and traveled to a doctor who could try it. It had cost a fortune, but James had done so well afterward, it had been worth every penny.

"Can we see him?"

His mother bit at her bottom lip, reminding him of Gretchen. "Visiting hours are over, but maybe we can talk to someone." His mother disappeared, returning a few minutes later with an encouraging smile on her face. "They're going to let the two of you go back now, but just for five or ten minutes. You'll have to come back again in the morning. He's in the bed at the far end of the unit on the right. I'll wait here for you and drink some more coffee. It's going to be a long night for me."

"Okay, we'll be out in a minute." Julian hugged his mother, then led Gretchen with him through the double doors of the ICU. They walked around the nurse's station and to the end of the hall. Taking a deep breath, he pushed back the curtain and found his identical twin lying in a hospital bed. It was such a familiar sight, he almost didn't react to it the way he should've. His brother's eyes fluttered open, then a lopsided smile spread across his face.

"Julian," he mouthed with a raspy whisper, breaking into a fit of coughing.

"Try not to talk too much, James. Use your signs." He let go of Gretchen's hand to walk to his brother's bedside. He scooped up James's clenched fist and patted it. Both the boys had learned sign language when they were young to help James communicate without speaking. It was helpful when the tracheostomy made it that much more difficult for him to speak. "Mom says you're having trouble breathing. Have you been sneaking pot again?"

His brother smiled at his joke and shook his head. "Can't get any. Mean nurses," he signed. James took a few rattling, wheezing lungfuls of air through the tracheostomy tube in his throat, making Julian more worried the longer he stood there.

Most people with a tracheostomy could speak by covering the tube with their finger or chin. Because James had such limited control of his hands and arms, that hadn't been an option for him. Instead, they'd adjusted the valve in his windpipe so he could get just enough air to whisper between breaths. Even then, his speech was limited by muscle control in his throat and face. He tended to sign most of the time to get his point across, but occasionally, he'd speak a few words. It had never taken much for Julian to understand him. They were identical twins; Julian knew his brother inside and out. He just couldn't help him.

"James, this is my friend Gretchen. She wanted to meet you."

James's head was almost always cocked unnaturally to the side with a pillow supporting his neck, but his gaze traveled past his brother to Gretchen. His left arm was drawn to his chest, but he waved his fingers at her. "Pretty," he signed.

"Yes, she is. She's very pretty."

"I'd hit that," James whispered with a smile.

Julian and Gretchen both broke into unexpected laughter. Despite everything, James always had a sense of humor. Whatever trauma that had impacted his ability to control his body had left his cognitive powers intact. He was smart and funny, and it made Julian sad that the world would miss out on what James could've done if he'd been born healthy like his brother.

"Uh, thank you, James," she said, blushing at his amusing compliment. "How are you feeling?"

James shrugged. His brother probably didn't know what it was like to feel good. He had okay days and bad days, but even his best days could be hard on him. Those were the days when he felt well enough to think about how he was trapped in a body that couldn't do what he wanted it to do.

A loud, wheezing breath rattled through James's trach tube, but it was quickly drowned out by a shrill beeping noise that sounded from the machine by James's bed. Julian looked up, noting that the blood oxygen percentage on the screen was blinking red.

The nurse came in a second later, checking the screens.

"You two will have to leave. We've got to get the ventilator hooked up."

Two other nurses and a resident came in behind her, and Julian was pushed out into the hallway with Gretchen. As he watched them work on his brother, Julian realized that his fantasies of doing serious films were just that—fantasies. Hard-hitting, low-budget indie films might reap all the awards and get the buzz at Sundance, but they wouldn't pay these bills. They wouldn't cover charter flights to Europe for experimental treatments. Giving James the absolute best quality of life was his number one priority. His vanity and his artistic needs would always take second place to that.

"We'd better go," Gretchen said, tugging at his arm.

Reluctantly, he followed her out of the ICU, dreading the news he'd have to share with his mother in the waiting room. The woman hadn't gotten a stitch of good news in almost thirty years. He hated to pile more on top of it.

But he knew that with the news would be his promise that he'd take care of it. Just as he always had. And always would.

They stumbled into a Louisville hotel room near the hospital at almost three in the morning. Gretchen was exhausted down to her bones, and yet too much had happened for her to sleep anytime soon. She could tell Julian was feeling the same way after how he'd paced in the hotel lobby while they got a room. Even if they went straight to bed, they'd both likely lie there with their brains spinning.

Gretchen flipped on the lights of their suite, revealing a tasteful and modern room. It had a separate sitting area from the bedroom, like Julian's room in Nashville. He carried her bag into the bedroom and laid it out on the bed. They'd left in such a rush, he didn't have a bag of his own. All he'd had was a small leather travel case he'd taken with him to the wedding chapel with things he might need throughout the day.

Now he stood at the foot of the bed, silently tugging off his bow tie and slipping out of his tuxedo jacket. She could tell he was distracted and worried about James. Gretchen knew that if one of her sisters were in the hospital, she'd be beside herself.

Instead of watching him undress, she took her bag into the bathroom to change. She'd spent far too many hours in this strapless bra, and she was ready to be done with it all. Unzipping her bag, she looked inside and groaned. Unfortunately, when she'd packed, she'd packed for a sexy night at his hotel. A detour to Louisville to see his sick brother hadn't been on the radar. The only pajamas she had were of the sexy red lace variety. With the dark cloud looming over Julian, she doubted he would be interested.

But with limited options, she slipped into the chemise and pulled the fluffy hotel bathrobe over it. When she returned to the bedroom, Julian's suit was lying across the chair and he was gone. She found him in the living room, standing in front of the minibar clad in just a pair of boxer briefs as he held a tumbler of golden liquid in his hand. Scotch, she'd guess.

"You're drinking?" she asked. That was the first thing she'd seen him drink aside from water since they met.

"Yeah," he said, looking thoughtfully at the glass. "My trainer can punish me later. That's the beauty of being able-bodied. I just... I just needed something to numb all the feelings inside me. A bottle of water and a protein bar wasn't going to do it."

Gretchen nodded. She hated to see him like this, but there wasn't much she could do. Instead, she sat down on the couch and beckoned him to sit beside her. He slammed back the rest of his drink and left it on the counter before he came over and collapsed onto the pillows.

Without saying anything, Gretchen snuggled up beside him. He wrapped his arm around her shoulder and hugged her tight against him.

"I want to talk about something other than my brother," he said after a long silence. "Tell me..." Julian hesitated. "Tell me about how someone so beautiful and full of life could be so awkward and inexperienced with men."

Really? That was the last topic she wanted to discuss, but if it would take his mind off James, she would confess it all. With her face buried against his chest, she started the not-so-interesting tale of her life. "My mother was a ballerina. She toured with a company for several years before she broke her ankle and retired. She met my father, a physical therapist, while she was doing rehab on her leg. She was tall and willowy, educated in the classics, and he was shorter and stockier, with more knowledge about football than anything else, but for some reason, they hit it off.

"They married and had three girls. I was the middle child. My sisters were always so much like my mother, so graceful and so skilled when it came to charming men. I took after my father. I was always chubby, always clumsy. I actually got kicked out of kinder ballet classes because I kept knocking over the other children. To say I was a disappointment to my mother was an understatement."

"Did she actually say that to you? That you were a disappointment?"

"No. But she always pushed me to be more like my sisters. She didn't seem to understand me at all. Even if I hadn't been stockier or uncoordinated, I was very shy. I was much more comfortable with my art and my books than with boys. I really didn't have much in common with anyone in my family. And when I got old enough to date, I don't know, I guess I sabotaged myself. I didn't feel pretty, I didn't feel confident and so guys never noticed me. I was so quiet, I could virtually fade into the background, unseen and unheard. It just continued on like that and after a while, I decided that maybe I was meant to be one of those suffering artists, destined to be alone."

"That's ridiculous." Julian eased back and lifted her chin with his finger until she had no choice but to look him in the eye. "There's no way a woman like you would end up alone. You're beautiful, talented, smart, passionate… You've got way too much to offer a man. He just has to be smart enough to see you when others don't. I'll admit that I probably wouldn't have been that guy. I'm always on the move, always too distracted to see things that aren't right in front of my face. And if Ross hadn't set up this date, I would've missed out on a wonderful few days because of my blindness."

Gretchen felt the blush of embarrassment rise to her cheeks. She wanted to pull away, to avoid his gaze, but he wouldn't let her.

"I mean it. You don't know how much it meant to

have you here with me tonight. I'm always the one that comes in to save the day. It was nice, for once, to have someone to hold my hand, to support me when I needed it. It's so hard watching James's health deteriorate, but having you there made all the difference."

"I'm glad I could be there. No one should have to go through that alone."

His blue eyes focused on hers, and she noticed for the first time that he'd taken out his contact lenses. The stunning Caribbean blue eyes she was used to looking at were now the soft blue-gray of the northern seas. The color suited him more, and she liked seeing him without part of his Hollywood facade. "Your eyes are a beautiful color," she said.

"They don't pop on camera," he said, deflating her compliment.

"That's the camera's loss."

He watched her for a moment before he spoke. "Gretchen, I don't want this to end."

The surprise shift in the conversation threw her off and she sat up, pulling away from him and taking a few seconds to respond appropriately. "Neither do I, but what choice do we have? You're going back to LA, and my business and my life are in Nashville."

He nodded in agreement, but he had a firm set in his jaw that told her he wasn't giving up that easily. "It would be complicated, yes, but I want to try. I can't just walk away from you like this. Say you want to be with me—no contracts, no faking it for the cameras."

Gretchen almost couldn't believe her ears. He was serious. He wanted to be with her, truly be with her, and not just because his manager was behind it or they were enjoying the benefits of their arrangement. A woman like her being with a man like Julian was some kind of fantasy come to life. How could she say no to that, especially when just a look from him could make her chest so tight she could barely breathe? She certainly wasn't looking forward to letting Julian go. She'd tried to keep her heart out of this short-term scenario, but with every minute that ticked by, she was losing the fight. Was it really possible that she wouldn't have to give him up when his plane took off on Monday?

"I want to be with you, Julian," she said, and she meant it. "I don't know how we'd manage, but I don't want to let this go, either."

"Then don't." Julian leaned into her and pressed his lips against hers. He kept advancing, easing her back until she was lying on the cushions of the couch. His hands fumbled with the tie of her belt, opening the robe and pulling back to admire what was beneath it.

"Holy hell," he said, running his fingers over the red satin-and-lace chemise. "You've had this on the whole time?"

"Just since we got here."

"And we've been talking? If I'd known what you had under that robe, we could've found some more pleasurable distractions than talking."

His lips met hers. Unlike the night before, there was less tenderness in his touch. There was a tension there, and she knew it was stress. He needed a distraction, and she was happy to be that for him tonight. She wanted him to lose himself in her and forget about all his troubles.

His hand glided up her outer thigh, pushing the robe out of the way and brushing against the lace edges of her negligee. "Did you know," he asked, as his hand ran across her stomach, caressing her through the fabric, "that red is my favorite color?"

Gretchen smiled, parting her legs for him to draw closer. "Is it really?"

"It is now." He punctuated the words by burying his face in her neck. He tugged at the plunging neckline of her nightie until her breasts were exposed and he could tease at them with his rough palms.

She still hadn't quite adjusted to the idea that she was a sexually active woman now. She still felt as though she was fumbling around, but being with Julian made it so easy. All she had to do was close her eyes and do whatever felt right. So far, that hadn't steered her wrong, and Julian certainly seemed to like it.

Drawing her leg up, she hooked it around his hip, pulling his firm desire closer to the slip of satin that separated them. Julian groaned when they made contact, rubbing himself across her most sensitive spot. The tiny panties that came with the chemise were hardly clothing, more an eye patch in matching fabric, but she supposed they weren't intended for everyday wear.

Julian gripped the panties in his fist and tugged at them. They tore away without hesitation, and he tossed them onto the hotel room floor. Gretchen gasped in surprise, then started to giggle. There was a reason they were so flimsy. The giggles were abruptly stopped when the panties were replaced by Julian's hand.

Her back arched up off the couch, her hips both drawn to and shying from the powerful feelings his touch roused inside her. It was amazing just how quickly he could bring her to the edge. He'd learned her body's responses after only a few encounters.

Gretchen clenched her eyes shut, hovering on the

verge of release, when she felt cold air rush across her skin. Her eyes opened and she found that Julian had pulled back and was watching her as he lay against the far arm of the couch.

He slipped out of his briefs and beckoned her to join him. "Come here," Julian said.

Gretchen shook out of the robe, nervously took his hand and covered his body with her own. "What are we doing?"

"I'm not doing anything," he said with a sly smile. "I'm going to lie here and watch you while you take the lead."

Her jaw dropped in surprise. They'd moved on to an advanced class without warning. The idea of sitting astride Julian during sex while he watched her was incredibly unnerving. And arousing. She knew instantly that she wanted to do this. She could do this. She wouldn't let nerves get the best of her.

Julian reached for his toiletry case sitting on the coffee table and pulled out a condom. "Care to do the honors?"

She took it from him, determination setting in her jaw. Opening the package, she put it in place and slowly rolled it down the hard length of him. Julian let out a hiss as her hands worked up and down. His jaw was tight, his body tense. It was then that Gretchen realized she liked being in charge. This might be nerve-racking, but it was also going to be fun.

She rose up onto her knees, and Julian helped guide her movements as she lowered herself onto him. She moved slowly, painfully slow, as her body stretched to accommodate him. Then, at last, she found herself fully seated. Her core was already throbbing and prickling with the sensation of his previous touches. She couldn't imagine she would last long like this.

Biting her lip, she braced her hands on Julian's bare chest. She leaned forward and rocked back once, testing the waters. It was a delicious feeling, and judging by Julian's fingertips pressing fiercely into the flesh of her hips, she was doing something right.

Gretchen did it again, this time faster. Gaining confidence, she fell into a pleasurable rhythm with Julian muttering encouraging words to her.

His hands stroked the silk-and-lace fabric of her chemise as she moved, rising up to cover her breasts as they spilled over the top. She placed her hands over his and thrust her hips harder and faster against him.

"Julian," she whispered as she felt the release building up inside her.

"Yes, baby," he encouraged. "Just let go. Take me with you."

So she did. With renewed enthusiasm, she moved over him, opening the floodgates so that every ounce of pleasure, every emotion she held back, rushed free. In the moment, it wasn't his touch or her movements that sent her over the edge, it was the warm heat in the center of her chest.

She'd never felt this sensation before, but she knew what it was. Now that she and Julian had a future, she'd finally allowed herself to feel what she'd been fighting. Love. It was love that pushed her over the edge, crying out his name as the tremors of pleasure washed through her. As he followed suit, thrusting into her one last time, she looked down at him, placing her hand over his heart until they were both still and silent.

It was then that she collapsed against him. Gretchen

buried her face in his neck, breathing in the scent she'd become so used to so quickly.

This. The sex was nice, but *this* was what she'd truly waited twenty-nine years for.

# Ten

Monday morning was a reality that neither of them really wanted to face. James's condition stabilized with the ventilator, and the doctors were extremely positive about his prognosis. He was moved out of the ICU, and his mother ushered Julian and Gretchen out the door and back to Nashville Sunday evening.

That night together had been a somber one, both of them knowing what Monday brought. Gretchen had to be in the office for her weekly staff meeting, so she slipped out of bed, leaving him a kiss as she ran out the door. She promised she would return after the meeting to say a proper goodbye before he had to leave for the airport.

They'd agreed they would give their relationship a real try, long distance be damned, but they both knew it would be hard. And different from how they'd spent the past few days. Julian worried about how they would pull it off. He had some time before his next film started shooting, but if he spent those weeks in Nashville, Ross would undoubtedly start complaining. He would want Julian in LA, doing readings, lining up his next part and being "seen." Unfortunately, he would probably want him being seen out on the town with a woman. That wasn't an option.

The only thing that got him up and dressed that morning was the knowledge that Ross was coming by to meet with him before he flew on to New York to arrange for a few press appearances. He'd much rather stay in bed and wait for Gretchen to return so he could make love to her one last time before he left.

He was drinking a protein shake he'd had stashed in his refrigerator when he heard his manager's knock on the door. Right on time, as usual. Julian opened the door, letting the short, squat man in the expensive suit into the room.

Ross wandered over to the sofa and sat down. "So, how'd the fake date go? The pictures I've seen looked pretty convincing, so good work. I know that couldn't have been easy to keep up."

Julian wasn't sure what his manager meant by that, but they should've been convincing. Every moment together was authentic and amazingly easy. "Actually, it was the easiest role I've played in years. After the first two days, I wasn't acting at all. In fact, Gretchen and I have really hit it off. I've asked her if I can continue to see her after this week."

The smug smile faded from Ross's face the longer Julian spoke. "Are you serious?"

Julian frowned at his manager. "I'm absolutely serious. She's a great woman. I've never dated anyone like her."

Ross sighed and ran his hand over his bald head. "I know that I set this up and I said that you dating a normal, everyday woman would be good for your image. But I never intended this to be a long-term arrangement."

"What does it matter if it's long-term or short-term? You wanted me to be with someone. I'm with someone. You should be happy."

"Not with her," Ross complained. "She's…"

Julian stared Ross down, daring him to insult Gretchen so he'd have a good reason to punch him. "She's *what*, Ross?"

Ross looked at him, preparing the words carefully. "She's not the kind of woman you'd want on your arm when you walk the red carpet at the Golden Globes. That's all I'm saying."

Julian snorted in contempt. "And when, in my illustrious career, have you ever booked me into a role that would get me invited to the Golden Globes?"

Ross shook his head. "You're missing the point. I'm sure she's a perfectly nice girl—the type you'd want to take home to meet your mother. But she's not the kind of girl that will take your career to the next level. Think Brad and Angelina. Tom and Nicole."

"Tom and Nicole are divorced."

"So it didn't work out," he said with a dismissive wave of his hand. "My point is that their high-profile marriage boosted their acting careers."

"There are plenty of famous actors and actresses with spouses that aren't in the business."

Ross leaned forward and rested his chin on his

pointed index fingers. "Julian, I'm your manager. You pay me to know what's best for your career. And I'm telling you—she is not the kind of woman Julian Cooper is supposed to be with."

If that was true, Julian wasn't certain if he wanted to be Julian Cooper anymore. His alter ego was becoming the kind of person he didn't even like. "You might be right, Ross, but I'm telling you that Gretchen is *exactly* the kind of woman that Julian *Curtis* wants to be with. This isn't a role, Ross, it's my life. I pay you to manage my career, but my private life is private. I'll date whomever I want to, and I'd appreciate it if you'd keep your mouth shut on the matter."

Ross's cell phone chimed and he looked down at the screen. Julian was happy for the interruption. The energy in the room had gotten far too tense. Ross was a good manager, but he needed to know he had boundaries.

Ross frowned at the phone and then let it down by his side. "You can date whomever you like, Julian, you're right. But you may want to reconsider choosing Gretchen."

"Why?"

"Did you tell her about James?"

Julian stiffened. "I had to. She was there when I got the call about him going into the hospital. But I told her she'd need to sign a confidentiality agreement."

"Did she?"

"Not yet. I was going to have you draw it up today."

Ross sighed and handed his phone over to him. "It's too damn late. The tragic story of Julian Cooper's secret twin has just hit the papers."

No. That wasn't possible. Julian scanned over the

article, looking for some kind of evidence that would prove that Ross was wrong. The sinking ache in his stomach didn't fade as he read the article. It was a huge, in-depth story about James, including his illness and recent hospital drama. Whoever had leaked the story had very up-to-date information about his brother.

"Who else knows about James?"

Julian shook his head. No one knew. "Just you and Murray. And Gretchen."

"Well, *I* certainly didn't leak the story."

He knew that was true, and with Murray on his honeymoon and worrying about anything but Julian and his brother, that left an unacceptable alternative. He just couldn't believe that Gretchen would sell him out and leak that story. She'd hardly seemed interested in the money he already owed her. But how much would the press be willing to pay for a story like this? Perhaps more than she could turn down?

"No," he insisted with a shake of his head. "I've been with her nonstop until this morning when she went to work. There's no way she could've contacted a reporter and sold that story without me knowing it."

Ross rolled his eyes. "Don't be so ignorant, Julian. You weren't with her every single second. You showered, you used the restroom, you slept. For all you know, she slipped out of bed in the night and emailed a reporter while you were satiated and unconscious."

Julian dropped into the chair beside him, the doubts finally creeping into his mind. He'd trusted her. Could Gretchen really have sold him out just like all the others?

A sad expression lined his manager's face as he reached out and patted Julian's shoulder. "I'm sorry, I really am. I know you think I'm a cold, heartless businessman, with all my confidentiality contracts and arranged relationships, but I've been in this business a long time. I've seen a lot of my clients get sold out by the people they trust the most. I try to protect my clients, but there's only so much I can do."

There was only one person who knew about everything that had happened with James over the past few days. The idea of that betrayal made his protein shake threaten to rise in the back of his throat. He didn't want to believe it. Every fiber in his being screamed that it couldn't be true. But Ross was right. There was no other answer.

"We've got to figure out how you want to handle this. Ignoring the article will make it seem like you're ashamed of your brother, which we don't want. It's probably best that we set up a tell-all interview of some kind, where you talk about him and explain why you tried to keep him out of the harsh spotlight."

"That sounds fine," Julian said in a flat tone. He really wasn't listening. At the moment, damage control was the last thing on his mind.

"While I'm handling that, you need to talk to Gretchen." He laid a fat envelope on the table. "Here's the money we owe her. Pay her and make her go away. Or I will."

Julian nodded. He knew Ross was right, but he didn't relish that conversation. "She's supposed to be coming over here today."

"When?"

Julian looked at the clock hanging on the hotel room wall. "Soon. She was coming back over before I left for the airport."

Ross nodded and stood up. "I'm going to head out, then. While I'm in New York, I'll see who I can talk to about that interview. When you get back to LA, call me and let me know how it went with Gretchen."

His manager slipped out of the room, but Julian hardly gave him any notice. The pain in his chest had subsided, leaving only the numbness of disassociation and the faint heat of anger licking at his ears. He knew what he had to do, and it was a role he didn't want to play. But play it he would to remove the malicious cancer from his life.

Gretchen had a hard time walking down the hallway to Julian's hotel room. A half hour ago, she'd damn near skipped down the same path, arriving earlier than she'd intended. She'd been so excited to see Julian one more time before he left that Natalie had let her cut out of the staff meeting early.

As she'd raised her hand to knock, she'd heard the sound of two men arguing loudly. She hadn't intended to listen in, but there was no way she was going to interrupt their argument. She'd decided to wait for a lull, then knock, but instead, she'd overheard more than she'd bargained for.

Ross's words haunted her, even now. *She is not the kind of woman Julian Cooper is supposed to be with,* he'd said. That hadn't surprised her. But when Julian said that he might be right, she'd felt her heart break. He'd done nothing over the past few days but tell her how beautiful she was, how worthy she was. To hear he really felt otherwise was a crushing blow to her fragile ego. She'd rushed to her car, sobbing against the steering wheel until she saw Ross leave.

She took a few minutes to recover from her tears and then headed back upstairs. She hadn't wanted to go back after that, but she knew it would be suspicious if she didn't show up. Taking a deep breath, she knocked on the door, more anxious than she'd been the very first day.

Julian was slow to answer, and when he did, she wished he hadn't. The light in his eyes was gone, his smile a distant memory. His jaw was tight in anger, his gaze burrowing into her as though he were searching her soul for some kind of guilt.

"Come in," he said, stepping back to let her inside.

This wasn't the reception she was hoping for, but she wasn't surprised. She sat down on the couch, clutching her purse in her lap. Without even speaking, she knew their relationship was about to unravel.

Julian picked up his phone from the coffee table and hit a few buttons. He wordlessly handed it to her, his blue eyes daring her to take it.

Gretchen hesitated, finally accepting the phone from him. When she looked down on the screen, she felt the air get sucked from her lungs. It was an article about James. She knew how hard Julian worked to maintain his brother's privacy, but now the secret was out. No wonder Julian was angry.

"How awful," Gretchen said, her hand coming up to cover her mouth. "How could anyone have found out about James? You were so careful. Could it have been one of the nurses at the hospital?"

"Good try," he said with a deadly cold tone. "I'm the actor in the room, not you."

Gretchen's gaze tore away from the phone to meet

his accusatory one. "What is that supposed to mean? Do you think I'm the one that leaked the story?"

Julian crossed his arms over his chest, looking larger and more intimidating than he ever had before. He looked as if he were about to mow down a field of terrorists with an automatic weapon, as in one of his films. "I don't have a lot of people to choose from, Gretchen. You're the only one who knows everything. You're the only one that's ever met my brother. No one else would have all these details."

Gretchen stood up. She was shorter than he was, but she couldn't just sit there and let him hover over her intimidatingly. "Just because I had the information doesn't mean I would've shared it. I told you that I wouldn't tell anyone about James and I meant it. I said I'd even sign your stupid agreement."

He nodded. "It never occurred to me that you'd manage to sell your story before I had time to draft the paperwork. A brilliant way to get around it, I have to say."

"Get around it?" she said, surprising herself with her own shrill tone. "I didn't get around anything, Julian, because I didn't sell this story. Did Ross feed you all these lies? I don't understand how you could think I'm capable of something like that."

"I didn't think you were capable of it, either." Despite his hard expression, Gretchen detected some hesitation in his eyes. He didn't seem to believe his own accusations, and yet he wouldn't back down.

"You're just using this as an excuse," she said, trying to bait the truth from him.

His brows went up in surprise. "An excuse for what?"

"To get rid of me," she accused. Ross's cruel words echoed in her head, fueling her own anger. "Despite all those promises you made in Louisville, you know I'm not the kind of woman that will boost your career."

Julian seemed baffled by her allegation. "What makes you say that?"

"I heard you talking to Ross," Gretchen said. "I got off work early and heard you arguing. I know I'm not the right kind of woman for Julian Cooper. I'm fat and I'm awkward. I don't have an elegant or graceful bone in my body. I know that. I don't need Ross or you or the press to point that out to me."

Julian shook his head angrily. "I don't know what you heard, but I can assure you that isn't what that discussion was about."

"It wasn't? Come on, Julian, be honest. As much as you claim you want to be this serious actor, you're hooked on that blockbuster lifestyle. You claim you can't quit because of your brother, but how much could his expenses possibly be? Are they as much as your Beverly Hills mansion? Your sports cars? Personal trainers and private chefs? Expensive baubles for your expensive women? I bet not. You're going to use this story to drop me because I don't fit into that lifestyle. I'm not going to help you become a bigger star."

"You know, this doesn't have anything to do with my lifestyle or my career. You obviously didn't hear the whole conversation with Ross or you wouldn't accuse me of such a thing. I would've happily walked the Gretchen I knew down any red carpet. I thought you were beautiful. Special. I meant every word I said to you, Gretchen. But that entire discussion I had with Ross is moot now, because I can't stand by and let you hurt my family."

Angry tears threatened to spill from Gretchen's eyes.

She didn't want to cry. Not in front of Julian, but the harder she fought it, the harder it became to hold the tears back. "I would never do that to you. Or to James. Or your mother. And if you think that I would, then you don't know me as well as you think you do."

"I guess not, but it's only been a few days, right? It's not like we were in love."

Gretchen flinched at how ridiculous he made the idea of love sound. She was grateful she had kept her budding feelings to herself. The last thing she needed was for him to throw that in her face.

"What did they offer you, Gretchen?" he taunted. His face was so twisted with anger and betrayal he didn't look anything like the Julian she knew. "Money? Was the ten grand I'm paying you not enough?"

"No, it isn't about the money. I don't care how much they would've offered me, I wouldn't have sold that story to the press. I don't even want the money from this week."

Julian rolled his eyes and picked up an envelope from the table. He thrust it into her hands and stepped away before she could reject the parcel. "Why don't you want the money? Don't need it after your big story payout?"

Gretchen was so upset, she didn't even look down at what he handed her. "There is no payout. There is no money. I don't know how to convince you of that. And I don't want your money because it feels wrong to take it when it felt like we were…more than just some fake Hollywood relationship."

His blue gaze tore away from hers, focusing on the beige carpet of the hotel room. "It was just acting, Gretchen. By making you think it was real, you were far more relaxed for the cameras. We never would've pulled this fake relationship off if you didn't think I really liked you."

That struck Gretchen dumb. Could he really mean that? Had he just played her because she was so stiff and awkward? She knew she wasn't good with men, but could she really be fooled that easily? He was an actor, after all, but she couldn't believe he'd misled her like that. He couldn't make eye contact when he said it. She was certain that there was more between them, but for some reason, he wouldn't let himself admit to the truth.

Her chin dropped to her chest, her gaze finally falling on the package in her hand. "What is this?" she asked.

"Ten thousand dollars, as agreed. You fulfilled your end of the bargain, and quite pleasurably at that." There was a gloating expression on his face that she didn't like. She'd been desperate to rid herself of her virginity, but she couldn't stand to have him gloat over taking it so easily.

"Obviously," he added bitterly, "the five-thousand-dollar bonus for keeping quiet about my brother was forfeited when you spilled your guts to that reporter."

Gretchen closed her eyes. She could feel her heart crumbling in her chest. There was no other explanation for the sharp sensation that stole her breath from her lungs. She had no words, but it didn't matter because she knew her words wouldn't make any difference. He'd decided she was guilty, and nothing would convince him otherwise.

And even if it did…what would it change? If he'd been pretending to like her just to get through the week, there was nothing between them to salvage. All she could do was hold it together long enough to get out of this hotel room with some of her dignity intact.

"Obviously," she said, steeling her nerves and matching his bitter tone.

When she opened her eyes, Julian was emerging from the bedroom with his rolling suitcase. Once again, he avoided her gaze, making a wide berth around her as he made his way to the door. "Enjoy Italy," he said. "I hope you can put that blood money to good use." Julian grabbed the handle of the door and flung it open, walking out of the hotel suite without so much as a backward glance.

Gretchen wanted to chase after him, to convince him that she was telling the truth, but her legs just wouldn't cooperate. She might not think much of herself, but she had too much pride to beg. Instead, her knees trembled and gave out, her body collapsing into the cushions of the couch. Her face dropped into her lap, this morning's second round of tears flowing freely and wetting the envelope in her hands.

She was a fool. A fool to believe that a man like Julian would ever want something to do with a woman like her. A fool to think that she could find happiness with a person so unobtainable. He was a fantasy.

And now, it had all come to an end.

# Eleven

Gretchen had buried herself in work this week. It was easy with her job—there was always a wedding to decorate for, a consult with a couple, some design work to finish and send to the printers. Thank goodness. She needed the distraction.

Her two days off had been awful. She'd pretty much sat in her apartment crying and eating cookies. That wasn't going to help matters at all. But by the time she returned to the office, she had that out of her system. She was ready to focus on work and forget all about Julian Cooper.

Unfortunately, it wasn't that easy. Not with three nosy friends and coworkers who immediately noticed that the romantic bubble had burst. She'd left their staff meeting on Monday almost beaming and came back Thursday morning in mourning. She'd fought off the questions but gave them enough information to satisfy them: it was over. She didn't want to talk much more about it when it was so new. So far, they'd backed off, but only because they were busy preparing for the next wedding, too.

When the time came, she wasn't entirely sure what she would tell them. Getting up from her desk and going into her supply closet, she pulled down the bin labeled for this weekend's autumn-themed wedding. As she sorted through the paper products, she tried to work out the tale in her mind.

"He accused me of leaking a story to the press and we broke up," she said aloud. "And really, we were never actually together. He was just playing me." That sounded silly, especially out loud, despite every word being true.

Of course, the supposed truth was nothing compared to her secret worry. Would he really have used all that as an excuse to break up with her because when it came down to it, he needed to date a pretty actress, not a frumpy artist? He'd insisted that wasn't true. He'd done nothing but tell her how pretty she was while they were together, but was he just buttering her up for the part? She couldn't dismiss what she'd heard between him and Ross.

The worst part of it was that she had to admit that Ross was probably right. She wasn't what people expected. Vain, painted-up Bridgette made a lot more sense in their business, even if Julian didn't like it. As hard as he worked to keep his brother and family out of the spotlight, protecting Gretchen would be harder. While early press might be positive, eventually, she'd find herself on a cover with a headline that declared Julian demands she lose weight or it's over.

It would never work between them; she knew that now. It was a pipe dream, a fantasy that lasted only while he was playing the role of the adoring, doting boyfriend.

Her fingers went to her throat and sought out the opal necklace. She'd worn it nearly every moment since he bought it for her. She loved it. But it was time to take it off. She unlatched the clasp and let it pool in her hand. Looking down at the beautiful, ruined necklace, she opened her desk drawer and dropped it in with her pens and paper clips.

That done, Gretchen picked up the box of paper products and carried them out of her office. She quickly divided them up among the chapel, the entryway table and the ballroom.

The ballroom was still bare bones. This weekend's wedding was smaller and far less grand compared to Murray and Kelly's event, but there was still plenty to be done.

"Gretchen?"

Gretchen set down the programs and turned to find Natalie in the doorway behind her. "Hey."

"The linen delivery is here. Do you need help?"

She shrugged. "Sure, if you've got time."

Natalie nodded and they both went to the back to get the cleaned, pressed linens from the delivery truck. They rolled the cart back into the ballroom and Gretchen started laying them out on the tables. She could tell Natalie was lingering purposely, but she wasn't about to start the conversation she was dreading.

Her coworker joined her in laying out linens, this wedding using a chocolate brown with an ivory-and-gold lace overlay. After a minute, Natalie said in a quiet voice, "Are you okay?"

Gretchen sighed and finished spreading out the tablecloth. "No, but I'm getting there."

Natalie nodded. The wedding planner at From This Moment was the quiet, observant type. She did a lot of listening, both in her job and in her daily life, something most people didn't really do. By listening, she noticed a lot, most importantly what people weren't saying.

"How long do you think I have before Bree and Amelia will try to fix me up with someone else?" Gretchen had hoped that losing her virginity would take that pressure off her friends and their quest to get her a man, but she doubted that would be the case. With that sexual burden gone, they could just hunt down a normal guy for her, not some superhero worthy of her first time.

"I think you're safe through the holidays. It's too busy a time to try fixing someone up, although I wouldn't put it past Amelia to throw a Christmas party at her house and casually try introducing you to a couple single guys while you're there."

Gretchen could handle some awkward conversations at a party. That gave her a few weeks at least. She always liked Christmas, so having that distraction would keep her busy. She'd just have to be super careful about how many sugar cookies she consumed. She didn't need these twenty extra pounds turning into twenty-five.

"You could always take a page out of my book and go into holiday hibernation. Don't surface until the New Year's Eve hangovers fade away."

Gretchen had too much family for that, as nice as it might sound. Natalie was different; she had divorced parents and a general disdain for the holidays, so it was easier to fade away for a week or so. "Not everyone hates Christmas, Natalie. I can deal with the matchmaking as long as all the holiday festivities distract me."

"Maybe you should take some of that money and go on a little trip. You don't have enough time for Italy, but what about New York City or Vegas?"

Gretchen chuckled. "After what happened to Amelia in Vegas? No, thanks."

"I doubt you'll elope while you're there. But maybe you'll meet a hot distraction and spend some time catching up on all those vices you've missed out on."

Gretchen eased down into one of the chairs and shook her head. "I don't think I can spend any of that money. It feels…tainted somehow."

"What about Italy?"

"I'll get there someday. Just not any time soon. If I go now, all I'll see is old ruins and shells of what was. But if I wait long enough, maybe I can go with a man that loves me and I'll be able to see the beauty in it again. That would make the trip better, don't you think?"

Natalie smoothed out the fabric in front of her. "It sounds nice," she said with a noncommittal tone. Natalie was nearly as enthusiastic about love as she was about Christmas.

"If this last week taught me anything, it's that I'm worth more than I think. I just need the confidence to put myself out there and maybe I can have a healthy relationship with a normal guy."

"Absolutely," Natalie agreed. She came over and knelt beside Gretchen, giving her a comforting side hug. "You'll find someone if you want to. You can do anything you want to."

Gretchen had said the words, but she didn't entirely

believe them yet. Not even Natalie's assurances convinced her, but she would try. She wouldn't let her heart be trampled on by someone like Julian. She'd just reached too high, like Icarus, and crashed to the ground. If she'd opted to date someone safer, it might not have hurt as much to fall.

"Thanks, Natalie."

"I've got an appointment in a few minutes, but I'll try to check back and help you later."

Gretchen waved as Natalie slipped out of the ballroom. She watched her go and let her gaze drop into her lap. She would go to Italy someday, she knew that. But she wouldn't do it with the money Julian gave to her. He thought she was a sellout, and if she spent it, maybe she was.

Getting up, she went into her office and sat down at her desk. She opened the bottom drawer and pulled out her purse. Inside, she could see the thick wad of cash she'd stashed there in an envelope. She felt ridiculous walking around with ten grand in her bag, but it was all she could do until she made her decision.

Bree insisted that she go to Italy and drown her sorrows in a hot Italian lover. Amelia suggested that she mail it back to him if it bothered her to keep it and take her trip. While the idea of sipping prosecco in Capri as a sexy man who spoke very little English rubbed suntan lotion on her body seemed nice, she knew she couldn't do it. But sending it back would likely result in Julian rejecting the delivery, and she'd never get rid of the money.

That left a third option—to do something positive with the money, so no matter what, some good would come from the whole thing. If Gretchen did something worthwhile with the money, maybe it would purify it somehow. Make the past week have purpose. Julian might think she was a sneaky liar willing to sell him out, but nothing could be further from the truth. There was one way to make sure he knew it, too.

Logging on to her computer, she looked up the website for the Cerebral Palsy Foundation. With just a few clicks she found what she was looking for—a solution and a little peace of mind. All she had to do was deposit the money in her account and put the wheels in motion.

She might not get to go to Italy, but she would get the final word.

This script sucked. Julian could barely stand to continue reading the crap that Ross had couriered over this afternoon. It made *Bombs of Fury* look like Shakespeare.

A week ago, he would've accepted the offer without question, but that was before Gretchen had gotten under his skin. She'd planted those seeds of hope that he could have a serious acting career, then turned around and poured gasoline on the buds as they broke through the earth. Ross and his publicist were already scrambling to shift attention away from James and find a way to suppress the story without making it look as if Julian was embarrassed of his brother. He was anything but. He just didn't want press camped outside the Hawthorne Community or reporters pressing Julian for a sob story. He'd already gotten a call from Oprah to share his secret pain.

Despite Ross's assurances that it was the right path to take, Julian didn't want to share his secret pain. He wanted to keep his brother out of the spotlight, and he'd failed when he'd spilled his guts to Gretchen. He'd trusted her. Those big brown eyes had pleaded with him to confide in her. Then she'd turned around and stabbed him in the back just like all the others. He still couldn't quite believe it.

He tossed the offensive script onto the kitchen table and shook his head. He'd do it. He knew he would. But he'd loathe himself even more than he already did. Getting up from the table, he planned to march into the kitchen and make himself a stiff drink when he heard the sound of footsteps on the tile of the entryway.

No one was in the house but Julian. Before he could react, the intruder sauntered around the corner in a crop top and a pair of yoga pants. Bridgette.

"What the hell? How did you get in here?" Julian clenched his teeth at her bold move.

"I still have a key," she said, swinging her blond ponytail over her shoulder and smiling at him with a sweetness he didn't trust. She held up a bundle of letters in her hand and set them on the counter. "I brought in your mail. I came by because I heard you were back from the wedding and I wanted to see you."

She took a step toward him, but Julian stepped backward. He didn't like this. Bridgette was far too calculating to just pop in to be sociable. "Why?"

Bridgette pouted, her collagen-plumped bottom lip thrusting out. "Because I miss you, Julian. These last few weeks have been really hard on me."

"We broke up six months ago. Last I saw, you had your tongue down Paul's throat. You didn't seem like you were suffering to me."

She frowned, but the movement didn't translate to a furrowed brow because of all the Botox she injected.

"I was using Paul as a rebound. I was just trying to get over you, and it didn't work. When I saw those pictures of you and that fat girl, my heart nearly broke. I—"

"Stop," he interrupted, holding up his hand. Julian might be upset with Gretchen, but he wasn't going to let anyone else tear her down. He'd lied when he said she hadn't meant anything to him. It hadn't been acting, but it was the best thing to say. It convinced her, and him, that there was nothing to fight for. But despite all that, she still meant something to him. More than Bridgette ever had. "Gretchen is a beautiful, smart, sensitive woman that I cared about quite a bit. Be respectful of her or leave." He preferred she just leave, but he doubted he'd get rid of her that easily.

"Cared for her?" Bridgette whined. "You barely knew her. She must've worked hard to get her hooks into you that quickly. I could tell she was up to no good. I knew I had to find a way to get you back."

"You don't know what you're talking about. Gretchen didn't have hooks, much less ones in me. And even if she did, I don't need you to save me. If the choice were between the two of you, Gretchen would win." Even with the media leak and the lies, she was more genuine than Bridgette. In fact, that kind of thing was what he would've expected from his ex, which was why he'd never so much as breathed James's name in her presence.

"How could you still think that way about her after what she did? Selling the story about your brother to the press is just unforgivable."

Julian was about to argue with her when he stopped short. The article never mentioned the source for the story. Even if Bridgette had read the magazine from cover to cover, why would she presume that Gretchen had been the one to spill the news? How could she even know that Gretchen had knowledge of James to begin with? There was only one good reason for that.

"You did it." The sudden realization made his heart drop into his stomach with a nauseating thud.

Bridgette eyed him, a practiced look of vague innocence on her face. "I did what?" she asked with all the sweetness she could muster.

He didn't know how she'd dug up the truth, but he knew down to the depths of his soul that Bridgette had been the one to betray him. "You're the one that leaked the story about my brother."

"Me? How could I do that when I didn't know you had a brother? You never mentioned him or anything else about your family to me. I read about it in the gossip pages just like everyone else."

"No. You did this." Julian wasn't about to fall for her protests; they were far too polished. She was an actress, after all. "There's no way you could know that I'd blamed Gretchen for leaking the story unless you'd deliberately set it up to look that way. You got so jealous you did it deliberately to break up Gretchen and me. Admit it, or I'll track down the journalist and find out for myself. And if it was you, and you lied to me, every secret you've ever told me will be front-page news."

Bridgette's mouth dropped open, her eyes darting around the room in a panic. Nothing here was going to help her now, unless she was willing to bludgeon him with the ceramic jar on the countertop.

"I had to," she admitted at last. "It was the only way to get you away from Thunder Thighs. I had a detective following you in Nashville. I'd hired him just to keep tabs on you and get a feel for whether or not we had a chance to reconcile. Then he tailed you to Louisville and uncovered the truth about your brother. I wouldn't have said a word about it, but then I realized that you took her with you. You'd never said a word about James to me in over a year together and yet you took *her* to meet him. I was devastated, Julian. I didn't know what to do. I thought if the story leaked, you'd blame her and come home so distraught I could comfort you and we'd get back together."

Bridgette was crazier than even he gave her credit for. "You plan is flawed, Bridgette. I did blame her and I did come home distraught, but I don't want you to comfort me. I want you to go away."

"Please, Julian. We could be a Hollywood power couple. Admit it, we just make sense together. A heck of a lot more sense than you and the pudgy artist."

"Get out!" he roared, his anger turning on like the flick of a switch. He wasn't going to have her in his presence insulting the woman he loved for one more minute.

"Julian, I—"

Julian lunged forward and snatched his house keys out of her hand. He wouldn't make that mistake twice. "Get out before I call the cops *and* the press so they can photograph you getting arrested for trespassing."

Her eyes widened. He could tell she was trying to figure if he was bluffing or not. After a moment, she decided not to press her luck. Flinging her hair defiantly over her shoulder, she spun on her heel and marched down the hallway, proudly displaying the word JUICY in big letters across her rear end. Julian watched as she opened the front door and looked back at him. "You'll regret losing me one day, Julian."

Instead of responding, he waved his fingers in a happy dismissal. She stormed out, slamming the door shut behind her. Julian followed her path down the hallway, flipping the dead bolt and arming the perimeter alarm system in case she tried to sneak back in and boil a rabbit or something.

With a heavy sigh of relief, he traveled back to the kitchen. He tossed the keys down by the stack of mail and started sorting through the letters that Bridgette had no doubt snooped through before bringing them inside. The last letter in the stack had the logo of the Cerebral Palsy Foundation on the front.

Setting the rest aside, he opened the envelope. It was a letter informing him that an anonymous donation had been made to the foundation in his and James's names. That brought a smile to his face. Perhaps having James's story hit the news wasn't bad after all. Now that it was done, perhaps being vocal about it would bring some much-needed attention to the cause. The foundation had even featured a story about them on the site with the link to donate to the cause in their name. If someone had seen the story and made a donation because of it, perhaps it was worth the angst that came along with it.

Turning to the next page, he saw that the amount donated was ten thousand dollars. That was no paltry donation. His eyes remained glued to the number, a nagging feeling prickling at the back of his neck.

Ten thousand dollars. That was exactly how much he'd left in cash for Gretchen when he'd stormed out. She'd said she didn't want his money, but he'd forced it on her. Was this her way of giving the money back and proving she was the bigger person at the same time?

Julian suddenly felt weak in the knees. He wasn't

used to experiencing that feeling outside of the gym. He slumped down onto a stool at the kitchen counter and looked over the letter again. The timing was far too perfect for it to be from anyone else.

He was a jerk. He knew that now. The only reason she'd gotten involved in this whole mess was because she'd wanted to take that money and go to Italy. All the drama and the heartache were for nothing. She'd handed the money away along with her dream.

Julian dropped the letter onto the counter and squeezed his eyes shut. Gretchen was the only person in his life who didn't want or need anything from him but his love and his trust. Without realizing the depths of his feelings for her, he'd given her both, then snatched them away, accusing her of terrible things and throwing cash at her as he left as though she were a common whore.

Picking up his phone, he dialed his travel agent. He didn't stop to think or worry about what Ross would say. He didn't care. All Julian knew was that he needed to get back to Nashville as soon as possible.

Once his arrangements were made, he started to formulate the rest of his plan. There were several hours before his flight, and he needed to make some important stops on the way to LAX.

He just prayed it wasn't too late to make this right.

# Twelve

The red-eye from Los Angeles landed Julian back in Nashville around sunrise on Saturday morning. He grabbed his rental car and tore off in the direction of the chapel.

He was expecting the place to be mostly empty given that it was just past 7:00 a.m., but the lot was filled with vans and trucks with vendor logos on the side. Wedding preparation apparently started early. Among them was Gretchen's green sedan.

Parking his rental out of the path of the big trucks, he followed a man with a giant vase of deep red, orange and yellow flowers through the back door and over to the ballroom.

The room was bustling with people. There were men on lifts adjusting the lighting in the rafters, at least half a dozen people handling flowers, an orchestra setting up on stage, and a few people setting out glassware and other table decor. In the middle of all the chaos was Gretchen. Despite everything going on around them, his eyes went to her in an instant.

Her hair was curly today. He'd gotten used to her straightening it while the cameras were around, but now that their farce of a relationship was over, she'd let it just be curly again. Julian liked it curly. The other style was chic and fashionable, but the wild curls were more suited to the free artist he saw in Gretchen.

She had on a pair of dark denim skinny jeans with ballet flats and a sweater in a rusty color that seemed to go with the fall decor of the day's event. Her back was to him when he came in. She was busily directing some activity in the corner where Murray and Kelly had placed their wedding cake.

With determination pumping through his veins and pushing him forward, he meandered through the maze of tables and chairs to the far corner of the room. No one paid any attention to him. He was only ten or so feet away when Gretchen finally turned around. As her eyes met his, she froze in place, clutching her tablet to her chest as though it was the only thing holding her on the Earth.

Julian smiled, hoping that would help soften the shock, but it didn't. She did recover, but it only resulted in a frown lining her brow and tightening her jaw. He wouldn't let that deter him, though. She was angry. She had a right to be angry after he turned on her like that. He'd expected this response when he got on the plane. But he would convince her that he was sorry and things would be okay. He was certain of it.

"What are you doing here, Julian?" Her voice was

flat and disinterested, matching the expression on her face. The only thing that gave her away was the slight twinkle in her dark eyes. Was it interest? Irritation? Attraction? Perhaps it was just an overhead pin light giving him hope where there was none to be had.

"I came back to talk to you," he said, taking a step toward her and hoping for the best.

Gretchen didn't retreat, but her posture didn't welcome him closer, either. "I think we've done plenty of talking, don't you agree?"

"Not about this." He took another step forward. "Gretchen, I'm so sorry about Monday. The whole situation with Ross, the news article... I know now that none of that had to do with you, and I'm sorry for blaming you for it. You were right when you said you would never do anything like that to me. And I knew it. But I've had so many people betray my trust in the past. Someone had to be to blame, and I didn't know who else could possibly be involved."

She nodded, setting down her tablet so she could cross her arms over her chest. "Jumping to unfounded conclusions tends to cause problems. I'm glad you found the real culprit. I hope you made them suffer the way you made me suffer the last few days. It seems only fair."

Julian watched a flicker of pain dance across her face, and he hated that he was the one to cause it. He had to fix this. "It was Bridgette," he admitted. "She had a detective following me around Nashville and up to Louisville. He dug up the whole story, and then she leaked it because she was jealous of you and wanted to break us up."

Gretchen snorted at his words. "Bridgette Martin...

is jealous…of *me*? How is that even possible? She's one of the most beautiful women I've ever seen."

"Like I told you before, Gretchen, it's all an illusion. I work in a business where everyone tries to tear you down. Even someone like Bridgette isn't immune to scathing critique, and their ego can be fragile because of it. You were a threat to her. She's a woman used to getting what she wants, and she was going to get me back by any means necessary."

"Those silicone implants must have leached chemicals into her brain."

Julian smiled. "Perhaps. But I wanted you to know that it didn't work. Even before I knew the truth about what she'd done, I didn't want her. I still wanted you."

Her dark gaze narrowed at him. "No, you don't," she said with certainty in her voice.

"I do," he insisted. "I did then and I still do. Even when I was angry at you, I only pushed you away because I knew I had to or risk another story in the papers. I didn't want to let you go, though. These days without you have felt so empty, like I've just been going through the motions. I miss having you in my life."

He expected Gretchen to echo his words, to say that she missed him, too, but she stayed silent.

"And then, just when I didn't think I could feel like a bigger jerk, I got the letter from the Cerebral Palsy Foundation. When I saw it, I knew the donation had come from you."

"How do you know it was from me? It was anonymous."

Julian shook his head. "It was, but it had you written all over it. I made you take the money when you didn't want it, so you returned it in a way that even I couldn't argue with. It was brilliant, really, but it just confirmed in my mind that I had been right about you all along."

Her brow went up slightly. "Right about what?"

"Right when I thought that you were one of the sweetest, most giving creatures I'd ever met. That you didn't want anything from me but my love, unlike so many others in my life. You could've taken that money and blown it and forgotten all about me. But you didn't. You couldn't return it, so you used it in the best possible way. A way that could help my brother."

"I hope it does," she said. "Something good should come of the last week's chaos."

Julian's chest clenched at her words. Did she really think what they had was nothing more than a muddled mess? "It might have been chaotic, but I loved every minute of it." Julian hesitated and took a deep breath before he said the words he'd been waiting to say. "And I love you, Gretchen."

Her eyes widened at his declaration, but the response stopped there. No smile, no blush, no rushing into his arms. She certainly didn't respond in kind, as he'd hoped. She just stood there, watching him in her suspicious way.

"I mean it," he continued in a desperate need to fill the silence. "You've changed me in such a profound way that even if you throw me out of here and never speak to me again, there's no way I can go back to living life the way I had before. I've told Ross that I want to take the role in that independent film we discussed. They're going to be filming in Knoxville, Tennessee, in the summer. I've got some re-shoots between now and Christmas, and then another shoot-'em-up movie to film this spring, but after that I'll be out this way for months."

Gretchen swallowed hard, her throat working before she spoke. "You'll like Knoxville," she replied casually.

"What I'll like is being closer to you."

"For a few months. And then what?" she pressed.

"And then I move to Nashville."

That got her attention. This time it was Gretchen who took a step forward, stopping herself before she got too close. "What are you going to do here?"

Julian shrugged. He didn't have all that worked out yet, but he knew that he wanted his home base to be here with Gretchen, even if he had to travel to the occasional movie set or publicity event. "Whatever I want to do. Theater. Television. Smaller-budget films. I could even teach. You were right when you said I was using my brother as an excuse. I have plenty of money to care for him. Even if I just invested the income from *Bombs of Fury* and never acted again, I could probably keep him comfortable for the rest of his life. The truth is that I was scared to try something new. Afraid to fail."

Gretchen's expression softened as she looked at him. "You're not going to fail, Julian."

"Thank you. You believe in me even when I have a hard time believing in myself. You give me the strength I didn't know I was missing. Having you there by my side when we visited James…you have no idea how much that meant to me. I need you in my life, Gretchen. I love you."

He reached into his pocket and grasped the ring he'd hidden there. As he pulled it out, he closed his eyes and sank to one knee, praying that his words had been sincere enough to quell her doubts so she could accept his proposal.

He opened the lid on its hinge, exposing the ring he'd

selected specially for her. The large oval diamond was set in delicate rose gold with a halo of micro-diamonds encircling it and wrapping around the band. The moment he saw it, he knew the ring was perfect for her. "Gretchen, will you—?"

"No!" she interrupted, stealing the proposal from his lips.

Julian looked startled at her sudden declaration, but Gretchen was even more surprised. The word had leaped from her mouth before she could stop it.

His mouth hung agape for a moment, and then he recovered. "The jeweler recommended this cut for a woman who was artistic and daring. I thought that suited you perfectly. Do you not like it? We can get a different one. You can pick whatever you want."

Of course she liked it. She loved it. It was beautiful and sparkly and perfect and she wanted to say yes. But how could she? "It isn't about the ring, Julian."

"Wow. Okay." He snapped the ring box shut and stood up. He glanced around the room nervously, as though he hoped none of the suppliers had witnessed his rebuff. Thankfully everyone was too busy to notice them in the corner.

"Julian." She reached out to touch his arm. "We need to talk about this."

His jaw flexed as he clenched his teeth. "It sounds like you've said all you needed to say. You don't want to marry me. That's fine."

"I never said that."

His blue eyes searched her face in confusion. "I proposed and you said no. Quite forcefully, actually."

Gretchen sighed. She'd botched this. "I wasn't saying no to the proposal. I wanted you to stop for a minute so I could say something first."

The lines in his forehead faded, but he didn't seem convinced that she wasn't about to drop him like a rock. "What do you want to say?"

"I care about you, Julian. I'm in love with you. But I'm not sure if that's enough to sustain a marriage. How can I know that you love me? Truly? How does either of us know that you don't just like the way I make you feel? Yes, I support you. I care about you and make you feel ten feet tall when everyone else is trying to tear you down or get something from you. Are you proposing to that feeling you get when you're with me, or are you actually proposing to me?"

"I'm proposing to you. Of course I am." He seemed insulted by her question, but it couldn't be helped. She needed to know before she fully invested not only her heart, but her life in this relationship.

"That all sounds wonderful. This whole speech of yours has been riveting. Award-caliber material. I think you'll do great in that independent film. But standing here, right now, how can I know that you mean what you say and that it's not some over-rehearsed script? You said that I wasn't the kind of woman Julian Cooper should be with. I heard you agree with Ross when you thought I wasn't listening. For you to turn around and propose not long after…it doesn't leave me feeling very confident about us. Are you going to drop me when the next hot young thing hits the scene and Ross pushes her at you?"

Julian closed his eyes a moment and nodded. "I did say that to Ross. You're not the kind of woman international action star Julian Cooper should be with. But if you'd stayed one moment longer, you would've heard me say that you're the perfect woman for Julian Curtis. And that Julian Curtis wasn't interested in his manager's opinion of his personal life."

Gretchen gasped. She didn't even know what to say to that. Could he really mean it?

"Gretchen," Julian said, moving close to her and placing his reassuring palms on her upper arms. "This isn't a rehearsed script. This isn't Julian Cooper standing in front of you right now reciting lines. This is Julian Curtis, a guy from Kentucky," he said with his accent suddenly coming through, "telling you how he truly feels and asking you to marry him. Do you believe me?"

Her head was spinning. With Julian so close, the warm scent of him was filling her lungs and his touch was heating her skin through her sweater. She could resist him from a distance, but when he stood there, saying all the right words the way he was now, she had no defenses. All she could do was nod.

Julian smiled and slipped back onto one knee. "Now, I'm going to try this again and I want you to let me finish before you answer, okay?"

Gretchen nodded again as Julian pulled out the ring box and opened it a second time. He took her hand in his and looked up at her with his soulful blue eyes.

"I love you, Gretchen, with all my heart. I know there are going to be people out there that think you're so lucky—a regular woman from Tennessee landing a big movie star—but they're wrong. If you accept my proposal and agree to marry me, I can assure you that I'm the lucky one. Every morning I wake up with you beside me is a day I count my lucky stars that you're in my life and have chosen me as the man you love.

Gretchen McAlister, would you do me the great honor of being Mrs. Julian Curtis?"

Gretchen waited half a heartbeat to answer. Not because she didn't want to say yes, but because she wanted to make sure she didn't interrupt him this time. When she was certain he was finished, she said "Yes!" with a broad smile spreading across her face.

Julian slipped the ring onto her finger, the tears in her eyes blurring her view of the sparkly jewelry. It didn't matter. She had a lifetime to look at it. Once he stood up, Gretchen launched herself into his arms. She wrapped her arms around his neck and pulled him close. There, with her nose buried in the hollow of his throat, she finally got to return to a place she thought she might never visit again.

Julian hugged her fiercely and then tipped her head up so that he could press his lips to hers. The kiss was gentler, sweeter, more wonderful than she could've expected.

What an emotional roller coaster the past week had been. She'd gone from the top of the world to the pits of despair and back in only a few days' time. Gretchen was no expert on this love business, but she hoped that it would level out. Her heart couldn't take the drama. But she could take fifty or sixty more years in his strong arms.

"We need to go to Italy," Julian proclaimed, drawing Gretchen from her spinning thoughts.

"Right now?"

Julian smiled and shook his head. "No, not right now. Unless you want to hop on a plane and elope… It might be the only way we can manage to get married without the press finding out."

Elope? She wasn't so sure about that. Amelia had not recommended her quickie Vegas wedding to others. "I'd rather not elope," she said, "but if you want to get married in Italy, that sounds amazing."

"That's what we'll do, then. You gave away your chance to go to Italy when you donated all that money, so it only seems right that we go there to get married, or at the very least, for the honeymoon."

Gretchen could just envision it in her mind. "A tiny rustic chapel in Tuscany. Or maybe a winery on a hill overlooking the poppies and sunflowers."

Julian tightened his grip on her waist. "Anything you want. You're marrying a movie star, after all. There's no cutting corners for an event like this. I can even call George to see if we can have it at his place on Lake Como if you want."

George? She blinked and shook her head. She would be perfectly comfortable as Mrs. Julian Curtis, but it would take a while for her to get used to the idea of their public lives as Mr. and Mrs. Julian Cooper, friends of movie stars, musicians and other famous people.

"That's probably a little more over-the-top than I was thinking," she admitted. Marrying Julian was enough of a fantasy come true. Having the wedding in Italy was more than she could ever ask for. She wanted to keep it simple, though. She didn't want to burn through a fortune on the first day of their marriage. They had a long life together ahead of them, and she wanted to celebrate every day, not just the first. "I just want something small with all our family, some amazing food and wine and scenery that can't be beat by any decoration you could buy."

"I think I can handle that. I'll add that I want to see

you in a beautiful gown that showcases all those luscious curves. I want flickering candles all over to make your skin glow like flawless ivory. And after we eat all that amazing food, I want to dance with you under the stars. This spring, I'll have a month off between filming. How does May sound to you? We can get married and then spend a few weeks exploring every nook and cranny Italy has to offer."

"Perfect," she said, and she meant it. She couldn't imagine a wedding or a husband any more wonderful.

A sound caught her attention. Looking around Julian's broad shoulders, Gretchen noticed three women hovering in the doorway of the ballroom, not working like the others. A blonde, a redhead and a brunette. Even from this distance she could hear the high twitter of their fevered discussion of Julian's return. He'd probably slipped in the back door, but it didn't matter. You couldn't get anything past those three. She also knew that they wouldn't go away until she told them what they wanted to know.

Raising her left hand in the air, she flashed the sparkling diamond at them and wiggled her fingers. It was a large enough setting that even from across the ballroom, the gesture was easily decipherable. A whoop and a few squeals sounded from the entrance.

Gretchen turned away to look up at her fiancé and smiled. "Block a week off the calendar next spring, ladies," she shouted while she focused only on him. "We're all going to Italy for a wedding!"

# Epilogue

"Christmas is coming."

Gretchen's brow went up at Natalie's morose declaration. "You sound like a character in *Game of Thrones*. Of course Christmas is coming. It's almost December, honey, and it's one of the more predictable holidays."

Her friend set down her tablet and frowned. Gretchen knew that Natalie didn't like Christmas. She'd never pressed her friend about why she despised the beloved holiday, but she knew it was true and had been since back when they were in college. Every year, the chapel would shut down for the week or so between Christmas Eve and New Year's Day. Natalie claimed it was a built-in vacation for everyone, but Gretchen wondered if there wasn't more to it.

Natalie was a workaholic to begin with, but when December rolled around, she redoubled her efforts. She claimed that she wanted to get a head start on the accounting and taxes for the end of the year, but Gretchen was certain that she was trying to avoid anything to do with Christmas.

While Bree might stroll into the office wearing reindeer antlers that lit up and Amelia might try to organize a holiday party, Natalie did not participate. She insisted they not exchange gifts, arguing they were just passing money around and it was pointless.

Natalie wasn't a Grinch, per se. She wasn't out to stop everyone from having a good holiday. She just didn't want others to subject her to their merriment. That usually meant she hid in her house and didn't leave for a solid week, or she went on a trip somewhere.

Even then, she couldn't avoid everything. Always the professional, Natalie usually had to coordinate a couple winter- or holiday-themed weddings this time of year. There was no avoiding it. Especially when one of this year's weddings was the wedding of Natalie's childhood best friend, Lily.

Natalie leaned back in her office chair and ripped the headset off, tossing it onto her desk. "It's bothering me more than usual this year."

"Are you taking a trip or staying home?" Gretchen asked.

"I'm staying home. I was considering a trip to Buenos Aires, but I don't have time. We squeezed Lily's last-minute wedding in on the Saturday before Christmas, so I'll be involved in that and not able to do the normal end-of-year paperwork until it's over."

"You're not planning to work over the shutdown, are you?" Gretchen planted her hands on her hips. "You don't have to celebrate, but by damn, you've got to take the time off, Natalie. You work seven days a week some-times."

Natalie dismissed her concerns. "I don't work the late hours you and Amelia do. I'm never here until mid-night."

"It doesn't matter. You're still putting in too much time. You need to get away from all of this. Maybe go to a tropical island and have some kind of a fling with a sexy stranger."

At that, Natalie snorted. "I'm sorry, but a man is not the answer to my problems. That actually makes it worse."

"I'm not saying fall in love and marry the guy. I'm just saying to keep him locked in your hotel suite until the last New Year's firecracker explodes. What can a night or two of hot sex hurt?"

Natalie looked up at Gretchen with her brow fur-rowed painfully tight. "It can hurt plenty when the guy you throw yourself at is your best friend's brother and he turns you down flat."

\* \* \* \* \*

## "A few hours till dinner? You must be home earlier than usual then."

She meant for the comment to be teasing. Evidently, Grant wasn't the workaholic she'd assumed he was if he ended his office hours early enough to have some relaxation time before dinner. The realization heartened her. Maybe he did have something in common with his twin.

But Grant didn't take the comment as teasing. "Yeah, I am, actually," he said matter-of-factly. "But there wasn't anything at the office I couldn't bring home with me, and I thought maybe you—and Hank, too, for that matter—I thought both of you, actually, might… um…"

Somehow, she knew he'd intended to end the sentence with the words *need me*, but decided at the last minute to say something else instead. Something else that clearly hadn't yet formed in his brain, though, because no other words came out of his mouth to help the thought along.

But Clara had trouble figuring out what to say next, too, mostly because she was too busy drowning in the deep blue depths of Grant's eyes to be able to recognize much of anything else.

\* \* \*

### A CEO in Her Stocking

is part of the Accidental Heirs duet:
First they find their fortunes, then they find love

# A CEO IN HER STOCKING

BY
ELIZABETH BEVARLY

Published in Great Britain 2015
by Mills & Boon, an imprint of Harlequin (UK) Limited,
Eton House, 18-24 Paradise Road, Richmond, Surrey, TW9 1SR

© 2015 by Elizabeth Bevarly

ISBN: 978-0-263-25286-6

51-1115

Harlequin (UK) Limited's policy is to use papers that are natural, renewable and recyclable products and made from wood grown in sustainable forests. The logging and manufacturing processes conform to the legal environmental regulations of the country of origin.

Printed and bound in Spain
by CPI, Barcelona

**Elizabeth Bevarly** is a *New York Times* bestselling and award-winning author of more than seventy novels and novellas. Her books have been translated into two dozen languages and published in three dozen countries, and she hopes to someday be as well traveled herself. An honors graduate of the University of Louisville, she has called home places as diverse as San Juan, Puerto Rico, and Haddonfield, New Jersey, but now writes full-time in her native Kentucky, usually on a futon between two cats. She loves reading, movies, British and Canadian TV shows and fiddling with soup recipes. Visit her on the web at www.elizabethbevarly.com, follow her on Twitter or send her a friend request on Facebook.

For David and Eli,
the people who made Christmas
even better than it already was.

# Prologue

Clara Easton was dabbing one final icing berry onto a poinsettia cupcake when the bell over the entrance to Tybee Island's Bread & Buttercream rang for what she hoped was the last time that day. Not that she wasn't grateful for every customer, but with Thanksgiving just over and Christmas barely a month away, the bakery had been getting hammered. Not to mention she had to pick up Hank from his sitter in… She glanced at the clock. Yikes! Thirty minutes! Where had the day gone?

With luck, the customer was someone who'd just remembered she needed a dessert for a weekend party, and *Hey, whatever you have left in the case is fine—I'll take it.* But the visitor was neither a she nor a customer, Tilly, the salesclerk, told Clara when she came back to the kitchen. It was a man asking for her as *Miss Easton.* A man in a suit. Carrying a briefcase.

Which was kind of weird, since no one on the island

called her anything but Clara, and few if any of her customers were business types—or men, for that matter. Moms and brides pretty much kept Bread & Buttercream in business. Clara was intrigued enough that she didn't take time to remove her apron before heading into the shop. She did at least tuck a few raven curls under the white kerchief tied on her head pirate-style.

Though the man might have fit right in on the island with his surfer dude good looks, he clearly wasn't local. His suit was too well cut, his hair too well styled, and he looked completely out of his element amid the white wrought-iron café sets and murals of cartoon cupcakes.

"Hi," Clara greeted him. "Can I help you?"

"Miss Easton?" he asked.

"Clara," she automatically corrected him. *Miss Easton* sounded like a Victorian spinster who ran a boarding-house for young ladies required to be home by nine o'clock in order to preserve their reputations and their chastity.

"Miss Easton," the man repeated anyway. "My name is August Fiver. I work for Tarrant, Fiver and Twigg. Attorneys."

He extended a business card that bore his name and title—Senior Vice-President and Probate Researcher—and an address in New York City. Clara knew probate had something to do with wills, but she didn't know anyone who had died. She had no family except for her son, and all of her friends were fine.

"Probate researcher?" she asked.

He nodded. "My firm is hired to find heirs who are, for lack of a better term, long-lost relatives of…certain estates."

The explanation did nothing to clear things up. From what Clara knew about the two people who had exchanged enough bodily fluids to produce her, whatever they might have for her to inherit was either stolen or conned. She would just as soon have them stay long lost.

Her confusion must have shown on her face, because August Fiver told her, "It's your son, Henry. I'm here on behalf of his paternal grandmother, Francesca Dunbarton." His lips turned up in just the hint of a smile as he added, "Of the Park Avenue Dunbartons."

Clara's mouth dropped open. She'd spent almost a month with Hank's father four summers ago, when she was working the counter of Bread & Buttercream. Brent had been charming, funny and sweet, with the eyes of a poet, the mouth of a god and a body that could have been roped off in an Italian museum. He'd lived in a tent, played the guitar and read aloud to her by firelight. Then, one morning, he was gone, moving on to whatever came next in his life.

Clara hadn't really minded that much. She hadn't loved him, and she'd had plans for her future that didn't include him. They deliberately hadn't exchanged last names, so certain had both been that whatever they had was temporary. They'd had fun for a few weeks, but like all good things, it had come to an end.

Except it didn't quite come to an end. When Clara discovered she was pregnant, she felt obliged to contact Brent and let him know—she'd still had his number in her phone. But her texts to him about her condition went unanswered, as did her messages when she tried to call. Then the number was disconnected. It hadn't been easy raising a child alone. It still wasn't. But Clara managed. It was her and Hank against the world. And that was just fine with her.

"I didn't realize Brent came from money," she said. "He wasn't… We weren't… That summer was…" She gave up trying to describe what defied description. "I'm surprised he even told his mother about Hank. I'm sorry Mrs. Dunbarton passed away without meeting her grandson."

At this, August Fiver's expression sobered. "Mrs. Dunbarton is alive and well. I'm afraid it's Brent who's passed away."

For the second time in as many minutes, Clara was struck dumb. She tried to identify how she felt about the news of Brent's death and was distressed to discover she had no idea how to feel. It had just been so long since she'd seen him.

"As your son is Brent Dunbarton's sole heir, everything that belonged to him now belongs to Henry. A not insignificant sum."

*Not insignificant*, Clara echoed to herself. What did that mean?

"One hundred and forty-two million," August Fiver said.

Her stomach dropped. Surely she heard that wrong. He must mean one hundred and forty-two million Legos. Or action figures. Or Thomas the Tank Engines. Those things did seem to multiply quickly. Surely he didn't mean one hundred and forty-two million—

"Dollars," he said, clearing that up. "Mr. Dunbarton's estate—your son's inheritance—is worth in excess of one hundred and forty-two million dollars. And your son's grandmother is looking forward to meeting you both. So is Brent's brother, Grant. I've been charged by them with bringing you and Henry to New York as soon as possible. Can you be ready to leave tomorrow?"

# One

Clara had never traveled north of Knoxville, Tennessee. Everything she knew about New York City she'd learned from television and movies, none of which had prepared her for the reality of buildings dissolving into the sky and streets crammed with people and taxis. Even so, as the big town car carrying her, Hank and Gus—as August Fiver had instructed her to call him—turned onto Park Avenue, Clara was beginning to get an inkling about why New York was a town so nice they named it twice.

Ultimately, it had taken four days to leave Tybee Island. Packing for a toddler took a day in itself, and Clara had orders that weekend for a birthday party, a baby shower, a bunco night and a wedding cake. Then there were all the arrangements she needed to make with Hank's preschool and covering shifts at Bread & Buttercream. Thank goodness the week after Thanksgiving was slow enough, barely, to manage that before the Christmas season lurched into gear.

Looking out the window now, she could scarcely believe her eyes. The city was just…awesome. She hated to use such a trite word for such a spectacular place, but she couldn't think of anything more fitting.

"Mama, this is *awesome*!"

Clara smiled at her son. Okay, maybe that was why she couldn't think of another word for it. Because *awesome* was about the only adjective you heard when you had a three-year-old.

Hank strained against the belt of the car seat fastened between her and Gus, struggling to get a glimpse at the passing urban landscape, his fascination as rabid as Clara's. That was where much of their alikeness ended, however. Although he had her black curls and green eyes, too, his face was a copy of Brent's. His disposition was also like his father's. He was easygoing and quick to laugh, endlessly curious about *every*thing and rarely serious.

But Clara was glad Hank was different from her in that respect. She'd been a serious little girl. Things like fun and play had been largely absent from her childhood, and she'd learned early on to never ask questions, because it would only annoy the grown-ups. Such was life for a ward of the state of Georgia, who was shuttled from foster home to children's home to group home and back again. It was why she was determined that her son's life would be as free from turbulence as she could make it, and why he would be well-rooted in one place. She just hoped this inheritance from Brent didn't mess with either of those things.

The car rolled to a halt before a building of a dozen stories whose stone exterior was festooned with gold wreaths for the holidays. Topiaries sparkling with white lights dotted the front walkway leading to beveled lattice windows and French doors, and a red-liveried doorman stood sentry at the front door. It was exactly the kind of place where people would live when they were the owners of an industrial empire that had been in their family for two centuries. The Dunbartons could trace their roots all the way back to England, Gus had told her, where they were distantly related to a duke. Meaning that Hank could potentially become king, if the Black Death returned and took out the several thousand people standing between him and the throne.

The building's lobby was as sumptuous as its exterior, all polished marble and gleaming mahogany bedecked with evergreen boughs and swaths of red velvet ribbon. And when they took the elevator to the top floor, the doors unfolded on more of the same, since the penthouse foyer was decorated with enough poinsettias to germinate a banana republic. Clara curled her arm around Hank's shoulders to hug him close, and Gus seemed to sense her anxiety. He smiled reassuringly as he rang the bell. She glanced at Hank to make sure he was presentable, and, inescapably, had to stoop to tie his sneaker.

"Mr. Fiver," she heard someone greet Gus in a crisp, formal voice.

Butler, she decided as she looped Hank's laces into a serviceable bow. And wow, was the man good at butlering. He totally sounded like someone who was being paid good money to be cool and detached.

"Mr. Dunbarton," Gus replied.

Oh. Okay. Not the butler. Brent's brother. She couldn't remember what Brent's voice had sounded like, but she was sure it hadn't been anywhere near as solemn.

Laces tied, Clara stood to greet their host, and... And took a small step backward, her breath catching in her chest. Because Hank's father had risen from the grave, looking as somber as death itself.

Or maybe not. On closer consideration, Clara saw little of Brent in his brother's blue eyes and close-cropped dark hair. Brent's eyes had laughed with merriment, and his hair had been long enough to dance in the ocean breeze. The salient cheekbones, trenchant jaw and elegant nose were the same, but none were burnished by the caress of salt and sun. And the mouth... Oh, the mouth. Brent's mouth had been perpetually curled into an irreverent smile, full and beautiful, the kind of mouth that incited a woman to commit mayhem. This version was flat and uncompromising, clearly not prone to smiles. And where Brent had worn nothing but T-shirts and baggy shorts, this man was dressed in charcoal trousers, a crisp white Oxford shirt, maroon necktie and black vest.

So it wasn't Zombie Brent. It was Brent's very much alive brother. Brent's very much alive *twin* brother. The mirror image of a man who had, one summer, filled Clara with a happiness unlike any she had ever known, and left her with the gift of a son who would ensure that happiness stayed with her forever.

A mirror image of that man who resembled him not at all.

She wasn't what he'd expected.

Then again, Grant Dunbarton wasn't sure exactly what he had expected the mother of Brent's son to be. His brother had been completely indiscriminate when it came to women. Brent had been indiscriminate about everything. Women, cars, clothes. Friends, family, society. Promises, obligations, responsibilities. You name it, it had held Brent's attention for as long as it interested him—which was rarely more than a few days. Then he'd moved on to something else. He'd been the poster child for Peter Pan Syndrome, no matter how old he was.

Actually, Grant reconsidered, there had been one way his brother discriminated when it came to women. All of them had been jaw-droppingly beautiful. Clara Easton was no exception. Her hair was a riot of black curls, her mouth was as plump and red as a ripe pepper and her eyes were a green so pale and so clear they seemed to go on forever. She was tall, too, probably pushing six feet in her spike-heeled boots.

She might have looked imperious, but she had her arm roped protectively around her son in a way that indicated she was clearly uncomfortable. Grant supposed that shouldn't be surprising. It wasn't every day that a woman who'd been spawned by felons and raised in a string of sketchy environments discovered she'd given birth to the equivalent of American royalty.

Because the Dunbartons of Park Avenue—formerly the Dunbartons of Rittenhouse Square and, before that, the Dunbartons of Beacon Hill—were a family whose name had, since Revolutionary times, been mentioned in the same breath with the Hancocks, Astors, Vanderbilts and Rockefellers. Still, Grant admired her effort to make herself look invulnerable. It was actually kind of cute.

And then there was the boy. He was going to be a problem. Except for his hair and eye color—both a contribution from his mother—he was a replica of his father at that age. Grant hoped his own mother didn't fall apart again when she saw Henry Easton. She'd been a mess since hearing the news of Brent's drowning off the coast of Sri Lanka in the spring. It had only been last month that she'd finally pulled herself together enough to go through his things. Then, when she came across the will none of them knew he'd made and discovered he had a child none of them knew he'd fathered, she'd broken down again.

This time, though, there had been joy tempering the grief. There was a remnant of Brent out there in the world somewhere. In Georgia, of all places. Grant had been worried they'd need a paternity test to ensure Henry Easton really was a Dunbarton before they risked dashing his mother's hopes. But the boy's undeniable resemblance to Brent—and to Grant, for that matter— made that unnecessary.

"Ms. Easton," he said as warmly as he could— though, admittedly, warmth wasn't his strong suit. Brent had pretty much sucked up all the affability genes in the Dunbarton DNA while they were still in the womb. Which was fine, because it left Grant with all the efficiency genes, and those carried a person a lot further in life. "It's nice to finally meet you. You, too," he told Henry.

"It's nice to meet you, too, Mr. Dunbarton," Clara said, her voice low and husky and as bewitching as the rest of her.

A Southern drawl tinted her words, something Grant would have thought he'd find disagreeable, but instead found…well, kind of hot.

She nudged her son lightly. "Right, Hank? Say hello to Mr. Dunbarton."

"Hello, Mr. Dunbarton," the boy echoed dutifully.

Grant did his best to smile. "You don't have to call me Mr. Dunbarton. You can call me…"

He started to say *Uncle Grant*, but the words got

stuck in his throat. *Uncle* wasn't a word that sat well with him. Uncles were affable, easygoing guys who told terrible jokes and pulled nickels from people's ears. Uncles wore argyle sweaters and brought six-packs to Thanksgiving dinner. Uncles taught their nephews the things fathers wouldn't, like where to hide their *Playboy*s and how to get fake IDs. No way was Grant suited to the role of uncle.

So he said, "Call me Grant." When he looked at Clara Easton again, he added, "You, too."

"Thank you…Grant," she said. Awkwardly. In her Southern accent. That was kind of hot.

She glanced at her son. But Henry remained silent, only gazing at Grant with his mother's startlingly green eyes.

"Come in," he said to all of them.

August Fiver did, but Clara hesitated, clearly not confident of their reception, her arm still draped around her son's shoulder.

"Please," Grant tried again, extending his hand toward the interior. "You are welcome here."

Clara still didn't look convinced, but the intrepid Henry took an experimental step forward, his gaze never leaving Grant's. Then he took a second, slightly larger, step. Then a third, something that pulled him free of his mother's grasp. She looked as if she wanted to yank him back, but remained rooted where she stood.

"My mother is looking forward to meeting you," Grant said, hoping the mention of another woman might make her feel better. But mention of his mother only made her look more panicked.

"Is something wrong, Ms. Easton?"

By now, Henry had followed Fiver through the door, so the three of them looked expectantly at Clara. She glanced first at her son, then at Grant. For a moment, he honestly thought she would grab her son and bolt. Then, finally, she strode forward. Again, Grant was impressed by her attempt to seem more confident than she was. This time, though, it didn't seem cute. This time, it seemed kind of…

Hmm. That was weird. For a minute there, he felt toward Clara the way she must have felt when she roped her arm protectively around her son. But why would he feel the need to protect Clara Easton? From what he'd learned about her, she was more than capable of taking care of herself. Not to mention that he barely knew her. And he wouldn't be getting to know her any better than he had to after this first encounter.

Sure, it was inevitable that their paths would cross in the future, since his mother would want to see as much of Henry as possible, and Clara would be included in that. But Grant didn't have the time or inclination to be *Uncle Grant*, even without the *Uncle* part. He and Brent might have been identical in looks, but they'd been totally different in every other way. Brent was always the charming, cheerful twin, while Grant was the sober, silent one. Brent made friends with abandon. Grant's few friends barely knew him. Brent treated life like a party. Grant knew it was a chore. Brent loved everyone he ever met. Grant never—

Clara Easton walked past him, leaving in her wake a faint aroma of something spicy and sweet. Cinnamon, he realized. And ginger. She smelled like Christmas morning. Except not the Christmas mornings he knew now, which were only notable because they were a day off from work. She smelled like the Christmas mornings of his childhood, before his father died, when the Dunbartons were happy.

Wow. He hadn't thought about those Christmas mornings for a long time. Because thinking about mornings like that reminded him of a time and place—reminded him of a person—he would never know again. A time when Grant had been staggeringly contented, and when his future had been filled with the promise of—

Of lots of things that never happened. He didn't usually like being reminded of mornings like that. For some reason, though, he didn't mind having Clara Easton and her cinnamon bun–gingerbread scent remind him today. He just wished he was the kind of person who could reciprocate. The kind of person who could be charming and cheerful and made friends with abandon. The kind who treated life like a party and loved everyone he met.

The kind who could draw the eye of a woman like Clara Easton in a way that didn't make her respond with fear and anxiety.

As Clara followed Grant Dunbarton deeper into the penthouse, she told herself she was silly to feel so intimidated. It was just an apartment. Just a really big, really sumptuous apartment. On one of the most expensive streets in the world. Filled with art and antiques with a value that probably exceeded the gross national product of some sovereign nations. She knew nothing of dates or styles when it came to antiques, but she was going to go out on a limb and say the decor here was Early Conspicuous Consumption.

Inescapably, she compared it to her two-bedroom, one-bath apartment above the bakery. Her furniture was old, too, but her Midcentury Salvage wasn't nearly as chic, and her original artwork had been executed by a preschooler. Add to that the general chaos that came with having said preschooler underfoot—and also rocks, puzzle pieces and Cheerios underfoot—and it was pretty clear who had the better living space. She just hoped Hank didn't notice that, too. But judging by the way he walked with his eyes wide, his neck craned and his mouth open, she was pretty sure he did.

"So...how long have y'all lived here?" she asked Grant. Mostly because no one had said a word since she and Hank and Gus entered, and she was beginning to think none of them would ever speak again.

Grant slowed until she pulled alongside him, which was something of a mixed blessing. On the upside, she could see his face. On the downside, she could see his face. And all she could do was be struck again by how much he resembled Brent. Well, that and also worry about how the resemblance set off little explosions in her midsection that warmed places inside her that really shouldn't be warming in mixed company.

"Brent and I grew up here," he said. "The place has been in the family for three generations."

"Wow," Clara said. Talk about having deep roots somewhere. "I grew up in Macon. But I've been living on Tybee Island since I graduated from college."

"Yes, I know," he told her. "You graduated from Carson High School with a near-perfect GPA and have a business administration degree from the College of Coastal Georgia that you earned in three years. Not bad. Especially considering how you worked three jobs the entire time."

Clara told herself she shouldn't be surprised. Families like the Dunbartons didn't open their door to just anyone. "You had me checked out, I see."

"Yes," he admitted without apology. "I'm sure you understand."

Actually, she did. When it came to family—even if that family only numbered two, like her and Hank—

you did what you had to do to protect it. Had August Fiver not already had a ton of info to give her about the Dunbartons, Clara would have had them checked out, too, before allowing them access to her son.

"Well, the AP classes in high school helped a lot with that three-years thing," she told him.

"So did perseverance and hard work."

Well, okay, there was that, too.

Grant led them to a small study that was executed in pale yellow and paler turquoise and furnished with overstuffed moiré chairs, a frilly desk and paintings of gorgeous landscapes. The room reeked of Marie Antoinette—the Versailles version, not the Bastille version—so Clara was pretty sure this wasn't a sanctuary for him.

As if cued by the thought, a woman entered from a door on the other side of the room. This had to be Grant's mother, Francesca. She looked to be in her midfifties, with short, dark hair liberally streaked with silver and eyes as rich a blue as her sons'. She was nearly as tall as Clara, but slimmer, dressed in flowing palazzo pants and tunic the color of a twilit sky. Diamond studs winked in each earlobe, and both wrists were wrapped in silver bracelets. She halted when she saw her guests, her gaze and smile alighting for only a second on Clara before falling to Hank...whereupon her eyes filled with tears.

But her smile brightened as she hurried forward, arms outstretched in the universal body language for *Gimme a big ol' hug.* She halted midstride, however, when Hank stepped backward, pressing himself into Clara with enough force to make her stumble backward herself. Until Grant halted her, wrapping sure fingers around her upper arms. For the scantest of moments, her brain tricked her into thinking it was Brent catching her, and she came *this close* to spinning around to plant a grateful kiss on Grant's mouth, so instinctive was her response.

Was it going to be like this the whole time she was here? Was the younger version of herself that still obviously lived inside her going to keep thinking it was Brent, not Grant, she was interacting with? If so, it was going to be a long week.

"Thanks," she murmured over her shoulder, hoping he didn't hear her breathlessness.

When he didn't release her immediately, she turned around to look at him, an action that caused him to release one shoulder, but not the other. For a moment, they only gazed at each other, and Clara was again overcome by how much he resembled Brent, and how that resemblance roused all kinds of feelings in her she really didn't need to be feeling. Then, suddenly, Grant smiled. But damned if his smile wasn't just like Brent's, too.

"Where are my manners?" he asked, his hand still curved over her arm. "I should have taken your coat the minute you walked in."

Automatically, Clara began to unbutton her coat… then suddenly halted. Because it didn't feel as if she was unbuttoning her coat for a man who had politely asked for it. It felt as if she was unbuttoning her shirt—or dress or skirt or pants or whatever else she might have on—so she could make love with Brent.

Wow. It really was going to be a long week. Maybe she and Hank should just head home tomorrow. Or even before dinner. Or lunch.

She went back to her buttons before her hesitation seemed weird—though, judging by Grant's expression, he already thought it was weird. Beneath her coat, she wore a short black dress and red-and-black polka dot tights that had felt whimsical and Christmassy when she put them on but felt out of place now amid the elegance of the Dunbarton home.

She and Hank should *definitely* leave before lunch.

Her plan was dashed, however, when Francesca, who had stopped a slight distance from Hank but still looked like the happiest woman in the world, said, "It is so lovely to have you both here. I am so glad we found you. Thank you so much for staying with us. I've asked Timmerman to bring up your bags." Obviously not wanting to overwhelm her grandson, she focused on Clara when she spoke again. "You must be Clara," she said as she extended her right hand.

Clara accepted it automatically. "I'm so sorry about Brent, Mrs. Dunbarton. He was a wonderful person."

Francesca's smile dimmed some, but didn't go away. "Yes, he was. And please, call me Francesca." She clasped her hands together when she looked at Hank, as if still not trusting herself to not reach for him. "And you, of course, must be Henry. Hello there, young man."

Hank said nothing for a moment, only continued to lean against Clara as he gave his grandmother wary consideration. Finally, politely, he said, "Hello. My name is Henry. But everybody calls me Hank."

Francesca positively beamed. "Well, then I will, too. And what should we have you call me, Hank?"

This time Hank looked up at Clara, and she could see he had no idea how to respond. They had talked before coming to New York about his father's death and his newly discovered grandmother and uncle, but conveying all the ins and outs of those things to a three-year-old hadn't been easy, and she still wasn't sure how much Hank understood. But when he'd asked if this meant he and Clara would be spending holidays like Thanksgiving and Christmas with his new family, and whether they could come to Tybee Island for his birth-day parties, it had finally struck Clara just how big a life change this was going to be for her son.

And for her, too. It had been just the two of them for more than three years. She'd figured it would stay just the two of them for a couple of decades, at least, until Hank found a partner and started a family—and a life—of his own. Clara hadn't expected to have to share him so soon. Or to have to share him with strangers.

Who wouldn't be strangers for long, since they were family—Hank's family, anyway. But that was some-thing else Clara had been forced to accept. Now her son had a family other than her. But she still just had—and would always just have—him.

She tried not to stumble over the words when she said, "Hank, sweetie, this is your grandmother. You two need to figure out what y'all want to call her."

Francesca looked at Hank again, her hands still clasped before her, still giving him the space he needed. Clara was grateful the older woman realized that a child his age needed longer to get used to a situation like this than an adult did. Clara understood well the enormity and exuberance of a mother's love. It was the only kind of love she did understand. It was the only kind she'd ever known. She knew how difficult it was to rein it in. She appreciated Francesca's doing so for her grandson.

"Do you know what your father and Uncle Grant called their grandmother?" Francesca asked Hank.

He shook his head. "No, ma'am. What?"

Francesca smiled at the *No, ma'am*. Clara supposed it wasn't something a lot of children said anymore. But she had been brought up to say *no, ma'am* and *no, sir* when speaking to adults—it was still the Southern way in a lot of places—so it was only natural to teach Hank to say it, too. One small step for courtesy. One giant step for the human race.

"They called her Grammy," Francesca told Hank. "What do you think about calling me Grammy?"

Clara felt Hank relax. "I guess I could call you Grammy, if you think it's okay."

Francesca's eyes went damp again, and she smiled. "I think it would be awesome."

Now Clara smiled, too. The woman had clearly done her homework and remembered how to talk to a child. A grandmother's love must be as enormous and exuberant as a mother's love. Hank could do a lot worse than Francesca Dunbarton for a grandmother.

"Now, then," Francesca said. "Would you like to see your father's old room? It looks just like it did when he wasn't much older than you."

Hank looked at Clara for approval.

"Go ahead, sweetie," she told him. "I'd like to see your dad's room, too." To Francesca, she added, "If you don't mind me tagging along."

"Of course not. Maybe your uncle Grant will come with us. You can, too, Mr. Fiver, if you want to."

Clara turned to the two men, expecting them to excuse themselves due to other obligations, and was surprised to find Grant looking not at his mother, but at her, intently enough that she got the impression he'd been looking at her for some time. A ball of heat somersaulted through her midsection a few times and came to rest in a place just below her heart. Because the way he was looking at her was the same way Brent had looked at her, whenever he was thinking about…well… Whenever he was feeling frisky. And, wow, suddenly, out of nowhere, Clara started feeling a little frisky, too.

*He isn't Brent*, she reminded herself firmly. He might

look like Brent and sound like Brent and move like Brent, but Grant Dunbarton wasn't the sexy charmer who had taught her to laugh and play and frolic one summer, then given her the greatest gift she would ever receive, in the form of his son. As nice as Grant was trying to be, he would never, could never, be his brother. Of that, Clara was certain. That didn't make him bad. It just made him someone else. Someone who should not—would not, could not, she told herself sternly— make her feel frisky. Even a little.

"Thank you, Mrs. Dunbarton," Gus said, pulling her thoughts back to the matter at hand—and not a moment too soon. "But I should get back to the office. Unless Clara needs me for anything else."

She shook her head. He'd only come this morning to be a buffer between her and the Dunbartons, should one be necessary. But Francesca was being so warm and welcoming, and Grant was *trying* to be warm and welcoming, so… No, Grant *was* warm and welcoming, she told herself. He just wasn't quite as good at it as his mother was. As his brother had been, once upon a time.

"Go ahead, Gus, it's fine," she said. "Thank you for everything you've done. We appreciate it."

He said his goodbyes and told the Dunbartons he could find his own way out. Clara waited for Grant to leave, too, but he only continued to gaze at her in that heated way, looking as if he didn't intend to go anywhere. Not unless she was going with him.

*He's not Brent*, she told herself again. *He's not.*

Now if only she could convince herself he wouldn't be the temptation his brother had been, too.

# Two

Unfortunately, as Francesca led them back the way they'd all come, Grant matched his stride to Clara's and stayed close enough that she could fairly feel the heat of his body mingling with hers and inhale the faint scent of him—something spicy and masculine and nothing like Brent's, which had been a mix of sun and surf and salt. It was just too bad that Grant's fragrance was a lot more appealing. Thankfully, their walk didn't last long. Francesca turned almost immediately down a hallway that ended in a spiral staircase, something that enchanted Hank, because he'd never seen anything like it.

"Are we going up or down?" he asked Francesca.

"Down," she said. "But it can be kind of tricky, and sometimes I get a little wonky. Do you mind if I hold your hand, so I don't fall?"

Hank took his grandmother's hand and promised to keep her safe.

"Oh, thank you, Hank," she gushed. "I can already tell you're going to be a big help around here."

Something in the comment and Francesca's tone gave Clara pause. Both sounded just a tad…proprietary. As if Francesca planned for Hank to be *around here* for a long time. She told herself Francesca was just trying to make things more comfortable between herself and her grandson. And, anyway, what grandmother wouldn't want her grandson to be around? Clara had made clear through Gus that she and Hank would only be in New York for a week. Everything was fine.

Francesca halted by the first closed door Clara had seen in the penthouse. When the other woman curled her fingers over the doorknob, Clara felt like Dorothy Gale, about to go from her black-and-white farmhouse to a Technicolor Oz. And what lay on the other side was nearly as fantastic: a bedroom that was easily five times the size of Hank's at home and crammed with boyish things. Brent must have been clinging to his childhood with both fists when he left home.

One entire wall was nothing but shelves, half of them blanketed by books, the other half teeming with toys. From the ceiling in one corner hung a papier-mâché solar system, low enough that a child could reach up and, with a flick of his wrist, send its planets into orbit. On the far side of the room was a triple bunk bed with both a ladder and a sliding board for access. The walls were covered with maps of far-off places and photos of exotic beasts. The room was full of everything a little boy's heart could ever desire—building blocks, musical instruments, game systems, stuffed animals… They might as well have been in a toy store, so limitless were the choices.

Hank seemed to think so, too. Although he entered

behind Francesca, the minute he got a glimpse of his surroundings, he bulleted past his grandmother in a blur. He spun around in a circle in the middle of the room, taking it all in, then fairly dove headfirst into a bin full of Legos. It could be days before he came up for air.

Clara thought of his bedroom back home. She'd bought his bed at a yard sale and repainted it herself. His toy box was a plastic storage bin—not even the biggest size available—and she'd built his shelves out of wood salvaged from a demolished pier. At home, he had enough train track to make a figure eight. Here, he could re-create the Trans-Siberian Railway. At home, he had enough stuffed animals for Old McDonald's farm. Here, he could repopulate the Earth after the Great Flood.

This was not going to end well when Clara told him it was time for the two of them to go home.

Francesca knelt beside the Lego bin with Hank, plucking out bricks and snapping them together with a joy that gave his own a run for its money. She must have done the same thing with Brent when he was Hank's age. Clara's heart hurt seeing them. She couldn't imagine what it would be like to lose a child. This meeting with her grandson had to be both comforting and heartbreaking for Francesca.

Clara sensed more than saw Grant move to stand beside her. He, too, was watching the scene play out, but Clara could no more guess his thoughts than she could stop the sun from rising. She couldn't imagine losing a sibling, either. Although she'd had "brothers" and "sisters" in a couple of her foster homes, sometimes sharing a situation with them for years, all of them had maintained a distance. No one ever knew when they would be jerked up and moved someplace new, so it was always best not to get too attached to anyone. And none of the kids ever shared the same memories or histories as the others. Everyone came with his or her own— and left with them, too. Sometimes that was all a kid left with. There was certainly never anything like this.

"I can't believe y'all still have this much of Brent's stuff," she said.

Grant shrugged. "My mother was always sure Brent would eventually get tired of his wandering and come home, and she didn't want to get rid of anything he might want to keep. And Brent never threw away anything. Well, no material possessions, anyway," he hastened to clarify.

When his gaze met hers, Clara knew he was backtracking in an effort to not hurt her feelings by suggesting that Brent had thrown away whatever he shared with her.

"It's okay," she said. "Brent and I were never... I mean, there was nothing between us that was..." She stopped, gathered her thoughts and tried again, lowering her voice this time so that Francesca and Hank couldn't hear. "Neither of us wanted or expected anything permanent. There was an immediate attraction, and we could talk for hours, right off the bat, about anything and everything—as long as it didn't go any deeper than the surface. It was one of those things that happens sometimes, where two people just feel comfortable around each other as soon as they meet. Like they were old friends in a previous life or something, picking up where they left off, you know?"

He studied her in silence for a moment, and then shook his head. "No. Nothing like that has ever happened to me."

Clara sobered. "Oh. Well. It was like that for me and Brent. He really was a wonderful person when I knew him. We had a lot of fun together for a few weeks. But neither of us wanted anything more than that. It could have just as easily been me who walked away. He just finished first."

She tried not to chuckle at her wording. Brent finishing first was pretty much par for the course. Not just with their time together, but with their meals together. With their walks together. With their sex together. Yes, that part had been great, too. But he was never able to quite…satisfy her.

"He was always in a hurry," Grant said.

Clara smiled. "Yes, he was."

"He was like a hummingbird when we were kids. The minute his feet hit the ground in the morning, he was unstoppable. There were so many things he wanted to do. Every day, there were so many things. And he never knew where to start, so he just…went. Everywhere. Constantly."

Brent hadn't been as hyper as that when she met him, but he'd never quite seemed satisfied with anything, either, as if there was something else, something better, somewhere else. He told her he left home at eighteen and had been tracing the coastline of North America ever since, starting in Nome, Alaska, heading south, and then skipping from San Diego to Corpus Christi for the Gulf of Mexico. When she asked him where he would go next, he said he figured he'd keep going as far north into Newfoundland as he could, and then hop over to Scandinavia and start following Europe's shoreline. Then he'd do Asia's. Then Africa's. Then South America's. Then, who knew?

"He was still restless when I met him," she told Grant. "But I always thought his restlessness was like mine."

He eyed her curiously, and her heart very nearly stopped beating. His expression was again identical to Brent's, whenever he puzzled over something. She wondered if she would ever be able to look at Grant and *not* see Hank's father. Then again, it wasn't as if she'd be looking at him forever. Yes, she was sure to see Grant again after she and Hank left New York, since Francesca would want regular visits, but Clara's interaction with him would be minimal. Still, she hoped at some point her heart would stop skipping a beat whenever she looked at him. Odd, since she couldn't remember it skipping this much when she looked at Brent.

"What do you mean?" he asked.

"I thought his restlessness was because he came from the same kind of situation I did, where he never stayed in one place for very long so couldn't get rooted for any length of time. Like maybe he was an army brat or his parents were itinerant farmers or something."

Now Grant's expression turned to one of surprise. And damned if it didn't look just like Brent's would have, too. "He never told you anything about his past? About his family?"

"Neither of us talked about anything like that. There was some unspoken rule where we both recognized that it was off-limits to talk about anything too personal. I knew why I didn't want to talk about my past. I figured his reasons must have been the same."

"Because of the foster homes and children's institutions," Grant said. "That couldn't have been a happy experience for you."

She told herself she shouldn't be surprised he knew about that, too. Of course his background check would have been thorough. In spite of that, she said, "You really did do your homework."

He said nothing, only treated her to an unapologetic shrug.

"What else did you find out?" she asked.

He started to say something, then hesitated. But somehow, the look on his face told Clara he knew a lot more than she wanted him to know. And since he had the finances and, doubtless, contacts to uncover everything he could, he'd probably uncovered the one thing she'd never told anyone about herself.

Still keeping her voice low, so that Francesca and Hank couldn't hear, she asked, "You know where I was born, don't you? And the circumstances of why I was born in that particular location."

He nodded. "Yeah. I do."

Which meant he knew she was born in the Bibb County jail to a nineteen-year-old girl who was awaiting trial for her involvement in an armed robbery she had committed with Clara's father. He might even know—

"Do you know the part about who chose my name?" she asked further, still in the low tone that ensured only Grant would hear her.

He nodded. "One of the guards named you after the warden's mother because your own mother didn't name you at all." Wow. She'd had no idea he would dig that deep. All he'd had to do was make sure she was gainfully employed, reasonably well educated and didn't have a criminal record herself. He hadn't needed to bring her— She stopped herself before thinking the word *family*, since the people who had donated her genetic material might be related to her, but they would never be family. Anyway, he hadn't needed to learn about them, too. They'd had nothing to do with her life after generating it.

"And I know that after she and your father were convicted," he continued in a low tone of his own, "there was no one else in the family able to care for you."

Thankfully, he left out the part about how that was because the rest of her relatives were either addicted, incarcerated or missing. Though she didn't doubt he knew all that, too. She listened for traces of contempt or revulsion in his voice but heard neither. He was as matter-of-fact about the unpleasant circumstances of her birth and parentage as he would have been were he reading a how-to manual for replacing a carburetor. As matter-of-fact about those things as she was herself, really. She should probably give him kudos for that. It bothered Clara, though—a lot—that he knew so many details about her origins.

Which was something else to add to the That's Weird list, because she had never really cared about anyone knowing those details before. She would have even told Brent, if he'd asked. She knew it wasn't her fault that her parents weren't the cream of society. And she didn't ask to be born, especially into a situation like that. She'd done her best to not let any of it hold her back, and she thought she'd done a pretty good job.

Evidently, Grant didn't hold her background against her, either, because when he spoke again, it was in that same even tone. "You spent your childhood mostly in foster care, but in some group homes and state homes, too. When they cut you loose at eighteen, where a lot of kids would have hit the streets and gotten into trouble, you got those three jobs and that college degree. Last year, you bought the bakery where you were working when its owner retired, and you've already made it more profitable. Just barely, but profit is an admirable accomplishment. Especially in this economic climate. So bravo, Clara Easton."

His praise made her feel as if she was suddenly the cream of society. More weirdness. "Thanks," she said.

He met her gaze longer than was necessary for acknowledgment, and the jumble of feelings inside her got jumbled up even more. "You're welcome," he said softly.

Their gazes remained locked for another telling moment—at least, it was telling for Clara, but what it mostly told her was that it had been way too long since she'd been out on a date—then she made herself look back at the scene in the bedroom. By now, Francesca was seated on the floor alongside Hank, holding the base of a freeform creation that he was building out in a new direction—sideways.

"He'll never be an engineer at this rate," Clara said. "That structure is in no way sound."

"What do you think he will be?" Grant asked.

"I have no clue," she replied. "He'll be whatever he decides he wants to be."

When she looked at Grant again, he was still studying her with great interest. But there was something in his eyes that hadn't been there before. Clara had no idea how she knew it, but in that moment, she did: Grant Dunbarton wasn't a happy guy. Even with all the money, beauty and privilege he had in his life.

She opened her mouth to say something—though, honestly, she wasn't really sure what—when Hank called out, "Mama! I need you to hold this part that Grammy can't!"

Francesca smiled. "Hank's vision is much too magnificent for a mere four hands. My grandson is brilliant, obviously."

Clara smiled back. Hank was still fine-tuning his small motor skills and probably would be for some time. But she appreciated Francesca's bias.

She looked at Grant. "C'mon. You should help, too. If I know Hank, this thing is going to get even bigger."

For the first time since she'd met him, Grant Dunbarton looked rattled. He took a step backward, as if in retreat, even though all she'd done was invite him to join in playtime. She might as well have just asked him to drink hemlock, so clear was his aversion.

"Ah, thanks, but, no," he stammered. He took another step backward, into the hallway. "I... I have a lot of, uh, work. That I need to do. Important work. For work."

"Oh," she said, still surprised by the swiftness with which he lost his composure. Even more surprising was the depth of her disappointment that he was leaving. "Okay. Well. I guess I'll see you later, then. I mean... Hank and I will see you later."

He nodded once—or maybe it was a twitch—then took another step that moved him well and truly out of the bedroom and into the hallway. Clara went the other way, taking her seat on the other side of Hank. When she looked back at the door, though, Grant still hadn't left to do all the important work that he needed to do. Instead, he stood in the hallway gazing at her and Hank and Francesca.

And, somehow, Clara couldn't help thinking he looked less like a high-powered executive who needed to get back to work than he did a little boy who hadn't been invited to the party.

Grant hadn't felt like a child since... Well, he couldn't remember feeling like a child even when he *was* a child. And he certainly hadn't since his father's death shortly after his tenth birthday. But damned if he didn't feel like one now, watching Clara and her son play on the floor with his mother. It was the way a child felt when he was picked last in gym or ate alone at lunch. Which was nuts, because he'd excelled at sports, and he'd had plenty of friends in school. The fact that they were sports he hadn't really cared about excelling at—but that looked good on a college application—and the fact that he'd never felt all that close to his friends was beside the point.

So why did he suddenly feel so dejected? And so rejected by Clara? Hell, she'd invited him to join them. And how could she be rejecting him when he hadn't even asked her for anything?

Oh, for God's sake. This really was nuts. He should be working. He should have been working the entire time he was standing here revisiting a past it was pointless to revisit. He'd become the CEO of Dunbarton Industries the minute the ink on his MBA dried and hadn't stopped for so much as a coffee break since. Staying home today to meet Clara and Hank with his mother was the first nonholiday weekday he'd spent away from the office in years.

He glanced at his watch. It wasn't even noon. He'd lost less than half a day. He could still go in to the office and get way more done than he would trying to work here. He'd only stayed home in case Clara turned out to be less, ah, stable than her résumé let on and created a problem. But the woman was a perfectly acceptable candidate for mothering a Dunbarton. Well, as an individual, she was. Her family background, on the other hand...

Grant wasn't a snob. At least, he didn't think he was. But when he'd discovered Clara was born in a county jail, and that her parents were currently doing time for other crimes they'd committed... Well, suffice it to say felony convictions weren't exactly pluses on the social register. Nor were they the kind of thing he wanted associated with the Dunbarton name. Not that Hank went by Dunbarton. Well, not yet, anyway. Grant was sure his mother would get around to broaching the topic of changing his last name to theirs eventually. And he was sure Clara would capitulate. What mother wouldn't want her child to bear one of the most respected names in the country?

Having met Clara, however, he was surprised to have another reaction about her family history. He didn't want that sort of thing attached to her name, either. She seemed like too decent a person to have come from that kind of environment. She really had done well for herself, considering her origins. In fact, a lot of people who'd had better breeding and greater fortune than she hadn't gone nearly as far.

He lingered at the bedroom door a minute more, watching the scene before him. No, not watching the scene, he realized. Watching Clara. She was laughing at something his mother had said, while keeping a close eye on Hank who, without warning, suddenly bent and brushed a kiss on his mother's cheek—for absolutely no reason Grant could see. He was stunned by the gesture, but Clara only laughed some more, indicating that this was something her son did often. Then, when in spite of their best efforts, the structure he'd been building toppled to the floor, she wrapped her arms around him, pulled him into her lap and kissed him loudly on the side of his neck. He giggled ferociously, but reached behind himself to hug her close. Then he scrambled out of her clutches and hurried across the room to try his hand at something else.

The entire affectionate exchange lasted maybe ten seconds and was in no way extraordinary. Except that it was extraordinary, because Grant had never shared that kind of affection with his own mother, even before his father's death changed all of them. He'd never shared that kind of affection with anyone. Affection that was so spontaneous, so uninhibited, so lacking in contrivance and conceit. So…so natural. As if it were as vital to them both as breathing.

That, finally, made him walk down the hall to his office. Work. That was what he needed. Something that was as vital to him as breathing. Though maybe he wouldn't go in to the offices of Dunbarton Industries today. Maybe he should stay closer to home. Just in case… Just in case Clara really wasn't all that stable. Just in case she did create a problem. Well, one bigger than the one she'd already created just by being so spontaneous, so uninhibited, so lacking in contrivance and conceit, and so natural. He should still stay home today. Just in case.

You never knew when something extraordinary might happen.

# Three

Actually, something extraordinary did happen. On Clara and Hank's second day in New York, the Dunbartons had dinner in the formal dining room. Maybe that didn't sound all that extraordinary—and wouldn't have been a couple of decades ago, because the Dunbartons had always had dinner in the formal dining room before his father's death—but it was now. Because now, the formal dining room was only used for special occasions. Christmas Day, Easter, Thanksgiving, or those few instances when Brent had deigned to make time for a visit home during his hectic schedule of bumming around on the world's best beaches.

Then again, Grant supposed the arrival of a new family member was a special occasion, too. But it was otherwise a regular day, at least for him. He'd spent it at work while his mother had taken Clara and Hank to every New York City icon they could see in a day, from the Staten Island Ferry to the Statue of Liberty to the Empire State Building to whatever else his mother had conjured up.

Grant had always liked the formal dining room a lot better than the smaller one by the kitchen, in spite of its formality. Or maybe because of it. The walls were painted a deep, regal gold, perfectly complementing the long table, chairs and buffet, which were all overblown Louis Quatorze.

But the ceiling was really the centerpiece, with its sweeping painting of the night sky, where the solar system played only one small part in the center, with highlights of the Milky Way fanning out over the rest—constellations and nebulae, with the occasional comet and meteor shower thrown in for good measure. When he was a kid, Grant loved to sneak in here and lie on his back on the rug, looking up at the stars and pretending—

Never mind. It wasn't important what he loved to pretend when he was a kid. He did still love the room, though. And something inside him still made him want to lie on his back on the rug and look up at the stars and pretend—

"It's pretty cool, isn't it?" he asked Hank, who was seated directly across from him, his neck craned back so he could scan the ceiling from one end to the other.

"It's awesome," the little boy said without taking his eyes off it. "Look, Mama, there's Saturn," he added, pointing up with one hand and reaching blindly with the other toward the place beside him to pat his mother's arm…and hitting the flatware instead.

Clara mimicked his posture, tipping her head back to look up. The position left her creamy neck exposed, something Grant tried not to notice. He also tried not to notice how the V-neck of her sweater was low enough to barely hint at the upper swells of her breasts, or how its color—pale blue—brought out a new dimension to her uniquely colored eyes, making them seem even greener somehow. Or how the light from the chandelier set iridescent bits of blue dancing in her black curls. Or how much he wanted to reach over and wind one around his finger to see if it was as soft as it looked.

"Yes, it is," she said in response to Hank's remark. "And what's that big one beside it?"

"Jupiter," he said.

"Very good," Grant told him, unable to hide his surprise and thankful for something else to claim his attention that didn't involve Clara. Or her creamy skin. Or her incredible eyes. Or her soft curls. "You're quite the astronomer, Hank."

"Well, he's working on it," Clara said with a smile. "Those are the only two planets he knows so far."

Grant's mother smiled, too, from her seat at the head of the table. "I have the smartest grandson in the universe. Not that I'm surprised, mind you, considering his paternity." Hastily, she looked at Clara and added, "And his maternity, too, of course!"

Clara smiled and murmured her thanks for the acknowledgment, but his mother continued to beam at her only grandchild. *Only* in more ways than one, Grant thought, since Hank was also likely the only grandchild she would ever have. No way was he suited to the role of father himself. Or husband, for that matter. And neither role appealed. He was, for lack of a better cliché, married to his business. His only offspring would be the bottom line.

"I also know Earth," Hank said, sounding insulted that his mother would overlook that.

Clara laughed. "So you do," she agreed.

Frankly, Grant couldn't believe a three-year-old would know any of the things Hank knew. Then again, when Grant was three, he knew the genus and species of the chambered nautilus—*Nautilus pompilius*. He'd loved learning all about marine life when he was a kid, but the nautilus was a particular favorite from the start, thanks to an early visit to the New York Aquarium where he'd been mesmerized by the animal. If a child discovered his passion early in life, there was no way to prevent him from absorbing facts like a sponge, even at three. Evidently, for Hank, astronomy would be such a passion.

"Do you have a telescope?" Grant asked Clara.

She shook her head. "If he stays interested in astronomy, we can invest in one. He can save his allowance and contribute. For now, binoculars are fine."

Hank nodded, seeming in no way bothered by the delay. So not expecting instant gratification was something else he'd inherited from his mother. Brent's life had been nothing *but* a demand for instant gratification.

Yet Clara could afford to give him instant gratification now. She could afford to buy her son a telescope with his newfound wealth, whether he stayed interested in astronomy or not. But she wasn't. Grant supposed she was trying to ensure that Hank didn't fall into the trap his father had. She didn't want him to think that just because he had money, he no longer had to work to earn something, that he could take advantage and have whatever he wanted, wherever and whenever he wanted it. Grant's estimation of her rose. Again.

As if he'd said the words out loud, she looked at him and smiled. Or maybe she did that because she was grateful he hadn't told her son that if he wanted a telescope, then, by God, he should have one, cost be damned. That was what Brent would have done. Then he would have scooped up Hank after dinner and taken him straight to Telescopes "R" Us to buy him the biggest, shiniest, most expensive one they had, without even bothering to see if it was the best.

As Hank and Francesca fell into conversation about the other planets on the ceiling, Grant turned to Clara. And realized he had no idea what to say to her. So he fell back on the obvious.

"Brent had an interest in astronomy when he was Hank's age, too," he told her. "It was one of the reasons my mother had this room decorated the way she did."

"I actually knew that," Clara said. "About the astronomy, not the room. He took me to Skidaway Island a few times to look at the stars. I've taken Hank, too. It's what started his interest in all this."

Grant nodded. Of course Brent would have taken her to a romantic rendezvous to dazzle her with his knowledge of the stars. And of course she would carry that memory with her and share it with their son.

"Hank is now about the same age I was when I started getting interested in baking," she said. "My foster mother at that time baked a lot, and she let me help her in the kitchen. I remember being amazed at how you could mix stuff together to make a gooey mess only to have it come out of the oven as cake. Or cookies. Or banana bread. Or whatever. And I loved how pretty everything was after the frosting went on. And how you could use the frosting to make it even prettier, with roses or latticework or ribbons. It was like making art. Only you could eat it afterward."

As she spoke about learning to bake, her demeanor changed again. Her eyes went dreamy, her cheeks grew rosy, and she seemed to go…softer somehow. All over. And she gestured as she spoke—something she didn't even seem aware of doing—stirring an imaginary bowl when she talked about the gooey mess, and opening an imaginary oven door when she talked about the final product and tracing a flower pattern on the tablecloth as she spoke of using frosting as an art medium. He was so caught up in the play of her hands and her storytelling, that he was completely unprepared when she turned the tables on him.

"What were you interested in when you were that age?"

The question hung in the air between them for a moment as Grant tried to form a response. Then he realized he didn't know how to respond. For one thing, he didn't think it was a question anyone had ever asked him before. For another, it had been so long since he'd thought about his childhood, he honestly couldn't remember.

Except he *had* remembered. A few minutes ago, when he'd been thinking about how fascinated he'd been by the chambered nautilus. About how much he'd loved all things related to marine life when he was a kid. Which was something he hadn't thought about in years.

Despite that, he said, "I don't know. The usual stuff, I guess."

His childhood love was so long ago, and he'd never pursued it beyond the superficial. Even though, he supposed, knowing the biological classification of the entire nautilus family—in Latin—by the time he started first grade went a little beyond superficial. That was different. Because that was…

Well, it was just different, that was all.

"Nothing in particular," he finally concluded. Even if that didn't feel like a conclusion at all.

Clara didn't seem to think so, either, because she insisted, "Oh, come on. There must have been something. All of Hank's friends have some kind of passion. With Brianna, it's seashells. With Tyler, it's rocks. With Megan, it's fairies. It's amazing the single-minded devotion a kid that age can have for something."

For some reason, Grant wanted very much to change the subject. So he turned the tables back on Clara. "So, owning a bakery. That must be gratifying, taking your childhood passion and making a living out of it as an adult."

For a moment, he didn't think Clara was going to let him get away with changing the subject. She eyed him narrowly, with clear speculation, nibbling her lower lip— that ripe, generous, delectable lower lip—in thought.

Just when Grant thought he might climb over the table to nibble it, too, she stopped and said, "It is gratifying."

He'd just bet it was. Oh, wait. She meant the bakery thing, not the lip-nibbling thing.

"Except that when your passion becomes your job," she went on, "it can sort of rob it of the fun, you know? I mean, it's still fun, but some of the magic is gone."

*Magic*, he repeated to himself. *Fun*. When was the last time he had a conversation with a woman—or, hell, anyone—that included either of those words? Yet here was Clara Easton, using them both in one breath.

"Don't get me wrong," she hastened to clarify. "I do love it. I just…"

She sighed with something akin to wistfulness. Damn. *Wistfulness*. There was another word Grant could never recall coming up in a conversation before— even in his head.

"Sometimes," she continued, "I just look at all the stuff in the bakery kitchen and at all the pastries out in the shop, and, after work, I go upstairs to the apartment with Hank, and I wonder… Is that it? Have I already peaked? I have this great kid, and we have a roof over our heads and food in the pantry, and I'm doing for a living what I always said I wanted to do, and yet sometimes… Sometimes—"

"—It's not enough," Grant said at the same time she did.

Her eyes widened in surprise at his completion of her thoughts, but she nodded. "Yeah. So you do understand."

He started to deny it. Was she crazy? Of course he had enough. He was a Dunbarton. He'd been born with more than enough. Loving parents. A brother who, had life worked the way it was supposed to, would have been a lifelong friend. Piles of money. All the best toys. All the best schools. Not to mention every possible opportunity life could offer waiting for him around every corner. And yet… And yet.

"Yeah, I do understand," he told her.

"So you must be doing something you love, too," she said.

Damn. She had turned the tables again. But his response was automatic. "Of course I love it. It's what I was brought up to do. It's the family business. Dunbartons have loved it for generations. Why wouldn't I love it?"

Belatedly, he realized how defensive he sounded. Clara obviously thought so, too, because her dreamy expression became considerably less dreamy. He searched for words that would make the dreaminess return—

since he'd really liked that look, probably more than he should—but he couldn't think of a single one. They'd already used up *magic*, *fun* and *wistfulness*. Grant wasn't sure he knew any other words like that.

Then he considered Clara again and was flooded with them. Words like *delightful*. And *luscious*. And *enchanting*. They were words he never used. But somehow, they and more like them all rushed to the fore, until his brain felt as if it was turning into a thesaurus. A purple thesaurus, at that.

Fortunately, their cook, Mrs. Bentley, arrived with the first course, and Clara was complimenting the dish and thanking Mrs. Bentley for her trouble. Grant started to point out that it wasn't any trouble, since that was Mrs. Bentley's job and had been for years, and she was being paid well for it. Then he remembered that Clara prepared food for a living, so expressing gratitude for it was probably some kind of professional courtesy. It also occurred to him that he was suddenly in a really irritable mood. But the subject of childhood passions evaporated after that, something for which he was grateful.

Now if only he could get rid of his troubling thoughts as easily.

Clara didn't think she'd ever been happier to see a salad than she was when the Dunbartons' cook placed one in front of her. Of course, the woman could have placed a live scorpion in front of her, and Clara would have been happy to see it. Anything to break her gaze away from Grant's. Because never had she seen anyone look more desolate than he did when he was talking about what he did for a living.

And he couldn't remember what he loved most as a child. Who didn't remember that? Everyone had loved something more than anything else when they were a kid. Everyone had wanted to be something more than anything else when they grew up. For Clara, it had been a baker. For Hank, at the moment, it was an astronomer. For Brent, it had been an astronaut. Even if it was something as unlikely as zookeeper or movie star, every child had some dream of becoming something. Of becoming someone. Every child, evidently, except Grant Dunbarton.

Then again, when a family had owned a business for generations, like the Dunbartons had, maybe it was just a given that their children's professional destiny lay in that business. Except that Brent hadn't gone to work for Dunbarton Industries. He'd been a professional vagabond, which was about as far removed from corporate kismet as a person could get. And he and Grant were the same age, so it wasn't as if taking over the business was a firstborn offspring responsibility for which Grant specifically had been groomed since birth. Nor did Francesca strike Clara as the kind of parent who would insist that her children pursue a preplanned agenda for the sake of the family. If Grant had shouldered the mantle of CEO for Dunbarton Industries, he must have done so because he wanted to.

Even if he didn't look or sound as if he'd wanted to.

The moment was now gone, however. Which was good for another reason, since it kept Clara from wondering if that was what the Dunbartons might have in mind for Hank. He was as much a Dunbarton as Grant and Francesca were. So he was as much a part of the family heritage—and family business—as they were. Surely they didn't have expectations like that for him, though. Although their blood ran in his veins, their society didn't. Nor would it ever, since there was no way

Clara would uproot her son from Georgia and move him to New York.

Even in Georgia, she planned to shield him from this world as much as she could. She didn't have anything against rich people—at least not the ones who earned their wealth and paid their employees a decent wage and gave something back to the community that had helped them build their empire. But the world those people lived in wasn't the real world or real life any more than Clara's upbringing had been.

And she wanted Hank to have a real life. One that involved both hard work and fun play, both discipline and reward. One where he would experience at least some anguish and heartache, because that was the only way to experience serenity and joy. It was impossible to appreciate the latter without knowing the former. And a person couldn't know the former if he was handed everything he wanted on a silver platter.

Maybe that was Grant's problem, she thought, sneaking another look at him. He was blandly forking around his salad, looking way more somber than a person should look when blandly forking around a salad. Maybe by having everything he'd ever wanted all his life, he was incapable of really *knowing* what he wanted. Except that he hadn't had everything he wanted, she thought. He'd lost his father when he was a child, and had lost his twin brother less than a year ago. He'd just told her how he understood what it was to not have enough, and she had a feeling there was more to it than just his personal losses.

She told herself to stop trying to figure him out. Grant Dunbarton's unhappiness and lack of fulfillment were none of her business, and they weren't her responsibility. She reminded herself again—why did she have to keep doing that?—that her life and his were only intersecting temporarily for now and would only be intersecting sporadically in the future. He wasn't her concern.

So why couldn't she stop feeling so concerned about him?

# Four

*Beware the Park Avenue doyenne with a platinum credit card.* That was the only thought circling through Clara's head at the end of her third day in New York, probably because she was so exhausted at that point that it was the only thought that *could* circle through her brain. Francesca Dunbarton was a dynamo when it came to spending money.

As Clara lay beside a sleeping Hank in Brent's old bedroom, she did her best to not nod off herself. No easy feat, that, since the three of them had hit every place Francesca insisted they needed to hit so her only grandchild would have all the essentials of other Park Avenue grandchildren: Boomerang Toys and Books of Wonder, Bit'z Kids and Sweet William, the Disney Store, the Lego Store...pretty much anything a three-year-old would love with the word *store* attached to it.

Then Francesca had insisted they *must* do the

Children's Tea at the Russian Tea Room, because Hank would find it enchanting. They just had *so* much catching up to do!

Hank had finally succumbed to fatigue on the cab ride home and hadn't stirred since. Not when the elevator dinged their arrival on the top floor, not when Clara laid him on the bed, not when Francesca brushed a kiss on his cheek, not when the doorman arrived to deliver all the bags containing his grandmother's purchases for him. And those bags had rattled *a lot*. And there were *a lot* of bags to rattle.

Now Clara lay beside Hank, her elbow braced on the mattress, her head cradled in her hand, and as she watched the hypnotic rise and fall of her son's chest, her eyelids began to flutter. Until she heard the jangle of something metallic and the fall of footsteps in the hallway beyond the open door. Grant, arriving home from work. He appeared in the doorway wearing an impeccable dark suit, tie and dress shirt, the uniform of the upper-crust environment in which he thrived. It was Clara, in her olive drab cargo pants and oatmeal-colored sweater, not to mention her stocking feet, who was out of place here.

When he saw her, Grant lifted a hand in greeting and was about to say something out loud, but halted when he saw Hank sleeping so soundly. Clara lifted her finger in a silent *Hang on a sec*, then carefully maneuvered herself around Hank until she could slide to the floor and tiptoe toward the door and into the hall.

"You didn't have to get up," he said softly by way of a greeting.

"That's okay," she told him. "I needed to get up. I was about to doze off myself."

"Go ahead. Dinner won't be ready for another few hours, at least."

She shook her head. "If I sleep now, I won't sleep tonight. And I'm already a terrible insomniac as it is. I have been since I was a kid."

Because growing up, there had just been something about sharing a room with other kids she didn't know well that lent itself to lousy sleep habits. Clara's experiences in foster care and group homes hadn't been horrible, but most of them hadn't been especially great, either. She'd been the victim of theft and bullying and rivalry like many children—even those who weren't wards of the state—all things that could create stress and wariness in a kid and contribute to insomnia. Sure, none of those things was a part of her life now, but it was hard to undo decades' worth of conditioning.

She and Grant studied each other for a moment in strained silence. It was just so difficult to take her eyes off him, just so strange, seeing the mirror image of Brent dressed in the antithesis of Brent's wardrobe. And the close-cropped hair, in addition to being nothing like Brent's nearly shoulder-length tresses, was peppered with premature silver. She wondered if Brent had started to go gray, too, in the years since she had seen him, or if Grant's gray was simply the result of a more stressful life than his brother had led.

Then the gist of his words struck her, and she smiled. "A few hours till dinner? You must be home earlier than usual, then."

She meant for the comment to be teasing. Evidently, Grant wasn't the workaholic she'd assumed if he ended his office hours early enough to have some relaxation time before dinner. The realization heartened her. Maybe he did have something in common with his twin.

But Grant seemed to take the comment at face value. "Yeah, I am, actually," he said matter-of-factly. "But I could bring the work home with me, and I thought maybe you—and Hank, too, for that matter—I thought both of you, actually, might…um…"

Somehow, she knew he'd intended to end the sentence with the words *need me*, but decided at the last minute to say something else instead. No other words came out of his mouth, though.

Clara had trouble figuring out what to say next, too, mostly because she was too busy drowning in the deep blue depths of his eyes. Looking into Grant's eyes somehow felt different from looking into Brent's eyes, even though their eyes were identical. There was more intensity, more perception, more comprehension, more, well, depth. She'd never felt as if Brent was looking into her soul, even though the two of them were intimately involved for weeks. But having spent only a short time in Grant's presence, she felt as if he were peering past her surface—or at least trying to—to figure out what lay in her deepest inner self. It was…disconcerting. But not entirely unpleasant.

"Um," she said, struggling to find anything that would break the odd spell. But the only thing that came to mind was something about how beautiful his eyes were, and how very different from his brother's, and how she honestly wasn't sure she ever wanted to stop looking into his eyes, and…well…that probably wasn't something she should say to him right now. Or ever.

Thankfully, he broke eye contact and glanced beyond her into Hank's room—or, rather, Brent's old room, she hastily corrected herself—and said, "Looks like my mother did her share to bump up the gross domestic income today."

Clara turned around to follow his gaze. The pile of bags on the floor seemed to have multiplied in the few minutes since she'd last looked at it. Once again, she was reminded of how much more the Dunbartons could offer her son than she could. Materially, anyway. They'd never be able to love him more than she did. But when one was three years old, it wasn't difficult to let the material render the emotional less valuable. Especially when the material included a toy fire truck with motion-activated lights and sound effects.

"I cannot believe how much stuff she bought for Hank," Clara said. She looked at Grant again. "She really shouldn't have done that. I mean, Hank is extremely grateful—and I am, too," she hastened to add. "But…" She couldn't help the sigh that escaped her, nor could she prevent it from sounding melancholy. "I don't know how we're going to get everything home."

"Leave most of it here," Grant said. "Hank can take home his favorites and play with the rest of it when he comes back to visit." He smiled. "That was probably Mom's intention in the first place."

The thought had crossed Clara's mind, too. More than once. As many times as she'd tried to excuse Francesca's excessive purchasing by telling herself Hank's grandmother was just trying to make up for lost time, Clara hadn't been able to keep herself from wondering if all the gifts were bribes of a sort, to ensure that Hank would badger his mother to bring him back to New York ASAP. Having Grant pretty much confirm her suspicions did nothing to make Clara feel better.

Hank stirred on the bed, murmuring a sleepy complaint, and then turned from one side to the other and settled into slumber again. So Clara pulled the door closed to keep him from being awakened by her conversation with Grant.

"We can talk in my room," he said.

Clara scrambled for an excuse as to why she wouldn't be able to do that, but couldn't come up with a single one. Then she wondered why she was trying, since there had been nothing untoward in his invitation. Brain exhaustion, she told herself. She was too tired to follow him, but too tired to find a reason not to follow him. It had nothing to do with the fact that she just maybe kind of wanted to follow him, for a reason that might possibly be slightly untoward on her part.

So follow him she did, to the room next to Brent's. Even though it was next door, it seemed to take forever to get there; this place was enormous. Grant's room was the same size as Brent's, with the same two arched, floor-to-ceiling windows looking down on the same view of Park Avenue and, beyond it, Central Park.

The similarities ended there, however. Where Brent's room was painted a boyish bright blue, Grant's was the color of café mocha. And where Brent's curtains where patterned in whimsical moons and stars, Grant's were a luxe fabric that shimmered with dozens of earth tones. The furniture was sturdy mahogany—a massive sleigh bed, dressers and nightstands, as well as the bare essentials of manhood: alarm clock, lamps, dish for spare change and keys.

The only bit of color in the room was an aquarium opposite the bed. It was far bigger than anything Clara had ever seen in a pet store, and it was populated by fish in all sizes and colors, darting about as if oblivious to the glass walls that enclosed them.

Clara was drawn to it immediately. Even living so close to the water, she'd never seen so many fish in one place, and the brilliant colors and dynamic motion captivated her. Vaguely, she noted that Grant entered the room behind her, tossed his briefcase onto the bed and approached a wooden valet in the far corner of the room. Vaguely, she noted how he began to loosen his tie and unbutton his shirt, and—

Whoa. Whoa, whoa, whoa, *whoa*. No, she didn't note that vaguely. She noted that *very clearly*. Grant undressing caught Clara's attention in much the same way a tornado swirling toward her front door would catch her attention, and she spun around nearly as quickly. Even if—she was pretty sure—he wouldn't go any further than unfastening his shirt a couple of buttons below the collar or rolling up his sleeves, he was still undressing. And that tended to have an effect on a woman who hadn't seen a man undress for a while. A long while. A *really* long while. Especially a woman who had always enjoyed watching a man undress. A lot. A *whole* lot.

Although his movements were in no way provocative, heat flared in her belly at the sight of him. With an elegant shrug, he slipped off his jacket, then freed the buttons of his shirt cuffs and rolled each up to mid-forearm, exposing muscles that bunched and relaxed with every gesture. As he slung his jacket over the valet, she noted the breadth of his shoulders, too, and, couldn't help remembering the last time she had seen shoulders and arms like his. Except those shoulders and arms had been naked, and they had been hot and damp with perspiration beneath her fingertips. They had belonged to Grant's brother, who had been lying on top of her, gasping.

She remembered, too well, how that had felt—too good—and her face grew warm as her blood rushed faster through her veins. The heat multiplied when

Grant lifted a hand to his necktie and freed it, and then slowly, slowly…oh, so slowly…dragged the length of silk from beneath his collar to drape it over the jacket. But it was when his hands moved to his shirt buttons, loosening first one, then two, then three, that Clara felt as if her entire body would burst into flame. Because she couldn't stop watching those hands, those big, skillful, seductive hands, and remembering how they had felt on—and in—her body.

No, not those hands, she reminded herself. It had been Brent's hands that made her feel that way. Even if, on some level, she suspected Grant was every bit as skilled as his brother when it came to making a woman feel aroused and sexy and shameless and wanton and… and…and…

Um, where was she? Oh, yeah. Fish.

Except she wasn't thinking about fish. Because she was too busy wondering if sex with Grant would be as fierce and incendiary as it had been with Brent, and if it would leave her wanting more—

"…and firemouth."

It took Clara a minute to realize it was Grant who had spoken, and not Brent, so lost had she been in her memories of making love to the latter. Apparently he'd been speaking for some time, too, and might have even called her something that sounded a lot like *firemouth*. But how could he have known what she was thinking?

She gazed at him in silence, hoping her expression revealed nothing of the graphic images that had been tumbling through her brain. But when his gaze finally connected with hers, his smile fell and his eyes went wide, and she was pretty sure he could tell down to the last hot, sweaty detail *exactly* what she had been thinking since she started watching him undress, which meant that whole firemouth thing wasn't too far off the mark. So she did the only thing she could.

She spun quickly away from him, focused on the aquarium, and asked, "What kind of fish are these?" In an effort to look as if she was truly fascinated by the little swimmers, she even bent over and brought her face to within an inch of the glass.

Belatedly, she realized the idiocy of the question. Not only because thanks to her, *both* of them were now doubtless thinking about sex, not fish, but also because asking it caused him to move closer to her. He did so slowly and uncertainly, as if he were approaching a barracuda, which wasn't that far off the mark, really, since, at the moment, she was feeling more than a little predatory.

*Breathe, Clara, breathe*, she instructed herself. *And calm down.*

Unfortunately, it was impossible for her to do either, because, by then, Grant had moved behind her, his pelvis situated within inches of her, well, behind. If he'd wanted, he could have tugged the drawstring at her waist and pulled down her pants right there. Then he could have tugged down her panties, too, to expose her in the most intimate, most vulnerable way. Then he could have unfastened his belt, unzipped his fly and freed himself. He could have gripped her naked flesh and pulled her toward himself, and then buried himself inside her, slowly, deeply, possessively. Over and over and over again.

If he wanted.

Because in that moment, Clara wouldn't have stopped him, since she suddenly wanted him, too.

*Oh, no. Oh, God. Oh, Grant.*

Instead, he stepped to her left and bent forward, his

face scant inches from hers, to gaze into the aquarium with her.

She told herself that had been his intention all along. He couldn't possibly have been thinking about doing all the things she had been thinking about him doing. Her brain was just a muddle of memories about her time with Brent—most of which had been spent in sexual pursuits, she had to admit—and was transferring those desires to Grant. She'd known the man a matter of days. Then again, she'd been steaming up the sheets with Brent within hours of meeting him…

"I was just telling you the names of the fish," he said. She could tell he was struggling to keep his voice even and quiet.

"The one in front," he continued, "well, the one that was in front a minute ago, when you were, ah, looking at him, is a firemouth."

Ah. So he hadn't been calling Clara that. At least she didn't think he had. Probably best to not ask for clarification. "This one," he said, pointing to a spotted one that had swum to the front, "is a Texas cichlid. *Herichthys cyanoguttatus*, if you want to get technical. From the family Cichlidae. Actually, all the fish in this tank are cichlids, but there are more than a thousand different species, and new ones are turning up all the time, so I only put a handful of my favorites in here. That one," he continued as another fish, this one speckled with purple, blue and green, darted by, "is a Jack Dempsey."

"Like the boxer?" Clara asked.

"Yep. That's who the species is named after. Because they have kind of a boxer's face, and they can be pretty aggressive in small groups. They're native to Central America—Mexico and Honduras specifically—so they get along well with the Texas cichlid."

The tension between the two of them was ebbing now, allowing Clara to breathe again. She smiled at the image of two fish from opposite sides of the border interacting without incident. Nice to know someone in this room could get along swimmingly. So to speak.

"And that one is called a convict," Grant said, indicating a fish that was black-and-white striped. "For obvious reasons."

"I'm sure he was framed," Clara said, doing her best to lighten the mood further. "He looks too sweet to be a criminal."

Grant identified a half dozen more species as they swam by, offering up snippets about the habits or personalities of each. The more he talked, Clara noted, the more he smiled. And the more he smiled, the more he relaxed. She gradually relaxed, too, until all traces of sexual awareness eased, and she was confident the charged moment they'd shared was only an aberration, never to be repeated.

At least, she was *pretty* confident of that.

As Grant wound down his dissertation on the fish, Clara waited for him to add something that would explain how he came by all his knowledge. But he never did. He only gazed into the aquarium, watching the parade of color. She caught her breath as she watched him, because in that moment, he looked exactly like Hank. Not just the physical resemblance, thanks to the identical genes, but the childlike fascination, too. He looked the same way Hank did when he found a particularly interesting bit of jetsam on the beach. Grown-ups—especially super serious, workaholic grown-ups like Grant—weren't supposed to be distracted by things like colorful fish. Grown-ups were supposed to be worried about stuff like whether or not they were getting enough vitamin D or how they were going to make rent this month.

Well, okay, that was why *some* grown-ups—like, say, Clara—couldn't be distracted by something like colorful fish. Grant hadn't had to worry about making rent his entire life.

"You know, for a guy who sits behind a desk all day," she said, "you sure know a lot about fish. I live just a couple of blocks away from the ocean, and the only thing I know about marine life is which ones are my favorite on any given menu."

He laughed lightly as the two of them straightened, the sound of his voice rippling through Clara like a warm breeze. "Well, that's important to know, too. And these are all freshwater fish. My saltwater aquarium is in my office. It's twice the size of this one, and you'd probably recognize a lot of the guys in there. Clownfish, damselfish, sea horses, grouper…"

"I love grouper," she said. "Grilled, with dill butter on the side."

He chuckled again, and Clara realized the reason she liked the sound of his laughter so much was because she hadn't heard it until now. Frankly, she'd begun to wonder if he was even able to laugh. But the knowledge that he could was actually kind of sobering. If he was able to laugh, why didn't he do it more often?

"You probably love more of them than you realize," he told her. "*Grouper* is a word that applies to fish from several different genera in the *Serranidae* family. There's some sea bass and perch in there, too."

"Wow, you really do know a lot about fish."

For some reason, that made him suddenly look uncomfortable. "It's kind of a hobby," he told her. "Left over from when I was a kid. Back then, I wanted to be a marine biologist and live in the Caribbean when I grew up. Maybe the South Pacific. I even picked out the colleges I wanted to attend. I had this crazy idea as a kid that I could start a nonprofit for research and conservation. My dad even helped me set up a business plan for the thing." He grinned. "I remember I wanted to call it Keep Our Oceans Klean. With a *K*. That way, I could say I worked for a KOOK."

Clara grinned, too. Ah-hah. So, as a child, he *had* wanted to be something specific when he grew up. He *had* had a passion like any normal kid. She was glad for it, even if she wasn't sure why he was sharing that so readily today when, just last night, he'd claimed no memory of such. And she could see him being the kind of kid who would prepare for his college future and make out business plans when most kids were trying to figure out where to go to camp.

"What colleges?" she asked.

He hesitated, and for a minute, she thought he would try to backtrack and tell her he couldn't remember again. Instead, quietly, he said, "College of the Atlantic in Maine for a BS in marine science, then on to Duke for my master's in marine biology. After that, it was a toss-up between University of California Santa Barbara and University of Miami for any postgrad work."

"Why didn't you go?" she asked. "Why didn't you start KOOK? It sounds like a lifelong dream if you're still keeping fish and know so much about them."

Now he looked at her as if she should already know the answer to that question. "There was no way I could do that after my father died."

Clara still didn't understand. For a lot of people, the unexpected death of a loved one made them even more determined to follow their dreams. "Why not?"

Once more, he hesitated. When he finally did speak again, it was in halting sentences, as if the information were being pulled from him unwillingly. "Well... I mean... After my father died, we all... And Brent..."

He halted abruptly, and then tried again. But he was obviously choosing his words carefully. "Brent was actually the one who was supposed to follow in my father's footsteps and run the business after he retired. He was the firstborn, technically, and he seemed to genuinely love the idea of going to work for Dunbarton Industries after he graduated from college. Even when we were little, he used to go in to the office with Dad sometimes, and it wasn't unusual for the two of them to hole up in the office at home in an unofficial Junior Achievement meeting. But after Dad died, Brent..."

He sighed heavily. "Brent reacted to our father's death by regressing. He started shirking responsibility, never did his homework, locked himself up in his room to play for hours on end. Instead of maturing as he aged, he only got more childlike. Even in high school. There was no way he could have gotten into a decent business school with his grades, which was just as well, since he made clear after our father's death that there was no way he was going to take over the company. And Mom wasn't much better. She retreated, too, after Dad died, from just about everything. And she let Brent do whatever he wanted."

It didn't escape Clara's notice that Grant had left himself out of the equation when describing how his family reacted to the death of the Dunbarton patriarch. She could almost see Grant as a child, feeling the same emptiness his mother and brother felt, but not wanting anyone to see him that way.

Before she could stop herself, she asked, "And how

did little Grant react after his father's death? You must have been heartbroken, too."

"I was," he said. "But with my mother retreating and Brent regressing… Someone had to be an adult. Someone had to make sure things got done around here. Mom wouldn't even pay the bills or our employees. The company almost went into receivership at one point. Some of my dad's colleagues stepped in and took over until I could graduate from college and step into the CEO position. So I majored in business and did just that. If I hadn't, the company would have been cut up into little pieces and sold off bit by bit. And then where would the Dunbarton legacy be?"

Clara wanted to reply that the Dunbartons would have made a boatload of money, so their legacy wouldn't be much different from what it was now, and Grant could have followed his dream. But she didn't think he would see it that way. He'd obviously started feeling responsible for his family and the family business when he was still a child himself. Clara got that. She'd assumed responsibility for herself as soon as she understood what responsibility was, and had done the same for Hank as soon as she realized she was pregnant. As a mother, she understood well what it was to put someone else's wants and needs ahead of her own. But she had still pursued her dream of doing something she loved for a living. And if she'd had hundreds of millions of dollars like the Dunbartons did, she'd now have a whole chain of Bread & Buttercream bakeries, and her home office would be in Paris.

"I guess legacies are important," she conceded half-heartedly—mostly because she knew Grant would think that, even if she wasn't quite on board with it herself. "Y'all have had your company for generations and everything. And you want to have something to pass on to your kids someday."

"Oh, I'm not having kids," he told her with conviction.

Too much conviction, really. Grant was only thirty-two. How could he be so sure of something like that? He still had plenty of time.

"Why not?" Clara asked.

Again, he looked at her as if the answer to her question should be obvious. "Because I don't want kids. Or marriage. I don't have time to be a father or husband."

Fair enough, she thought. But… "Then why do you need a legacy? If you're going to be the end of the line, that's even more reason for you to go after your dreams. You could sell the business now, go back to school to major in marine biology and study every ocean on the planet."

Of all the questions she'd asked and observations she'd made, that one seemed to upset him most. "That's not the point," he told her tersely.

"Then what is?"

He waved a hand in the general direction of the aquarium. "The point is that being an aquarist is a hobby. Not a career."

Clara was going to argue with him, since hobbies rarely included knowledge of Latin, never mind use of the word *aquarist*, which she'd sure never used in her life. But he truly did look kind of angry—and not a little distressed—and she didn't want to prolong an exchange that was threatening to become adversarial. So she tried to lighten the mood.

Smiling, she said, "Well. I don't know about you, but I suddenly hope we're having fish for supper."

At first, her attempt at levity seemed to confuse him.

Then it seemed to make him relax. Then he looked kind of grateful that she had relinquished the matter. He even smiled, but it wasn't like the smiles when he was watching his fish, and it never quite reached his eyes. In fact, his eyes were pretty much the opposite of smiling.

"I think it's going to be kebabs," he said. "But we can certainly put in a request for grouper at some point this week. Or next, if you and Hank want to stay a little longer."

Was that an invitation? Clara wondered. Because it kind of sounded like one.

"We can't," she told him. "I don't want Hank to miss too much school, and the bakery will be super busy the closer it gets to Christmas. I just can't afford to stay away any longer," she added when it looked as if he would take exception. "I'm the only full-time baker I have."

But instead of taking exception, he said, "No one would object if you needed to withdraw funds from Hank's trust to help you out with the business. It's there for his needs, but until he's an adult, his needs are joined to yours. If expanding your business and hiring more people would make you more money and increase the quality of Hank's life, then it would be a perfectly acceptable use of the trust."

Clara was shaking her head before he even finished talking. "That's Hank's money," she insisted. "He'll need it for college and for starting his life afterward, whether that's on his own or with someone he loves. Or he'll have it in case of emergency."

"But—"

"I've been taking care of myself and him for a long time, Grant. I've managed fine so far, and I'll continue to manage fine."

"But—"

"You and your mom have been great to both of us, but we'll be heading back to Georgia as scheduled. Thanks, anyway. Now, if you'll excuse me," she continued when he opened his mouth to object again, "there are a couple of things I need to do before supper."

And without waiting for a reply, Clara headed for the door. She assured herself she hadn't lied when she told Grant there were a couple of things she needed to do before dinner. The first was to make sure Hank didn't sleep too long, or he'd be even more insomniac tonight than she was. The second was to remind herself—as many times as it took—that Grant Dunbarton wasn't his brother, and that she needed to stop responding to him as if he were. Because although it hadn't broken her heart when she parted ways with Brent, if she got involved with Grant and then parted ways with him…

She thought again about the happy, childlike look on his face when he was talking about his fish, and the way his expression sobered and grew withdrawn when it came to talking about his work. Well. Something told Clara that if she got involved with Grant and then they parted ways, her heart might never be the same.

As Grant watched Clara leave, he did his best— really, he did—to not stare at her ass. Unfortunately, that was like trying to not breathe. Because the minute his gaze lit on her departing form, his eyes went right to the sway of her hips. And then all he could do was mentally relive that beyond-bizarre moment when he'd been standing behind her by the aquarium, wondering what she'd do if he pulled down her pants, tugged down her panties, freed himself from his trousers and buried himself inside her as deep as he could. Hell, he'd been hard enough to do it, thanks to the expression on her face when he'd looked up from unbuttoning his shirt to find her gazing at him as if she wanted to devour him in one big bite. There was just something about a woman with hungry eyes that made a man's body go straight to sex mode.

Besides, she had a really nice ass.

This was not good. It had been a long time since Grant had been this attracted to a woman this quickly. In fact, he wasn't sure he'd ever been this attracted to a woman this quickly. And the fact that the woman in question was Clara Easton made things more than complicated. He couldn't just have sex with her and then move on. She was going to be a part of his life, however indirectly, for, well, the rest of his life. She would be accompanying Hank to New York whenever he came to visit until the boy was old enough to travel on his own. Hell, she'd be coming to New York with Hank even after he was old enough to travel by himself, because his mother would insist that Clara come, too. She'd also insist Clara and Hank be included in all future holiday gatherings. Hell, knowing his mother, Grant wouldn't be surprised if she convinced Clara and Hank to move into the penthouse at some point. She might even ask Clara to change her name to Dunbarton, too.

Even if none of that did happen, Grant couldn't do the "Yeah, I'll call you" thing with Clara that had always worked well for him in the past, since he was excellent at avoiding women who wanted more than sex and even better at avoiding the ones who wanted a family. After having sex with Clara—who came readymade with a family—he wouldn't be able to escape seeing her again with some regularity. And *seeing a woman again,* never mind *with some regularity,* was something that wouldn't fit Grant's social calendar.

He wasn't good at relationships. Not family ones, not social ones, not romantic ones. And Clara was threatening to be all three. He couldn't afford responsibilities like that. He had too many other responsibilities. And none of them included other people. Even people who had a great ass. So no more thinking about Clara in any way other than the mundane. Which should be no problem.

All he had to do was make sure he didn't think about her at all.

# Five

Grant wasn't surprised when he woke up in the middle of the night. It had taken him forever to get to sleep, thanks to his inability to banish thoughts of Clara from his brain, and he'd slept lightly. Nor was he surprised that when he awoke, it was from a dream about Clara, since he'd still been thinking about her when he finally did go to sleep. He likewise wasn't surprised that the dream had been a damned erotic one, since his last thoughts of her before going to sleep had mostly revolved around her ass. What did surprise him was that he awoke to the smell of cake. Probably chocolate cake. Possibly devil's food cake. Which was easily his favorite.

He glanced at the clock on his nightstand. Three twenty-two. He didn't doubt that there were a number of bakers already up and plying their trade this early in the morning in New York City. However, none of them should have been plying it in the Dunbarton kitchen.

Either someone got seriously lost on their way to work, or Clara was awake, too.

He told himself to go back to sleep. She had said she was an insomniac, so her reasons for being up were probably totally normal and had nothing to do with damned erotic dreams like his. But was it normal for her to be baking at three in the morning? Didn't insomniacs usually just read or watch TV until they fell back asleep?

With a resigned sigh, Grant rose from bed and pulled a white V-neck T-shirt on over his striped pajama bottoms. Then he padded barefoot down the hall toward the kitchen, the smell of cake—oh, yeah, that had to be devil's food—growing stronger with every step. When he finally arrived at his destination, though, he saw not cake, but *cup*cakes, dozens of them, littering the countertops, all with red or green icing. He also saw Christmas cookies and gingerbread men bedecked with everything from gumdrops to crushed peppermint. There were bags of flour and sugar—both granular and powdered—strewn about untidily, as well as broken eggshells and torn butter wrappers, whisks, spoons, spatulas and other things he hadn't even realized they had in the kitchen.

In the middle of it all was Clara, dressed in red flannel pajama pants decorated with snowflakes and an oversize T-shirt bearing the logo for something called the Savannah Sand Gnats. It also bore generous spatters of chocolate and frosting. On her feet were thick socks. Grant had never known a woman who slept in socks. Or flannel. Or something emblazoned with the words *Sand Gnats*. Of course, whenever he was sleeping with a woman, she wasn't wearing anything at all. In spite of that, strangely, there was something about

Clara's socks and frumpy pajamas that was even sexier than no clothes at all.

Her mass of blue-black curls was contained—barely—by a rubber band, but a number of the coils had broken free to dance around her face. Another streak of chocolate decorated one cheek from temple to chin, and when his gaze fell to the ceramic bowl she cradled in the crook of her arm, he saw that it was filled with really rich, really dark chocolate batter, something that meant—*Who's the man?*—the cupcakes in the oven were indeed devil's food.

"Um, Clara?" he said softly.

When she glanced up, she looked as panicked and guilty as she would have had he just caught her helping herself to his mother's jewelry. "Uh, hi," she replied. "What are you doing here?"

"I live here," he reminded her.

"Right," she said, still looking panicked and guilty. "Did I wake you? I'm sorry. I was trying not to make any noise."

"It wasn't the noise. It was the smell. Devil's food, right?"

She nodded. "My favorite."

Of course it was. Because that just made him like her even more. "Were the pecan tarts we had for dessert tonight not to your liking?"

Instead of replying, Clara chuckled.

"What?" he asked.

"Pecan," she repeated, pronouncing it the way he had—the way he always had—*pee*-can. "The way you Northerners say that always makes me laugh."

"Why?"

"Well, first off, because it's wrong."

"No, it isn't."

"Yeah, it is." Before he could object again, she continued, "Look, we Southerners claimed that nut as our own a long time ago, and we say 'pi-*cahn*.' Therefore, that's the correct pronunciation. Also, in case you were wondering, *praline* is pronounced '*prah*-leen,' not '*pray*-leen.' That's another one that really toasts my melbas."

"But—"

"And second of all, I laugh because it always seemed to me like it should be the other way around. Saying 'pi-*cahn*' sounds so hoity-toity, like you Northerners, and saying '*pee*-can' sounds so folksy, like us Southerners." Instead of taking issue with the whole pecan thing—everyone knew the correct pronunciation was "*pee*-can"—he repeated, "So you didn't care for the tarts?"

She started spooning batter into the cupcake pan, an action that delineated the gentle swell of muscles in her upper arms and forearms. Grant wouldn't have thought muscles could be sexy on a woman. But on Clara, muscles were *very* sexy. Then again, on Clara, lederhosen and waders would have been sexy.

"They were delicious," she said. "But I couldn't sleep. And when I get anxious, I bake."

He wanted to ask her what she had to be anxious about. Her son was worth a hundred and forty-two million dollars. She'd never have to be anxious about him—or herself—again. Instead, he asked, "How long have you been up?"

She looked around for a clock. Or maybe she was just gauging the piles of cupcakes and cookies and trying to calculate how long it took to produce that many. "I don't know. What time is it?"

"About three-thirty?"

Now she looked shocked. "Seriously? Wow. I guess I've been up a few hours, then."

She'd been in here for a few hours? Dressed like that? Baking devil's food cupcakes? And he hadn't known it? He was slipping.

In an effort to keep his mind where it needed to be, he focused his attention on the bowl of batter still folded in her arm. Unfortunately, it was way too close to where her T-shirt strained over her torso, offering a tantalizing outline of her breasts and—

"So, what's a Savannah Sand Gnat?" he asked, driving his gaze up to her face again.

"It's our baseball team," she told him as she went back to scooping batter into the cupcake pans.

"Savannah's baseball team is called the Sand Gnats? Seriously?"

She looked up again, narrowing her eyes menacingly. "You got a problem with that?"

"No," he quickly assured her. "But sand gnats aren't exactly endearing, are they? I mean, they might as well have named the team the Savannah Clumps of Kelp."

She shook a chocolate-laden spoon at him. "Don't be dissing my team, mister. I love those guys. So does Hank."

He lifted his hands in surrender. "I apologize. Let me make amends. Dunbarton Industries has a suite at Citi Field. I can take you and Hank to a game someday. Maybe when the Mets play the Atlanta Braves."

And holy crap, did he just invite her to something that was months away and would bring her back to New York for a specific reason to do something with him and not because his mother wanted to see Hank? What the hell was wrong with him?

She dropped the spoon back into the bowl. "See the

Braves play? From a suite? Are you kidding me? Hank would love that."

Grant wanted to ask her if she'd love it, too. Instead he said, "It's a date, then." Crap. Putting it that way was even worse than asking her out in the first place. Quickly, before she could think he meant a *date* date— which he absolutely did not—he added, "For the three of us. Maybe four. Mom doesn't care for baseball, but if Hank is coming, she'll probably want to be there, too."

The comment made Clara's expression go from elated to deflated in a nanosecond. But she said nothing, only went back to furiously spooning the last of the batter into the last cups in the pan, as if wanting to put too fine a point on the whole baking-when-anxious thing.

"Clara?" he asked as she scoured the last bit of chocolate from the bowl. "Is something wrong?"

She didn't look up, only continued wiping the bowl clean, even though she had already scraped it within an inch of its life. Softly, she muttered, "What could possibly be wrong? My three-year-old just became a tycoon. That's every mother's dream, right?"

"I don't know," Grant said. "I'm not a mother. But I would venture a guess that, yes, it would be every mother's dream. You won't have to worry about his future anymore."

At that, Clara did look up. But she no longer looked anxious. Now she looked combative. "I wasn't worried about his future before," she said tersely. "Why would I be?"

Clearly, Grant had hit a nerve, though he had no idea how or why. Clara, however, was quick to enlighten him.

"Look, maybe I've been struggling financially since he was born. Maybe I was struggling financially before he was born. I still manage. I always have. I started a college fund for him as soon as I found out I was pregnant, and I make a deposit into it every month. He's never missed an annual checkup at the pediatrician or twice-yearly trips to the dentist. He gets three nutritious meals a day, clothes and shoes when he needs them, and although Santa may be at the bottom of his toy sack by the time he gets to our apartment, Hank has never had a Christmas morning where he wasn't delighted by his take. No, I can't lay down my platinum card whenever I feel like it and buy him anything he wants, but I give him more love and more time than anyone else ever has, and I will always give him more love and more time than anyone else, and that's way more important than anything a platinum card could buy."

The longer Clara spoke, the more her voice rose in volume and the more vehement she became. By the time she finished, she was nearly shouting. Her eyes were wide, her cheeks were flushed, and her entire body was shaking. When Grant only gazed at her silently in response— since he had no idea how else to respond—she seemed to realize how much she had overreacted, and she slumped forward wearily.

"I'm sorry," she said. She turned around and set the now-empty bowl on the countertop. But instead of turning around again to say more, she only gripped the marble fiercely, as if letting go of it would hurl her into another dimension.

Grant tried to understand—he really did. But the truth was, he had never loved or feared for anyone as much as Clara obviously loved and feared for her son. Grant got how she felt obligated to be the one to provide for Hank. But he didn't understand how she could not be overjoyed about the windfall he had received.

Especially since it could ease significantly all those obligations that could sometimes feel so overwhelming.

As if she'd heard the thought in his head, Clara finally turned slowly to face him. Thankfully, she no longer looked combative. Nor did she look anxious. Now she only looked exhausted.

"I've always been the center of Hank's world," she said quietly, "the same way he's always been the center of mine. Now, suddenly, he has family besides me. He has people to love him and provide for him besides me. And even if they can't love him more than I do, they can provide for him better. There's no way I can deny that. At some point, he's going to realize that, too. If he hasn't already." Her eyes grew damp, but she swiped them dry with the backs of her clenched fists. "There's already a part of me that's afraid he'll want to stay here instead of go home when the time comes for us to go back to Georgia."

Ah. Okay. Now Grant understood. She was afraid of losing her son to his grandmother, because his grandmother was, at this point, pretty much the equivalent of Santa Claus. Actually better than Santa Claus, since Santa evidently arrived at the Easton home having to scrape the bottom of his bag. Grant wished he knew what to say to ease her fears. But the fact was, his mother *could* give Hank anything he wanted, and Clara couldn't. Not that he would ever say that to Clara.

He just wished he did know what to say to her.

He was spared from having to figure it out, however, because the timer went off on the oven, and Clara sprang to grab two oven mitts and remove the pans of cupcakes from inside. Just as deftly, she inserted two more and closed the door, setting the timer again. When she spun back around to face him, she still looked troubled. So much for baking alleviating her anxiety.

"This money from Brent is just going to be so life changing for Hank," she said.

"But it will change his life for the better," Grant told her.

"Will it, though?" she asked. "With so much money comes so much responsibility. And people treat you differently when you have that much money. You treat yourself differently when you have that much money. And I don't want Hank to change."

"Everyone changes, Clara. Change is inevitable."

Without removing the oven mitts—and damned if there wasn't even something about those on her that was sexy—she wrapped her arms around herself, as if physically trying to hold herself together.

"But change should come gradually and naturally," she said. "I don't want Hank to be robbed of a normal childhood or adolescence. I want him to have a childhood where he can go barefoot all summer and catch lightning bugs and put them in a jar with holes punched in the lid and have a lemonade stand on the sidewalk and eat peaches picked right from the tree. I want him to have an adolescence where he works a crappy part-time job and drives a crappy car but loves both because they give him his first taste of freedom. The kind of childhood and adolescence I always wished I had when I was a kid. Hell, I just want Hank to *be* a child and adolescent. I don't want him to grow up too soon. Kids who get thrust into adult positions too early in life…"

When her gaze lit on his, Grant was knocked off-kilter again by just how huge and haunting and bewitching her eyes were. They were even more so when she was so impassioned. He found himself wanting to reach out to her physically, to curl his fingers around her nape and pull her close, and—

"Kids like that," she continued before he could act on his impulse, "kids who are cheated out of a normal childhood, they never grow up to be truly happy, you know? They don't learn how to play as kids, so they never relax or feel joy as adults. They don't make friends as kids, so they never trust or love other people as adults. They just never become the kind of person they might have become if they'd had the same upbringing and chances that regular kids have, and they never stop wondering what kind of person they might have—should have—been, if they'd just been able to grow up at a normal pace. They never stop feeling like, no matter what they have, it's not…" She shrugged, but the gesture was more hopeless than it was careless. "It's not enough."

Grant knew she was talking about herself. He knew everything she said was based on her own experiences growing up, and on her own reality as an adult. He knew she was worried Hank would end up like her. There had been nothing in her monologue that was directed at him, not one thing he should take personally.

For some reason, though, he did take it personally. He took everything she'd said personally. Her comments just struck a chord inside him, too. Discordantly at that. Because although Clara's reasons for being denied a normal childhood were nothing like the reasons he had been denied one, they had both ended up in the same place. That had been made clear at dinner the night before, when both had chorused the same sentiment.

But his life *was* enough, he told himself. Even if, sometimes, it felt as if it wasn't. He wouldn't change a thing about the way he'd grown up, because *his* experiences had made him who and what he was today. And he liked who and what he was. He didn't want to relax—relaxing wasn't in his nature. And he didn't want to love other people—love only complicated otherwise satisfactory relationships. He didn't care if he hadn't grown up to be the person he might have—should have—been, if he'd been allowed to grow up at a normal pace. He liked the person he was just fine. No, not just fine. A lot. He liked the person he was a lot.

But in spite of all his self-assurances, he still sounded defensive when he said, "There's nothing wrong with growing up too soon." Because he said it a little too quickly. A little too tersely. And he couldn't rein it in when he added, "What? Would you rather Hank be like his father and never grow up at all? Spend his life running from one hedonistic adventure to another, leaving before he's done any good, never making a difference anywhere?"

"Of course not," Clara said. "But—"

"At least now Hank has a future," Grant interrupted her. "He can even work in the family business if he wants to. *He* could be the Dunbarton legacy. He could become CEO of Dunbarton Industries after I retire."

Instead of looking pleased, or even intrigued, by the suggestion, Clara looked horrified. "Oh, God, no," she said. "The thought of sweet, happy-go-lucky Hank becoming a joyless, relentless, workaholic CEO who only cares about money is just so…so…"

She shook her head without finishing, obviously unable to find a word abhorrent enough to convey her disgust at the prospect of Hank following in his uncle's footsteps.

She seemed to realize exactly what she'd just said because she immediately told him, "That came out wrong.

I didn't mean *you're* a joyless, relentless, workaholic CEO who only thinks about money. I only meant…"

"Actually, Clara, I think you did mean that," he said.

For some reason, though, Grant couldn't stay angry about the comment. Which could only mean that, on some level, he agreed with it. Not so much that he was joyless. He knew how to enjoy himself. The opportunity for enjoyment just didn't present itself all that often. Nor was he relentless. He could relent under the right circumstances. The need for it just rarely materialized. And he thought about a lot more than money. But money was what kept business in business, and it was as essential to maintaining a quality of life as food and drink were.

So it must be the workaholic part of Clara's accusation that hit home. And, okay, maybe that part was true. Maybe he did work more than the average person did. He had an important job, and it was one no one else in the company could do, because, in spite of its huge size and profits, Dunbarton Industries was still a family business. His position didn't afford time for slacking off. Or, okay, being particularly yielding. Or finding a lot of enjoyment. And it meant he spent a lot of time thinking about the bottom line.

But Clara must understand those things. She was, in effect, the CEO of her own company. Hers was an important job, too, that no one else could do. She must put in longer than usual hours and take work home with her in the form of books to keep and orders to place. She was the last person to be pointing a finger at someone who worked too much at a joyless, relentless job and kept his eye on profitability. She must be as joyless and relentless and profit minded as he was.

But she was doing the thing she had always wanted

to do, he reminded himself, noting the streak of chocolate on her face again…and battling the urge to draw
nearer and wipe it—no, lick it—off. She had followed
her childhood dream. And she made time for her son.
She'd taken off work to bring him to New York to meet
the family they hadn't realized he had. Grant thought
back on how she'd sat on the floor in Brent's room to
play with Hank, and laugh with him, and share an affectionate embrace.

Maybe Clara thought she'd grown up to be unhappy
and unfulfilled as a result of being denied a "normal"
childhood, but she hadn't. She had learned how to play
and to love. Hank had made that possible for her.

So there was really only one joyless, relentless, workaholic CEO who only thought about money in the room.
And it wasn't Clara Easton.

She opened her mouth to say something else, but
Grant held up a hand to halt her. Nothing she said at
this point would ring true. She thought all he did and
cared about was work. Which shouldn't have bothered
him, since work was pretty much all he did or cared
about. It hadn't bothered him when that was his own
opinion of himself. But knowing Clara felt that way
about him, too…

"Um. Well," he said. "I'll leave you to it."

She hesitated, and then said, "I promise I'll clean up
my mess before I go back to bed."

He nodded. "Mrs. Bentley will appreciate that."

"And I'll put some cupcakes and cookies in the
freezer, since there are so many. Maybe that will get
you and Francesca through Christmas after Hank and
I go back to Georgia."

"Mom will appreciate that."

"And you?" she asked.

He looked at her again. "What about me?"

"Will you appreciate them, too?"

He found the question odd. "Of course."

This time Clara was the one to nod. But there was something disingenuous about the gesture. As if she were trying to make him think she believed him, but she really didn't.

"Good night, Clara," he said before turning toward the door again. "I hope you get some sleep."

"Good night, Grant," she replied. Then she said something else he didn't understand. "I hope you get some, too."

# Six

The good news was that Clara would have no trouble avoiding Grant the day after calling him a joyless, relentless, workaholic CEO who didn't think about anything but money. The bad news was the reason: as soon as she and Hank had woken up, Francesca announced that the three of them would be spending the day together again, this time at the Bronx Zoo, because Hank loved *Madagascar* so much when he and Francesca watched it together. They might also go to the New York Aquarium if they had time because it had been one of Brent and Grant's favorite places when they were Hank's age.

Although Clara would be able to avoid Grant for the day, she wouldn't be able to avoid him for the morning, since, as she and Hank and Francesca sat in the smaller dining room near the kitchen eating breakfast, Grant joined them.

It quickly became clear that he wasn't exactly happy to see her, either, and wanted to bolt from the house as soon as he could. He was dressed for work in another one of his pinstripe power suits and had his briefcase in hand and a trench coat thrown over one arm. And he barely acknowledged Clara and Hank with a quick "Good morning" before turning to his mother.

"Don't forget you need to look over and okay next year's revised budget before you go out," he told her. "The board is voting on it tomorrow."

Francesca waved a hand airily at her son. "Oh, I'm sure it will be fine. Hank and Clara and I are spending the day together again."

Grant looked surprised by his mother's lack of interest in the corporate budget. "You need to read it, Mom. And you need to be at the meeting to vote on it. We need a quorum, and some of the other board members are—"

"All right, all right," Francesca interrupted him. "I'll read it tonight, I promise. And yes, I'll be at the meeting. Nine o'clock," she said quickly when he opened his mouth, presumably to remind her. Then she looked at Hank and Clara again. "I'll arrange for you and Hank to tour the company while I'm in the meeting tomorrow. It's never too early for a child to learn the ropes of the family business. You could come and work for us someday," she said directly to Hank. "Wouldn't that be fun?"

Clara couldn't help the way her back went up— literally—at Francesca's suggestion. And she could tell that Grant had noticed. Francesca, however, seemed oblivious. As did Hank. At least, he was oblivious to what exactly *coming to work for the Dunbartons* meant, because he jumped on the opportunity faster than a person could say *corporate drone*.

"Okay," he agreed around a mouthful of waffles. "Do you work there, too, Grammy?"

Francesca smiled. "No, but I used to. I was the vice president in charge of public relations before your father and Uncle Grant were born. After that, I helped their father when he was the boss and needed my advice on something. Nowadays, I help the company make money by sitting on the board of directors."

"Are you the boss now?" Hank asked.

"No, sweetheart, your uncle Grant is the boss."

"But you're his mom," Hank objected. "That makes you his boss."

Francesca smiled again and looked at Grant. "Well, in some things, maybe," she said. "But even moms stop being the boss of most things at some point. Uncle Grant is the one who runs Dunbarton Industries." She winked at Grant, and then looked at Hank again. "For now, anyway. But maybe you'll be the boss there someday, Hank. Wouldn't you like that? With your own office and a big desk and lots of people calling you *Mr. Easton*?"

*And migraines and chest pains and high blood pressure?* Clara thought before she could stop herself. *And no life outside the office whatsoever?*

Grant seemed to know what she was thinking, because although he addressed his next comment to his mother, it was clearly intended for Clara. "Don't push him, Mom. Hank might not want to grow up to be a joyless, relentless, workaholic CEO who only thinks about money. He might want to be a professional beach bum like his father."

Now Francesca threw her son a puzzled look. "What on earth are you talking about? Brent wasn't a beach bum." But she didn't repudiate the first part of Grant's statement.

"Right," Grant said. "Well, then. I'll just head to work to be joyless, relentless and profit obsessed. Have a fun day seeing the sights."

The remark had the desired effect. Clara felt like a complete jerk. She scrambled for something to say or do that might make for a reasonable olive branch. "Grant," she said before he could make his escape. "Don't you want to come with us today? I bet you haven't been to the aquarium in a long time."

He had started to turn away, but halted when she said his name. It was only when he heard the word *aquarium*, though, that he finally turned around.

"It has been a long time," he said. He thought for a minute. "Before my father passed away, in fact."

Clara had figured it had been a while, but even she was surprised to hear it had been decades since he visited a place that must have been a utopia for him when he was a child.

"Then you should take the day off and come with us," she said.

Francesca looked surprised when Clara extended the invitation, but said, "Oh, do come with us, Grant. You loved the aquarium when you were a little boy." Now she looked at Clara. "He would have gone there every day if he could have. I remember there was this one thing he loved more than anything else. We could never pull him away from it. Brent and I could see the entire aquarium in the time Grant took to look at that one thing. What was it called, dear?"

"The chambered nautilus," Grant said in the same tone of voice people used when talking about deities or superheroes. Clara half expected the skies to open and a chorus of angels to break into song.

"That was it," Francesca said to Clara. "I always

thought it was kind of creepy and macabre myself, but Grant was enchanted by it."

"It's a living fossil," he said. "It hasn't changed in four hundred million years. And it lives almost two thousand feet deep and can use jet propulsion to move more than sixty meters per minute. What child wouldn't be enchanted?"

Or what adult? Clara wanted to ask. Since Grant was still obviously enchanted.

"Then you should come with us," Clara said. "You two have been apart for too long."

For one brief, telling moment, Grant's expression changed to the same one that came over Hank whenever Clara took a pan of baklava—his absolute most favorite thing in the world—out of the oven. Then, just as quickly, Grant changed back into businessman mode.

"There's no way I can take today off for that," he said. Though there was something in the way he said it that indicated he really wished he could.

"We could go another day," Clara said. "One you *could* take off."

For a moment, Grant only looked at her in an almost anguished way that seemed to say, *Don't. Just... don't.* But all he said was, "There are no days I could take off for that."

For some reason, Clara just couldn't let it go. "How about Saturday?" she asked. "You don't have to work Saturday, do you?"

His *don't* expression didn't change. "Not at the office, but I'll have plenty to do here."

She opened her mouth again, but he cut her off.

"I can't take time away from work. For anything," he said tersely. Adamantly. Finally.

"Okay," she said. "I just thought maybe—"

"Now if you'll excuse me," he interrupted her, "I have to get to the office. Enjoy the zoo." Almost as an afterthought, he added, "And the aquarium."

And then he was gone, before any of them could say another word. Like "Goodbye," for instance. Or "Have a nice day." Or even "Don't work too hard. Or too relentlessly. Or too joylessly." Though it was clear that Grant Dunbarton didn't have a problem with any of those things.

It was dark when Grant got home from work that night. As it always was this time of year. As it was some days in summer, come to think of it, when he worked especially late. But always, in winter, it was dark. There was a part of him that liked the shorter days. It was quicker to get through them. In summer, when the sun didn't set until eight or nine o'clock, it just felt as if that much more time was wasted somehow. Dark was good. Dark meant night. And night meant the day was almost over.

As he headed through the penthouse toward the stairs, he heard voices coming from the direction of the living room and turned in that direction instead. The room was lit up like, well, a Christmas tree, even though the Christmas tree twinkling in the corner offered the least amount of light. The main illumination came from the two lamps on the tables bookending the sofa, where his mother was sitting reading next year's budget, as she'd promised to do. Although the glass of wine she held and the pajamas and slippers she was wearing seemed incongruous with her reading material, seeing her there reminded Grant of occasions in the past when she'd been more involved with Dunbarton Industries.

She'd always enjoyed working, he remembered, even if she had left the day-to-day operations of the business behind years ago. She still seemed perfectly comfortable now, going over the budget for next year.

On the floor not far from where she sat, Clara and Hank lay on their stomachs with coloring books open before them and crayons littered about. Hank was in his pajamas, too, but Clara was still dressed as she'd been that morning, in khaki cargo pants and a black sweater, her shoes discarded now to reveal socks patterned with images of Santa Claus. Grant smiled at seeing them.

Mother and son were chattering about their individual coloring book creations, Clara saying something about how the jungle animals on her page were conspiring to escape from the zoo, and Hank telling her his had already done that and gone to Madagascar, like in the movie. Clara replied that her animals weren't going to Madagascar. They were going to open a vegetarian café on Fordham Avenue, and that way, they'd be close enough to still visit their animal friends who stayed behind. Hank deemed the plan a solid one, then went back to coloring his own pages, which seemed to consist mostly of jagged lines of, if Grant's Crayola memories served, Electric Lime, Hot Magenta and Laser Lemon. They'd been some of his favorite colors, too, when he was a kid. He was surprised he was able to remember their names so easily. Funny, the things the brain stored that then returned to a person out of nowhere like a surprise birthday present.

"You all look busy," he said as he strode into the room—and wondered when he had decided to do so. His original plan had been to retreat to his office before anyone saw him, the way any self-respecting workaholic CEO would. Not that he was still bothered by Clara's comment or anything. So why was he wading into this patently domestic scene where the only work getting done was by his mother—who tempered her work with wine and did it in her pajamas.

"Hello, dear," his mother said without looking up from the budget. "How was your day?"

He figured he'd played the relentless, joyless workaholic card as much as he could, so he only said, "Fine. Yours?"

"It was lovely," she told him. Finally, she looked up from the budget. "Until I started reading this. There are some huge problems here, you know."

"I know," he said. "That's why I wanted you to look it over before the meeting tomorrow. Have any ideas for where to make improvements?"

"Dozens," she told him. She pointed to the tablet sitting next to her on the sofa. "I'm making notes. Lots of them."

"Good. I've made some, too. We can compare later."

"Uncle Grant!" Hank piped up before Francesca had a chance to reply. "We saw that thing you like so much. At the aquarium. It was awesome!"

Grant smiled. "The chambered nautilus?" he asked. "What did you think of him?"

"I think he winked at me."

Grant chuckled. He'd thought the same thing the first time he saw it, even though that was impossible for the animal. Even so, he told Hank, "That means he likes you. They don't wink for just anyone, you know."

"Really?" Hank asked, sounding genuinely delighted that he had left such an impression.

"Really," Grant assured him. "I bet he's telling all the other cephalopods about you right now, and they're all hoping you'll come back soon to see them." Which was what Grant had always imagined them doing when he was little. He'd completely forgotten about that until Hank mentioned the winking thing. Huh.

Hank looked at Clara. "Can we go back tomorrow, Mama?"

Grant looked at Clara, too, only to find she was already looking at him. And even though her son had asked her a question, she continued to look at Grant. She was smiling at him, too. Smiling in a way that made his heart rate quicken and his blood warm. Not in a sexual way, as usually happened when he looked at her. But in a way that was…something else. Something he wasn't sure he'd ever felt before. Something that almost felt better than sex.

"We can't go back tomorrow, sweetie," Clara told her son. Though she was still looking at Grant and smiling in that…interesting…way. "Grammy wants to show us the place where Uncle Grant works. Where your grandfather used to work. But maybe the next time we come to New York, we can go back."

*The next time we come to New York*, Grant echoed to himself. How could Clara be talking about leaving already? They'd just gotten here.

Then he remembered they were on day four of their visit. Halfway through the week and a day Clara had said she and Hank could stay in New York. When Gus Fiver had told him and his mother that, Grant had been thinking a week and a day would be more than enough time for an introductory visit. He'd figured all of them would need to take things slowly, that there would have to be a number of such short visits to gradually welcome and include Hank and Clara into the family. But only four days in, Hank and Clara already felt like part of the family. They seemed to be right where they belonged. Their leaving in four days felt wrong somehow.

But they'd be leaving next Monday evening. And who knew when they would make it back?

"Okay," Hank said glumly in response to Clara's promise that they would visit the aquarium on their—admittedly nebulous—return. He went back to his coloring, but his crayon strokes were slower and less enthusiastic than they'd been before.

"Want to join us?" Clara asked.

When she tilted her head toward an assortment of coloring books on the floor that had yet to be opened, it took a moment for Grant to realize her invitation was to lie down beside her and Hank and start filling one in. Yet she had extended the invitation in all seriousness, as if this was the sort of thing people their age did all the time. And, okay, maybe it was something Clara did all the time, being the mother of a three-year-old. It wasn't something Grant did all the time. Or ever. Even if there was something about the idea that sounded kind of fun at the moment.

"Um, thanks," he said. "But I'll pass." Then he couldn't help adding, "It isn't something CEOs do."

"Oh, sure they do," Clara said. She smiled that interesting smile again. "They just color everything the color it's supposed to be and never go outside the lines."

"Very funny," Grant replied dryly. Though, actually, he did kind of find the remark funny.

Ha. He'd show her. He'd lie right down beside her and grab a coloring book and a handful of crayons—Atomic Tangerine, Sunglow and Purple Pizzazz had been other favorites, he recalled—and color all over the damned page, going out of the lines whenever he felt like it, and—

Or, rather, he would do that if he could. If he didn't have so many other things he needed to do. Like go over the budget again so he and his mother could compare notes. Even if he had gone over it twice already. The meeting was tomorrow. He should refresh his memory. Even if he did remember everything pretty well.

"Thanks," he told Clara. "But I have some other things I need to get done before tomorrow."

Because tomorrow was always another day. Another day of things he needed to get done before the next day. Because that day would have things that needed to get done before the day after that. Such was life for a high-powered CEO who didn't have time for things like going to aquariums and coloring zoo animals and having a life outside the office.

"You two have fun," he said to Clara and Hank. To his mother, he added, "I'll be in my office whenever you're ready to go over your proposed changes."

His mother nodded. "Give me another hour or so."

"That's fine," Grant told her. Because that would mean they were an hour closer to the end of the day. An hour closer to bringing on tomorrow. An hour closer to getting done all the important things that needed to get done before other important things took their places.

An hour closer to when Clara Easton would leave New York to return to Georgia.

For the first time in a very long time, Grant was suddenly much less eager to see the day draw to a close.

# Seven

By Friday evening, day five of her "vacation," Clara was more exhausted than she was after a full week at her physically demanding, labor-intensive, stress-provoking work, even after sleeping a full five hours later than she normally did on Friday morning. Because the moment she swallowed the last bite of her bagel and the final sip of her coffee, Francesca had hustled her and Hank out of the house to tour Dunbarton Industries' headquarters while she and Grant attended their meeting. Clara had to admit, the tour had been eye-opening and surprisingly interesting. But upon the meeting's conclusion, Francesca had swept the two of them off again, this time to zigzag across Central Park, from the zoo to the carousel to the castle to the Swedish Cottage and its marionettes. Though Clara might just as well have stayed at the penthouse the whole day for all the attention Francesca and Hank had paid her. The majority of her day had been spent catching up with the two of them.

Clara understood. Really, she did. Hank was Francesca's only grandchild, and he was all she had left of Brent. She had a lot of lost time to make up for with him and was trying to squeeze the three and a half years of Hank's life she'd missed into a week's worth of shared experiences that could tide her over until she saw him again. And it was the first time Hank had been the center of someone's universe who never said the word *no*. Yes, he and Clara had plenty of fun together, but there were a lot of times Clara had to tell him no, either because of time or money constraints. Francesca had neither of those, so she was completely at Hank's disposal. And, boy, was he learning that fast.

By the time they returned to the penthouse—after, oh, yeah, dinner at Tavern on the Green—Grant had shut himself up in his office.

Clara grimaced as she thought back on when she'd accused him of being a corporate drone the other night. She hadn't meant to insult him. The words had just popped out. She could hardly be held responsible, because she'd been A) anxious, B) exhausted, C) in the middle of baking enough cookies and cupcakes to feed the United Nations—and their respective nations—and D) trying not to notice how sexy Grant Dunbarton was in a V-neck T-shirt and striped pajama bottoms.

Seriously, when that guy dressed like an ordinary person, he was extraordinarily hot. She was still thinking about just how hot as she sat in the spectacular Dunbarton library to which she had escaped for a little peace and quiet, sipping a glass of luscious pinot noir she hoped would help her forget how hot Grant Dunbarton was. *No!* she immediately corrected herself. The wine would help her relax after yet another day of worrying that her son would abandon her in favor of his grandmother. *No! Not that either!* She was just having a glass of wine to—

Oh, bugger it.

She was having a glass of wine because she really needed a glass of wine—thanks to her growing anxiety over Hank's allegiances *and* her growing attraction to Grant. But where she could pretty much convince herself that Hank would never abandon her, she was less successful convincing herself that her attraction to Grant would go away. Because she was definitely attracted to Grant. Very attracted to him. And the attraction had nothing to do with any misplaced affection for Brent that might still be lingering somewhere inside her. What Clara was feeling for Grant wasn't the breathless infatuation a girl had for a cute guy who was funny and charming and a great kisser. It was... something else. Something she wasn't sure she even wanted to identify, because that could make things even more complicated.

Maybe Clara was only four years older now than she was when she met Brent, but they'd been years filled with mothering and working and trying to build a life for herself and her son. Years of taking on responsibilities and obligations she would have for the rest of her life. The easy, breezy girl who'd fallen for Brent was gone, as were the fast, fun feelings she'd had for him. But the woman who was coming to know and care about Grant? She was another story.

And the last thing Clara needed was to fall for Grant Dunbarton. She shouldn't even find him hot. Sex with him wouldn't be like sex with a guy with whom she'd had no future—precisely because, with Grant, she did have a future. Even if it wasn't a future together, he'd still be in and out of her life thanks to Hank's ties to the family. It was already awkward enough between them. Throwing sex into the mix would only make it more so. Wouldn't it? Of course it would. So she had to keep her distance from the other Dunbarton brother.

"I'm sorry. I didn't know anyone was in here."

As if conjured by her thoughts, Grant spoke from behind her. Clara was so jumpy from both the day and her thoughts that she simultaneously leapt up from the settee and dropped her wine, which crashed into the spectacular Dunbarton coffee table before shattering and sending shards of glass and seemingly gallons of wine—red, of course—falling onto the spectacular Dunbarton Oriental rug.

She cried out at the mess she'd made, then, "Quick!" she shouted at Grant. "I need a towel and some club soda!"

Without questioning the order, he hurried to a bar in the corner of the room and collected the requested items. When he returned, he was already pouring club soda onto the towel and looked even more panicked than Clara was. Damn. The rug must be worth more than she thought.

"Should I call nine-one-one?" he asked.

Well, she didn't think it was worth *that* much.

She grabbed the towel from him, dropping to her knees beside the stain. Grant dropped with her. He wrapped one arm around her shoulders as he withdrew his phone from his pocket. "My God. Are you okay? I'm calling nine-one-one."

"Don't be silly. It's just wine," she said, trying to ignore the heat that seeped through her at the feel of his arm around her shoulder. Why was he doing that? "I can get the stain out, I promise. Or I'll pay to have it professionally cleaned."

He had pressed the nine and the first one, but halted. "You're not bleeding?" he asked. "You didn't fall because you're lightheaded due to blood loss?"

Only then did Clara realize he thought she'd cut herself badly on the broken glass. Meaning his concern wasn't for the rug—it was for her. Which was saying something, because the carpet was massive, stretching from one side of the library to the other, and it could very well have been here since the penthouse was built. It had to be worth a fortune. But he hadn't given it a thought. Some joyless, relentless, workaholic CEO who only thought about money he was.

"I'm fine," she said. She held up her hand for inspection, and realized it was covered with red wine. Hastily, she wiped it off with the towel. "See?" she said, wiggling her fingers to prove it. "Not hurt. Just clumsy."

He took her hand in his and turned it first one way, then the other, just to make sure. Heat shot through Clara from her fingertips to her heart, then seeped outward, into her chest and belly. If she didn't remove her hand from his soon, that heat was going to spread even farther, right down to her—

Oops. Too late.

She tugged her hand free and went back to work on the stain. But Grant circled her wrist with sure fingers again and drew her hand away. Once more, Clara was flooded with sensations she hadn't felt for a long time. Too long. She'd honestly forgotten how nice it could be, just the simple touch of a man's bare skin against her own.

"There could be broken glass in there," he said from what sounded like a very great distance. "I'll call someone tomorrow to have the rug cleaned professionally. Until then, we can close off the room to make sure Hank doesn't wander in here."

"But—"

"It's okay. Really. We don't use this room that often anyway."

"You were about to use it tonight," Clara pointed out.

"No, I wasn't. I just came in to fix a drink." He smiled. "The good bourbon is in the library."

She smiled back. "Right. All that stuff in the kitchen pantry must be complete rotgut."

His smile grew, reaching all the way to his eyes, and the bubbling heat in Clara's torso bubbled higher. "We only keep that for the servants, so they'll have something for when we drive them to drink."

So much for his being humorless, Clara thought. When he put his mind to it, Grant could be every bit as funny and charming as his brother. Though he was being a bit relentless about not letting go of her wrist. Not that she really minded, even though she should.

"But club soda is amazing," she objected halfheartedly, trying to focus on something other than the gentle feel of his warm fingers around her wrist. "It'll work. I swear."

He didn't reply, but didn't let go of her hand, either. In fact, he ran his thumb lightly over the tender flesh on the inside of her wrist, making her pulse leap wildly. Something he probably felt, since his thumb stilled on her skin right about where her pulse would be. He continued to watch her intently, his lips parted, his eyes dark. For one tiny moment, Clara thought he might actually lean in to kiss her. For one tiny moment, she really wished he would. Then, suddenly, he freed her wrist and reached for the towel in her other hand, pressing it carefully into the stain.

"Club soda is good for stains, is it?" he asked as he worked. He picked up pieces of glass where he found them, setting them on the coffee table.

Clara nodded. Then, realizing he couldn't see the gesture, because he was still dabbing at the rug and picking up glass, she said, "Uh-uh." Mostly because that was the only sound she could manage.

"Spill wine a lot, do you?" he asked, smiling again, more softly this time. But he still didn't look at her as he continued to work on the stain.

"Well, not as often as juice," she said, "which club soda also works great on. But I am a harried mother of a toddler, so there are days when wine is one of the four basic food groups."

"They don't use the four basic food groups anymore," he said. Still cleaning up her mess. Still smiling. "It's the food pyramid now."

"Actually, that's been replaced, too," she told him. "By something called MyPlate. Which is pretty much the four basic food groups again, except they separated fruits and vegetables, and they put dairy in a cup."

Having evidently decided he'd done as much as he could to control the damage, Grant looked at Clara again. But his eyes were still dark, and his mouth was still much too sexy for her well-being. "So what are the four basic food groups of the harried toddler mother?" he asked.

Clara was tempted to say merlot, Chardonnay, pinot grigio and Cabernet, but stopped herself. She almost never drank pinot grigio. So she said, "Smoothies, whatever's left on the toddler's plate when he's done eating, Lärabars and wine."

Grant nodded. And still looked as though he might kiss her.

So she said, "Really, just give me ten minutes and I can have this rug looking good as new."

"You'll have your work cut out for you," he told her. "It's more than a hundred years old."

Clara closed her eyes. "Wow. That so doesn't make me feel better."

He chuckled at that. "It should. Can you imagine how much stuff has been spilled on this rug in that length of time? In my lifetime alone? Brent and I weren't exactly clean kids."

His expression cleared some at the mention of his brother, and Clara was grateful for the change. He picked up a few more pieces of glass and gave the rug a few more perfunctory pats, then left the towel over the stain to alert any unsuspecting library visitor of its presence. Then he rose from the floor and held out a hand to help up Clara. But she pretended she didn't see it and stood on her own.

"'Clean kids' is an oxymoron," she said when they were both vertical again. "I can't imagine having two of them underfoot at the same time. Francesca must have had her hands full with the two of you."

Grant smiled again. "Yeah, well, I think the fact that she and my father never had any more kids after the two of us speaks volumes."

Clara waited for his expression to cloud over again at the realization that he was the only Dunbarton child left. Instead, he still seemed to be steeped in fond nostalgia for their childhood. He looked past Clara, gesturing at a chair near the fireplace.

"I remember once, my dad was sitting over there reading an annual report when Brent and I came tearing through here. I don't remember which one of us was chasing the other. Maybe we were racing or something. Anyway, my dad was also enjoying what was probably some ridiculously expensive brandy—he did love his Armagnac—and Brent knocked it off the table and onto the hearth. Broke the snifter into bits, which probably added another couple hundred bucks to the damage. Then he tried to pass himself off as me, so I'd have to take the blame."

"You don't sound too mad about that."

Grant shrugged. "It was only fair. I'd passed myself off as him at school the week before when I got caught in the halls during class without a hall pass. Problem was the teachers really did have a tough time telling us apart. But Mom and Dad never did. Brent had to pay for that snifter out of his allowance. But I paid for half. Least I could do."

Now Clara chuckled. "Did you guys do that often? Pretend to be each other?"

Grant smiled again. "Only when we were absolutely sure we could get away with it."

She could believe that about Brent, mischievous guy that he was. But she was having a hard time imagining Grant as the naughty child.

"Come on," he said, tilting his head toward the bar. "I'll pour you another glass of wine. There's a really nice Harlan Estate in the rack. So much better than that rotgut from the pantry."

She was about to tell him the rotgut in their pantry cost about five times what she had in her own pantry, but halted. Who was she to turn up her nose at a really nice Harlan Estate?

He opened a bottle and poured them each a generous serving of dark red wine. He handed one glass to

Clara and then, almost as an afterthought, picked up the bottle to take it with them.

"Is Mom with Hank?"

Clara nodded, her stomach knotting with anxiety again. This was the first time Hank had spent more of his day with someone else than with Clara. For his first two years, he'd stayed in the bakery with her, playing in a part of the kitchen the then-owner had childproofed for him. Everyone who worked there had looked after him. When he'd started preschool at two, he'd still spent the bulk of his day with Clara at the bakery. Since coming to New York, though, Francesca had clocked more time with him than Clara had. And Clara still wasn't quite okay with that. But she couldn't bring herself to deny Francesca all the time with Hank she wanted, knowing it would be months before they could come back to New York for a visit.

"The marionette show was 'Jack and the Beanstalk,'" Clara said. "Francesca told Hank it was his father's favorite book when y'all were kids, and promised to read it to him when we got ho— Ah, back to the penthouse."

After mentioning his brother, Clara waited to see if Grant would revisit memories of his childhood again, but he only said, "The living room, then. It will be quiet in there." He hesitated for a moment before adding, "You look like you could use some quiet."

Was it that obvious? But all she said was, "Thanks. Some quiet would be good."

The Dunbarton living room was even more spectacular than the Dunbarton library, with its veritable wall of windows on one side looking out on the nighttime skyline and a dazzling blue spruce trimmed with glittering decorations and seemingly thousands of twinkling lights. The furnishings were elegant and tailored, the color of luscious gemstones, and the walls were painted a deep, rich ruby. The only other illumination in the room came from a fire someone had set in the fireplace, warmly crackling in invitation, and a half dozen candles in a candelabrum placed on the center of the mantelpiece amid pine boughs and holly berries.

Grant must have seen how her gaze lingered there, because he told her, "Mrs. Weston always lights the place up before she retires for the day. And then we just let the fire burn itself out."

Clara marveled again at the lifestyle the Dunbartons enjoyed. The lifestyle Hank might enjoy someday, if he wanted. She just couldn't jibe the life he'd led so far with the one that awaited him. Every year it was going to be harder to tear him away from this and get him to return to their modest life in Georgia. Living here was like living in a Hallmark Christmas card, Clara thought. Until she sat down on the sofa and noticed there wasn't a single present under the tree.

"Someone needs to start shopping," she said. "There are only twenty-two shopping days left until Christmas."

Grant smiled as he placed the bottle of wine on the end table beside him. "No worries. We stopped exchanging gifts years ago. Bonuses for the servants, doormen and concierge, but that's about it."

"You and Francesca don't exchange gifts?"

He seemed to find the question odd. "No."

Maybe when people reached a certain income bracket where they didn't really need anything anymore, they stopped buying Christmas presents for each other. Clara supposed it was possible. But it seemed unlikely. There was more to Christmas than getting stuff, and there was more to gift giving than simply supplying someone with an essential item—or even a luxury.

Gifts under a Christmas tree weren't meant to replace love and attention. They were meant to symbolize it. That was why even the poorest families struggled to put *some*thing under the tree. To show the other members that they were important and cherished. To find an empty Christmas tree in a home like the Dunbartons', who should find gift giving effortless and enjoyable, was just… Well, it was kind of heartbreaking, truth be told.

"Why not?" she asked. She told herself she should just let it go. It was none of her business why Grant and Francesca didn't exchange gifts. For some reason, it just bothered her that they didn't. A lot.

But he didn't seem bothered at all. He just shrugged and said, "I don't know. We just don't. We haven't since…" He thought for a minute, clearly not able to even remember when the tradition came to a halt. "I guess since Brent left home. He always bought gifts for me and Mom, so we always got him something. After he left, we just…didn't do it anymore."

Meaning that, if it hadn't been for Brent, they would have stopped even before then.

"But there should always be gifts under a Christmas tree," Clara objected. "Even if there are only a few. It's naked without them."

Grant didn't seem to take offense. "Okay. I'll tell the service who decorates for us that next year, they should wrap some boxes and put them under the tree when they finishing decorating it to add to the holiday mood."

Clara gaped at that. "You don't even put up your own Christmas tree?"

He shook his head. "Mom hires a service to do that every year."

Clara gaped wider. "There are people who get paid to put up other people's Christmas trees?"

"Sure. And the wreaths and the garlands and everything else." When he finally realized how appalled she was by the concept of a Christmas-for-hire, he added, "I mean, they do use our stuff. We're not renting from them the way a lot of people do."

"People *rent* their Christmas?" Clara asked, outraged. Why bother decorating at all if you weren't going to do it yourself?

Instead of being offended by her tone, Grant just shrugged again. "Welcome to the twenty-first century, Clara. And to New York City. A lot of people like to have their houses decorated because they entertain friends or clients. But they don't want the hassle of doing it themselves."

"But putting up the tree is the best part of Christmas. Well, after opening presents, at least." Then she thought about that some more. "No, it is the best part. It still feels Christmassy before and after the presents are opened. But it can't feel Christmassy without a tree."

"I bet Hank's favorite part is the presents."

Clara shook her head. "Oh, don't get me wrong. He loves the loot. But that part only lasts one day. The tree stays up for a month. And decorating it is easily the funnest thing of all. Don't you miss that part?"

"What part?"

"How every year, when you take out the ornaments, you remember some of them you forgot you had, and then you remember where you got them and what you were doing then and how much has changed. Putting up a Christmas tree is like revisiting your whole life every year."

Grant looked dubious. "Correct me if I'm wrong, but you and Hank have only had…what? Four Christmases together?"

"But even before Hank," she said, "I always put up a tree, starting with my freshman year in college. My dorm mates and I pooled our funds and bought a tree, and we found ornaments at thrift shops and discount stores. We split them up after we graduated. I still have mine," she added. "And when I put them on our tree every year, I remember those dorm mates and being in college, and that first breath of freedom where I could do anything I wanted without permission." She smiled. "Like put up a Christmas tree in my own place, with my own stuff, and if I fell in love with one of the ornaments, no one could say it didn't belong to me so I couldn't take it with me when I went to live somewhere else."

Grant had been smiling while she talked, but he sobered at that. "Did that happen to you?"

She hesitated, wondering why she had even brought the incident up. Wondering, too, why it still hurt nearly twenty years after the fact. "Yeah," she said softly. "When I was eight. Looking back, the ornament wasn't all that great, really. A little plastic Rudolph with a broken leg whose red nose had been rubbed white over the years. I painted him a new one with some red nail polish, and I glued his leg back on with way more glue than was necessary, so it left a gigantic lump. Then I put him back on the tree and admired him every day. I don't know why I loved him so much. I guess I felt kind of responsible for him or something. I was moved to a new place the week before Christmas that year, and

I wanted so badly to take him with me. But my foster mother said no."

"Why?"

This time Clara was the one to shrug. "I don't know. She didn't say. A lot of questions I asked back then never got answered, though. It wasn't unusual."

He looked as if he wanted to say something else, but instead, he only gazed at her in silence. Long enough that the air around them began to grow warm. Long enough that she thought again he might kiss her. Long enough that she wished he would.

"Um, I should go check on Hank and Francesca," she said. "If he likes a story enough, he wants it read over and over again, and it can get kind of annoying."

She stood before Grant had a chance to say anything and hurried out of the living room. Only after she was heading down the hall toward Hank's room—she meant Brent's old room—did she realize she hadn't even tasted the glass of wine Grant had poured for her.

# Eight

Grant went into the office the day after his and Clara's heart-to-heart by the Christmas tree, even though it was a Saturday. Not because he had a lot of things to do he hadn't finished during the week. On the contrary, things slowed down a lot between Thanksgiving and New Year's. He just figured he would take advantage of the weekend to catch up on some email and other things. It had nothing to do with how he wanted to avoid Clara, because she might still look the way she had last night. Not just when she'd shown her distress that the Dunbartons didn't do Christmas the traditional way. But when she told him about the Rudolph ornament at her old foster home. She might as well have been eight years old again, being shuttled to a new, strange place, so lost and lonely had she seemed in that moment.

Once he arrived home, Grant still wanted to avoid her, and for the same reasons. He sighed as he tossed his briefcase onto his bed and then went about the motions of undressing. After slipping into a pair of dark wash jeans and a coffee-colored sweater, he headed to the library for a bourbon. The rug cleaners had already come and gone, and the carpet looked good as new again. Well, okay, good as a hundred years old again. He poured a couple of fingers of Woodford Reserve into a cut crystal tumbler and headed out to the living room. It, too, looked exactly as it had the night before, minus Clara, a glaring absence that made the whole room seem off somehow. He was about to turn and make his way somewhere else, somewhere that wasn't so quiet, when his gaze lit on something that hadn't been in the room the night before—four gifts under the Christmas tree, each wrapped in a different color of foil paper, topped with curly ribbon.

Although he was sure he knew who had left them there, he couldn't help moving to the tree for a closer look. When he stooped, he saw that each bore a tag and that two were for him and two were for his mother. The larger ones were from Clara, the smaller ones were from Hank. Not that Grant thought for a moment that Hank had shopped and paid for them. But he wouldn't be surprised if Clara had asked the boy for final approval.

He set his drink on the floor and reached for the gift that was addressed to him from Clara. It was cube-shaped, large enough to hold a basketball and heavy. Unable to help himself, he gave it a gentle shake. Nothing. Whatever was in there, she'd packed it well enough to keep it from moving. He replaced it and lifted the one to him from Hank. It was square and flat and much lighter. But it, too, was silent when he gave it a shake. He set it next to the other one, palmed his drink and stood.

Damn. Should he give gifts to them in return? Not that Grant minded giving gifts. He just didn't want to brave the crowds to shop for them. Especially since he had no idea what to get a three-year-old boy. Or Clara, for that matter. The only time he'd bought gifts for women, they were to make up for some oversight. A date he'd forgotten, a wrong word at the wrong time, taking too long to return a call, something like that. He generally bought jewelry, because that was always a safe bet with women. At least, it was for the women he dated. Clara, though... For one thing, she didn't seem to wear much jewelry. For another, jewelry seemed like the kind of thing you gave a woman when you didn't know what else to get her. It was his go-to gift because he'd never wanted to work that hard to figure a woman out. Clara, though...

Clara. For some reason, he did want to figure her out. He just had no idea how to go about it. And he couldn't help thinking it would be a bad idea to try. Because the more he'd learned about her over the past few days, the more he'd liked her. And the more he'd wanted to learn. And he just couldn't risk getting involved with her, not when he wouldn't be able to make a clean break after whatever happened between them came to an end.

Because it would come to an end. It always came to an end. Grant wasn't the kind of man to make a long-term commitment to a woman. Not when he already had a long-term commitment to his work. Besides, in spite of the undeniable attraction he and Clara felt for each other, they weren't well suited. She'd made clear she wanted what she considered a "real" life for her son, one in her small town, surrounded by simple pleasures. She wanted to temper her work with play and her reality with dreams and her sense with sensibility. And that just wasn't Grant's way. At all.

Sure, they could potentially engage in a sexual liaison. Sure, it could potentially be incredible. But it wouldn't last. He was sure of that, too. He and Clara were too different from each other, and they both wanted entirely different things from life. Getting involved with each other would only make life more difficult for them both when their paths inevitably—and regularly—crossed in the future.

The living room, like the library, was too quiet. The whole house was too quiet. Where was everybody?

He wandered into the kitchen to find it empty, though there were signs someone had been snacking in here not long ago. There were cookie crumbs on the counter, and an empty milk glass in the sink. Suddenly, he heard laughter that sounded as if it was coming from the dining room. He headed in that direction and found Clara and Hank lying on the floor on the other side of the expansive table, gazing up at the planets on the ceiling. Clara was pointing at one of them, and Hank was still laughing at something one of them must have said.

Neither of them had seen or heard him come in, so Grant stood still and silent in the doorway, watching them. Hank was already in his pajamas, blue ones dotted with some cartoon character Grant had never seen, and Clara was in a pale green sweater and blue jeans. But the sweater was cropped at the waist, and riding higher because of the position of her arm, revealing a tantalizing bit of naked torso between its hem and the waistband of her jeans. Grant did his best not to notice how— Oh, hell, no he didn't. He zoomed right in on the milky skin and wondered if it felt as soft as it looked.

"No, not Plu-*toad*," Clara said, sending Hank into

another fit of giggles. "Plu-*toh*." But she was laughing, too, by the time she finished.

"I think it should be Plu-toad," Hank said. "And only frogs should live there."

"You know, Hank" Grant said, "frogs and toads aren't the same thing."

Both Hank and Clara scrambled up off the floor as if it had caught fire, looking guiltily at each other before turning to Grant.

"Don't worry," he hurried to tell them. "I used to lie in here looking at that ceiling all the time. Go back to what you were doing."

"That's okay," Clara said. "We were finished."

"Anyway," Grant said to Hank, "If you want frogs to live there, you should call it Plu-frog."

That made the boy giggle again, which gave Grant an odd sense of satisfaction. He didn't recall having put *Make a child laugh* on his bucket list, but now that he'd accomplished the feat, it seemed like something everyone should attempt at least once. It felt kind of good, having done it.

When it seemed as if none of them was going to ever speak again, Grant said, "So I noticed someone left some presents under the Christmas tree today."

"We did!" Hank cried. "Mama and me went out this morning and—"

Clara clamped a gentle hand over her son's mouth and shot him a meaningful look. "And got coffee," she finished for him. "Right, sweetie?"

Hank hesitated, and then nodded vigorously, so she removed her hand. "Right," he agreed. "Mama got coffee, and I got hot chocolate. And then we didn't—"

Clara clamped her hand over his mouth again. "We have no idea how those gifts got under the tree."

"Funny," Grant said, "the tags said they were from you and Hank."

Clara and her son exchanged another look, this one full of comical wide-eyed innocence. Then they both shook their heads in exactly the same way and stretched out their arms in identical comical shrugs. Then they looked at Grant again.

"No clue," Clara said.

"No clue," Hank echoed.

"Then I guess it would be okay if I open mine now?" Grant asked.

Clara shook her head. "No, that would not be okay. You have to wait until Christmas morning, just like everyone else."

"I can't even open it Christmas Eve?" he asked.

"Don't worry, Uncle Grant," Hank said. "Mama never lets me open my presents till Christmas morning, either." He threw his mother a chastising look as he added, "Even though *all* my friends get to open one on Christmas Eve."

"Oh, and if all your friends jumped off a bridge, would you do that, too?" Clara asked him.

"Maybe," Hank told her. "If it was on Plu-toad!" He punctuated the statement with a childish laugh. Clearly this was high humor for three-year-olds.

Actually, Grant wanted to laugh, too, but Clara gave her son a stern look that silenced them both...until she groaned and started laughing, too. Then the three of them made a few more jokes about Plu-toad, until the humor just became so weird, only a three-year-old—or a couple of especially silly adults—could understand it.

"Enough," Clara finally said to her son with one last breathless chuckle. "You're never going to get to sleep tonight. Go brush your teeth and tell Grammy good-night. If she doesn't have time to read you a story, I can. But bedtime is in thirty minutes!" she called after him as he scampered off. "I mean it, Hank!"

She looked exhausted when she turned back to Grant. "He's been sneaking out of his room...I mean, Brent's room...after bedtime to watch TV with your mother. He's fallen in love with *Oliver and Company*, which is probably one of the movies Disney just stuck back in the vault, so I won't be able to find it on Tybee Island, or it will cost a fortune on eBay, so I won't be able to afford it, which is just one more way your mother will lure us back here. I don't know which one of them I want to ground more."

Grant smiled. "Take away her Bergdorf's card for a week. That'll teach her."

Instead of laughing, Clara sat down on the floor and lay back again to gaze up at the ceiling. Not sure what made him do it—maybe it was the way her sweater rode up again—Grant lay down beside her.

And looked up at the star- and planet-studded ceiling from that vantage point for the first time in twenty years. Wow. He'd forgotten how much cooler it was from this angle. He really could almost pretend he was lying in a field out in the middle of nowhere, the way he had done when he was a child.

"We have to go home in two days," Clara said abruptly.

The comment surprised him, even though she wasn't telling him anything he didn't already know. Somehow, it just felt as if she and Hank had been here for months. It felt as if they should be here for more months. Surprising, too, was how melancholy she sounded about going home. She'd made no secret of her fear that Hank wouldn't want to leave after spending time with his grandmother. Grant would have thought Clara would be relieved to be going home in a few days. Of course, he thought he'd be relieved about that, too, since it meant he would stop entertaining such ridiculous ideas about the two of them. But he didn't feel any more relieved than she sounded.

"Maybe you can come back after the holidays," he said, intending the comment to be casual and perfunctory. Realizing after he said it that it was actually serious and hopeful.

She said nothing at first, just looked up at the stars. Then she turned her head to look at him full on. She was so close. And her eyes were so green. Her black curls were piled on the floor, scant inches away, close enough for him to reach over and wind one around his finger. Would it be as silky as it looked? It was all Grant could do not to find out for himself.

"It's going to break Hank's heart to leave," she said. "He's fallen in love with your mother, and she's been so wonderful with him. And between his school and my work, it's going to be summer before we can get back for a visit."

"What about spring break?"

She shook her head. "Too close to Easter. It's super busy at the bakery then. No way could I take the time off. Especially after taking this week at Christmastime."

"Then Mom can come visit Hank in Georgia."

Clara looked fairly panicked at that.

"Is that a problem?" he asked.

"Well, our apartment is just so small. There's only the two bedrooms. And only one bathroom. No way would Francesca be comfortable staying with us."

Grant smiled. Of course Clara would assume that family would want to stay with, well, family. "She'd stay in a hotel, Clara. They do have hotels on Tybee Island, I assume?"

Clara nodded earnestly, thinking he was serious about asking if there were hotels in a popular seaside destination.

"She'd probably prefer that, anyway," he said. "She does like her room service."

For some reason, that made Clara look even more panicked. "Hank might want to stay with her at the hotel. He loves hotels. We hardly ever get to stay in one. Especially the kind that have room service. He'd be thrilled."

"Then his staying with Mom would give you some time to yourself. Surely, it would be nice to have a break."

She sighed and looked at the ceiling again. "Yeah."

Funny, she didn't sound as if she thought it would be nice.

She was still worried about losing Hank to the Dunbarton lifestyle. Still worried his mother would take her place in Hank's heart. Which was crazy because, number one, no child who had a relationship like Hank clearly did with Clara would put anyone else before his mother. And number two—

Number two, Grant really, really wanted to tangle his fingers in her hair and trace the elegant line of her jaw with his fingertip, and then, when she looked at him again, roll toward her and cover her mouth with his, and then cover her body with his, and then—

"Breaks are good, right?" she said softly. She was still gazing at the stars overhead, but she seemed to be seeing something else entirely.

It took him a minute to rewind to the point in the conversation when they'd been talking about his mother visiting her and Hank in Georgia. But even when he remembered, the thought fell by the wayside, because he was still too focused on one strand of hair that had stayed pressed against her cheek when she turned her head to look back up at the ceiling.

Without thinking about what he was doing, he reached across the few inches separating them and tucked a finger beneath the sable curl. He told himself it was just to free it from her skin—her luscious, glorious skin—since hair stuck in place like that could be pretty damned annoying. But his gesture left the back of his knuckle pressed against her cheek—her luscious, glorious cheek—and the moment he realized her skin was indeed as soft as it looked, he couldn't quite pull his hand away again. Instead, he grazed his finger lightly along the elegant line of her jaw, once, twice, three times, four, even after the strand of hair had fallen away.

At first, he thought he must be touching her so lightly that Clara didn't even notice he was doing it. Then he glimpsed a hint of pink blooming on her cheek and noted how the pulse at the base of her neck leaped higher. Her lips parted softly, and her chest rose and fell with her more rapid respiration. Grant noted then how his own breathing had hitched higher, how his own heart was racing and how heat was percolating beneath his own skin, too. When she turned her head again to look at him, her pupils were expanded, her cheeks were ruddy and her lips parted wider, as if she would absolutely welcome whatever he wanted to do. And what Grant wanted to do in that moment, what he wanted more than anything in the world, what he wanted more than he'd ever wanted anything in his life was to…

Slowly, he pulled his hand away from her face and settled it on his chest. "Your hair," he said, having to push the words out of his mouth as if they were two-ton boulders. "It…it was caught on your, um…your cheek."

Clara continued to gaze at him in silence, looking as if she couldn't remember any better than he did where they were or what they were supposed to be doing.

He tried again. "I just wanted to, um… I know how damned annoying that can be."

She nodded slowly, but said nothing for another charged moment. Then, softly, she told him, "Thanks. Yeah. I hate when that happens."

But she didn't stop staring at him. And she didn't stop looking sensuous and desirable and hot as hell. And he didn't stop wanting to…

He had to stop thinking about her this way. It really was ridiculous, his pointless preoccupation with Clara. He should be happy she was leaving in a few days. After she was gone, he could go back to being preoccupied with other things. Things that were actually important. Like work. And also work. And then there was work. And he couldn't forget about work. All of which were really important, something he wished Clara could understand. Maybe if she realized just how important his work was, she wouldn't be so quick to dismiss a position at Dunbarton Industries, working toward CEO, as a possible future for Hank. Who knew? Maybe the boy would end up being more like his mother than his father and actually enjoy running a business. Just because it might not be the business he originally wanted to run… Just because it wasn't, say, Keep Our Oceans Klean… Hank could adapt.

"It's good that you're here now, though," Grant told her. "And you know, it just occurred to me that the company holiday party is tomorrow night."

Which actually hadn't just occurred to him. He'd

known it was on his schedule for some time. And he'd thought about asking Clara if she wanted to come, but had decided she wouldn't want to because of her less than warm and fuzzy feelings about the corporate world. Suddenly, though, for some reason, inviting her seemed like a really good idea. For Hank's sake. Not for Grant's.

"It's a family friendly event," he added. "We encourage all of our employees to bring their spouses and kids. I'm sorry I didn't invite you before now. I wasn't sure you'd be interested. Mom and I go every year. Kind of necessary for us, me being the boss and her being on the board of directors. But you and Hank should come this year, too. You can see what Dunbarton Industries is really all about."

"You mean I can see what Hank's legacy could be," she amended.

"Okay, that, too," he admitted. "Maybe you'll see that it's not as joyless and relentless as you think."

She sighed softly, meeting his gaze earnestly now, something that somehow made her seem even more accessible than her heated looks had a moment ago. Something that somehow doubled his desire to reach for her.

He really, really had to stop thinking stuff like that.

"I truly am sorry about saying that, Grant. I didn't mean I thought you were like that."

Yeah, she did. But maybe her coming to the party would change her mind. Instead of saying that, though, he only said, "Apology accepted." Then, because she still hadn't accepted—or declined—his invitation, he asked, "So do you and Hank want to come to the holiday party with me and Mom?"

She hesitated only a moment—but it was still a moment, which was telling in itself—then replied, "Sure.

Why not? It's probably the only holiday party I'll get to attend this year. With grown-ups, anyway. I'm going to be swamped at the bakery after we get back." Then she smiled, and her distress seemed to evaporate. "Thanks for inviting us, Grant."

She was thanking him? For what? He was the one who had just received a gift in the form of her acceptance. And it was the nicest gift he'd received in years.

"It'll be fun," he told her. Which was something he always automatically said about the Dunbarton holiday party, even though he never meant it. This year, he did mean it. And for that, he was grateful to Clara Easton, too.

Okay, so the corporate headquarters of Dunbarton Industries wasn't as sterile and soul-sucking as Clara had assumed it would be before her first visit here with Francesca. So the main offices looked as if they'd been designed by Frank Lloyd Wright, with open spaces, organic lines, satiny woodwork and sleek Prairie School furnishings. So Grant made sure that a sizeable chunk of the company's profits went toward making its employees more comfortable and happier in their work environment. She still couldn't see Hank working here someday.

But then, she couldn't really see Grant working here today. As nice as the place was, and as upright, forthright and do-right as he was, he still seemed out of place here, even after having helmed the corporation for nearly a decade, and even though his employees clearly liked him. Francesca, yes, Clara thought. She was totally at home here, not just amid the polished, sophisticated surroundings, but also in flitting from one person to another, saying hello and chattering about their work and their families and ensuring that everyone was happy at their jobs in general and having a good time this evening. But Grant?

Although he, too, had spent much of the evening moving from one person to another to speak to them all, there had been no flitting or chattering on his part. He'd seemed reserved without being standoffish, serious without being stodgy and businesslike without being self-important. Which, okay, were all good traits for a boss to have.

He still seemed out of place here.

And Clara felt out of place, too, even having been here twice now. She just wasn't used to being in a workplace that was so...clean. Her professional environment was always scattered with utensils and dusted with flour and sugar. Stains in a rainbow of colors were an integral part of any shift. By the end of her workday, there was confectionary chaos to clean up, and she was a sticky mess. And she liked it that way. All of it.

She would never go into her workplace dressed as she had for the party tonight, in a formfitting, claret-colored, off-the-shoulder velvet cocktail dress and pearl necklace and earrings—even if they were faux. And black stilettos? Uh-uh. Not unless she wanted to break her neck on some spilled pastilles or frosting.

Grant, however, wore another one of his dark power suits and looked perfectly normal—if not quite comfortable—in it. His only nods to festivity were in his necktie—one that was dark red and spattered with tiny bits of holly—and a small boutonniere of evergreen and berries that his mother had affixed to his lapel before they left the penthouse.

He'd been much less restrained with the office decorations—or, at least, whomever he'd put in charge of decorating had been, but they'd obviously met with his approval. Everywhere Clara looked, she saw signs of the season. A giant Christmas tree in the corner was lit up like, well, a Christmas tree. A shiny silver menorah was ready for lighting when Hanukkah began. Not far from it was set up an mkeka for Kwanzaa, along with a kinara set to be lit the day after Christmas. She'd learned a lot about Kwanzaa as the room mom planning the holiday party for Hank's class last year and through orders at the bakery. And the oversize ice bucket with the magnum of champagne had to be for New Year's. Someone had even installed a plain metal pole for the observers of Festivus. The only decorations Clara hadn't been able to figure out yet were the—

"Pentacles?" she asked Grant, who had affixed himself to her side since concluding his rounds of guest-mongering. He was lifting for a sip from the tumbler of bourbon he'd been nursing all night before lowering it again to look at Clara with confusion.

"What pentacles?" he asked.

She gestured toward the display on the other side of the room near the rest of the holiday icons.

"Oh, those pentacles," he said. "For Solstice. The incense, too. Don't want to leave out the Wiccans."

"I wondered what that was I smelled."

"Mostly frankincense and myrrh, I think," he said.

"Which brings it all full circle," Clara replied with a smile.

She was about to say something more about how there really were a lot of December holidays when Hank ran up, clutching a misshapen paper star that was painted bright purple, sprinkled with neon pink glitter and tied with a chartreuse ribbon. He thrust it up toward her.

"Mama, look! Another ordament for our Christmas tree!"

"Or-*na*-ment," Clara corrected him automatically as she took the star from him, knowing she'd probably be correcting him another dozen times before Christmas actually arrived. "And it's beautiful, sweetie. I like the colors you picked."

"The or-*na*-ment lady helping us said we could pick whatever colors we want. I made another one that's orange and blue, but it's still drying."

Clara held up the ornament for Grant to see. "Now every year when we hang this on the tree, I'll think back on this moment and remember I was standing here with you when we got it."

It was true. Every year, when she or Hank hung it on the tree, she would be thinking fondly about the time she had spent with Grant this year, even if nothing ever came of it. She also knew she would be thinking about how she wished something *had* come of it, something that went beyond fondness, because that way, she would have another memory to carry with her.

Hank fairly beamed. "I made the other one for Grammy. Now she can think about me every year when she hangs it on her tree."

Without awaiting a reply, he spun around and ran back toward the room where the party organizers had set up the children's crafts. Which was just as well, since Clara had no idea how to tell him that his grandmother hired out their tree decorating, so she wasn't sure his star would even make it onto the Dunbarton tree. Though maybe now that Francesca had an original work of art from her grandson, she'd go back to doing their trimming the old-fashioned way.

"I guarantee you that Hank's star will be on our

tree every year," Grant said, clearly knowing what she was thinking. "And it will probably hang somewhere in Mom's office or bedroom the rest of the time."

Clara smiled. "Thanks. I kind of figured that, but it's nice to hear reassurance." She looked at the star again, then at the tiny cocktail purse she'd brought with her. "Now if I could just figure out what to do with it till we go home, so it doesn't get wrinkled. Well, any more wrinkled," she amended with a sigh.

"Here, let me have it," Grant said.

He took it from her hand and draped the loop of ribbon around his boutonniere, so that the garishly painted paper star—larger than his hand—dangled on his chest against his expensive suit for all the world to see. And if Clara hadn't already been halfway in lo— Uh, if Clara hadn't already been halfway enamored of him, that gesture would have finally put her there.

"There," he said. "That should keep it safe for the rest of the evening."

Yes, it should, she thought. Now if only Grant would do the same thing for her heart.

# Nine

It was nearly midnight by the time the partygoers left for home. Hank was sacked before the car pulled away from the curb, so when they arrived back at the penthouse, Clara handed him over to Grant to carry upstairs. Hank murmured sleepily at the transfer, then looped his arms around his uncle's neck, nestled against his shoulder and fell asleep again. Clara tried not to notice how easily Hank curled into Grant or marvel at how much trust he had placed in him in such a short time. Instead, she battled another wave of affection for the man who had won that trust and showed such tenderness for her son.

Grant carried him effortlessly up to the penthouse and, after Francesca murmured her good-night to her grandson and gave him a kiss on the cheek, continued the journey back to Hank's...or rather, his father's—why did Clara keep making that mistake?—old bedroom and laid him carefully on the bed. Then she removed Hank's shoes and the little clip-on necktie decorated with snowmen that his grandmother had bought for him—she'd also bought his little man suit that was a miniature version of Grant's—and tucked him in. It was no problem to let him sleep in his clothes. Hank wouldn't be wearing them again before they went home. Tomorrow, she thought further. No, today, she realized when she noted the time on the little rocket ship clock sitting on the nightstand. Which had arrived much too quickly.

In fact, she might as well just leave Hank's new outfit here, since she couldn't see him having an opportunity on Tybee Island to dress like a tiny businessman—unless it was for Halloween. But she could see Francesca finding lots of reasons for Hank to dress like his uncle here in New York.

Clara swallowed against a lump in her throat, brushed back his dark curls and pressed a light kiss to his forehead. She whispered, "Good night, Peanut," which was the nickname she'd given him when he appeared on her first ultrasound looking like one, but which she hadn't used since she'd decided on a name for him, before he was even born. Then she turned toward the bedroom door to leave.

She was surprised to see Grant leaning in the doorway, waiting for her, but was happy that he had stayed. As exhausted as she was from the evening and the hectic week before it, she was entirely too wound up to sleep. Or maybe it was something else that had put her in that state. Some churning eddy of emotions that wouldn't stay still long enough for her to identify any of them, but which were pounding against her brain and heart with the ferocity of a tsunami.

"Nightcap?" Grant asked when she was within whispering distance.

"Oh, yes. Please."

She followed him to the library and waited while he fixed their drinks. He poured a bourbon for himself, then reached into the wine rack for what was sure to be another very nice red for her. But Clara halted him. A very nice red wasn't going to cut it for her tonight.

"I'll have what you're having," she told him when the bottle was barely halfway out of its slot.

He looked surprised, but tucked the wine back into its resting place and tugged free the cork from the bourbon again instead. She watched as he splashed a few swallows of the amber liquor into a cut crystal tumbler like his—at home, Clara would have poured a drink like that into a juice glass decorated with daisies whose paint was beginning to fleck—and looked at her for approval. She shook her head.

"I'll have what you're having," she repeated. "Same generous two-and-a-half fingers."

"Okay," he said, pouring in a bit more. "Funny, but I didn't take you for a bourbon drinker."

"Normally, I'm not," she said. "But nothing in my life has been normal since August Fiver showed up at the bakery."

And nothing in her life would ever be normal again. That, really, was the reason Clara needed something a little more bracing tonight. She didn't know if it had been seeing Hank dressed like a little millionaire, or how out of place she'd felt in Dunbarton Industries' offices, or how out of place she still felt here in the penthouse, or a combination of all of those things and a million more to boot. But tonight, more than ever before, Clara felt the need for something to dull a reality that was too fast closing in. Her son had become part of a world that wasn't her own, and he would be spending much of his future living a life that had nothing in common with hers. And it would be that way forever.

When Grant turned around holding both their drinks, looking as much a resident of this alien world as her son was now, Clara realized he was part of the problem, too. Because over the past week, especially the past few days, it had become clear that Grant didn't belong in this world, either. Not really. He may have been born to it, and he may be reasonably comfortable in it, but he wasn't truly, genuinely happy here. As a child, he'd had much different plans for himself, and passions that had nothing to do with the existence he was plodding through now. He was living his life out of obligation, not because it was the one he had chosen for himself. With each new day, that had become more clear.

But what was also clear was that he had no intention of leaving it.

Clara thought back to the way he'd been when he answered the front door upon her and Hank's arrival. Had that been only seven days ago? It felt like a lifetime had passed since she had stepped over the Dunbarton threshold. Grant's reception that day had been formal and awkward, and he'd seemed to have no idea how to react to Clara *or* Hank. Since then, he'd taught her about aquarium fish, had made jokes about Plu-toad and had lain on the floor, gazing up at the stars with her. And tonight, he'd hung a gaudy child's creation from his lapel as if it were the Congressional Medal of Honor. That first day, he hadn't seemed capable of laughter or whimsy. That first day, he hadn't seemed capable of happiness. But tonight...

She looked at the star, still dangling from his lapel,

then at the careless smile on his face. Tonight, he seemed very happy indeed. And Clara would bet everything she had in the world that it wasn't because the office holiday party had gone off without a hitch. It was because, at some point over the past few days, Grant had gotten in touch with something in himself that had reminded him what his life could have been like if he hadn't turned his back on his childhood to dive headfirst into adulthood decades before he should have. Maybe it was having Hank around that had done that. Or maybe it was something else. Clara just hoped Grant kept in touch with that part of himself after she and Hank were gone.

They made their way into the living room in time to see Francesca in front of the Christmas tree, admiring the star from Hank that she had hung on it front and center. She turned when she heard them approach, and she was smiling, too.

"You know," she said, "maybe next year we should put up the tree and decorate the house ourselves instead of hiring the service."

"I think that's an excellent idea," Grant told her.

He unlooped the star from his boutonniere and placed it beside the one Francesca had hung. "Just for now," he told Clara. "You can take it home with you tomorrow. But they do look good there together."

"Yes, they do," Clara had to admit. She was going to hate breaking the two of them up.

Francesca looked at Clara. "Maybe you and Hank could come for Thanksgiving next year," she said. "And we could all decorate the day after. That's when the service usually comes."

Clara started to decline, since it had been tough enough to swing a trip during the holidays this year. But the hopeful look on Francesca's face made her hesitate. The bakery was closed on Thanksgiving—and on Mondays, too, for that matter—and it wasn't especially busy the day after, since most people had so many leftovers and were out raiding the shopping malls. She could maybe close that weekend, too, without taking too big a financial hit. Things didn't really start hopping until a few weeks before Christmas. Her employees would probably like having the extra time off after Thanksgiving, too. It might be possible.

"Let me crunch some numbers," she told Francesca. "And look at the calendar for next year. I'll see what I can do."

Francesca smiled. "It would be lovely to have you both here. Grant and I usually go out for Thanksgiving dinner, since Mrs. Bentley has the day off. But we could have her prepare something the day before and put it all in the fridge. Then we'd just have to heat it up."

Clara shook her head. "I'll do the cooking on Thanksgiving." Hastily, she amended, "I mean, I *would* do the cooking on Thanksgiving. If we're able to come. Which I'll see if we can."

Francesca looked both delighted and a little appalled. "But that's so much to do! And you don't want to have to work on a holiday."

"It wouldn't be work for me," Clara said, knowing that was true. "I enjoy it. I always cook for Hank and me and some of our friends who spend Thanksgiving with us."

Funny, but she suspected that, as much fun as it was to cook for friends, she'd enjoy it even more cooking for family. Even if the Dunbartons weren't, technically, her family. They were Hank's family. So, in a way, that made them her family, too. Extended family. But still family. Kind of. In a way. More than anyone else had ever been family to her.

Francesca smiled again. "That really would be lovely," she said.

She told them both good-night and cautioned them not to stay up too late, because she had plans for Clara and Hank tomorrow before they headed to the airport in the late afternoon. Clara waited for the internal cringing that usually came with the prospect of enduring more of Francesca's gadabout tourism, but it never materialized. Interesting. Or maybe not. In spite of not belonging here in the Dunbarton world, Clara was beginning to kind of like it. New York had turned out to be not such a scary place, after all. And Central Park, right across the street, was as lush and bucolic as anything she'd ever found in Georgia. Hank could still climb trees here, even if he couldn't pick fresh peaches from them. And he could still go barefoot from time to time. And who knew? Maybe there were even fireflies in the summer that he could catch in a jar.

As she and Grant moved to sit on the sofa, he loosened his tie and unbuttoned the top two buttons of his shirt, then shrugged off his jacket and tossed it over the arm. Clara toed off first one high heel, then the other, immediately after sitting down. It was then that she noticed the additional gifts under the tree. The last time she'd been in here, there had been only the four she and Hank secretly placed there. Now there seemed to be dozens.

"Wow. Francesca's been busy," she said.

Then she noted that the tag on the gift nearest her was addressed to Hank from "Uncle Grant."

"She even did some shopping for you," she added.

Grant looked mildly offended. "Hey, I'll have you know I did my own shopping."

Clara was even more surprised. He hadn't asked her for suggestions as to what Hank would like. That first day, he hadn't even seemed to know how to talk to a three-year-old. Now he was Christmas shopping for one? He really had come a long way over the past week.

"I'm sure he'll love whatever you got him," she said.

"Yes, he will," Grant replied with complete confidence.

"It was nice of you to think of him," Clara said. Then she looked at the pile of gifts again. "It was nice of Francesca, too."

She didn't add that Francesca shouldn't have overdone it the way she had. Somehow Clara knew Hank's grandmother would always overdo it where he was concerned. Funny, though, how that didn't bother her quite as much as it would have a week ago.

"Hank won't know what to think when he sees that all those gifts are for him," Clara said.

"Well, not *all* of them are for him," Grant told her.

Right. There were the ones from Hank and Clara to Grant and Francesca under there, too. Somewhere.

"I just hope you and Francesca like yours from us as much as I'm sure Hank will like his from y'all."

Grant said nothing in response to that, only gazed at her looking... Hmm. Actually, he was looking kind of smug. Happily smug. Maybe he'd had more to drink at the party than she'd thought.

Clara lifted her own drink to her lips and sipped carefully, letting the bourbon warm her mouth before swallowing, relishing the heat of the liquor as it passed through her throat and into her stomach, spreading warmth throughout her chest. "Oh, yeah," she mur-

mured. "That's what I needed. It has been such a—"
She stopped before saying that it had been such a long
week. Because, suddenly, the week hadn't seemed long
at all. She and Hank really were leaving much too soon.
Finally, she finished, "Such a busy week."

"I guess you'll be happy to get back home," Grant
said softly. "Back to your routine."

Clara wanted to agree with him. And she did agree
with him. To a point. Yes, she would be happy to get
back to Tybee Island. She'd be happy for her and Hank's
lives to go back to normal. She'd be glad to get back
to work at the bakery. She'd even be glad to return to
their tiny apartment. Regardless of where or what it
was, there really was no place like home.

She should have been glad to be leaving New York.
But she actually kind of liked New York. Even more,
she kind of liked what New York had to offer. The parks
and museums and fun stuff, sure. And the lions at the
library and the pear blinis at the Russian Tea Room.
But more than any of those, Clara liked the Dunbartons.
Especially Grant Dunbarton. And even having only
been here for a short time, it was going to be strange
returning to the place where she had lived her entire
life. Because now she had experienced life away from
home. And strangely, life away from home, as weird
and foreign as it was, was starting to feel a little like,
well, home.

"Yes, it'll be nice to get back to Tybee Island," she
said. "But it'll also be…"

"What?" he asked when she didn't finish.

She sighed. "I don't know," she said honestly. "It
kind of feels like we'll be returning to a different place
from the one we left."

She was about to say more—though, honestly, she

still wasn't sure what she was thinking or feeling at the moment—when something over Grant's shoulder caught her eye. Beyond the windows, fat, frilly flakes of white were tumbling from the night sky.

"Oh, look, Grant! It's snowing!"

She set her drink on the end table and rose from the sofa, crossing to the window as if drawn there by a magic spell. Snow was magic. At least, in her part of Georgia it was. As rare a sighting as Santa Claus himself. The flurry of white seemed to pick up speed as she gazed through the glass, blowing first left, then right, then spinning in circles. Beyond the snow, the lights of New York sparkled merrily, making the scene even more entrancing.

She sensed more than saw Grant move alongside her at the window, but she couldn't quite tear her gaze away from the falling snow. Or maybe there was another reason she didn't want to do that, a fear that if she looked at him in that moment, she might very well succumb to the enchantment of the snow, of New York, of the Dunbarton world and of Grant himself. And Clara couldn't afford to be enchanted. Not by any of it. Because enchantments were only as good as their magic. And as bewitching as it was, at some point, magic always failed.

"It doesn't snow down in Georgia?" he asked softly.

She shook her head. And focused on the snow. Because it kept her from focusing on the soft velvet of his voice that was as magical as everything else.

"Not where I've lived," she told him, keeping her voice quiet, too. "Not much, anyway. For sure, it never did like this. I kind of hoped it would snow while we were here—for Hank, I mean," she quickly amended, even though it was only a half-truth, "but the weather was so mild when we got here, and then I didn't check again to see if it was going to stay that way or get colder." Not that it seemed to have gotten colder. On the contrary, it was getting warmer all the time…

But then, Clara hadn't checked a lot of things this week, she realized now. Not the weather, not the time, not—

She looked at Grant again. Not her heart. And now it seemed as if it might be too late for all those things. Unless…

Not sure why she did it, just knowing she had to, Clara cupped her hand over his cheek, pushed herself up on tiptoe and pressed her mouth to his. She had thought he would be surprised by the kiss. She certainly was, and she was the one who instigated it. But he returned it as swiftly and intimately as if it was something the two of them did all the time. Then he wrapped his arms around her waist and pulled her against him, seizing control of the embrace completely. And for the first time in her entire life, Clara knew what it was to feel as if she was home. Really home. In the place she belonged more than anywhere else in the world. Grant kissed her as if she were a part of him, a part he'd lost a long time ago and only just regained. He kissed her as if she was as essential to life as the air he breathed. He kissed her as if he couldn't not kiss her. So she looped her arms around his neck and kissed him deeper still.

She didn't know how long they stood there embracing in front of the window—maybe seconds, maybe centuries. She only knew she never wanted to move away from him again. He kissed her mouth, her temple, her cheek, her jaw, her neck. And when Clara tilted her head back to give him better access, he drew his mouth lower, along her bare shoulder and back again, over her collarbone and down her breastbone, skimming his lips over the top of one breast where it was revealed by her dress and then the other. She tangled her fingers in his hair and relished the feel of his warm breath against her sensitive flesh. Then she gasped when he cupped a hand over her breast.

He turned to move them out of the window, pressing her against the wall as he pushed his body into hers and kissed her more deeply still, covering her breast again, scrambling her thoughts and heating every part of her. When he raked his thumb over her nipple through the fabric, she tore her mouth from his and cried out. So he buried his head in the curve where her neck joined her shoulder and dragged open-mouthed kisses over both. Clara was so lost in sensation that she barely noticed when he dropped a hand to the hem of her dress. But when he tugged it up over her thigh, then her hip, and bunched it at her waist, she gripped the back of his shirt in both fists, holding on for dear life. Her legs nearly buckled beneath her, though, when he cupped a hand on her fanny over the lace of her panties.

"Oh, God, stop," she gasped. "Grant, we have to stop."

He lifted his head to look at her, and for a moment, it was as if he'd never seen her before and couldn't imagine how they had become so passionately entwined. Then realization must have come crashing down on him. Hastily, he removed his hand from her bottom and pulled her dress back down over her legs. But he didn't move away from her.

"Right," he whispered. His breathing was ragged and labored. "I guess it's not a good idea."

Clara smiled at that. "Oh, it's a very good idea," she assured him.

At least, it was right now. And *right now* was all she

wanted to think about. Because it was the only thing she could be absolutely sure of. And right now, she wanted Grant absolutely.

His gaze locked with hers. "You're sure?"

"Yes," she said. "This just isn't a good place for it. Let's go to your room." When he still didn't move, and only continued to study her face as if he couldn't quite believe she was real, she added softly, "Now, Grant. I want you now."

He nodded, then, with clear reluctance, pushed himself away from her. He took her hand in his and led her out of the living room and down the hall to the spiral staircase that led to the bedrooms below. Clara had no idea how she was able to make it without stumbling, so shaky was her entire body, but finally, finally, they made it to his bedroom. It was dark, save the soft blue light of the aquarium that threw wavy white lines on the wall behind it, giving the place an otherworldly aura that was strangely fitting. Clara felt as if she was in another world at the moment. One she never wanted to leave.

He closed the door behind them—locking it, she noted gratefully, clearly thinking about Hank sleeping so close by—then turned to her again. Before she could say a word, he pulled her back into his arms and kissed her, taking up exactly where they left off. Except this time, when he moved his head down to trail soft, butterfly kisses along her neck and shoulder, he tucked his fingers into the top of her dress and nudged it down to bare her breasts. As he covered one with a big hand, he dropped his other hand to her hem again, drawing the garment up over her thighs and hips once more. Blindly, Clara jerked his shirttail from his trousers and freed the buttons one by one, pushing it open so she could rake her fingertips over the warm skin beneath.

Grant Dunbarton may have been a workaholic, she thought as she touched him, but he clearly worked out, too. She traced the elegant cant of his biceps and triceps, then ran her fingers along the bumps of muscle on his shoulders, chest and torso until she reached the buckle of his belt. Instead of unfastening it, though, she drove her hand lower, over the swell of his erection beneath his trousers. He was already hard and ready for her. She need only unfasten his fly to enjoy him flesh on flesh. But she waited on that, pressing her hand against him to palm him through his clothing, marveling at how he grew harder still.

He pulled his mouth from hers and sucked in his breath at her caress, but didn't stop her. He only stroked her breast with sure fingers, thumbing the nipple and tracing the curve. Every time Clara moved her hand on him, he drew his thumb over her, until they were both panting with desire. Finally—quickly—she unbuckled and unzipped him, dipping her hand into his trousers and through the opening in his boxers to wrap her fingers around him. He was…oh. So hard. So stiff. So big. She drove her hand down the solid length of him, then pulled it back up again, loving the way his entire body reacted to the stroke. So she did it again. And again. And again.

Until he wrapped his fingers tight around her wrist and halted her motions. Until he told her, "Your turn."

Before she could object, he cupped his hands over both her shoulders and spun her around so she was facing away from him. Then he gripped the top of her zipper and lowered it until he could push her dress down over her hips and legs to puddle around her ankles. Her bra went just as quickly—a simple flick of his fingers did it—then he pulled her against him, back to chest, and looped an arm around her waist to anchor her there. Good thing, too, since the heavy weight of him pressing into her fanny through her underwear made her legs go weak.

He dipped his head to her neck again, skimming his lips lightly along her shoulder, then moved his free hand back to her breast. For long moments, he only held her close and caressed her, then he moved his hand lower…and lower…and lower still, easing his fingers into the juncture of her thighs. Then he was touching her there, through her panties, fingering the damp fabric and folds of flesh beneath, pushing and pulling to create a delicious friction she never wanted to end. As she grew wetter, he ducked his hand under the lacy garment and rubbed her more insistently, until his fingers were sliding against her and in and out of her with an easy rhythm. Clara matched it with her hips, pushing back against him when he entered her and levering forward when he withdrew, her bottom rubbing his erection with every motion.

As they moved that way, his breathing became as ragged as hers. Then he was pulling her panties down along with his trousers, rolling on a condom and sliding himself between her legs. Finally, he pushed himself into her as easily as he had done with his fingers. Only this time, he filled her deeply. She sighed at the sensation of him inside her. So full. So thorough. So complete. She had forgotten how good it felt to be joined to another human being in the most intimate way possible. Oh…so good. She picked up the rhythm, once more, taking all of him. He opened his hand over her back, splaying his fingers wide, and pushed her forward, bending her at the waist so he could enter her more deeply still. All Clara could do was go along for the ride.

He pumped her that way for long moments. Then, just when she thought they would both go over the edge, he slowly—and with clear reluctance—withdrew. They shed what little clothing remained and made their way silently to the bed. He shoved back enough covers to make room for them, then sat on the side of the bed and pulled Clara toward him. When she was sitting in his lap, straddling him, he pulled her breast to his mouth and tongued its sensitive peak. Then he moved to the other. Then back to the first, sucking her deep into his mouth and raking her with his teeth. As he did, he traced the delicate line bisecting her bottom, up, then down, then up again.

Just when she thought she would explode with wanting him, he pulled his mouth away from her breast to look at her face. She threaded her fingers through his hair and gazed into those blue, blue eyes, nearly drowning. She wanted desperately to say something. Something he needed to know. Something she needed to tell him. But she couldn't find a single word to tell him how she felt. So she kissed him, long and hard and deep, and hoped it would be enough.

He cupped her face in his palms and kissed her back, with a gentleness and tenderness that was at odds with their steamy passion and the carnality of their position. Sex had never been like this for Clara, a balance of hot and sweet, of need and generosity, of take and give. It had always been too much of those first things and too little of those last. Until now. And now...

Grant moved his hand between her legs and began the sweet torture of his fingers again. Oh, *now*. She never wanted to leave this bed. This room. This place. She never wanted to be with another man again.

Just as that thought formed, he lifted her up and over his heavy length again, entering her more deeply than ever. As he curved his palms gently over her bottom, she twined her fingers possessively around his nape and her legs around his waist. Their bodies merged as one a second time, each complementing the other perfectly, each completing the other irrevocably. He was hers. She was his. At least, for now.

In one last, fluid motion, Grant turned their bodies so that Clara was lying beneath him. He braced his elbows on the bed by each of her shoulders and dropped his thumbs to her jaw. Then, as he caressed her face and gazed into her eyes, he buried himself as deeply in her as he could go. She wrapped her legs around his waist again and lifted her hips to meet him, sliding her hands down his slick back to hold him there. Over and over, he thrust into her. Over and over, she opened to him. Then, as one, they came, each crying out in their climax before slowly descending again.

Grant rolled his body to lie on his side next to her. He smiled as he looped a damp curl around his finger, and kissed her one more time. Sweetly this time. Chastely. As if the whole world hadn't just shattered beneath them.

And it occurred to Clara in that moment that *right now* with Grant would never be enough.

# Ten

Grant awoke the way he did every morning—alone in his bed during the dark hours just before dawn, to the beeping of his alarm clock. No, wait—that wasn't actually true. Yes, he was alone in his bed, and yes, it was still dark, and yes, he had to slap his hand down on the alarm to shut it off. But usually he woke up rested and clearheaded and ready to rise from bed, then immediately launched into a mental rehearsal of all the things he had to do once he arrived at work. Today, he was anything but rested and clearheaded, and the last thing he wanted to think about was work. The first thing he wanted to do was make love to Clara again. Then he wanted to spend the rest of the day thinking about her. And work? No way. He'd much rather spend the day with Clara. Doing whatever they felt like doing. Even if that was nothing at all. And then he wanted to go to bed with her at day's end and make love with her again. Then he wanted to do the same thing the next day. And then the one after that. For weeks and months and years on end.

Oh, this wasn't good. Grant needed to wake up the way he always did. Because that was the way he lived his life. Every day. All day. Day in. Day out. One day at a time. If he ever strayed from his routine…

Well. He just might not make it through the day.

He rolled onto his side and stared at his aquarium, its pale blue night-light a soft counterpoint to the tumble of thoughts bouncing around in his brain. Normally, the sight of his fish gliding about in blissful ignorance of the world and its constant pressures made Grant feel calm. Normally, watching the slow parade of myriad colors and elegant motion put him in touch with a part of himself where lived all the merriment, fancy and simplicity he'd stowed away decades ago and never allowed to roam free. Normally, that was enough to keep him going for another day. But this morning, watching the dappled, indolent to-and-fro, he knew that a momentary reconnection with what he'd left behind wouldn't be enough. Because he'd awoken alone. And in the dark. And where those two things had never bothered him before, this morning, they bothered him a lot.

He rolled over again, to the other side of his bed, where Clara had slept for an hour or so, before waking up and telling Grant she needed to finish the night in her own bed. Before Hank awoke and went looking for her, she'd said. Before his mother awoke and saw the door to the guest bedroom open and the bed still made. Clara had kissed him one last time on the mouth, and smiled in a way that could have meant anything. Then she'd slipped back into her dress and stolen away like a thief in the night. Which was appropriate. She was a thief. She'd stolen something from Grant he might never get back. Especially if she took it with her when she returned to Georgia.

He lay his head on the pillow where hers had been only hours ago and inhaled deeply. Yeah, there it was. The faintest hint of cinnamon. The merest suggestion of ginger. And something else, too, something that was inherently Clara Easton. Something that could never be bottled the way spices were and opened whenever he wanted to enjoy it. Something he would never find anywhere else, no matter how hard he tried. And now she was going home, and she would be taking that with her, too.

He looked at the clock on the nightstand. 6:17 a.m. Seventeen minutes later than he always got up. Usually, by now, he was in the shower, readying himself for another day of running the family business that he'd never really wanted to run, but which had to be run by someone in the family because...

Because. He was sure there was a reason for that. He was sure there had been one when he shouldered the responsibility so many years ago. But he couldn't quite remember now what that reason was. There was one, though. There must be. He was sure of it.

He couldn't take the day off, as much as he might want to. Even being the boss had its limits. Grant had a meeting this morning that had been on his agenda for weeks, a meeting that had been nearly impossible to organize in the first place, thanks to the schedules of everyone involved. He couldn't miss it. He was the one who had called for it. Clara's plane didn't leave until this evening. He could head home after the meeting and be back in time to take her to the airport himself. It shouldn't go past noon. One at the latest. Two at the outside. Even that would give him a two-hour window to get her and Hank to LaGuardia. But he wouldn't make the meeting at all if he didn't get a move on and get into the shower now.

He rose and shrugged on his robe, then headed for the bedroom door to make the short trip up the hall to the bathroom. Instead of heading left, however, he turned right. He strode past the closed door to Hank's room and paused at the one opposite. He started to knock quietly, then figured he probably shouldn't wake Clara. Just because he wanted to see her before he went to work. Just because he was having trouble thinking about anything but her. Just because it would be nice to have a smile from her to carry with him for the rest of the day.

He should leave her a note, he thought. To tell her he would be home in time to take her to the airport for her flight. No, to tell her how much he'd enjoyed last night, and that he would be home in time to take her to the airport for her flight. There was just one problem. How could he possibly convey how much he'd enjoyed last night in a note?

He'd call her before the meeting. There would be just enough time after he got to work. It would be good to hear her voice, anyway. It had been hours since he'd heard her voice. Eons. Just hearing her say "Good morning" would be enough to get him through the day. At least until he saw her again this afternoon.

For a moment, Grant only stood with his open palm against the bedroom door. He really wished he didn't have to go to work today. He couldn't remember a time when he'd ever felt that way. But he did today. Then he reminded himself that the sooner he got to work, the sooner he could call Clara. So, morning planned, he headed down the hallway again.

So he wasn't going to call or anything.

Clara looked at the pile of bags by the Dunbartons' front door—the two she and Hank had arrived with and two additional, newer and bigger ones for him, thanks to his and Francesca's negotiations about what he would be taking back to Georgia with him right away because he just couldn't live another minute without it. Would that Clara was able to do the same. But Grant probably would have objected to being packed up in such a way. Then she looked at Hank, who was giving his grandmother one final hug before they left. Then she looked at Renny Twigg, who had arranged for a car from Tarrant, Fiver & Twigg to take Clara and Hank to the airport, the way Gus Fiver had arranged for one to pick them up there…had it only been a week ago? Funny, Clara felt as if it had been a lifetime since she and Hank showed up at the Dunbartons' front door like a couple of secondhand relations.

"We should get going," Renny said gently. "Traffic and all."

Clara nodded. "Hank, sweetie," she said, "it's time to go."

Francesca had wanted to come to the airport with them, but Clara had told her it was okay, that if she did, it would be hours before she got back home, and that it would be easier for all of them if Renny had the driver just drop her and Hank off. A long goodbye wouldn't be good for any of them.

Of course, if Grant had been there—or if he had, oh, Clara didn't know…maybe offered to drive her and Hank to the airport himself, say—it would have been a different story. She would have taken the longest goodbye she could get from him. Evidently, though, he wasn't going to give her a goodbye at all. He'd already left for work by the time she woke up, and she hadn't heard a word from him all day. No text. No call. No email he could have fired off from his desk. She hadn't expected sonnets from him. Or even a haiku. But she would have liked to hear *some*thing. A few words or emojis to let her know he was thinking about her and that last night had meant more to him than...

What? she asked herself. The way she was thinking, it almost seemed as if it had meant something more to her than...well, whatever it had meant. A physical reaction to a sexual attraction they'd both been feeling all week. Her attempt to exorcise a bundle of turbulent emotions that had been bouncing around in her head and heart demanding release. An effort to make sense of something that defied sensibility. She still wasn't sure what last night had been, so how could she expect Grant to think it was more than any of those things? Still, it would have been nice if he had at least acknowledged that it happened, if he had let her know he'd thought about her once or twice today.

Because she sure hadn't been able to stop thinking about him.

She'd hated leaving his bed to return to her own last night. But she had been afraid Hank might wake up fretful, which he sometimes did after going to bed so late following a highly stimulating event like the party. And if he'd come looking for her in the guest room and seen she wasn't there, or that her bed hadn't been slept in...

Well, she just hadn't wanted to make him think she wasn't there for him when he needed her, that was all. And at the other end of the spectrum, if Francesca had seen that Clara never went to her own bed, she might have thought something was going on between her and Grant that would...

Well, she just hadn't wanted to make Francesca think there was a chance Clara was falling in love with her other son, thereby ensuring her grandson would be linked to her more decisively than before. Even if Clara was kind of falling in love with Francesca's other son.

That was obviously a pipe dream. Grant hadn't even waited around long enough to tell her good morning. How could she have expected him to be here to say goodbye?

"You've been wonderful, Francesca," Clara said as she and Hank finally ended their hug. "I can't thank you and Grant enough for making us feel so welcome here."

"But you *are* welcome here," Francesca told her, sounding vaguely alarmed that Clara might not think so. "Any time, under any circumstances. I'm already making plans for your next visit. Can you believe we never made it to a show?" she added, sounding scandalized. "How can anyone come to New York and not see a show? You must come back as soon as it's convenient."

Clara forced a smile. "We'd like that."

She looked down at her son, who had moved away from Francesca to affix himself to Clara's side the same way he had that first morning. Except this time, any apprehension he might be feeling was because he didn't want to leave. Neither did Clara. But there was no way she could take any more time from the bakery, and Hank needed to get back to his routine before he forgot what it was.

"Maybe you could come visit us on Tybee Island," she told Francesca. That way, there wouldn't be the risk of running into Grant. "Hank's preschool has spring break in April. Come down for Easter. I'll bake a giant ham and a sweet potato casserole, and we can have bacon-braised green beans and cheese grits for sides and banana pudding for dessert. How does that sound?"

"It sounds like my cholesterol will go through the roof," she said with a smile. "But I'd like that very much. Maybe I can convince Grant to take time away from work to come with me."

Clara started to object, then decided it wouldn't be necessary. There was little chance Grant would take time away from work for anything. So Clara said nothing at all.

"I'll miss you, Grammy," Hank said.

His eyes grew moist, but he swiped at them with one fist. It was all the encouragement Francesca needed. Her eyes went misty, too. Not that Clara could blame either of them. She felt like crying herself. Though maybe for a slightly different reason...

Hank broke away for one more hug, then Renny Twigg echoed their need to leave. At the same time, the doorbell rang, heralding the arrival of their driver and a doorman with a luggage cart to carry down the bags. Francesca promised again to pack up the gifts under the tree and ship them to Tybee Island tomorrow, though Hank had opened one this morning after she had insisted. Inside had been a plush, squishy planet Jupiter, complete with arms, legs and smiling face, that Hank hadn't put down since. He'd also kicked science to the curb by naming it Plu-toad.

The flurry of bag-gathering and final goodbyes dried whatever tears were left, and then Hank, Clara and Renny were in the elevator with the driver and doorman, heading down to the lobby. Clara surreptitiously checked her phone as they descended, to see if there were any new texts. There weren't. Then she checked to see if she'd missed a call. She hadn't. Email? Nope.

Then the elevator doors were opening, and she and Hank and Renny were following their driver and luggage toward the door. Once through it, Clara looked up and down Park Avenue. But there was no handsome, dark-haired, blue-eyed man in a power suit running toward them shouting, "Clara! Wait!" the way there would have been if this were the Hollywood version of the story. So once she and Renny were settled inside the car with Hank fastened into his car seat, there was no reason for her to look back.

This wasn't Hollywood, Clara reminded herself as the car pulled away from the curb. And, like Hollywood, it wasn't real life, either. The Dunbarton family lived in a way few people were able to manage, in a world few people ever entered. Hank may have been her ticket into it, but she would always be here temporarily, and always as a fringe dweller. She would never be a permanent resident, and she would never really belong. It was time she started accepting that and went back to the life she knew. The life to which she'd been born. The life where she belonged. The life she—usually—loved.

The life that would never be the same again.

Grant sat at the head of the giant table bisecting the boardroom of Dunbarton Industries, glaring at the man seated halfway down the left side. Not just because he was the reason this meeting had gone on hours too long—so long that Clara and Hank must, by now, be on their way to LaGuardia without him—but because he had spent the majority of those hours contributing to the very problems Grant had called this meeting to avoid. He hadn't even had a chance to slip out and call

Clara to tell her goodbye, because the meeting had become so contentious he hadn't wanted to risk making it worse by breaking for anything. He'd even arranged for lunch to be brought in, because by that point, he'd been worried everyone might leave and not come back.

It had been that way since the moment Grant arrived at work. He'd exited the elevator to hear voices raised in controversy and had entered the reception area to see that two members of the meeting had already arrived and were engaged in not-so-civil debate over the only item on the agenda—Dunbarton Industries' acquisition of an abandoned wharfside property in an area a group of historians had halfheartedly slated for revitalization once upon a time. But the Waterfront Historical Society had been forced to scrap the project when the economy tanked, and the massive warehouse complex had been sitting vacant and decaying for years. Grant wanted to buy and revamp all of it to make it a safe, environmentally friendly work and living space, the centerpiece of what could potentially become an industrial-retail-entertainment-residential complex. He'd invited a handful of the city's leading developers to attend today, knowing a number of them would be interested. All he should have had to do was iron out a few minor problems that might arise with Dunbarton Industries and some of the other involved parties, and they'd be set. He'd figured that part of the meeting would take, at most, a couple of hours. Then it would just come down to a matter of which developer could offer the most attractive package to all involved, which should have taken no time at all.

Unfortunately, the developer he had considered the best fit for the enterprise had, unbeknownst to him, already had a number of run-ins with the Waterfront

Historical Society that had either ended very badly or hadn't ended at all. Both sides had used the first part of the meeting to try to iron out those problems instead of the ones they were supposed to be talking about. It hadn't taken long for everything to escalate to the point where now *everyone* at the table was bickering about past wrongs. Every time Grant thought he had things back on track, someone—usually the man half-way down the table on the left side—drove everything over a cliff again. Try as he might to point out how well his proposal could benefit most of the people present, most of the people present preferred to talk about—or argue about—something else instead.

Sometimes Grant felt like the world of big business was populated by nothing but three-year-olds. No, wait. That wasn't true. Hank Easton was three, and he behaved better than anyone currently seated in the Dunbarton Industries boardroom. At this point, it was beginning to look as if Grant would never see Hank or his mother again.

Then again, whose fault was that? Grant was the boss here. He was the one who called the meeting. He could have also called an end to it any time he wanted today and then tried to reconvene at some point when everyone was more amenable to making progress. But he hadn't. Instead, he'd done everything he could to en-sure it *didn't* end. At least not until he achieved the out-come from it he hoped—no, needed—to achieve. The acquisition of that property could ultimately be worth billions in company revenue. It could be the biggest success Dunbarton Industries ever had. They weren't the only company interested in it. Waiting even a week could mean another company swooped in and grabbed all that potential for itself. Grant needed to act quickly if he wanted this thing to succeed for them. And, hey, wasn't success the whole point to life? Wasn't that why he worked as hard as he did? So that the family business would thrive?

Yes, yes and yes. At least, all of that had been true before. Before Clara Easton and her son showed up at his front door.

He looked at the group of people surrounding the table again. There were eight of them. At least four of them besides him would be affected positively by this arrangement if he could pull it off. Those four represented dozens more who would become involved further down the road and benefit. From those dozens, hundreds more. In the long run, if this project worked out the way Grant envisioned it, it would create thousands of jobs, most of them permanent. A dangerous public eyesore would become a safe, walkable area with green space. Property values would rise. Investors would reap rewards. From a business standpoint, it could be a massive success.

From a business standpoint.

But what about other standpoints? What about other successes? Clara was on her way home to Georgia, and Grant hadn't even told her goodbye. And who knew when he would see her again? She had a business to run eight hundred miles away from the one he had to run here. They both had commitments to their work that were equally demanding. And hell, it wasn't as if they'd made any commitments beyond those. It wasn't as if they'd made a commitment to each other. On the contrary, Clara had told him last night she wanted him "now." Maybe that meant she wanted him in the heat of that moment. Maybe it meant she only wanted him that once. She had left his bed to return to her own afterward. Sure, she'd had a good reason for it. But she had left his bed to return to her own.

And he hadn't stopped her.

No commitment. From either of them. No promises. No plans. No talk of the future at all. But that was good, right? It meant neither of them had expected anything more from last night than one night. Yes, they would see each other again eventually. They would have to, since Hank was a part of the Dunbarton family now. But Clara...

Clara had offered no indication that she wanted to be part of the family, too. At least in any capacity beyond the one that included her son. She'd had to get back to Georgia for her work. She couldn't come visit New York over Hank's spring break because of her work. Grant couldn't visit her in Georgia for the same reason. Both of them had put their work first. Both had made that their priority.

He could still end this meeting now. If he hurried, he might even make it to LaGuardia before her plane left. If nothing else, he could call for a ten-minute break that would allow him to retreat to his office long enough to call Clara and tell her goodbye.

He glanced at his phone, sitting on the table to his right. It had gone off a number of times during the meeting, but always with notifications he knew he could attend to later. Not once had it gone off with a notification from Clara. She was leaving without telling him goodbye, too.

And maybe that, really, told Grant everything he needed to know. About himself and Clara both.

"All right," he said to the group seated around the table. "Let's start from the top. Again."

* * *

"Did you have a good time in New York?"

It took a moment for Clara to realize Renny Twigg was speaking to her. Hank had been chattering at the other woman ever since the car pulled away from the curb, recapping everything he'd done with his grandmother over the past week. And Renny, bless her heart, had hung on every word. Funny, but Clara wouldn't have pegged her as someone who would respond as well as she did to a toddler. Not that the high-powered lawyer life seemed especially fitting for her, either. Renny definitely gave off a vibe that made her seem as if she was more suited to a life away from suits. Clara had no idea why, but somehow, she pictured her being the kind of woman who would be happier in a job where she could corral livestock.

"I did," Clara said in response to her question. Because she had mostly had a good time in New York. The fact that her heart had been broken there at the end didn't change that.

"Was it your first time?" Renny asked.

Once again, it took a moment for Clara to reply. Because for a moment, she thought Renny was referring to something that really wasn't any of her business and frankly should have been obvious with Hank, the fruit of Clara's loins, sitting right there. Then she thought maybe Renny meant something else that still wasn't any of her business—jeez, Clara was just realizing herself that it was hard to recognize the first time you fell in love with someone. But of course, Renny was talking about coming to New York.

"Yes," she said. "It was my first time." In New York *and* in love.

"What did you think?" Renny asked.

"It's not what I expected at all," Clara told her. Not New York. And not love, either.

"It always surprises people," Renny said.

Well, Clara could certainly understand why.

"They expect it to be this huge, overwhelming thing where they'll never feel comfortable or safe."

Yep, that was pretty much the way Clara had always thought about love.

"They're scared they'll get robbed or end up so lost they'll never be able to find their way."

Exactly, Clara thought.

"But after a while, they realize it's not so scary. And it can be...*so* wonderful. And then people can't believe they waited so long."

Well, Clara didn't know about that. New York, sure. She agreed with everything Renny said. But love? Not so much. Because Clara had indeed been robbed while she was here—Grant had stolen her heart. And she was certain she'd never be able to find her way back to the place where she was before she came here. And she definitely didn't know if she'd ever feel comfortable or safe again. Not the way she'd felt comfortable and safe with Grant. So for now, the score was New York, one, Clara nil, and Grant...

Well, Grant had certainly scored, she couldn't help thinking. Unfortunately, it was looking as if, now that he had, he wanted to drop out of the game completely.

Gee, he had a lot more in common with his brother than she'd thought.

Their arrival at the Delta terminal of LaGuardia airport came way too quickly for Clara's comfort. So much for New York City's notorious rush hour traffic. Then again, when she glanced down at her watch, it was to see the trip had taken them more than forty-five minutes. She'd just been so lost in her thoughts, she hadn't even noticed the passage of time.

With any luck, it would continue to pass quickly once she and Hank were back on Tybee Island. She'd just have to make sure she threw herself into her work once they were home. Work was good for passing time and keeping her focused on the things she should be focusing on. And it was good for making her forget the things she should be forgetting about.

Things like the pale blue eyes of a man who refused to let himself be happy.

# Eleven

Clara did her best to take a page from the Grant Dunbarton workaholic playbook when she got back to Tybee Island, throwing herself into the ebb and flow of the bakery to the point where she thought about nothing else—save Hank, of course. But now that Hank was inextricably tied to the Dunbartons, thinking about him—and talking to him and being with him—meant she would always be thinking about them, too. And thinking about them meant thinking about Grant, which then made her all the more determined to throw herself into her work and think about nothing else save Hank.

Which only started the cycle all over again.

It was exhausting, frankly, trying to focus on nothing but work, from the moment she rose in the morning until she switched off the light at night. She didn't see how Grant lived this way. No wonder he'd been so joyless.

No, she told herself. That wasn't right. He wasn't joyless. At least, he hadn't been at the end of her time in New York. But more than a week had passed since she and Hank had left, and Clara hadn't heard a word from Grant *or* Francesca, save a quick call to the latter immediately after their arrival back in Georgia to let her know they'd arrived home safely. Silence from Grant hadn't surprised her. Well, okay, it had. Part of her had thought he was starting to break away from the relentless CEO who had usurped his childhood and get back in touch with the little boy who'd wanted to head up a nonprofit called KOOK. But silence from Francesca? The mother of all grandmothers? That had surprised Clara a lot. She would have thought Francesca would be calling every day.

But it was Christmas, she reminded herself, and people got busy over the holidays. She knew that, because she felt as if she was single-handedly catering every holiday party on the island. Francesca was probably just so bogged down in entertaining and being entertained that she didn't have a minute to spare for anything else.

The timer on the big oven went off, pulling Clara's thoughts back to the matter at hand—snowman cookies. Two dozen of them. For starters. They were destined for the holiday party at Hank's preschool tomorrow—the last day of class before Christmas, which was scarcely a week away—along with dozens more. Clara had baked Christmas tree cookies, too, along with dreidel cookies and kinara cookies and New Year's baby cookies and pentacle cookies.

Well, who knew? She didn't want to leave out the Wiccans. Or maybe she'd just been thinking too much about the last night she'd spent in New York. And not just the party at Dunbarton Industries. About making love with Grant, too.

But she wasn't going to think about him, she reminded herself. Again. She was going to think about work. Unfortunately, going back to work meant looking at two dozen Rudolph cookies she'd frosted earlier that were set enough now to go into one of the cases in front. And seeing those just reminded Clara of Grant all over again, and how she'd told him the story of the Rudolph ornament in her former foster home that she'd nurtured and repaired and hadn't been allowed to take with her when she'd been reassigned. What had possessed her to tell him that story? She'd never told that story to anyone.

*Stop. Thinking. About. Grant.* She really did need to focus on work. Which, naturally, made her think of Grant. Gah.

Hastily, she picked up the tray with all the Rudolphs staring at her and carried them out to the shop. The bell over the door was ringing to announce yet another customer—gee, she hoped they could fit another customer in here, since the shop was already full to the gills—so Clara threaded her way through her three busy salesclerks, toward the cookie case, to tuck the tray into an empty spot. And wow, there were a lot of empty spots. At this point, she was going to be baking until midnight Christmas Eve if she wanted to have something for Hank to leave out for Santa.

She slid the Rudolphs into the case and was heading back to the kitchen to retrieve more cookie dough from the walk-in when Tilly cupped a hand over her shoulder to halt her.

"Is it too late for someone to place a special order?" she asked.

Well, it was, Clara thought. Christmas was only eight days away, and she'd taken on about as many special orders as she could manage for what was left of the holidays. But depending on what the customer wanted, she might be able to squeeze in one more.

"Maybe," she told Tilly. "What does she need?"

"It's not a she," Tilly said. "It's a he."

The comment immediately carried Clara back to the day Gus Fiver entered the bakery and turned her world upside down. She pushed the thought away. Her world would get back to normal, she told herself. Eventually. Someday. Okay, it would get back to a new kind of normal. She just had to figure out what it was going to be.

"All right, what does *he* need?" she asked Tilly.

Before the salesclerk could respond, a voice—much too deep to be Tilly's, but infinitely more familiar—replied loudly enough to be heard over the buzz of the customers, "You, Clara. He needs you."

The crowd went silent at the announcement, every head turning to see who had spoken. When Clara followed their gazes, she saw Grant on the other side of the counter, standing head and shoulders above and behind the group of women who had been waiting to be served. Though they now seemed much more interested in waiting to see what happened next. They parted like the Red Sea to reveal him from head to toe, then, as one, looked back at her, to see how she would respond.

"Uh, hi," was all she could manage.

The heads turned toward Grant.

When he realized they had an audience, he grinned. With absolute, unadulterated joy and genuine, unbridled playfulness. Which, Clara couldn't help thinking, wasn't exactly the reaction she might have expected from a joyless, relentless, workaholic CEO. He wasn't dressed like one, either. He wasn't even dressed like a CEO on vacation. No, Grant Dunbarton looked like any other island local, in knee-length surf jams, a Savannah Sand Gnats sweatshirt and Reef Rover shoes.

"Hi yourself," he greeted her in return.

If Clara didn't know better, she could almost believe it was Brent Dunbarton, not Grant, who had ambled into her bakery. Except for one noticeable difference. She'd never come close to being in love with Brent. But the man standing in her bakery now?

Well, there was a time when she had thought she might love him. Before he'd chosen his work over his own happiness. Before he'd chosen his work over her and her happiness, too.

The heads had turned again, to get Clara's reaction. But she wasn't as comfortable being the center of attention as Grant obviously was, so she tilted her head toward the door that connected the shop to the kitchen in a silent invitation for him to follow her. The disappointment of the crowd was palpable—a couple of women even *Aww*ed or muttered *C'mon, Clara*, but she didn't care. She was happy to provide them fodder for their holiday parties. Not so much to provide fodder for the coconut telegraph.

She trusted Grant to follow, because she wasn't about to turn around and look at all those speculative faces. The only speculation she was interested in the moment was her own. What was he doing here? Dressed the way he was? Why hadn't he called first? Or texted? Or, jeez, sent up a flare? He could have at least given her some small notice, so she wouldn't have to be greeting him in her once-white-now-rainbow-hued baker duds of formerly white pajama pants, T-shirt and head scarf. And— *Oh, no*, she thought when she saw her wavy reflection in the silver door of the walk-in—her now rainbow-hued face, too.

She grabbed a towel from the counter and did her best to scrub the remnants of frosting and chocolate from her face. Then she spun around to face Grant... who had somehow become even more handsome and sweet looking in the handful of seconds it had taken them to escape the crowd.

But she wouldn't succumb to a sweet and a handsome face. Especially one that couldn't even be bothered to call her. Still, he had come here for something. She couldn't imagine what, but the least she could do was hear him out.

"Okay, let's try this again," she said. "Hi."

He grinned again. "Hi yourself," he repeated.

An unwieldy silence ensued. Mostly because Clara had no idea what to say. Seriously, why was he here? And how could a man who had rejected her in favor of a corporate conglomerate still stir so many feelings inside her she didn't want to feel? She needed to get back to work. *Best wind this up ASAP.*

In spite of that, she asked lamely, "So... How's things?"

He chuckled. Honestly, she could just smack him for looking so—

Happy. Oh, God, he looked *happy*! How could he be so happy when he'd made her feel so lousy?

"Um, different," he said.

She gave his outfit an obvious once-over. "So I see."

He sobered a little at that. "Yeah, I guess I look a lot like Brent, don't I? I didn't mean to—"

"No," she interrupted him. "You don't. I could easily tell the two of you apart. You look nothing like Brent. You *are* nothing like Brent. But you know, for all his faults, at least your brother followed his heart and fulfilled his dreams and lived his life in a way that made him happy. But you... You'd rather..."

When she trailed off without finishing—mostly because she was afraid she wouldn't be able to do that without revealing just how hurt she was—he asked, "I'd rather what?"

She shook her head, still not trusting her voice or herself to answer.

He took a step closer. She took one in retreat. He frowned at her withdrawal.

"C'mon, Clara," he said softly. "I'd rather what?"

She inhaled a deep breath, crossed her arms over her midsection, arrowed down her brows and tried again. "You've buried your dreams, Grant. Your life is nothing but your work. It means more to you than anything—anyone—else ever will. And your heart? Jeez, there's a part of me that sometimes wonders if you really have one."

He winced at that last, closing his eyes and turning his head as if she really had smacked him. Then he opened his eyes and looked at her again, his gaze unflinching this time.

"Why didn't you call me to tell me goodbye before you left New York?" he asked.

It wasn't exactly what Clara had expected him to say. Nor was it a question she knew how to answer. So she only said, "What?"

He shrugged. "Why didn't you call me to tell me goodbye before you left New York?"

She studied him a moment longer before answering. Finally, truthfully, she said, "I don't know."

He was right. She could have called him to say goodbye. Or she could have texted him. Or sent him an email. She just…hadn't. She'd been too focused that day on getting herself and Hank packed and ready for their flight back to Georgia. Because she had needed to get Hank back into his routine here, and because she had needed to get herself back to…

Work. She hadn't been able to spend any more time in New York, because it had been too important for her to get back to the bakery, which would be incredibly busy before Christmas. There was no way she'd have any time for things like…

But she had a business to run, she reminded herself. And she had employees who depended on her for their weekly paycheck. It wasn't that she had chosen her work over Grant. It was that…

She sighed again. It was that she had chosen her work over Grant. Because her work was important. Because she had obligations. Because people were relying on her.

"Wow," she said softly. "I guess we're both a couple of workaholics, aren't we?"

He nodded slowly.

"And I guess we've both sort of lost sight of what's really important."

He took another step toward her. This time, Clara didn't take one in retreat. "So what are we going to do about that?" he asked.

She shook her head and replied honestly again. "I don't know."

He studied her again. But he didn't say anything.

So Clara did the only thing she could. She nodded toward his shirt and said, "I thought you were a fan of the Savannah Clumps of Kelp."

He expelled a single chuckle—it was a start. To what? She still wasn't sure. But something inside her that had been wound too tight gradually began to unknot. "What, those losers?" he asked. "Nah. The Sand Gnats are where it's at."

She braved a smile. "I'm glad you've seen the light."

Now he sobered again. "Yeah, I have. And not just there. A whole lot of things have come clear to me in the last couple of weeks." He took a step closer. "Thanks to you."

Clara took a step closer, too. He was trying to meet her halfway. That was a little better than a start. The least she could do was help him get there. "Oh?" she asked.

He moved closer. "Yeah."

She did likewise. "In what way?"

By now, they were nearly toe-to-toe and almost eye to eye thanks to Clara's height in her work clogs. There was still an inch or two separating them—both distance-wise and stature-wise—but it wouldn't take much work for either of them to close that distance. Should either of them want to. Grant seemed to be trying to do that. Clara wished she knew how to help him.

"I resigned from Dunbarton Industries," he told her. "Effective immediately."

Her mouth dropped open at that. She couldn't help it. He might as well have just told her there was a giant squid dancing the merengue behind her, so astonishing and fantastic was the announcement.

But all she managed for a response was, "You did?"

He nodded. "I did. But it's taken some time to get the kinks ironed out of the arrangement, and I didn't want to say anything to anybody until we knew it would all work out the way we wanted it to."

"We?" Clara asked.

He nodded again. "Mom and I. She's taking over as CEO." He smiled again. "Effective immediately."

Clara's mouth almost dropped open again. Almost.

But somehow that news wasn't quite as astonishing or fantastic as the other had been. She'd seen for herself how at home Francesca was at the Dunbarton Industries holiday party, and how much the employees liked her. And she'd seemed to really know what she was doing when she went over the budget. From what Clara had seen, Francesca had been passionate about her ideas for keeping the company running. She'd been one of its vice presidents once upon a time. And she was a Dunbarton. Why shouldn't she run the family business if she wanted to? As long as she wanted to.

"And Francesca is okay with that?" Clara asked. Even with all the other considerations, Francesca hadn't exactly been Ms. Corporate America while Clara and Hank were in New York. She'd been much more Ms. Grandmother America.

"Yeah, she is," Grant said. "The minute you and Hank left, she started feeling aimless. She wanted to call you two the day after you left but was afraid you'd think she was being intrusive and trying to insinuate herself into your life down here or trying to bribe Hank to tell you to bring him back to New York."

"I would never think that about Francesca," Clara protested.

When Grant raised a single brow in response, she relented. "Okay, maybe I thought that about Francesca at first," she admitted. "But that was just the leftover foster kid in me being insecure and fearful."

"Anyway," Grant continued, "When I told her I wanted to step down from the company—hell, not just step down, but leave it completely—she just kind of smiled and told me it was about time. She'd always known following in my father's footsteps hadn't made me happy, but that it had seemed so important to me, she didn't question it. She said she'd always known I would finally figure out what I really wanted and pursue that instead, and wondered what took me so long. She'd always planned to take over for me when that happened, and that was why she stayed on the board and kept a finger in what was going on in the business. Now she'll have something to keep herself occupied so she won't miss Hank as much." His grin returned as he added, "And, unlike *some* CEOs, she'll be the kind of boss to give herself time off for the things she really wants to do. Like be with her grandson when he comes to visit."

Clara grinned back. "So you finally figured out what you want?"

"Yeah," he said. "And I wonder what took me so long, too. Then I remembered what I want didn't come into my life until recently, so there was really no way I could know that. Not until…"

"Until?" Clara asked.

"Until I met you."

She smiled.

"And Hank, too," he added. "But mostly you. The day you left New York was just…" He blew out an exasperated breath. "Actually, the day at work was like every other day. Except that by the end of the day, I knew there was something besides work I could be doing. Something I *wanted* to be doing. A lot more than I wanted to be working, that's for damned sure. Before you, Clara, I could pretend my work gave my life purpose, that it was important …" He made that exasperated sound again. "Before you, I could pretend I was happy," he finally said. "Or, at least, happy enough."

"'Happy enough' doesn't sound like happy," Clara told him.

"It's not. I know that now. I could never go back to

being the workaholic CEO after that night you and I…"
He halted, and there was something in his eyes that
made her heart turn over. "I couldn't be that again after
that night, Clara. Hell, I could barely maintain that ve-
neer the whole time you were in New York. The minute
you stepped through the door, you started reminding
me of too many things I'd made myself forget. Things
that made me happy when I was a kid. Things that made
me want to be happy as an adult. But I felt like I could
only go after those things if I turned my back on what
I thought was my duty to my family. I'd completely forgotten about my duty to myself."

Wow, did that sound familiar. Not the part about being
reminded of a happy childhood, since Clara's hadn't exactly been that. But the part about wanting to be happy
as an adult. She, too, had convinced herself she was
"happy enough." She had Hank and a reasonably solid
business, and she kept a roof over both. But she'd been
pretty driven to ensure things stayed that way. She put
nearly every hour of her day into something else—being
a mom or being a businesswoman, thinking she could
only do those things by not thinking about herself. When
was the last time she had been just Clara? Really, had
she *ever* been just Clara?

"So what will it take to make you happy as an adult?"
she asked him.

"I think you already know that," he said.

"I'd still like to hear you say—"

"You," he told her without hesitation.

"—it."

Wow, this was going to work out so well. Because
the only other thing she needed to be happy—happy
for just Clara—was Grant.

She took a final step forward that literally brought

her toe-to-toe with him. And then she tipped herself up on her toes and pressed her mouth to his. It was a glorious kiss, even better than the first one they'd shared. Because this time, there was no doubt. This time, there was only…

Joy. Complete, unmitigated, take-no-prisoners joy. And if there was one thing the world needed more of at Christmas—and one thing Clara and Grant needed more of forever—it was joy. Lucky for both of them, it could be found just about anywhere. All you had to do was look for it. Or, if you were very lucky, joy came looking for you. Clara was just glad it had found her and Grant both.

It was snowing in New York City, Clara saw as she sipped her coffee and looked out the window of the Dunbarton living room onto a Central Park that was completely cloaked in white. Which was the way it should always be on Christmas morning. The way it would be every morning, if she had her way, since she would forever associate snow with the first time she and Grant made love. Of course, she'd also think about him whenever she saw stars in the sky. And whenever she saw Christmas cupcakes. And fish. And chambered nautiluses…nautili…those macabre floaty things. And—

Well, suffice it to say she'd think about Grant a lot. Pretty much all the time. Since they would have so much time now that they had *both* abandoned their workaholic ways. Clara had even closed the bakery for the week between Christmas Eve and New Year's Day—with full pay for everyone—so that she and Hank could spend the holiday here in New York with family. It was the least she could do in light of Grant's giving up his position at Dunbarton Industries to ensure his own happiness. Learning how to let herself be happy was, hands down, the nicest gift she'd ever received for Christmas.

She turned to look at the pile of unopened packages under the tree behind the dozens of toys Santa had left for Hank. She didn't care what was in any of those boxes. Nothing could be better than what she'd already been given this year. Even so, she couldn't wait to open them. Just looking at them made her feel like… Well, like a kid at Christmas. Grant wasn't the only one who'd needed to get in touch with his inner child. Clara had needed to do more of that, too. Because she wanted to give that child the kind of Christmas she'd never had as a kid. And from here on out, she would.

True to her baker's hours, Clara had woken before everyone else. So the coffee was made, cinnamon buns and gingerbread were warming in the oven and a fire was crackling in the fireplace. She was still in her pajamas—the red flannel ones with snowflakes, identical to Hank's, which was a Christmas tradition for the two of them—and planned to stay in them all day. That was a Christmas tradition she and Hank had created, too, one she would introduce to the Dunbartons along with the handful of others she and her son had forged. They'd go nicely with the Dunbarton traditions, especially now that Grant and Francesca were planning to return to the ones they'd embraced when Grant was a child. Hence the cinnamon buns and gingerbread warming in the oven, something Grant had told her they'd always had for breakfast on Christmas morning when he was young.

As if conjured by her thoughts of him, he strode into the living room with a cup of coffee in one hand and a hunk of gingerbread in the other. He was still disheveled from sleep in dark green-and-gray-striped pajama bottoms and a gray T-shirt. Next year, he and Francesca would be in red flannel with snowflakes, too. This family was going to be so obnoxiously sweet in their Christmas clichés that they would gag a cotton candy factory. Because they all had a lot of time to make up for.

Grant smiled when he saw her, then held up the gingerbread. "I couldn't wait for breakfast. It smelled so good. Just like Christmas."

Clara smiled, too. "The best Christmas ever."

"How do you know?" he asked. "It's barely started."

"Doesn't matter," she told him. "I'm with you. That makes it the best Christmas ever."

He seemed to suddenly remember something, because he hurried to the end table and placed his coffee and gingerbread there, then headed for the tree and began sorting through the gifts.

"While it's just you and me," he said, "I want you to open your present. Well, one of them," he amended. "This one," he added when he located a small square box wrapped in shiny green paper.

"Okay, but you have to open one from me, too," she told him as she moved toward the tree to look for the one she wanted. She found it quickly, flat and rectangular and wrapped in bright blue. Like the ocean, she'd thought when she saw the paper. The perfect color.

For a moment, each of them knelt on the floor by the tree, clutching the packages they'd picked out for the other, knowing this first official sharing of Christmas gifts was a precedent for them both. She and Grant were family now. Not just through their ties to Hank. But through their ties to each other. Family ties didn't have to be blood ties. They didn't even have to be matrimonial ties. They just had to be love ties. And even if neither of them had said the actual words yet, she and Grant definitely had those.

As if decided upon in their mutual silence, they each thrust their present at the other. Then, as excited as children, they began to tear the paper to shreds.

Grant finished first, opening the box to reveal a trio of coloring books Clara had bought him at the New York Aquarium, along with a box of twenty-four crayons. At first she feared he was disappointed, because he just looked at them without touching them, not even to see what other books were under the one on top, which was called *Under the Sea* and was the most generic of them. She really wanted him to see the one on the bottom, called *I Am a Cephalopod*, because that was the one she knew he'd love most.

"Are there not enough crayons?" she asked. "I mean, I almost got the sixty-four count, but that just seemed so ostentatious, and I—"

"It's perfect, Clara," he said. When he looked up, his expression was absolutely sublime. "The twenty-four pack has Blue Green, which is what I always colored the ocean. And there's Red Orange for the firemouth cichlid. And Brown for the nautilus. You've given me everything I could ever need. Everything I could ever want."

She smiled at that. It was all she could ask a gift to do.

"Now finish opening yours," he told her.

She looked at the box in her lap, now completely freed of its wrappings. It was plain white, with no logo to give her a hint as to what it might be. Carefully, she pulled off the top. Beneath it was a crush of glittery tissue paper. She withdrew that, then caught her breath at what lay under it. A Christmas ornament. Rudolph the Red-Nosed Reindeer. Plastic with chipped paint and a red nail polish nose and a gigantic lump of dried glue on one leg. Her eyes filled with tears as she lifted it from its tissue paper bed, as carefully and reverently as she would have held the Hope Diamond.

"I can't believe you found this," she said. "Where…? How…?"

He grinned. "Would you believe…the magic of Christmas?"

She grinned back. "Gee, I don't know. Something like this would take an awful lot of magic."

"Then how about a friend who's a high-ranking member of the NYPD and married to a social worker who knew who to call to ask about your file in Georgia and find out who you were living with when you were about eight years old?"

Clara shook her head in astonishment. "I can't believe you went to all that trouble."

"It was no trouble," he said. "Anything to make you as happy as you've made me."

"It doesn't take a Christmas ornament to do that," Clara told him.

"Maybe not," he said. "But if it makes you happy…"

"Very happy," she assured him.

"Then I'm happy, too."

Clara was leaning in to give him a kiss when she heard the patter of Hank's feet slapping down the hall toward them, followed by an admonishment from Francesca to *Wait for me!* Hah. Not likely. No kid could wait on Christmas morning. Not for anything.

"You started without me!" Hank exclaimed when he saw the evidence of opened presents littering the floor between her and Grant.

But he was quickly sidetracked when he saw the toys from Santa scattered about and headed immediately for those. Francesca dove in right behind him, her merriment rivaling his.

Clara and Grant looked at each other. And she knew in that moment that they were both thinking exactly the same thing. Yes, they had started without Hank this morning. But that was just the point. They had *started*. Finally. They had started living. They had started loving. They had started feeling happy. Really happy. The kind of happy that only came in knowing they were exactly where they wanted and needed to be. Exactly where they belonged.

"Merry Christmas, Clara," Grant said softly. "I love you."

Had she just been thinking that learning how to let herself be happy was the nicest Christmas present she'd ever received? Gee, she'd been mistaken. That was the second best. The first was sitting right across from her, telling her he loved her.

"Merry Christmas, Grant," she replied just as quietly. "I love you, too."

And amid the ringing of laughter and the aroma of evergreen and gingerbread, closing their fingers over remnants of their childhood that now brought joy instead of sadness, Clara and Grant shared another kiss. The first of many they would share that day, Clara was certain. The first of many they would share in life. Because that was what life was. Sharing. Living. Loving. From one Christmas morning to the next.

# Epilogue

Clara was dabbing a smile on the last of two dozen dolphin cookies when the bell over the entrance to Cairns, Australia's Bread & Buttercream rang for what she hoped was the last time that day. Not that she didn't love every customer who came into her new digs in Clifton Beach, but with the grand opening just over and Christmas only a few weeks away, the bakery had been super busy. Not to mention she had to pick up Hank from Camp Australia for first graders—um, she meant year one students—in… She glanced at the clock. Yikes! Less than an hour! Where had the day gone?

She placed the dolphin on a rack with the rest of his pod to let the glaze dry, setting aside a basket of papayas that she and Hank had picked fresh from a tree in their backyard yesterday evening, before they'd stopped to catch fireflies in a jar. Then she wiped her powdered sugar–dusted hands on her white apron, which was easier now with the soft curve of her baby bump rising up to greet them.

She let her hands linger over the slight swell. She was barely four months along, but had already outgrown some of the maternity clothes that were supposed to last till her third trimester. Her ob-gyn had said they were going to do an ultrasound next visit to check for twins, something that still made Clara a little woozy. Still, Hank was already jazzed about the prospect of having one little brother or sister. Two might very well make him Big Brother of the Year.

She heard her salesclerk Merindah greet someone out in the shop with a happy hello, then Grant's voice replying. Clara smiled. He always took off from work early on Friday to meet her at the bakery so they could pick up their son together and get an early start on the weekend. He'd been busy, too, the past few months, getting his nonprofit, A Drop in the Ocean, off the ground. Okay, so it wasn't as catchy as KOOK, but it still had a certain whimsy. And already, it was making a difference. The organization employed more than two dozen people here and would be helping to preserve ecosystems from the Great Barrier Reef to Nauru and the Cook Islands. For starters. Although Grant had chosen Cairns for the main headquarters, he wanted to open satellite sites for A Drop in the Ocean all over the world. He'd funded much of its endowment with his own money, but thanks to his contacts in the business world, he had regular—and substantial—donors from some pretty major sources. Yes, he was the organization's CEO. But he wasn't relentless. He wasn't joyless. He wasn't a workaholic. He'd taken his dream and run with it. The same way Clara had. But they both made sure those dreams included time for each other.

After ensuring that Merindah and Clara's part-timer, Susan, didn't need anything before the bakery's close, she kissed her husband and asked him about his day.

"It was busy," he said.

But it was a good busy, Clara could tell. In the three years she'd known him, she'd never seen Grant look happier than he had since their move here. His skin was burnished from his time outdoors, and his hair was longer and less tidy than it had been when she first met him. He lived in Hawaiian shirts and cargo shorts these days, and he drove an old, army-green Range Rover—the kind he'd said he always wanted to have when he was a kid. They lived in a big house on the beach, surrounded by palm and mango trees, where they were occasionally visited by dolphins and goannas. The night sky was amazing, completely different from the one Hank had learned when he was little. And there were a million things to explore. It was a better life than Clara could have ever imagined for her son. Or for Grant. Or for herself.

She'd never been happier, either.

Grant helped her into the Ranger Rover, and after she was buckled in, he placed his hand gently over her swollen abdomen. "Think there are two in there?" he asked.

"Could be," Clara told him. She suspected there were, and her doctor had all but said she thought there were, too, but they wouldn't know for sure until after the ultrasound. "Would you be okay with that?"

He grinned. "Totally. And Mom would be beside herself. She's sure if we just have enough kids, one of them is bound to inherit the CEO gene, and then she can train them to follow in their grandmother's footsteps."

Clara grinned, too. "So she's coming next week, right?"

He nodded. "She gave herself the rest of December off, flying back to New York the day after New Year's."

Clara looked up at the sun and swiped at a trickle of perspiration on her neck. "Guess we can forget about white Christmases here." Funny, though, how that didn't bother her as much as she might have thought it would.

Grant closed the door of the Range Rover and, through the open window, told her, "We don't need snow to make it Christmas."

And that was certainly true. They could make it Christmas anywhere. And everywhere. And not just at Christmastime, either. All it took was knowing they were together. Exactly where they wanted to be. Exactly where they needed to be. Exactly where they belonged.

\* \* \* \* \*

*If you loved this story,*
*pick up the first* ACCIDENTAL HEIRS *book,*

*ONLY ON HIS TERMS*

*and these other stories of billionaire heroes*
*from* New York Times *bestselling author*
*Elizabeth Bevarly:*

*THE BILLIONAIRE GETS HIS WAY*
*MY FAIR BILLIONAIRE*
*CAUGHT IN THE BILLIONAIRE'S EMBRACE*